Heart & IRON

by

Andrew Huddleston

PublishAmerica
Baltimore

© 2004 by Andrew Huddleston.
All rights reserved. No part of this book may be reproduced, stored in a retrieval system or transmitted in any form or by any means without the prior written permission of the publishers, except by a reviewer who may quote brief passages in a review to be printed in a newspaper, magazine or journal.

First printing

ISBN: 1-4137-5397-3
PUBLISHED BY PUBLISHAMERICA, LLLP
www.publishamerica.com
Baltimore

Printed in the United States of America

*Dedicated to my loving wife, Denise,
my parents and children.
Thank you for the family, love, patience
and history.*

Chapter 1

There were many who came before him and his wife and many would come after. Mother Scotland would always be with him but the new land promised a better life. He loved and so he boarded that small craft of wood, rope and sails to cross the large ocean. Seven men and women of the McCray Clan brought faith and hope to live those months at sea under his watchful eye; many other families would come for the life and work America promised by way of the same sea-lanes and charts. Many would die at the cruelest junctures during moments of forgetfulness or weakness or by means none could control.

The hearty and lucky made a home beyond the stretch of the east. Disease, weather, the mines of Kentucky and Tennessee, the natives who owned the land—all exacted a toll in blood and they paid generously, willingly, with little rest or comfort. Taken by the arrow and sword or by the cave-ins or swallowed by sickness, still they came. Their quest for this place called America, its freedom and its neverending room and beauty was worth the price. And as it was, even the seemingly constant, ever-present harbingers of terror in every form that took the most from them could not defeat their faith in their God and in themselves.

America's bounty in grains and game was theirs to use, the new land's warmth overshadowed its harvest of blood and toil and sheltered the many that came from Scotland and many impoverished origins. Lucious McCray left the old country with his mother and father, three brothers and their one sister. He left the old country as a seasoned seventeen year old, older man, striking out with the rest to find some portion of a fortune—something he could send back—and a life rich in consequence.

He worked bone hard and deep in the belly of those mines. His father was promised a farm just south for two years of their labor. The Company would feed and house both of them between the fourteen-hour shifts in the black.

Katy of an old Irish clan was in those mountains with her father; they suffered the ruin of family because of the loss of her grandmother on the voyage that brought them into Virginia where they left for land westward. Each day the dolor gripped and took away all joy and never released them. The silent, agonizing hurt to their spirits never ceased, never slowed, and never yielded its piercing punishment.

Regret overtook him and he wallowed in strong ale while lines began to tear deep in her young face. Lucious was there and took her. *He wasn't her knight; he was lonely while she was stricken and God made them to be together.* They were to begin a new family in the new country and in a year, he and his father were to make the claim for the small farm Creeless wagered in return for many tons of the black harvest. Lucious would take Katy with him to do their Father's will as best they could in every way. Both were taught the faith and fear and were sure to devote all honor and glory to Him.

Lucious picked and shoveled, happily spreading his sweat and skin and blood inside the dark, dusty bowels of American earth to make a life. Katy prepared bread, soup, and when the hunting was good, she cooked rabbit or deer flesh to fill their sparse table. Much of the coal he worked was hauled to young Pittsburgh where foundries surrounded by clapboard buildings appeared to be burning themselves like every piece of coal in the furnaces as each huge barrel of melt slowly belched the spew.

Weak humans poured the iron. The men inside the filthy, gagging smoke burned and cradled and turned the guts of each furnace along with the sweat of the men who tore the recipe out of earth by hand to make the iron and steel. It was transformed to implements of expansion and some certain to be used near Mexico as weapons of death, destruction and freedom by taking.

There was trouble down that way for the people known as Texicans who would be fighting and dying before a score had passed. Lucious heard little about it and didn't have time to ponder; staying the course his God directed him. He was to grow food one day and provide for a family with Katy. There was family though that took for the territory on the promise of land straightway. His brother Luther went on to the region called Texas to begin his farm on a larger portion of the earth. Within the first year he would not have that farm owing to poor weather and failure of his crop.

Luther became a tavern keeper near the muddy banks of the Buffalo Bayou in a new city they named for Sam Houston. He was killed there, impaled through the heart by the force of frightened horses; he stopped the runaway carriage that day and saved the terrified child passenger. One of the wooden yokes struck a post and splintered to a spearhead and the carriage pushed the sharp end into Luther's chest. He was carried to his tavern and laid on a tabletop to bleed out and die, escaping the pain. Few people came to the funeral. Most of the family was several hundred miles east. Lucious would learn of his brother's courage six months after when he received one of the few letters. His tears were fresh as though he lost Luther the day he read the letter. The man quickly went to his wife, beautiful Katy, who could finally smile and give of her warmth and manner to lift his spirits.

She delighted all those who knew her. His pride was a pride beyond measure and capacity. Soon he would give her that place and many children, God willing, and they would have a family to stay. He looked on his wife every day and savored in silent joy over her, his fortune. Not a day passed when he didn't think of her in the most affectionate terms, not a minute passed did he consider he was alone. She was his world, his dream, and his beautiful island in this strange country and together they loved each other. He would make his due within the year to set south for the area on top of a mountain in north Alabama. There he was told he could farm nearly fifty acres.

The snow came plenty that year and laid everything under frozen white. The heavy skies, solid in an ugly bluish gray yielded the covering, making the land even colder than it would be. Lucious held Katy under the few blankets she brought; old, worn, true blankets in sack and patched quilt work, warm by two and comely in shape, lacking but theirs, the holy covering aided the couple that night neither slept. They loosed the bindings of all clothing and laid next to each other in total honesty and relished the warmth of each other's body.

"Lucious, dear heart, I believe the Lord will surely bless us with a child," Katy said as she cocked her head upward, mooneyes, sadly opened, fearful but steady. She was waiting for him to agree. Being months away from their leaving this place and many more months before the farm would yield even if the best conditions were found on the land, she knew the task to be monumental, perhaps beyond their capacity soon. She feared the future would cause them to feel what the thousands had in her father's Ireland. Hunger with no escape, no repast to save them.

Many died. She worried he may be in the mine longer if she had conceived; would he love her for that? Lucious was quiet. Slowly breaking a smile, he gazed on Katy through the dimness of the cabin.

"My fine Katy." He smiled the words. "If you come to expect, so will I. It would be the best day!" He kissed her hair and brought her to him with a tighter hold. She again settled the blankets around them. The small ball the couple formed gave them comfort as the outside wind loudly announced its presence and potency. The force compressed through every small breech in the walls bringing some white ice inside.

"Through all the troubles, a child would truly be a gift and treasure. We would be set to be sure."

"We should prepare, Lucious. This could be ours soon."

"Are you telling me we are going to have a child?" he asked broadly smiling.

"No, dearest. I'm not certain. I don't know but could be ... Would it not happen for us most untimely if it were soon?"

"Sure it's not the best time. But have no worry; it would be a grace on us, Katy," he said.

"But I do worry. There's so much to do and I sure want to go to our farm when we planned it."

"It's only this spring, dearest. We can go then."

Braxton Creeless summoned Lucious to see him after another month passed and taken the cold and snow. He had put away anticipation because Katy had yet to announce and there were no signs. He had taken more hours in the mines to weigh more for an exchange; the move was closing on him to be able to plant that spring. His handiwork with the chisel and lathe when he wasn't underground, gave him musket stocks, shelves, and other things made of wood another desired and willing to trade for tools and linens along with a few household fineries.

"You're close to completing your contract with us, Mr. McCray."

"Yes, sir. I trust you've found my work satisfactory."

"I have. Indeed, I have." Creeless looked on the young man. His full head of gray and wild hair that passed his neck and fell patternless against his high collar moved as he spoke.

When the awful news that Lucious' father was killed in one of the Creeless mines, there were no apologies, but there had been a heartfelt and sincere expression of grief by the roughly hewn, loud owner. What the mines took was the fault of the mines; no one questioned fate in those days. Creeless remained the proprietor of McCray's wages and held the contract of the young man he had come to be very fond.

"I know you've been taking a fair amount of more weight."

"Yes, sir. I do what I can since I have a Wife."

"Here's something for your new family to be, Lucious." He handed over a small leather bag of silver dollars. "You'll need this. Mrs. Creeless wanted to be sure you and Katy had it." He smiled.

"But, sir! I haven't yet earned this money." Lucious turned nervously with the bag clutched in his outstretched hand.

"Sure you have. Besides, it's a gift from us. We think a lot of your family and want you to have it."

"Thank you, sir! You're most kind and generous."

"Enough! I'm not! You're new in country and I want you to make it well. We have enough barbarians and thieves and ner-do-wells, so many ... You have to be careful, mind you."

"Yes, sir," the young Lucious said.

"This country must have fine, strong, God fearing people of families or we will all perish, and you and Katy are of such stock." He smiled.

"I want you to look up my brothers' straight way down there. They know you're coming. They have a farm and a mill near the plot I promised you."

"Gladly, Mr. Creeless."

"Gregory and Zechariah will help you start."

"I'm indebted, kind sir," Lucious said meekly.

"You done some good work. I want another dozen men like you! With them, we'd mine the mountain clean in a year and leave this dread!" he said as he laughed slyly but friendly. Lucious wondered for a moment, *if the man was of clear thinking*. Perhaps his kindness was a measure of recompense; he felt a twinge of guilt. The profit he had been given was profit at the expense of his father's and other men's lives. *But it was the same all round in this new land.*

"I wish you well, Mr. Creeless." He saw the dirty boards of the floor.

"Thank you, young McCray. I figure in four weeks the trails and roads will by dry enough and you and Katy should go as soon as they are. I'll not be holding you to the last day."

"Thank you more, sir!"

"And Godspeed. We'll miss you here. Take care of your wife. I know your father would have expected no less," the older man said.

"I will, sir. I'm taking the river tomorrow and will be absent here until summer."

"I hope you have a safe journey, sir."

"And I for you, Mr. Creeless."

"Thank you, Lucious. There's a deal I must make at the fort on the southern edges of Ohio and beyond. The Army is building more up river and some west, you know. And they be needing coal and iron for sure. Many are trespassing through the cold gates of a hellish north or wanting the dangerous skies of the Indian's west. It seems to be they must all want to die," he laughed again the strange laugh. "Damn lunatics they are!"

"Well, sir. I suppose they're people looking for a little bit of earth," Lucious said.

"Maybe so, young McCray, but no one must tell them it already belongs to another people ... Like where we are now! Hell, it wasn't ours!" He laughed. "In this country, you've got to make for yourself. We did and you have to yet. Many of those who were here before us died because they didn't leave. You best be ready to defend yourself. I don't care where you go!"

He left him with the small sack safely tucked in his shirt. Creeless frightened him with his demeanor and seemingly morbid taste. His brothers would surely be like him, he thought, and he would see them soon enough. He was also happy to know he had been released and could plan their travel.

His father passed into the next world when the hole he worked in the earth not one hundred meters from the pit Lucious worked yielded no air to breathe and he and eight others were taken quickly. Lucious knew him as a man of the strongest character who lived what he taught all of them and never took for himself the larger share, instead giving to his family his all, his most, and stayed the course through his forty-six years; he was every day the same. He loved America.

Mother McCray followed him and made the children the same; she was a quiet woman, well mannered and not given to argue, but when she spoke, every child respectfully latched to her every word. She never spared the rod and could use it while loving every new body and soul she delivered to work the earth. Lucious learned from and was of both. She had not expected to lose her husband ever; to her they would leave this world together as they practically started when she was fourteen and he a boy of sixteen in the fields of Scotland. Married in the church, she felt they were promised, but the Lord must have a different plan for her. She wanted to return to one place of her happiest memories—the day she stepped off that ship with her husband.

After her husband's death Mrs. McCray left with her youngest son, Thomas, who returned her to Boston. The cold bay had been the family's port of entry such a short, such a long time ago. The family became scattered, so much like the seed of corn when strong winds take it causing a crop to fail but spreading the earth's treasure for other life. It was like that for Lucious and sweet Katy. They were but simply two more people of many from the

Highlands and old Ireland; scattered folk like leaves but taking on the task of living in a foreign land.

So many came slowly, through the mountains, across the plains, and into places where swamps sucked down hope or where the sun took everything as it's toll for the audacity of any newcomers to tread into it's hallowed deserts where it was king; not them, but the fire and heat of that which ruled the vastness. The owner of the mines put on a dance in the large barn that doubled as a church and their dry goods store for the work party. Every Christmas, he brought the miners and their wives to the social. Wild pheasant, turkey, and venison were served by several of the camp's women volunteers. They also cooked the beans, breads, pies and puddings to complete the full meal few enjoyed except on these occasions.

Lucious groomed his long black hair fixed over a strong, angular face and pulled on the new boots Katy made for him some months back. She dressed in her finest flow, the yellow material her mother left had been cut and sewn by her own hand to a long, billowing dress. Her dark blonde hair and new smile set off the dress causing it to look even finer. She was a beautiful, sweet, engaging woman. They walked from the one room cabin down the trail toward the barn where hymns were sung every Sunday and prayers delivered for sick friends and family, especially her father who was bound to die young by his own vice.

Tonight they would dance together like he did in old Scotland with his mother who taught him and little Cassy of the same green, fertile valley where her family raised sheep. He saw them moving their feet in unfamiliar patterns and to musical instruments that were played differently. The rhythm had a certain flair and life to itself, traces of what he heard before were there and he found he liked the mostly makeshift sounds the fellows produced with steel, strings and small boxes.

He followed old Jeb and McNulty as they took to the floor and in what he heard as a mix of minuet and jigs, sustained a regular pattern by foot and hand with their women.

"This coming spring, we'll be moving further south, you know, Mr. McNulty. I'll be taking only one sire and filly and me lovely wife."

"So I understood it, Mr. McCray. Good fortune to yer now when yer do. You be fine farmer. I'm sure of that. The weather's more comforting for growing yer crop," the crusty Scott said.

"Aye, it is indeed. We're blessed people now and need to make the better of it here."

"This new country surely will be that."

"Aye, sir. I'll miss all when we go. I know it'll be fine though because I'm following Him."

"Don't ever lose your faith, young Lucious McCray. Those who do, die, yer know."

"I won't do that."

"Now take yer beautiful wife and dance with her. I believe she's tired of waiting while yer idle with an old man," he laughed loudly, loud enough to be heard throughout the barn.

"I tried and do have troubles with the footwork, you know."

"Yer have to go on. Yer have to put yerself right in the center and you'll learn, to be sure." He laughed with the young Husband and they toasted to each other's success with a tip of the cider brew the owners kegged last year.

"I don't think I can drink much of this, Mr. McNulty. Forgive me for stopping."

"Go on now, son, and take yer wife." He laughed heartily, causing his fully protruding belly to jiggle and move faster than the music.

He'd been a miner for years and now worked as a bookkeeper. Since being given that job, Andrew McNulty had grown fat on opossum, sugar, and sow belly. His work in the mine ended when his back gave way and he couldn't move very much without paralyzing pain crippling him to his knees. He was lucky for the time the owner Creeless needed someone to make entries as his business grew from serving some of the new northern industry rather than only moving mule wagons of southern heat out of the heart of Tennessee.

"Please favor me, Katy, and dance if you will," Lucious said. He smiled on her glow made slowly brilliant by the light of the well-placed lanterns. Her look reminded him of their wedding night and how the lightest reflection of light barely showed her skin she reserved for him. He held that fond memory in detail of their beautiful night when he first loved her and took her body as his own. She nodded quiet affirmation as she did that night and followed him by hand to the floor again.

This time he had to more forcefully control his limbs and learn this dance. It may be a long time before there would be another or an occasion for another. He knew that and he knew all she had in this world was her faith in him and the most profound hope God would favor them with children and sustenance.

"Katy, dear Katy. You're such a wonderful prize! Have I said how very much I love you?" he whispered through the noise of the hall. "Have I even begun to tell you?"

"You don't have to worry yourself, sweet Lucious. I know you do and will always as I you," she said softly.

"When we go to Alabama, I don't know how we'll fare, you know."

"We'll fare well, husband, because you and I are wed in His name and are bound. He'll not let us falter to be sure. Now, go to the corner you see McNulty and start when he starts," she said and smiled generously toward her groom reassuring him with a slight squeeze on his hand.

"Very well, dear wife. I won't make a fool. You'll see this time." He smiled back and turned toward the corner as the musical group of miners was set to begin another tune by sounding a long, warning stroke on one violin.

That summer he heard the settlers in Texas were talking of independence. His brother should have lived to see it happen. As he and Katy loaded their belongings on the backs of two horses to meet a caravan headed southerly, he heard Luther's voice. A deep echo of words whirled in hard brogue he hadn't heard since Boston; his snarl telling him of war and sons as though a warning he could hardly heed was being put in his soul.

This wild country was plenty violent and it didn't take much effort to find it. One so inclined could relish any sort of inward and outward fight he wanted. If it weren't the stubborn trees and felling them one at a time to scratch a plot that would grow a little so the land that could yield, it was the many wars, small and large.

Quietly, slowly, for God's sake, there were also growing clamors in turn over slaves. Other storms were also gathering strength beyond Mexico and north of her, growing near every McCray; there was the wretched struggle of both the blighted natives and newcomers and the desperation of other settlers with far less honed and kept character. There was the struggle to eat and stay warm.

Lucious hoped to find peace on top of the mountain as his father desired and take up his father's dream as his own and go where the family could prosper humbly yet sufficiently and for their children to inherit a richer life. His was to begin the legacy and chisel forever a place for the McCray clan. Theirs would be a family of honor, goodness and faith and of the mountain. It was for this, God's favor, and to make for Katy a better life than she had, that through the clouds of any danger and destroyer, his was to grip hope out of all of it, tighten the clinch until it yielded unbreakable steel and force his thrust of a single spiritual man to prove again what others who came before him proved.

Chapter 2

Lucious was a man who blended in a crowd; there was no extraordinary look about him nor did he carry any unusual feature. He was plain like his father. His arms were hardened by the work of the pick, his brow furrowed by the sweat creasing his young face in his long thirty years, and he was humble in sway and demeanor, as he'd been taught. Lucious was courteous as most and walked and attended his Katy always as a gentleman.

He brought his wife to the train of souls passing from Richmond headed south where the main body would settle in Louisiana where rumor was there was a better chance to live in peace with the Indians. The McCrays would attend as far as the Alabama mountain and bid the rest well in their journey; he knew his and Katy's would be a short, safer trip and those who ventured further, wagered their very lives with each passing mile until they arrived at the few clusters where there were many others like them.

Brother Arthur and Sister Rebecca left their mother with Thomas and took leave to travel a hundred miles north of Tennessee that same spring. Arthur found work as a boot maker and Rebecca began to clean the houses of prosperous merchants who used the river to float foodstuffs and fabric to the ever-increasing number of people spreading along the basin and westward. The fort in Ohio, where the wide river of the gateway ran in spiral spilling its muddy banks for untold miles, gave up fertile growing fields in return for its occasional wrath and the new town was growing large. After a year, one of those merchants persuaded her to lay with him and afterwards left fifty silver dollars by the bed. She found a new way to make a living and spite the God who took her father.

Make good, the words echoed inside Arthur's skull as a command without choice. His father would expect no less of him. Lucious thought of all of them often and during the quiet times, missed Arthur and Rebecca's company. Arthur had been a poorly prepared child and sickness kept him down through most of his early years. Now that he was a grown man of twenty-three, he received some measure of health as recompense and also the responsibilities he must inherit as one no longer needing care. He gladly shouldered every burden and pleasure of his open gate.

Rebecca had been at her father's side continuously while he was alive; she was strong and fetching as a child and could cook everything her mother could by the time she was a young lady of twelve. When she reached sixteen, she was thinking of marriage but in the day Lucious and Katy left for Alabama, she had yet to meet the right man. Lucious loved their letters and treasured them above any belonging. He boiled their coffee as the Company slowly moved livestock and horses, wagons and dogs toward their new home.

There was little time ahead of him; the work that waited loomed fearful. He had yet to begin that which he was commissioned the still many miles away and wondered how well Katy and he would fare. Lucious thought they were moving much too slow and every day with only a few miles past, their party would take the night. Every day his burden compressed.

"Why am I drawn into this damnable fit, sweet wife? We're stalled again unlike the sea I remember that carried us steadily. I worry."

"Lucious, take your leave! We'll be fine." She turned her face away from his stare. "Do you know I'm bearing our first child? I tell you, don't worry. This baby is a sign," she said and smiled her own delicate smile that never failed to warm Lucious.

"There's much to do, Katy." Her words escaped him for a bit.

"And we will. I'm so very happy. Ours will be a good home with no contempt, you know. Smile for me, Lucious, so that I know you're happy too."

"Me, a father! Oh, how I feel so much a man like my father. We must take special care for your safe delivery, dearest. God, I wish I knew what to do!"

"Don't worry anymore. There's nothing for you to do…Just be near me, Lucious."

"Are you able to take a tin of this coffee?"

"Certainly. It's so good on this cool night. Sit beside me now and listen to all that's in the air." Without a word, he took his place beside her and smiled. From despair and worry, her few words, her announcement, made him feel the proudest and richest and the most blessed man on earth. He dared not share any such thoughts with his wife directly and he'd rather have his skin tortured with fire and ants than show any tears.

That night and those few precious minutes with his wife was pure joy. Somehow he must pen letters to his mother, Arthur and Rebecca and send them on a true course. They had to hear of his gladness and their new, larger family. Mother McCray would be fiercely angry if she didn't hear of his fortune away from Boston. He smiled over the prospect. It meant she cared a whole world for them; her family was her world. He would see the Creeless Brother, not for charity but for his child. He knew if he couldn't start his crops soon enough, he could work. His strain left him. He felt at ease and better able to bear the slow journey for what lay ahead was a man's heaven.

After seven days, he was summoned to report to the front oxen carriage. It was raining the day the land bound captain directed him to a cut, well-worn road. He was to take that road alone with Katy while the rest of the party made its way deeper across the Mississippi territory toward New Orleans.

"And about one day east you'll see the water where you're to take the way around it, McCray. Godspeed. I'm you don't find the mill; you'll be needing to ask closely. If you go on, you can't miss the farms," the captain said.

"Thank you. And may the rest of your own journey go on without incident. You're a good captain to deliver us."

The talk on the captain was that he was a direct descendant of one of the old Jamestown survivors and it seemed to fit. Generations removed from the few, his grandfather had taken an Indian maiden as his wife and the hardened lines of her forefather's special courage showed in his face. It was born from those very early years when the people placed their very lives in the hands of the Great Spirit.

Lucious announced their departure to Katy who broadly smiled and reassured him they were close as promised through her prayers. Alone now, they set off with the few things they had and the horse. He didn't rest until they made the whole leg, forcing each late step through the night and well into the next day when he found renewed energy.

He easily found Creeless the next afternoon by asking a merchant in the small town about him. The brother was a cheerful, kind sort with gray and wiry brush covering his face and, like his brother in Tennessee, a gray main falling to his shoulders. He directed him to their own acres with a few kind words and a simple arm gesture.

"You're next to me, Mr. McCray, and will take the land to the first hill. Not the second mind you, because it's easily confused and old Collins wouldn't take kindly to anyone's trespass."

Lucious went straight to the land he'd till and work and make yield bounty for his own use and for others he could trade with to fetch things his wife needed. Having paid his penance, they started with little more than the threads they wore to protect them from the cold rain. Katy brought a skillet and two pots, bowls and forks that were all her father could give her and a small chest of possessions closer to heart than useful.

Her mother's Bible and last tapestry where she knitted the hills and green of Tennessee; the woman's expression of hope before she died was done with poor yarn but in rich splendor. Katy kept those things and the short diary her mother managed to record their start since the Virginia shores and the boundless love expressed for her family, certain to provide the strength they needed. Now it was only she and Lucious. By the name McCray, their lot was to meet and embrace the dream, grasp the country and shake the land to feed them. Nothing could stop them and it had to be for both; it was certain.

"Take this!" Katy said as she handed over her chest with a tired motion of a wilting hand, fingers curled downward by the pain in her body. "Should this not go well, make sure you see my brother."

"Don't worry. You'll be fine," he tried to comfort her. "Sarah Creeless is coming to aid." She closed her eyes across a face no longer smooth but furrowed and bent to ripples.

Their first child was an agonizing day away but would be born before the hour the sunset again behind the broad towers of pines and oaks. Sarah Creeless had performed for all the women on the mountain and saw only one lost in her twenty years of service. During the quiet moments when her body didn't rebel against her, Katy wondered if she were ready to be a mother. She aspired to be as good of a teacher and parent as hers but the inescapable doubt haunted the young woman as she lay so near. Lucious wondered too and did not speak of it—whether he was man enough to be the father like his seemed overly presumptuous, an evasive overture.

The new life they were bringing into the world must have the best, the most caring and kind, be kept warm and fed and taught well. He nervously fetched Mrs. Creeless who told them they must summon her for the birth during a Sunday church meeting weeks ago. By September, Lucious, Katy, Gregory and Zechariah Creeless had built a cabin to face their first winter. Judge Hornsby, the County Administrator, pitched in and with his knowledge of roofing and hearths, made certain the build would keep any weather from encroaching inside the newcomer's place. The small structure was tightened by red clay and grass mortar and the fire pit in slate and limestone covered the length of one of the four walls. The hearth was a single monolith of rock that raised above the roof just enough to draft the smoke away.

He cleared part of the acreage to build the cabin but had planted barely enough to hold them until the next April. Neighbor Collins traded a cow for some of his cut timber and a month in days of the newcomer's labor. Seeing the new family, old Collins presented them a blanket and a carton of candles, some broadcloth his wife wanted to give the McCrays and a few worn but still good implements.

Collins wasn't the rascal Creeless warned him of after all. He and Creeless were the closest of friends and played that way. Sarah came and tended to the woman in a fashion that could have put Lucious off if he didn't know she was thinking of the best for Katy. He happily yielded to her every demand and ran out when she loudly told him to go and returned when she commanded.

Events were beginning to take form quickly and he moved and delivered things he was asked to deliver like a puppet on a tight string controlled by a boss who seemed she would hurt him more than a scolding if he failed her. As she had him going to and fro, he held his urge to laugh away from Miss Sarah out of fear she would punish him for that too. She named the first child Jacob and held the precious gift to her breast. The tenderness and love that filled the cabin overshadowed the joy and there was plenty of joy. Lucious could hear his heart beating and feel every push of blood to his head as he gazed on his wife and beautiful son. Miss Sarah embraced him.

"Take care now, Father. You have a family. Now let them rest. Go to John and he'll boil some coffee for you while I stay a while," she said and finally smiled for him. Her reassuring eyes erased any doubts.

Her strength and talent gave him pause and another reason to be thankful. He loved her as a sister, a dear, wonderful, spirited older sister whom he could rely on to be in their home when they needed her. Creeless was pitching hay where Lucious found him. His sons were helping. They were two young men born on the mountain ten and twelve years ago, but who could work as men twice their age. He left the mule and walked toward them.

"Mr. Creeless! I want to thank your family!" Tears came to his eyes he couldn't stop. "Miss Sarah has seen my Katy through the birth of a son and…" He brought his hand to a reddened face.

"That's good news!" The man stopped work and turned toward his neighbor, sweat pouring from him; he wiped his eyes clear and extended a hand toward Lucious. "Your wife?"

"She's fine and resting now with little Jacob. He's such a fine one! I've brought this. 'Taint much…only a small way to thank you and Miss Sarah and the boys here." Lucious handed over a basket with muscadine jelly, bread, and a glass full of cream butter.

"Thank you," he said softly as the boys approached the conversation. "It's a fine gift. Thank you! Here, Zechariah, take your brother and eat. Leave some for me!" he laughed and his smile was continuous.

"This is a happy day, young McCray. Sarah and I will bring your supper at dusk."

"You've done so much. Thank you, sir!"

"Please. You call me Zechariah. It's a grand day for our mountain you see. Having children makes us prosperous and I hope you have a full house!"

"You and Mrs. Creeless have been so generous. I'm taking some trees to build a barn and want to bring you wood for your hearth. Don't worry your mind, Lucious. The Judge and I will help you with that," he laughed. "A barn raisin' is a good reason to drink some spirited corn! We'll be there with others, be assured! Just be the good neighbor you are." His smile was a smile that quickly steeled Lucious' confidence.

He told himself that he had to load the man's barn with enough wood to see him through two winters.

"I hope Katy's in the best of health!"

"God willing, sir." He smiled then returned to Katy.

"Lucious...Miss Hornsby brought these things," Katy said as she rose, asking her husband to survey all that was placed on their broad oak tabletop. There was a basket of vegetables and fruit, a neatly folded stack of swaddling clothes, oil, and a leather pouch of money.

"She's so nice. The church folk took the collection for Jacob to have a good start. She said to tell you she's sorry she missed seeing you, but the Judge needed her...he's down sick."

"I'll have to thank them, Katy. May I fix you something to eat yet?" He slowly attended her side and held her hand while gently stroking the baby's forehead. His emotions were once again overwhelmed. He and Katy suddenly had the most important job.

Thomas worked on the docks and kept their mother warm in a small tenant nearby. He walked the mile to his job while she took laundry and cooked meals for gatherings. Boston was a beautiful town and full of history as the seat of the great revolution. The place suited her better than the edges of America's frontier—and bore a climate she was more accustomed. She felt safer there and at home in the church she gave thanks for the family's safe voyage. It had been months at sea and Boston was dry and warm and her fondest memory of Lucious and his smile.

Thomas pulled his weight and rose to a position of foreman to take charge of other men loading and unloading shipments. He noticed Mabel Hoban from Ireland early in their stay and would pass more minutes in the sundry she clerked than he had to, making himself a nuisance until she took notice. Her open eyes and slight body were beautiful. He dreamed of holding her tightly next to his body and knew the feeling would be heaven. He dreamed of kissing her beautiful lips, proudly walking with her and more. His shyness kept him from talking much but he was drawn to her. The sundry was in a row of closely built buildings on a narrow busy road nearby where all kinds passed—too closely to suit him. The seamen and roughnecks who worked around the docks posed a danger to her or to his chances. One day he stopped by the store after the last load of the day and he saw her talking to a taller man, more handsome he thought and knew he must take the chance or perhaps lose her.

He stood by until they were finished and he left.

"Mabel…how you be, today?"

"I'm fine, Thomas McCray. And you? Do you want your usual pan of meal?"

"Fine, fine. No, ma'am. We're fixed for meal. Mother is preparing a feast for the assembly and we're to dine on some that's over tonight."

"Okay, then. And what can I get for you?" she asked the shy stranger. He stammered and hesitated but finally summoned the courage he needed.

"Mabel…I want to call on you. I would very much like to have some time with you," he said as he looked at the floor.

"Well, stop staring at the floor then, Thomas. I was wondering if you'd ever ask!" she laughed. "Why are you so shy?"

"That's wonderful, sweet Mabel. May I call on you this Sunday?"

"Surely. You can attend Mass with us and then eat."

"I would like that. Are you close?"

"Aye, we are. My family is just outside the city on a place."

"Is that where your father tends iron and smiths?"

"Aye. His shop is alongside of our home." She smiled. "And the pigs are in the back!"

"I'm greatly honored, Mabel. I'll ride out before the hour of ten."

"Do come, Thomas, and bring your mother if you will…we'll enjoy the day I'm sure."

Through their twenty-two planting seasons, Katy and Lucious became new parents to Jebediah, a sturdy one, Rachel with her full hair at birth, John the smaller, and then Carl. Jacob and Jebediah were friends as well as brothers and were the first to learn work. They learned to ride and shoot by the time they were of ten years, another gift from Judge Hornsby who taught them while teaching his daughters. His experience in Texas convinced him every American should know.

Zechariah taught Lucious and his sons how to tend cattle and sow to make sure the livestock grew fat and healthy. Rachel learned to cook and mend. They were all taught to love the land. Lucious thought of himself as prosperous and blessed and during their eighteenth year on the mountain, he purchased a fancy carriage for the family. There was a brisk trade for the swine he farmed south of Gunters Crossroad and fair barter closer to them for the hay, oats, and corn he tilled every year.

Katy became known as the finest seamstress for miles stretching past several counties and every bride who was able to go to her had her make up her wedding gown. Old Higgins distilled corn and made a fine whiskey behind his sawmill. His roughened skin and hairless scalp rumored taken by the Creeks caused him to be a strangely imposing figure whether intended or not.

Some said he had been a river man and lost his hair in a drunken fight over a woman with a mad Frenchman. He never told anyone the truth about it and no one dared to ask. Lucious came to know of him and began having the trees he felled cut into smoother timbers by the crusty temper of a man who hardly spoke. He left him be otherwise and directly warned his sons to stay away from the man of doubtful character.

The church on the mountain was a Methodist group formed by Jonathon Walker who rode his stallion across and back two hundred miles of counties to tend to the spiritual needs of all who would listen. Town folk started a school and used the church building. Every McCray child had to attend; the farm was second. Katy knew in her heart the schooling of their children was most important and Lucious never protested.

The McCrays attended services and sang the hymns; the children had to also learn the Bible and faith in God.

"We're going to see a nice profit, Katy. The Creeless family will do me the honors," Lucious said.

"That's grand! Do you think we'll be able to buy some cloth—enough to fit up each child for Sundays?"

"Yes—and enough to get you a pretty dress and hat from McCullough's store."

"I don't need that, but I'd surely buy a doll for Rachel and perhaps a new iron and churn. Those things would suit us well."

"Surely. And I'll be adding stock. There's a good place down from the barn for sow, you know. I'll be building a smokehouse before next winter," he said as he put the ledger down.

"Miss Rutledge said Jebediah is doing very well in school, Lucious. She told me she thinks him to be exceptional."

"He's like each of our children." He smiled. "And he'll be a fine man with a future. I think all of them will be the finest citizens."

"We're a blessed lot." He paused. "I was thinking of traveling to meet my brothers if it can be arranged. It's been well past ten years since I've seen them."

"I'd truly enjoy going. Do you really think it's possible?"

"Yes. Certainly it is now with the rail from all points east—even past here. We can go by way of steam." He lit a stick in the hearth and brought it to a pipe packed with tobacco.

He took the smoke in the evenings after settling for the dinner Katy prepared every day. If no animals left the fencing, he'd be able to rest. The children were reciting to each other in preparation for Miss Rutledge's class the next morning. Hearing them was happiness to Lucious and Katy. The couple was proud of their brood and it was a good day. Everyone was well and laughing inside the home. Storms brewing on earth between people caused Katy and Lucious to hold fast to the church and clutch Brother Walker's every word in the hope of salvation from every calamity. Madness seemed to take hold and fester a most ominous presence in every corner of men's minds and they heard it was in every place.

From Kansas to Boston town, Virginia and Missouri, people were angry and humankind seemed postured to die. In Alabama and Georgia, there was talk, dangerous talk. Lucious and Katy didn't want to hear of it, didn't want troubles, and never understood how and why there could be such a horrid disease of minds to cause them to think they can own another. Slavers were determined. Men of faith were determined. Their causes were against each other in a campaign presently of rhetoric, but fiery and perilous talk it was. His iron seemed colder to Lucious. Some were talking of killing to defend their claim of ownership of people while others of killing every semblance of the unrighteous, inhuman, wrong notion of titling human beings to another.

There was a horrible stain in their country, one so powerful and rich, it was impossible to imagine, let alone cause a cleansing of hearts. Katy had it come to her in an awful dream. Her sons would be taken with Lucious in a single moment of this insanity and be given over lifeless to the dirt and worms. She prayed every day the talk would remain mere words until men tired of it and stopped talking of war.

Lucious kept to himself during those days and began tending a fire to bend iron. He learned by doing when his blade fractured, and after sealing the first edge, went on to fix, reshape and mend old tools and soft iron skillets for neighbors. The small hearth he fashioned inside the barn and a homemade bellows of canvas allowed his own inferno and scorch with coal to fuel his flaming tempest—a burn he could control. During those days he hid his mind in work.

There were always fences to build or replace, plenty of time needed on the till, and late hours consumed in a smoking barn. He thought of his sons when he couldn't escape and their age. Jacob and Jebediah were men now and bolstered with all the fire and energy young men possess. They would surely want to go when called; he could hardly stop them from living the idea of protecting their home. He would rather go himself—another Southern man simple in principles—swallowed by events others controlled but knowing his lot was to stay.

Thomas and Mabel wed that spring and moved with his mother into a small house built next to the Hoban's place. There were a few clear acres easing to the north from the city where the family could grow cattle fat while her father taught Thomas the trade. Their house began with two rooms and grew to four within three years as they had their first child. Mrs. McCray doted on her grandchild and wrote to Lucious and Katy every week telling them of his latest.

Thomas was able to realize the warmth of her body and heart next to him and the best life has. During the winters he made sure the hearth was always fired and she made sure there were plenty of heavy and plump quilts. While Mother McCray was sleeping in the next room, she and Thomas would love under the covers. Their son Peter grew and learned to farm swine and cattle; when he reached thirteen, he was brought into the blacksmith's shop, which was beginning to become part of the town now as more city buildings were built around them. Their acreage like others became but a spear northward, with people and traffic coming closer and deciding the edges of their property. Father Hoban and Thomas knew it was a matter of time and it was drawing near when they would have to move further out or forfeit the livestock. Boston was growing along with their business, which consumed more of their time. There were a steady and increasing flow of people who needed wheels repaired, horses shoed, and implements made. The men built a second hearth and bellows and put Peter to work when he was not in school.

They enjoyed reading of Jacob and Jebediah for their family in Alabama and sorely missed them. Thomas began to plan a trip now that many rail lines ran deep through the south. Their mother was near the age when she would be unable to travel. The time was short for her to see her elder son and her southern grandchildren. It would take a day over a week to make the trip and then another few hours' carriage to the mountain. Thomas and his mother planned to stay for a month before returning.

The family ate cornbread and bean soup with a portion of salted ham that day and began the journey. The way would pass through Maryland and to Virginia and then on to Chattanooga, with a change of trains at each town. Along the way, Thomas saw the beauty of the mountains and hills he hadn't seen since moving to Boston and remembered the snow caps, the never ending tree line and rivers and towns along the way. The country was a wonderful place to live and love, he thought. And how truly fortunate the McCrays were that their father brought them to the new land. This fall was another kaleidoscope of warm colors and nature's best dress.

As they came down toward Harpers Ferry armed soldiers delayed the train on the tracks. Their wait was not long so Thomas thought little about it. Word came through the coach; the rumor of a figure he read about as some distant fighter from Kansas, John Brown, was that he and his gang had brought violence to Maryland. The soldiers kept them well away from the trouble and then let them go on without a word.

They arrived in Alabama and found their way to the McCray farm where Katy and the boys met them and brought out the cake and biscuits. The party went into the night; Lucious brought in several friends from the mountain and they ate and laughed. The celebration went into the night and the next morning before everyone gave it up for sleep. Mother McCray held her grandchildren close and watched them play. She was proud of her sons and their families and prayed the Father who was lost to them saw. She felt he did and must be smiling for them.

The few weeks went quickly and as the fall settled in the family returned to Boston where Mabel and her father had been forced to sell. The levy was too high to take year after year and it cost them the small farm and the shop. They planned to talk to Thomas when he returned about some acreage further east, a half-day from Boston by horse. There was an old sod house but only two small rooms made up the space. Father Hoban figured he and Thomas could build more space in a matter of days and set a larger hearth before the worst of the winter.

Thomas missed Mabel so much he could barely think and the days required for them to return were long. He wanted her voice and touch; he wanted to see her. He wanted to hold her and bring her body to his in sweet closeness of hearts and souls, lips and breasts. While away he kept a journal of his thoughts about her and was able to record his loss of half of whom he became while away from his wife. The train took them northward slowly, agonizingly slowly. Loving her meant loving Boston and he came to that quickly.

Homecoming meant sweet warmth and happiness. It was good to see family but it was better for him to see Mabel, feel the crunch of fresh snow, and breathe the cold air. Working the bellows, watching Peter begin learning to walk and talk and having her waiting for him at the end of each day was the favorite part of his life. The train made its way along the wind of rail and finally Boston was in sight and close enough to smell.

Chapter 3

"Dear heart, you're beautiful and I cherish you. Have you been happy?" Lucious asked his wife.

"I'm happy for our years, but presently I'm very tormented by all the talk."

"Ours is a worry to be sure, but we have to go on," he said as he rose to her, taking her downcast eyes as a certain sign. Little could he say to remedy her sickness of heart on things so solemn and weighty. Still, she expressed love for him. That was one special part of her nature he adored.

"Let me kiss your beautiful lips and bring us together. Even amidst our hour of urgency, allow my arms. These events will go on, you know. And all we have is prayer. I'll never want you to suffer a hurt and I do so wish to make all your worries depart," he said.

That winter was mild but the summer was the hottest and reminded her of the summer she gave birth to Jacob nineteen years past. It didn't seem so long ago when she nursed baby Jacob. Lucious did his work the same as he did then, clearing, tilling, mending, and forcing what he could from the stubborn earth while losing more of himself under the broil of an unforgiving and constant sun. He tended Katy and she tended him through their toil. In the quiet moments of late evening the marriage often quietly recounted their blessings of children. Jacob and Jebediah were strong men now, Rachel was close to marrying age and very able, John and Carl were catching up quickly and becoming good hands. Lucious Brother Thomas, an avid student, could recite every line of the constitution and bill of rights by the time he was seven years old and remained studious and reserved another twenty years before the move north. The family often remarked he was much too serious for his age; he was in boyhood a man in little and growing skin.

The family took their carriage ride that Sunday like many Sundays before to listen to Jonathon Walker pronounce every passage to illustrate the narrow way; clearly and loudly he spoke of sin, death and forgiveness, heaven and hell, righteousness and redemption. That day the larger congregation brought food and a guest from South Carolina who was riding across the northern tier of his home state, Tennessee and Alabama then back again to deliver the call. Lucious knew of him from Collins and sent Katy home with the younger ones while he stayed to listen. As much disdain as he had for politics, it was still important to know of his neighbors and their intent. He was part of the country and would never have his family consider him or their own different; he saw it simply. He must raise his voice as, thanks to God, is allowed, but when determined by most; he had to go with them in full spirit because it was right.

Lucious noticed even old Higgins came to the meeting and slept through most of Brother Walker's message, apparently waiting for after. The hat he wore never came off and his scowl silently stayed fixed, as did an immovable expression through glassy eyes. A faint scent of corn liquor surrounded him; Lucious thought he may be drunk on the brew, but he was there and with them nevertheless, keeping a distance from the ladies and children as though he knew the protocol to adhere. After the hearty meal provided by the women of every house, Katy drove the younger ones back toward their home. Lucious, Jacob, and Jebediah remained with the men to hear from their guest. He gathered them around the large stone outside the building that once held a modest sign signifying the faith.

After a heavy storm blew a wooden sign away, a large stone was brought to the church and provided a natural speakers stand for talk of secession and forming armies. The South Carolinian spoke of their need to frighten the rascals across the Potomac from even contemplating enslaving the south further than the chains already forcibly anchored around the heel of the region under the guise of protecting the federation as founded under the constitution. During his spirited and optimistic speech, he said it wouldn't take much and it wouldn't be a long wait for the southern states to have freedom and live the proper way of the document penned by Jefferson. He asked everyone to sign for the militia as a showing and stretched out a large ledger.

"You all be kildt," Higgins abruptly pronounced in a slow draw and black tone of foreboding for all to hear, including the speaker who was speechless for the while. The Saw Miller looked straight into each set eyes and didn't flinch, didn't blink, nor did he utter another word. He was the first to leave them; the gathering fell silent until he was out of view. Lucious stared at the ground beneath him while both sons stood in the human queue forming in front of the stone. Jacob and Jebediah could not know, but he did.

There was a certain dark wisdom within that river man, born from years of experience and first hand knowledge of what lies beyond the shadow of their mountain; the humanity and strength of a country growing wildly and recklessly with ever more far-reaching power in industry, ships and armies that even the English couldn't hold and Mexico couldn't defeat. He knew America was more than a place; it was an event, a sanctuary for all and they were still coming. The young country was a marvel unlike the world had ever witnessed and possessed the sure strength and might that could never be beaten by any other challenge.

Whether the speaker was true or not wasn't known by those at the meeting. Most thought he was. But Higgins knew of other places and had seen more of America. He knows about the free states as he'd been along the Potomac to see the fortifications of men and material. As much as Lucious wanted to believe their farms would always be theirs by simply showing unity toward Washington, the spew from Higgins caused him painful pause. If there were such designs by those powerful men, their protests would favor a much crueler rejoinder. Katy could be feeling it right.

"They say a showing of war is coming, Katy. Men from all around are talking of it," Lucious said to Katy.

"With those from the North?"

"Yes. The man has said the same I've heard before, that the President has taken from us in the south unfairly by the high tax."

"Tax? I know nothing of this, Lucious."

"They want to leave the union and form their own country using the Constitution. They say Washington has thrown it out for the South."

"All this talk is an awful way, Lucious. I don't believe they hate us to do these things you say."

"The man spoke of only wanting fair treatment and it doesn't look good for them to change their views up there. He also said many he knows hate the abolitionists too. They're forcing things …"

"Do these same men hate us too?"

"They say the Yankee will take our farms for freed slaves. A sworn punishment of the South should they carry the day," he said painfully unsure.

"I don't believe him. Such foolishness! This doesn't become our folk. I pray it'll stop."

"Many think it's true. We signed the petition for the militia today, Katy, and I hope nothing comes of it. A fight is not a certain thing."

"Fight our own Country?"

"Aye. Those who would come here. And if that be true, we've had too many hard years to let anyone take it. Can't allow it," he said and turned his head down.

Several peaceful months passed but the fervor and fear was growing through every home on the mountain. The pitch of the rhetoric they heard and read took on an energy that enveloped most men who wanted to show their bluster and courage. Jacob returned from an absence of three days, which was unusually long for him and respectfully asked his mother to sit.

"Momma … I want to join a Calvary they're forming close to here."

"Oh? I don't want you to leave us, Jacob." She said with fear in her voice.

"Near every fit man is doing his share and I have ability to bring to our noble cause."

"I know, son, but your father and I worry so," she cried.

"Please. It'll be over quickly and I'll be home before spring."

The thought of any one of her children dying was like her own death but she sadly knew she couldn't hold him. She wouldn't. To strip him of his manly intent and cut such a pure heart would be stealing honor, pride and purpose away from a beloved son. She knew she could temper him still if she were wont to meddle with the precious principles she and Lucious taught him.

Another full year passed making a mockery of many fools' predictions. After the Fort Sumpter chorus, Katy received three letters through two planting seasons from Jacob to soften the quiet terror during those long craving months. Her son was in a bloody war and it would soon be Jebediah's turn. He was grumbling as his voice was changing from boy to man and she feared his intent. She and Lucious could do little but think of the other children to render health to their heavy hearts.

Jebediah became a soldier of the South in the spring and was transported by train deep in South Carolina for training with others to form the Eleventh Alabama Company. The men and boys emerged out of the northern Alabama foothills of the Appalachian range to fight the Yankees as part of a glorious redoubt against aggression.

Each donned their hand made blouses proudly, the gray and butternut colors new and bright. It would be weeks of marching and drills for combat, learning how to reload quickly and fire from a disciplined line of flesh standing tall and exposed. It was weeks of bread and beans, grainy coffee and hard tack and occasional forays into town for cider.

He had not seen a battle and thought of war as an adventure with other men set to make things right. He thought of being in the service was a wonderful change from the farm where the chores were different and less taxing. Learning military bearing was new and an exciting thing for the boy and it all made him feel more the man than he had known before. One morning he came to know it was far more serious.

The veterans marched in formation into the heart of the camp; solid, dirty, dangerous looking men on either side of two prisoners marched in with no smiles that could be seen. Jebediah, Jim Payne, and Earl watched them and wondered what this was to be. Sailor and Preacher were sitting at the fire with them. Men of Jeb's Company who came to know each other some, new and there because they felt their Country calling them to serve were watching in silence and wonder.

"What do ye suppose this is?" Jeb asked the crowd.

"I haven't heard, young feller," Sailor said. "It 'pears those two have committed an offense."

"I believe them to be deserters. See, they are in a mere portion of the uniform. I suspect they tried to leave."

"We need to get on with the business of readying for drill," Jim Payne said dryly. "Forget them," he muttered as the men were marched passed them beyond sight.

"Poor devils. Brought shame on their families," Preacher said. Jeb looked at him, his mouth turned down, hoping he would never do the same.

The cadre turned to, checked their dress and took their new rifle barreled muskets up to report as the same it had been every morning. They knew it was the parade ground, a field cleared but pocked with small thatches of growth where feet hadn't already killed it and earth ready to slime up when it rained.

Before they made their way, the captain's courier stopped them and said it was the company's order to appear in line at the northern edge of the camp.

"You must form up near the breastworks on the other side, gentlemen. Captain's orders."

"We be on our way," Sailor assured the fifteen-year old clerk whose oversized uniform hung on him like scarecrow. Jeb and the rest followed him through the tents and found a large body of troops standing at attention facing the earthen and timber wall built for the recruits to learn of quick fortifications. In less than ten minutes, there were five hundred southern troops formed as thick blocks of gray in their companies surrounding the face of the breastworks. In the center were two hastily placed timbers piercing upward, standing out from the wall and shorter in height. The battalion stood in silence waiting for their orders. An hour passed and no one moved. There was a pall and aura over the field that day; the men knew this was to be an extraordinary morning. Finally the captains of each company marched out of the near tent together and split off to face their respective men. A colonel and his aides marched to the center and front and turned to face all of them. Quickly behind the colonel a group of veterans cadenced by an older crusty and tough looking sergeant marched the prisoners to stand and face the companies. Jeb began to realize what was to happen as soon as he saw them.

"Gentlemen! You soldiers of Alabama, South Carolina and Georgia hear this!" the Colonel read from a group of papers held with both hands. "Know ye today these two stood accused and found guilty of desertion in the face of the enemy. Their sentence to be carried out today is death. Today the great Confederacy takes no contentment, but rather umbrage in her duty," he said then paused and retrieved another page. "The guilty are Jody Fogle and Adolphus Greene who have been sentenced to die by firing squad by the military court convened in Charleston on the 20th day of August this year."

His full-mouthed voice resonated through the ranks. The two doomed men stood there weakly looking out to their fellows with sad eyes. One was smaller and began to faint; a veteran caught him and helped him remain upright. Their arms were then tied behind them to the posts putting both facing the troops and Jebediah saw them as lonely stick figures roughly resembling other soldiers from his distance, their faces a blur and indistinguishable.

Two of the veteran troop tied rags around each man's head and a preacher of the Gospel offered words of reassurance then left them. Ten of the veterans and their Sergeant had formed a line thirty feet in front and were ready to carry out the sentence. Jeb thought, *this is hard to believe—why anyone would find himself in such a dire place!* He prayed neither had simply wanted to return home to tend to a sick family member or something like that and they were true cowards who let their fellows down when it counted most. Surely, he thought, there is good reason for them to die. Jeb closed his eyes and prayed for them.

"Fire!" He heard the command and saw the figures slump dead and thought, *the poor sons of mothers somewhere who most sorely are missing them were taken on purpose for their deeds maybe done before they thought about it much. And for this they were killed—eternal punishment for men who failed their task—maybe they simply had no stomach for it.* Jeb thought it a terrible conclusion to that which must have been their good intentions early. He promised God and himself he would never do the same.

Chapter 4

It all had what was to become a familiar look and feel. An awful odor of rotting and burning flesh hung heavy in the air all around them. Nothing they could do now could save any one of those lying singly and in heaps before them. There was no taking back—no way to undo what happened here. The ditch splitting a field of an unknown Virginia farmer and the field itself took the place of center in every man's world. There had been human gallantry and honor displayed unmatched in the history of a country so young.

Their bravery would hardly be known; only a few of their stories would be retold that could preserve some purpose for their deaths and—for a little while. Most had their lives stopped at once, many lingered in agony until the numbing influence of death finally yielded the last measure of mercy. After a generation, there would be little remembrance, little appreciation for their sacrifice, and their names would be forgotten in the circle of living.

Jebediah left his mother and father when the call went out from the Eleventh Alabama. Captain Stewart organized a new company for the regiment in sore need of replacements. The band of men formed out of their red clay farms and small towns was part of the reinforcements ordered up by the south's new commander, General Lee. They were late for this battle, having been in training while Stewart mustered new recruits.

Not one knew what war meant. Left to their conjuring, weak imaginations, not one saw beyond the boredom of camp, and their drills and practice. The quick spectacle before them defined war and washed them in blood at once. The filth left over hadn't been known, the smell never experienced. Private McCray pondered first on Jacob. To every man and boy, the truth now lay in front of them; they were dispatched to bury the dead on the way to the forward campaign. All were feeling and not thinking the same in the first awful minutes of their arrival. With one mind, one smell, one hearing and sight— they were small, trifling, insignificant observers coming to that work left for them in a field. All were changed.

The undefined gripped every man of Captain Stewart that day and they were violated seeing their comrades reduced to refuse of bone and blood. They were suddenly scorched, deflowered and their innocence gone forever. Their day was the sight of a pile of burning men in the ditch, drooped over one another in grisly embrace and, close by, others lay in solitary repose where they fell. The replacement Company to a man learned that day. Limbs and heads and tethers of streaming flesh were all but indistinguishable black against blackened ground.

Most in their party of internment became sick and lost their stomachs on the whole sight or as pieces were stumbled upon in their start of work to dignify the fallen. In Gunters Crossroads, the Town of Guntersville, Katy McCray cried reading every posting in the church of the dead and missing. Lucious cried when he was alone in worry over Jacob and Jebediah when he could steal away and take up the dark. Part of them was in peril forced by the way of man; the hollowness and agony of being impotent in its face tore at their hearts and both were of poor heart.

Yankees could counterattack and move back to the pasture any time so the respects afforded could be little except for hastily prepared graves and markers. There was no dignity in piles of human carnage and the vomit and blood and little pride found in yards of entrails leading to half of what was a farmer with a family, an educator or blacksmith, or a fine preacher or someone's beloved brother. Jebediah found one lifeless form bloated to the seams and gazed on him to respect for a while. He thought of this poor man to recapture his control and forbearance in the glorious cause. He wondered what he could have been and done, who he was, and whom he left behind.

An ominous gray smoke settled over most of the field and extended to the hills much further away where he heard the Yankees were lingering for them. Fueled by streams of darker smoke, it lingered still; it gave voice to a sadness felt on earth that day. To a man, the company felt its unwelcome advance and saw it take posture, moving slightly but dwelling as a rancorous setting; man made that uninvited stranger of consummated evil. One full week had yet to pass beyond the grumbling among their new troop of boredom and of their wanting to get into the fight.

Jeb felt the strain of routine at camp like the others and longed to get on with the grand adventure. When orders finally came down to them, there was jubilation and laughter and drinking. Every man was happy. They were still convinced the war against Lincolnism would be short and exciting and not so bloody. Fort Sumpter had been easy enough.

Rather than tending to fence rails and gathering feed, Jeb followed his brother to fight for their noble cause. He yearned to see other people and visit larger towns he only heard and read about in the occasionally printed newspaper in Guntersville in what would become the seat of Marshall County. He wanted to see, taste and hear the offerings of cities like Atlanta, New Orleans, and Richmond that had been described as so pleasant.

Listings of the dead failed to dissuade his youthful optimism of the war being an adventure and over quickly. He worried he would miss the engagement entirely. He did march through Richmond on the way; it was the closest he came. The anticipation and curiosity he felt at eighteen years, when innocent and sheltered and wide-eyed gentle, was all gone the instant his Company became part of Beaver Dam Creek. More than a brief skirmish, the creek had been a fierce, desperate battle, gory beyond description between countrymen.

This must be worse than foreign soil, young Jeb thought as he considered the sights before him. People were crueler to those they knew it seemed, than to those they didn't. He couldn't imagine the carnage was the same toward the British or Mexicans. Surely he would have heard had it been so. *How can men do this to other men?*

Dying for loyalty and honor among men took them. Jeb felt those words were important that day; these brave souls must have thought it worth the forfeiture. Not a man could waiver as the line bore toward certain death for many; gray and blue waves advanced for their prize and took their wage. His order was to rest the ones whose reward was final. He had to begin thinking of Mary Hornsby instead of pride and honor and kept her face in his mind's view through the job. Those he was to silently receive would never know more of life's pleasures. *The poor wretches would never see or hear or taste anything good; they'd never know anything precious of this earth and never enjoy delights of family and friends. Theirs,* he prayed, *was now found in Heaven.* They were like him and he learned that day, could have been him except for circumstance. The vision of her face composed him steady and whipped the weakness growing within his legs.

"Mister Stewart! Bring the wagon up!" Lieutenant Colonel Hulles shouted over toward the young Captain. Marcus Stewart brought his palmetto around and rode quickly past the line of men who stood in silence. The horse drawn wagon carried a cache of tools and digging implements, ammunition, and a few bulk provisions for the company.

"We're to dig for our friends, Jeb," an older soldier muttered reverently for the young McCray to hear. "They is goin' to have to be put in the ground and we're goin' to do it."

"Yes, sir. I guess that's 'bout all we can do for them," the man who spoke had volunteered at forty years and became a friend in the early camp with whom Jebediah spent most of his time. Jim Payne was more like an uncle to the young adventurer from Alabama and quickly became his counsel.

"We'll be in the thick of it soon, Jebediah. We'll be required to have our soul's right." Jeb heard his words and didn't want to think of them. Looking at the task before them and the appalling reality gripped more of him and caused him to begin to shake uncontrollably.

"So it comes to this, Mr. Payne."

"Steady now, boy. Don't think about it and bother you now. Stay with me."

Captain Stewart and other officers were conferring beside a slight knoll that overlooked much of the grisly scene, which was the Eleventh Alabama's portion. Distant thunder shook the air and ground in a frequency only mankind would conjure. Jeb began to feel very small; he recognized for a moment that he had not a clue what future there may be for just another son of farmers. There were several hundred thousand like him and who left home and family—the mothers and fathers and clans who supported the war by offering their own and the blood of treasured members.

"I can at least work hard for them, Mr. Payne. These are brave souls who came before us."

"Yes, they were. We'll remember them well."

"I don't know what I'll be in battle."

"You'll be as brave."

The men had been ordered to stand by and were allowed to sit and rest near the creek. A few had taken handkerchiefs and fixed them over nose and mouth in a vain attempt to escape the stench. Most were gathered with their backs to the scene and trying to make conversation about anything else they could think of; the men around Jeb talked about hunting, home, sweethearts, but war emerged between them causing theirs to be brittle talk not nearly sufficient.

The captain called to his lieutenant and the sergeant major and told them to detail the men toward the base of the knoll and begin digging a trench parallel to the creek. Jeb looked into Mr. Payne's eyes for reassurance. The older gentleman gently smiled and then stoically turned to stare at the black earth leading to the knoll. As soon as the order was given, the Company stood in unison and crossed muskets. A trail of the reinforcements slowly made their way toward the wagon and stood to draw the instruments of internment. Another trail formed beyond the wagon and slowly walked toward the lieutenant.

Lieutenant Padgett called out to three of the troops to report to him. He was overheard by Jim Payne and Jebediah instructing the small squad to assist him in the removal of those fallen who ranked captain and higher. They were separating the higher ranks for graves. The rest was to be put together in a trench after every effort to identify each one is made. Some of the men were assigned to make out markers and put a name and date on each one; little else would be left to distinguish a forever lost, loved one. Not one of the fathers, sons, and brothers expected to die like this.

They started digging the trench, following the mark made by the captain and lieutenant.

"We need to make certain we have it far enough, men," the captain announced as he moved his mount further away from the rocks that marked the end of the trench. "Come to this point and go as deep as five." Jebediah noticed the captain bending toward the earth from his saddle to place a stick. For an instant, he thought it would be good if he fell off his horse and ate part of the ground.

He quickly snapped back to his loyalty and better morality. As if trying to escape in some way from the awful job, he had to silently acknowledge Captain Stewart had been a fair captain. He was firm but he made sure the men had in his charge had enough to eat and enough rest. He'd done the best he could that circumstances and orders allowed. Jeb and the company knew that.

McCray saw it wasn't unusual though for orders to be questioned. Far different than what he was accustomed to, discipline was loose and he heard it was the same way in every unit. Most officers were elected and each of them expected questions and grumbling. Captain Stewart had the ability to out-argue and out-shout the men who challenged him and he made it clear to the Company early, he was in charge. Jeb knew someone would raise an issue and it wasn't long.

"Aye, Captain! Is this the Christian burial for these brave lads?"

Stewart didn't notice who had been so bold so he guided his mare toward the cluster where the voice came. His voice was gravely serious. His message was for all of them.

"Yes, it be so! You men must do this for it's all we can do! My whining boys! Do ya'll hear that thunder yonder? We must be up there tonight so we have not the time to do this more proper. Now, you get to it!" He turned his horse and galloped to the far edge of the company where a small stand of seedlings somehow survived the musket fire, canister, and grapeshot. The men watched him as he tied the mare and picked up a shovel with a broken handle thrown near the place.

Without a word, he began to chip and claw the earth near the stick. One hour of digging yielded the outline and after two more, the sweating confederates finished a five-foot deep by fifty-two foot long ditch. Their most difficult task now lay before the troop and was one Jeb dreaded the most. Handling their remains, some only pieces, and the gut-wrenching act of a last bit of care, brought every one of them to the limit of what they or any man could handle. Quietly, slowly, the troop moved toward every patch of honor, the men who lay swollen in silence, the lonely place where each of them died.

"Well, at least I'm happy we got to them before the Yankees did," Jim said softly to Jeb.

"They would have taken from them I heard…And still left our boys out for the critters."

"Yes, sir, Mr. Payne. And I heard old Albert say General Lee is getting McClellan backed up so they won't be getting here! We'll sure help him take it to them! Reckon they'll surround Washington to keep us out." He managed a tinge of laughter to take up part of the overwhelming sadness he was unable to loosen.

"Hell, we don't want any of it, anyhow. Can't plant on brick."

"No, sir. Can't do that." He clutched the collar of another and pulled.

"Don't say anything, Jeb. Just do."

"It's hard, Mr. Payne."

"It's ours today. Tomorrow, ours will be worse."

"I fear the sight of these men is doing me badly. This vile theater has taken all from the poor wretched boys beneath us and we're the same. This fate could be ours."

A detail of three was tasked with recovering weapons, caps and balls, and anything of serviceable condition. The pile of stores that had been used in the fight and now harvested for others, gave some measure of testimony for their worthy cause. A few sabers, many pistols and forty-three muskets were found to be in good condition. To a man, the small cadre of rebels in Company B became more willing to battle the Yankees as the dead were moved and their armaments picked.

There had been and was an irrepressible wave of group movement and singular thought. Many may die and they were willing. Events from

Mannases to the creek bore out the good chance they had of succeeding if they were willing to meet the threat with every drop of sweat and blood like those did before them.

While pulling the fallen toward the ditch where most would lay together, the warrior's determination gripped every man of the Eleventh Alabama. Clutched in heart and soul and knowing they were in the inescapable throws of their own legacy, they knew death may be their reward, but it was theirs to spend to save the sweet essence of the south. It fell to Jebediah since he was the closest to follow a crimson path to a sunken place in the earth where he found the shreds of an arm next to where a soldier fell. He gathered the man's collar with a strong grip and pulled him to the trench. His mind numbed as the area began to look cleaner and yield little evidence of what happened in its hardened space. He thought of their faces. He saw each lifeless face cut down before fully working a life; in front of him now, presently and forever these were gone to dirt. He remembered Mary, his mother and father, Jacob, Rachel, John, and Carl.

The pitiful face bore extreme suffering. His arm had been taken at once; it was quick. His chin had been nearly shot off and one of his eyes dropped out and yet there were signs etched on the remainder of his face that he may have lived tortuous hours after taking the hot, destroying balls of iron.

"Wonder if he lingered long?"

"Don't matter, Jeb. He's at peace now."

"Maybe the agony and misery is released to the air waiting for another."

"Stop such talk young McCray and fetch the lad yonder."

Jeb went to one intact except for the red stained holes in his coat and began to move him; flies and bugs were moving inside the open wounds and in the deep cut lacing the length of his arm. Death is final and awful and worms are real and he was again powerless to find comfort in remembrances. His mind was in a back and forth whirl of emotion one minute, abandoned the next. The drummer boy he left for another had met and lost to destiny as well those who died older.

Every man who saw him cried out loud at first glance; every one who wore the gray tried in vain to hide unbecoming tears. He must have seen only twelve or thirteen years. No one knew him and no one from his family could be there to grieve more and protest. He still needed his mother for many things; he needed his father. The Eleventh Alabama finished the job by replacing dirt, covering the trench in minutes. Markers were carefully placed topside over the location where each was laid.

The chaplain held a prayer service and reminded the men, the prospects for heaven for the brave were good. He asked God for mercy and forgiveness and for kind treatment for each new, poor soul entering his heavenly domain. It was to be called the battle of Gaines Mill. Ahead of them, the rebels were in a deadly struggle day and night except for brief repasts for both sides to collect their dead and wounded. They were cordial toward their enemy brothers when not facing each other to perform the decreed by circumstance and time.

It was life and death during battle and even as it was carried on, it wasn't for them to hate those wearing different uniforms except during those accursed moments when comrades fell. Jeb wasn't angry with any one camped in the distant hills. The Eleventh Alabama infantry unit was typical of every confederate group; the men took pride in their Regimental Colors and battle standard. Each knew his day was upon him. Each knew he would be thrust into the chaos and carnage to leave more behind. The guns in the distance told them all before the colonel or lieutenant or sergeant major said as much.

It was quiet in the ranks as they gathered their weapons and formed a scraggly line. The men were all standing, a few checking over musket lengths while others were to themselves, waiting in prayer or trying to straighten muddled thoughts. Memories of South Carolina and the training camp were gone and replaced by the new reality. Solemnly, they waited for the command.

"Mister Stewart! Move the men to the road double quick. We're going in," the captain said and gave Lieutenant Colonel Hulles a quick salute then raised his arm and circled an empty hand in the air to signal their march. Mounted on his horse, he moved to the first men and began leading the way. Within a few minutes a long gray line was stepping out.

Jeb knew every man's best performance was expected on the field of battle; in every contest, the rebels before them formed convention out of the extraordinary. The success at Mannases bolstered their ideas of victory. He heard many brag about the southern farmers and how they could out-march, outwit, and out-fight the Yankees. Such hardy talk from some out of their smaller numbers against a better-armed foe failed to surface now. In Carolina, no true exposure of substance taught them while they played in camp, safe, deep and far away from the killing. The lofty enterprise didn't require much tribute from any except for sworn words, sore feet, sweat, and tired eyes. To a man, they'd learn the cry on the morrow; a guttural hail squeezed powerfully through each throat to both frighten those across from them and bolster their own courage. Only by fire and test, the piercing and horrific rebel yell was learned and used as it compelled them forward to kill the disciplined and finely uniformed soldier of the North.

Jeb hoped he'd meet that test when he thought of it. But those around him absorbed lingering doubts as bread; to be a coward was worse than dying. As a Southerner, the yoke of their heavy burden and expected performance weighed him forward; it weighed each one of them. He must do well or suffer no face to his family, Mary, or any. The company left the field to link up with General Longstreet's command and follow through under General Lee. Whatever they'd be asked to do, Jeb thought, it would take them to another victory.

General Lee was the brightest, the best, and he was with them. They quickly marched in each other's shadows toward their Confederate Army.

The double quick march caused them all to breathe hard, each face pushed wind to bring new air to lungs that were biting heat, saving the survivor for his day in a lawless court. Cannon fire began to subside after the company put six miles behind them; intermittent shakes of the earth caught them, as they were closer now. They were led off the road by their captain and across another field planted in corn.

"It's a very good farm here and he's got strong, healthy pecan trees," Jim calmly said toward Jebediah.

The place was sullied with remnants, marking those who came before them and forced a union retreat. An overturned caisson, satchels, blankets and caps bore evidence of deeper scars the earth of one man's farm took that day. A small party of union soldiers was attending to the last of their fellows; searching for dead and wounded they missed during a first pass. The white flag furled easily in the quiet breeze through their uneasy calm; they were the first Yankees Jeb had seen. Company B was still moving but slower now; each step was wearier as they passed the blue detachment.

"They look like us."

"Yes, young man. And they be like us 'cepting the uniform," Payne sighed.

"I suppose they must have high-tailed it through here. Reckon our boys were after them directly." Jeb searched the ground with his eyes.

"Yes. Those up yonder who we'll joining." Jeb's shirt felt uncomfortable, scratchy and wet at the same time, plied to his skin like an unwelcome second covering. His trousers bothered his walk and the cupie he wore seemed to clinch the crown of his head. He felt the sweat running down from his temples and from his waistline. His matted hair was stinging him.

One foot in front of the other, he commanded himself. *Got to keep going. Must walk with them.* As much as he tried to lay home out of mind for a while, clouded images of the sweet refuge distracted Jeb. He longed to be there and the images were suddenly beyond his capacity to refuse.

He saw his mother working between their hearth and table lovingly preparing a fine meal and quickly, warm pictures of every brother and precious little sister caused a strained kaleidoscope to take on unwelcome and unwanted power of remorse. He saw his father and brothers cleaning scatter guns for a hunt, laughing and joking about which would first fire and miss the rogue buck this time they'd been after for years. He saw his brother Jacob pitching hay and for a second, swore he could smell home. He saw Mary Hornsbys' face. He watched as the preacher baptized little John, an event that brought out the cakes last year. He listened as the family laughed and sang together while Father struggled with an old banjo. He followed every detail of the worn and scratched places on the instrument Mr. Creeless shared with him back when momma had them all celebrate Jacob's tenth year. He felt the work of the field, the jerks and pulls and his muscles behind their mule. He saw his mother cry when Miss Sarah passed on and watched a quiet Zechariah Creeless stand with Gregory and his father so humble and heavyhearted. He saw Jacob when he enlisted in the southern Calvary and remembered how excited he was for Brother. The last he heard, he was in the Ninth Virginia. He'd always been better on a horse and frightened Judge Hornsby more than many times.

Lord, I hope he's well, he prayed. *Them Yankee balls don't know how good a brother he is and I sorely want to see him.*

At once Jebediah noticed movement in the wood-line ahead of them. It was a body of troops serving General Hill and as their column moved closer, more could be made. It appeared the woods were alive with men, horses, and weapons. It was the largest force Jeb had ever seen in one place; as far as his eyes could take the scene, there were troops. He was far removed from his family and felt it.

It was a long way too from the Marshall County courthouse where he signed up and caused his mother to cry again. He remembered the celebrations and goings-on around their little town and happily became part of it. The jubilant spirit that gripped most of the citizenry gripped him. Picturing a battle line such that laid before him could not have been done by any of them in those days.

War wasn't known; protecting their homes with rattling and showing seemed easy enough. Jebs' father expressed the same in those early days as many did. A government brought about by revolution couldn't object to the desire of a portion of its own people wishing to form their own for better reasons without suffering perfect ambivalence. It was hypocritical of Washington to hold fast all lands and territories through force. The government had become impoverished with greed and oppressive and had to be dealt with force.

"These are our homes!" The cry was heard and the blustering took. "These are our lands, our factories, our lives! We are the people defending every corner of the frontier south and west and our very right to live in peace and govern our own affairs is threatened!"

There was no question in the McCray home about the validity of their first cause. The family and community showered his older brother being the first of the sons to honor this belief with attention and gratitude. Parents McCray were proud of Jacob and hid their pain. Jebediah saw all of this and heard those feelings and his youthful desire quickly stirred action for himself.

The very idea of a Confederate States of America was enough to motivate him. It was the dawn of freedom for them; an event few in history ever chance to feel. It could hardly have been predicted the generations of exploitation their brave actions would cause. Before them lay the heart of a freedom worth dying for.

Now the June brought more than heat and blossoms and stalks and Southern men were formed by the tens of thousands in northeast Virginia and across from them were northern men. Ordinary men from Alabama, Georgia, Texas, and the rest of the south were engaged in a mortal contest with men from New York, New Jersey, Pennsylvania and other states of the north. Liken to each other, separated by fate, their enemy was their own to meet in the cruel, convoluted exercise of battle.

Jebediah's spirit of adventure gave way to a hope of survival when he dug and saw that trench. His mind was fed in the hours; he grew up that day. Ordered to stand picket left and behind troops already occupying the wood, the Eleventh Alabama spread their thin offering toward the western edges of the forest. Hot, wet, and worn, they quietly checked over their equipment. New knowledge was before them and their survival depended on chance and arms. Each man recounted powder caps, loads, and balls carefully. Some of the rebels appeared to have already been part of the campaign for months as their frayed likeness adjusted bed rolls in longing and carefully sipped precious water.

Jebediah took the wet cloth passed and wiped his brow. Relieved to be at rest while uneasy about being this close, he joined laughter when old Henry loudly complained the graybacks would best him before any Yankee could have a chance.

"They may find me squalling on me back to pinch the largest of the beasts! That'll give the first bluecoat an easy target on the ground! Damn, wretched sons they be!" Henry said with a sneer and a laugh.

"Quiet yourself, Henry!" a voice came from the left. "Only a gravely starvin' grayback would eat on you!"

"Aye! And one void of self respect for sure!" came another.

"What the insects take from you will leave less for us to smell, Henry! Leave them be!"

The moment took Jeb home and he forgot circumstance. As the formation fell silent, they felt manly. Soon they would prove to themselves and those next to them how strong and skillful they were as fighting men. Jebediah too allowed an unbridled, limitless sense of might fill him. The time was near and he would fight for his country. He would meet his appointment in good faith and nurture the gift of strength as others do from other men in the thick.

"Reckon we'll attack?" he asked Jim Payne who was quietly viewing the horizon.

"Don't know, Jeb. We very well may be but I hope not soon, dad gum. My feet are sorely in need of rest."

"Mine too. Reckon they'll say soon what plans they have for us," he said and smiled. "At least we're stopped for a while."

Jim reached into a trouser pocket and pulled out pieces of corn bread. He divided the fare with young Jebediah. "Here, boy. This'll settle our stomachs."

Sergeant Major Terry walked the length of the company reporting they would stay in those woods for the night and to use their time well.

"Well! That's good news," Jim sighed. "I'm relieving these boots and gettin' off'n my feet for a while!" he said and smiled at Jebediah.

The night air was pleasantly warm with a breeze winding through trees, gently touching each face. Sweet pine had replaced gunpowder and filth in the air. Those who weren't on duty slept on top of blankets and the roots, brush, and rock where they stood, but given some hours to sleep was a prize that overcame their every discomfort. Jebediah and Jim Payne laid out their blankets and set to turn in for the night.

"A prayer would do us good."

"Yes, sir," he said. Jeb's eyes were closing on their own through the silent period of their very human appeal.

"Have a good night too."

"Amen, Mr. Payne. Thank you," he managed the words. "Jim."

Chapter 5

Y a'll get to these coordinates by five. We'll chase 'em...When you're there, Captain, you'll be dispatched with orders," the colonel spoke within earshot of a group of rebels that included Jebediah. He was taking some coffee and sharing a fire with Jim Payne and several others. It was their breakfast and the black grounds from the boiling pot were riding with every sip as the solid part of their morning meal. Promised provisions were on the way by wagon but the Army always moved faster.

The wagons were late—and would appear only when possible because the soldiers traveled any terrain; the Army made often-mere paths where the wagons couldn't follow in straight line. The hungry southern men waited patiently until their food reached a junction of roads or a town. Many died with empty stomachs.

He gingerly touched his lips to and away from the edge of the tin cup. The coffee was hot; it could scorch one's tongue if the black liquid wasn't partially inhaled. A privileged connection the coffee, a steaming remembrance of his own civilization when he thought of Mary and the church meetings where she came so beautiful and he bashfully watched her from afar. He wanted to court her but she had a suitor, Thomas Stamps, who was a steady and good man of her class.

He could only dream and admire her from a distance; separated by the gulf of distinction and tending manners, he had to wait, perhaps forever, in the shadows of desire. He welcomed her into his mind that cool morning through the fog while waking out of a labored sleep and the sleep that left imprints of stubble and minute indentations across his back. Though he dared not approach her, he didn't want her to leave his mind; where he could not go, his eyes compelled him.

He worried some that if he didn't let her go, he'd be ill prepared for the coming action. Maybe he wouldn't hear orders well or react fast enough on the field if she occupied the most space. And he sadly knew he was in love with one, which there was little chance. As much as he wanted her to stay, he knew his fancy could hasten his death. He would soon learn the risk first hand.

The schooling that started at the ditch would be continued in fast and loud completeness during the challenge for land. He turned and faced Jim Payne, catching eyes in warm friendship and felt sturdy. He silently prayed they'd both live another day. The sight of the troops they just buried brought him closer to the real possibility of his own death, but they were others, men he didn't know. They were more vulnerable perhaps by being in the place at that time. He figured a life after the war and although waning a bit, he was confident he was picked to make it through. He was meant for more than this.

"Press to your right! Get ready to move on, gentlemen!" the order was shouted and heard as it was delivered with authority by an indistinguishable, unrecognized voice from the wooded veil ahead of where they sat. Jim Payne and Jeb didn't have to know where it came from. There was little time. They quickly gathered their belongings and tied what they could in the wrap of bedrolls and were fitted to move within minutes. There was no time to think and that was a good thing. As the order resounded in repetition from others to make certain it was heard throughout the pines, cannon fire erupted and pounded the earth a short distance away.

They were the batteries of General Hill and the Yankees returning shot for shot. The woods came alive as the gray presence moved forward to its jagged edges. The lieutenants and sergeants led them out as one to the open field. Not much further and they'd be killing and dying in a naked pasture that stayed the two armies. Gritty, wet, groggy some of them—the confederates walked in concert shoulder to shoulder to meet the enemy of their people.

Most of their minds were numb, some clutched a Bible and said prayers asking forgiveness and secondly for safety. Some of them made vows to the Almighty while others purpose was to ask for nothing more than for Him to accept their humble thanksgiving for their lives to this day. All asked Him to look over those they left behind. Step by step they marched forward. No one fell behind lest he be thought of as less a man. They swelled onto the tillage, eyeing only the lay of earth where they were to foot ahead. The veterans on either side of the Eleventh were walking in unison and ready. Jim Payne had a notion of the burden ahead and thought to comfort his young friend who he was certain walked in dread.

"Steady, Jeb. It'll be good. Let the Lord's will be."

"Godspeed, Mr. Payne. I'm praying for yer safety."

"And I, yours. Take cover behind me when it starts—I'd be honored if'n you'd do."

"No, thank you, sir. We'll both be taking coffee tonight after." They heard the order to prepare muskets and to make certain their bayonets were fixed to stay.

"Shoot true, men of the South! Leave them with little, hit your mark, and don't forget yourself!" the voices repeated. They were expected to kill and would be held accountable if they didn't.

Distance helped; it was better not to see the faces of men they caused a family to lose. Their fathers, husbands, and brothers would fall; both family protectors and family shames would succumb. There could be no choosing between good and bad during battle. *Who am I, a boy from Alabama, to take rights of a man's life?* He thought who was he to kill the father of children who waited his return—*but he won't return because mine was the finger to touch it off with a straight aim!"* The spark and flash would put a hole through his chest, wounding that moment and forever his every child's heart. *Could I see them? How would I be in their eyes? I'm to be the fault for every cruelty they know.*

He had to quickly levy those beliefs over for he had to kill to live. If it wasn't fair for a vision to die at his hand he forced, it wasn't for him to die. Tears welled and he couldn't stop the flow; the prospects were set. *How in the name of the Lord am I to pull my first shot into them?*

"Does God forsake us in this?" he hurriedly asked Jim, his nerves boiling, confused, scared, horrified, and depressed at once over the lunacy. "It shouldn't have to be," he thought. "God, forgive me."

"No, son. The Lord's with us always. He's also with them." Jim pushed his musket in two short jabs toward the federal line. "God bless you, Jeb."

"God bless you, Mr. Payne," he answered.

They stepped deeper into the field and there was no time left to talk. Jeb saw the stars and stripes at a distance among the bluish presence that stretched as far as he could see to both sides in front of him. He glanced for their own flag and found one raised high in the queue past Jim. He and every one of them proudly marched into range of cannon under the stars and bars.

Shot could be seen clearly now and fifty yards more would choose some of them. Captain Stewart and the lieutenant walked the length of the company's stretch and repeated the same message.

"Steady now, lads. We'll show 'em what the Eleventh Alabama is made of…Ready to double quick on command!"

"Yes, sir!" many voices shouted their chorus of acknowledgment and determination.

"Let's show 'em, lads! Double quick when you hear!" the captain's voice cracked by its own passionate bidding to march men into the throws of hellfire. The methodical drumbeat prodding each step suddenly stopped; bugles calling out shrill commands replaced the slight sound of stretched canvas in the midst of powder furry. The orders were trumpeted and shouted immediately as was the envelop of sheer, numbing terror.

"Double quick! Charge!"

He could hear himself breathe; every take of air kept and every desperate exhale drove him onward as they all hurled their fragile bodies deeper toward the fusillade. He couldn't fall behind or show any weakness or hesitation. And so he ran with them stride for stride with the long musket ready to fire, its honed wood wrap and narrow stem of iron the only protection across his heart. The balls could be heard passing them among the thunderous and murderous blasts of union artillery. White smoke invaded the path before him and beside him. They were running, charging their enemy—an enemy that stayed and fired. Jeb felt some fall as they did; out of the corner of his fixed eyes, he saw them die.

On they went, their colors dropped then picked up again. On they went. The blue line was nearer now and he heard their confederate volley finally begin and saw it disrupt the incoming fire; finally, there was a slowing. He leveled his musket to steady a shot and fired into the faceless wall of men ahead of him. He watched the veil of shot and shell take many of them down in an explosion no one could survive but many more did than he expected. Stopping as those beside him did just long enough to quickly reload, he was still part of the advancing gray. He didn't know if he'd hit someone, killed someone, or missed entirely—it was instinctive to fire and he didn't hesitate to fire again.

The cannon took toll and had the Federals confused and more wary than they should have been. Jeb felt his face crack into a smile as he watched blue backs leaving the place he was to be running through. It appeared the day would belong to the south except for a stubborn core of indigo that stayed in their fire and smoke, still shooting heavy lead into the gray ranks. Jeb and the Eleventh were close enough to see their hair and beards. Their line was halted to a walk to enable them to put a fiercer thicket of fire to their front. Every man loaded and fired as fast he could move his hands from satchels to muzzles. Each man took his pause and powder, patches and balls to quickly handle each of the damn things his best for the extreme purpose and resolve of the unit.

Jeb took aim and knew he killed his first man for certain and took no wait in contemplation but reloaded to fire again. The man he killed could be like Thomas he pondered and save circumstance could have been his brother, but he had to fire. He had to keep firing, as it was his duty and orders. Beside him, inches away from his shoulder, without a sound to mark, the corner of his eye took the split second Jim Payne's head exploded with blood. Down he went, a gentle bundle—his confessor, mentor and fellow patriot fell forward with the next step Jeb took. The violence took him in a field somewhere above Mechanicsville and in an instant; Jeb lost his friend without as much as a cry.

Vengeance ran its sharp scarlet sword through him in a fury of flame and he screamed. He howled, deranged and full, to the men in blue only steps ahead, setting off those around him; the Rebs began running without an order toward the Yankees and their meager breastworks. They took as many as they could reach. Shooting and swinging, stabbing, clubbing, and killing every soldier in a different uniform, they forced their way and took the costly space as theirs. As many were spared who were fast enough, those who stayed to reload or wielded bayonets were killed two and three times over.

The Eleventh Alabama's grisly initiation was like those who came before them and proved equal to the task. Jeb knew himself as perfectly capable of killing. The enemy was gone except for their dead and a few prisoners. The proven took time to regroup, take an inventory, names, and write the difficult letters.

"Take count, men. I must know our losses. Lieutenant, take charge and report to me directly," the captain ordered with a loud voice.

"Yes, sir," Padgett answered, posting Jeb and the sailor to form two groups for a quick number of those standing. Although wounded grievously in his shoulder and arm, the captain remained with his company as long as he could before the last transport was loaded for Richmond.

Stewart looked much older than his years; the captain's beard was matted on his left side with blood above a shrunken, motionless shoulder. The captain's glance of hollow eyes toward him caused Jeb to ponder the man's elusive glory and the nobleness of those cut down by following his commands. The deep, dark cavities told of leadership, responsibility; his job was to carry out orders by giving orders and he sent many to their death that day. From his small but sturdy frame, he led and performed without doubt and accepted the torment; the death of even one haunted him and forced his melancholy. He couldn't prepare his heart to lose troops he drilled and trained those solitary weeks when he taught them discipline and resolve and along the way, mediated their minor squabbles.

It all had value. He was proud of the men in his command. They responded well before and in their first taste and drank it without hesitation, in full gulps, at full speed. He was proud of Company B; he was proud to be part of the Eleventh. The sultry day of fire and smoke had seasoned him as well; his sense of loss was equal. Company B emerged with sixty percent of its strength. A small cadre of the wounded made up for some as they were helped to the rear for field dressings before their transport to Richmond. There had been twenty-three killed outright.

"I'll be back, Tom. Ya'll save some for me," Jeb heard one of them say, but it rang hollow because he knew many of their wounded would be returning to the earth instead.

They knew it too. They saw the refuge from the Richmond hospital every day while they were camped. The fresh dirt in rows of man-sized mounds a quarter mile away and the daily wagon trips to that place was clear enough. He didn't want to be in the party that recovered Jim Payne. But he knew there were others who must feel the same about another, and he forced his steps. He put on a mask to hide his frailty and went; he could do no less for Mr. Payne.

"Poor Jimmy," Earl Hudgins, said to Jeb as the two of them picked him up to carry to the mark. "He got his luck today…Nothing in him now."

The words sickened Jebediah. He didn't want to hear about him and didn't have the heart to stop Earl.

"I didn't know him well, Earl," Jebediah said.

"Yeah. Kept to himself mostly. He came from near about Gadsden, Alabama, that place down near a river."

"I know where it is, Earl. Ain't too far from mine."

"They'uns have a lot of men in the service from down there?"

"A fairly number."

"Not many from where I come from. A lot of rich folk at the northern part of my county who paid for someone else to do their fightin' you know."

"I've heard of such." He turned his eyes downward. Solemnly the men of the company completed their chore. Preacher Smith, as he was called because he helped at a small church in Jefferson County before the war, held a service after their comrades were gathered. Not a single man missed it, not a single man failed to follow his prayer.

Earl Hudgins started an apprenticeship with a blacksmith and was making good progress before the secession. He had taken to the craft following two failed seasons of raising bean and okra crops; the bank had taken his small farm. In his late thirties with a wife and five children from one year to fourteen, Earl was a hand carved, tough and lean rebel of five foot, ten inches who never shied from a fight. He sent all of his pay home and from the time of his induction and lost twenty pounds he didn't have to spare from the beginning. He managed to get by eating very little; only that which the service provided kept him alive. He spent most of his time with a different group of Company B than Jebediah.

They were an older set unlike Jebs' friends except Jim Payne who adopted the youngsters to help them along. Earl took a liking to the young farmer who demonstrated he could fight and knew how to mind his manners.

"You all may join us at the fire tonight, Jeb."

"Thank you, Earl. I be doing that. Thank you."

"Lost a friend today, you did."

"Yes, sir. Mr. Payne ... He's in the fore line up yonder," he said, pointing to his mentor lying a number of feet away.

"His family would want to hear from you, Jeb. That's the way. The man closest writes a letter. Tell 'em all you know," he said. Jeb lowered his head again.

He knew it was true. Somehow he'd have to set his mind to a letter. He didn't want to write anything that wouldn't fit Mr. Payne well and do him justice; any words he chose could never match the man. The language couldn't do it.

His weakened fingers drew up in a smarting knot; the man spent most of his time listening to the younger and rarely talked about his family or himself. Jeb slowly walked toward his body. There should be some belongings that would reveal more of who he was. Letters, pictures, and a Bible—something had to be; he must fetch them away from Jim before he was covered.

In a fragrance of guilt for not knowing more, he took one dreadful, shaking step after another. He was lying straight, arms and legs closed together in a quiet repose; the flesh had begun to swell to the seams of his britches. He carefully looked on Mr. Payne's face; there were changes that made him appear almost different enough to think his friend had escaped and was coming back to them. Any moment, he'd appear and tell them he was glad he found them all again. But the blackened and puffed out flesh of what was left of the man's face was real, and he was Jim.

Jeb found a Bible inside the wet and stained jacket and gently pulled it away. Inside roughly sewn pockets laced with worn leather strips fashioned within both covers, he retrieved some letters. He carefully laid the materials aside and weighted them with a stone. The fragile paper, painted with his friend's life, had been kept these months protected by a piece of red handkerchief cut into squares. It was the same cloth Jeb saw him wearing when he reported the first day to camp. He used force to pull a scratched and dented wedding band off his fingers and felt the pain. All the personals were separated and put down beside the Bible; surely there would be an address of family.

He remembered his own and Mary to embrace his thinking. *Oh, Mary, sweet Mary. How I do love you... Oh, God, I wish I were holding you. I want you to know me and I would have it different if I could. I want you to stand at the alter with me. Your fairness causes my heart to melt away like so much sweet butter...Your charm and grace...Your lovely hair so beautifully adorning your head that cannot turn for me. I wish I were with you. Could such a dream ever be? Can it ever be?*

He felt tears uncomfortably running down either side of his chin. His weak eyes made a vain effort to see as he gathered up all that was left and clutched them tightly to his chest. Blindly, Jeb stumbled away from him and toward his Company. Some quickly turned away as he neared. The order came they were to rest and eat and the time Jeb needed. He had to get to it. He had to do his best to put himself aside and console those Jim Payne left and report to them the bravery of a good man.

Captain Stewart allowed himself to be taken by ambulance, having felt the strength slip away from every muscle over the course of a fast hour. He could barely hold his head up from the affect. He had lost a goodly amount of blood by the time he wheeled himself into the bed of one, loaded nearly full with gray.

The lieutenant was given command of the company and Sergeant Terry began arranging for the election of another lieutenant to fill in for a time.

Jebediah left them, having little preference and a greater desire to sort out Mr. Payne's life than vote. He reverently started revealing the contents of his find—luckily not lost to the hole. The first pages of the Bible yielded his wife's name, Tess, but also an unsteady note scribed alongside. *Tess, beloved Wife; born December 24, 1823. Died of consumption, June 30, 1859.*

Jeb knew why he never spoke of her and when asked about his family, would simply say they're doing well and he would return to them. He never heard Jim moan or complain of a sad and pitiful life—and it must have truly been one by assignment of such preordained deprivation and loss. Further entries explained well why he never sought counsel; there was tremendous joy found in the steadier handwriting more. *James Payne, born April 29, 1849; Darling Aimee Payne, born December 15, 1851; Richard Payne, born September 25, 1853. Pride of my life in God's name, may He always protect them.* And it was signed simply, *Jim Payne.*

Jeb felt him writing the simple postscript to his family. They were a young group; they must be with another part of his family. The Bible, worn from use and having been generously underlined throughout its thin pages had no other written entries so he set it carefully beside his knee and picked the few letters. He figured surely he would find more. *Poor young 'uns,* he thought and tried to prevent tears from welling up again. This time he was partly protected by the shadows of a sun pitched well past noon and setting toward evening.

In a while it would be dusk, then night, and then he would hide completely. The first letter had a return address prominently written out but in a set smear. He made out *Mabel Ferguson* and the town of Mobile. The street was more difficult to be sure of his deciphering but appeared to be closer to *Allen Street, number 14.*

Uncovering the rest of the six letters, he saw they were all from the same household except one. Thankfully, he had a clear person and place to write as his guess was confirmed. The other paper was different *Tess* was written on the back and there was no address. It was his writing to his deceased wife. He didn't want to violate a trust if he were to open it nor could he not do what Mr. Payne would have him.

Sailor rustled the fire and added pieces of wood; through the cracking and spitting smoke, Jeb stopped and took the last swallow of water from his canteen and used it to clean his hands again. The reading of the revered sanctum put near dirt and fire had to be his and so he scrubbed furiously. The callused and hardened skin of his fingers became reddened between streaks of crust and he was unable to clean them well enough; nothing he could do would make ready.

He set Mr. Payne's pen to his wife aside and unfolded the others. He read, *My Dear Brother,* and quickly learned Mabel Ferguson was his sister. He followed the woman's flowing cursive and although he couldn't make out some of what she sent, there were words and phrases about the children with her. James, Darling, and Richard were each named accompanied by entries of their triumphs and travails. *James junior,* she wrote, *is doing well in school as you would have it; he knows what you expect.* She went on to describe how manly he is for thirteen and how he had taken to be a father to his eleven-year-old sister and nine-year-old brother. She wrote how their reaction was, *at first a worry without you being here and they needed him to look after some of the things a father looks after.* Little Darling and Richard were described as missing him and their mother sorely, but were, *as respectful and well-mannered children unlike I've ever seen.* She went on to write they were all most thoughtful children, that between work and play, regular times were taken when each of them seemed immersed in deepness.

Jeb found the one to write of the tragic news. He knew he would have to tell her; it would fall to her to tell the children. She had the graver task; his was nothing compared to that and he felt foolish for his lack of courage. He asked the Lord to guide his hand though for Mr. Payne's sake so that he would use good words. With tearful and glassy eyes, he began the new venture, one that took as much courage to do as it took to wander into battle.

June 27, 1862

Dear Mrs. Ferguson,
    With a heavy heart and saddened mind I must write to tell you the Lord took Jim today. Nothing I can put down on this paper will bring you sufficient solace and comfort. He is a beloved brother and father. It is within my heart to say how great a man he was to all of us too. He was a good friend and helped in every way a man can help those of us who are weaker. He was truly admired and loved here and we will miss him. He was one of the South's finest men. I pray for you and the children. I reverently pray you will take heart from what he was and is still to those he loved.
    He lost his life as the Regiment was ordered to take a federal position near Gaines Mill and in that field of glory he is buried. He was beside me the whole way as we marched into the enemy's fire and I saw him die with honor just before we captured our cause. I have sent all his personals in a parcel to arrive with this. I am truly sorrowful for your loss and ours. I am humbled to have known him.
                      In God's love and blessed name,
                        God bless you all.
                        Jebediah McCray of Marshall County.

He carefully penned the address, convulsively touching the end of the quill on the tip of his tongue before each word and dip. His tongue filled with ink and the blackened spit mixed and ran with his tears out of the corners of his mouth. The oddly colored mix streaked his chin and finally melted into his stubble. Jeb thoughtfully left it as part of him; in a display of tribute to Mr. Payne, he left it.

The other letters were friendly greetings and more descriptions important to a father. He had them close to his heart by keeping the Bible against his chest. There were accounts of Darling's birthday, Richard's newfound interest in ships and the sea and James Junior's serious approach to his schooling and his job at the docks to contribute to their keep. He piously unfolded the last envelope and read his reflections on Tess. The page flowered with purity and love and deep, profound respect.

Jeb could hardly fathom how much Jim had missed Tess and longed to be with her again. The language was beyond his capacity but he did know what was written. In a hurried pen, his soul was poured out to Tess; his very human emotion poured out in every line. He described how Jim felt when he held her as though he was holding her as he wrote. He crafted prose telling of how he longed for her to this day and how she was his life. He wrote she was still with him and for that would never look on another.

Jeb decided not to read past the first page; he *was* with her, he thought as his stomach turned and his head took to ache severely because there was little contentment. Good people like Jim and Tess Payne shouldn't be taken before their years, he purposed, while so many others are left who aren't worthy of even stepping where their shadows graced. He thought of the awful day his mother may receive a letter about him.

He gathered the package and made it ready to send. There were several days of the same for Jebediah after that night; a defensive battle had begun where they were encamped. The defense of Richmond and the push to deliver the Yankees across the Potomac had become a strategic obsession with General Lee and every commander it seemed. The troops heard the call of purpose every day, several times a day; they were admonished they must hold fast for the sake of their wives, homes, children and all that was precious to them, to a man.

The soldier on foot didn't mind the prodding much; it was better not to be marching though each of them knew their time was coming. The war was young and much work lay ahead for all of them to take their fill. It would be costly and grind up many of the South's finest and many of the North's best.

Jeb wondered about Jacob and how he was faring and whether he had been through what he saw yet. He wanted to see and talk to him and find comfort with him, but there was little time to look back regardless of the stall. Each day was still hazardous with the threat of pain and death looming constant; there was no time of safety, no places to hide sufficiently.

The noise of war was all around as a reminder and their fight could begin in a heartbeat. Friendships formed fast and often lasted only a little while. They were heartfelt and treasured by all the men when they could, while they had each other. Jeb said a solitary and silent good-bye to Jim Payne as he presented the parcel that evening while others shoveled the dirt. Giving it up with outstretched arms, the quartermaster took and heaped it with the others. The wagon was full; precious evidence of honor and faith were left by men who feared but were unafraid, who desired to postpone death but were taken—not at their chosen time if given a choice—and of some who were taken slowly after enduring very individual time in agony, willingly taken as due for that which bore out of the one heart of the South.

The letters and parcels were stacked over the bloodstained boards. Jebediah clinched his teeth and grounded them together; he bound himself to fight hard when it was time.

The sultry evening hours were punctuated with soft breezes too gentle to be of value by the troops; the trails slightly carved in air carried smoke from the cook fires in thin wafts of satiny streamers. The entrenched Southern lines were preparing meals, checking weapons and putting off tomorrow until tomorrow.

Jebs' company shared some fried pork and potatoes procured by Captain Stewart from the stores wagon while most were sleeping. Sailor took charge at their fire and began to proudly demonstrate his skill. His given name was Taylor Smith, but he earned the common one when he fell out of a boat on the river back home twice during the same day of fishing. His partners, an uncle and a neighbor, labeled Taylor with the watery nickname and Sailor stuck.

Sailor had proven himself hard during the campaign and seemed to thrive in war; he was in his glory and seemed happy. He smiled broadly when he formed a line with the rest. This peculiar man put off all but his closest friends. Aroma filled the bivouac area; the sweet appetizing air of meat and spices alerted the hungry bunch of a few hours of coming ease and pleasure.

Fiddles and harmonicas could be heard playing as men took turns filling their cups. Each cup meant the strength of full bellies, the satisfaction of life. Jebediah sat on the ground beside Sailor and preacher Smith. Earl Hudgins was with them—the last to fill his bowl.

"I heard Gerald Judson is on the way," Hudgins said with a hopeful tone.

Men of the Eleventh Alabama passed the rumor before they were chewed up in the earlier fight.

"Yeah…Heard he's suppose to be here and help move McClellan out of Virginia and back to where he come from," Hudgins pretended bravado in his laugh.

"Ain't no telling what all they run into up there! Hope they make it in," Preacher sighed.

"With good ole Jackson, them Yankees are in for a fit… And it be fitting for them to get their comeuppance, I tell you," Hudgins said.

"They'll make it in. Ain't no Army that'll stop 'em," Sailor said, somberly squinting toward the west.

We're lucky he's part of us. Jeb imagined their arrival. His brother should be with them unless the strength of the union forces so easily dismissed by Sailor caused an unbearable loss to the family that would have to be shouldered by every one of them. He worried the costs could have been high; he had no way of knowing for certain. *Too little chance to see him,* Jeb thought, *but it'd be so good to hear his voice and shake his hand…a little time.*

Hungry animals barred from hunting on their own lapped up every drop of grease left from the pork flesh. Not a crumb was wasted as they'd eaten their portions, rinds, fat and all. The fare was fine to them; it was better than they had in a while and as rewarding as the best meal served in the finest café of Richmond.

"Yes, sir. We be moving into it soon. Could be tonight, could be tomorrow, but we're going again, gents."

"Don't want to talk about it, Earl."

"You're thinking about it like every man here. Why put us off?"

"I'm not fussing with you, Earl. It's not like I thought it would be and don't want to live it more than called to. The Lord will make us all ready when it's time," Preacher said and lowered his head to let out a breath. Jeb looked at Earl and tried to smile as a compromise.

"Yeah, Jeb. I know. Look at Sailor. He don't seem too bothered by any of it."

"Well…There's no point in frettin' about things. We can fight them in the thickets or on the mountainsides and we'll do it soon enough. Let Preacher be."

"Guess this war may not be over too soon," Jeb whispered.

"No, maybe not. But don't ponder that way, Jeb," Earl said as he tapped his powder pouch out of habit to settle its contents.

The four men sat and were distinctively silent. Earl lit up a pipe and leaned back on the soft brush covered ground to settle a while and enjoy the feeling of a full stomach. Each of them was aware it might be his last meal if his turn was next. If he lived, it may be his last fill for a while. The gray line was formidable, although thin compared to the nation's vision of a people defending their homelands.

The Yankees seemed a neverending accumulation of mankind that poured out of the cities and farms somehow that must be infinite in numbers. They were well equipped and ate regularly and well. The Army of the Potomac had all the showings of superiority; even their battle standards were professionally done.

The Army of Virginia had been quickly assembled from all the small hamlets and farms, mines and harbors south of Maryland and as quickly trained in only the most fundamental disciplines of an Army. Most were dependent on their homegrown skills of stalking on foot for game and riding the long spaces between virgin forests and buyer towns. The hearty bodies of farmers could bear up and set the standard for all to meet.

Enthusiasm rooted in their souls and hearts born from belief in their cause—even though many were not fully aware of it—was the great source of their advantage if there was one. Hard and forceful, absolute and sacrificial, their cause was feelings. It would have been unseemly to fail, unmanly to avoid; their test was battle and time after time, walk after walk, each was expected to enter the fire of death and each man did so willingly pulled by the invisible hand of a most honorable cause.

Jebediah sipped his coffee slowly in anticipation. His body was wretched with a vigilant rash caused by his soiled clothes. Dirt and blood, sweat and urine dressed his uniform, the makeshift patches of cloth sewn quickly together by hopeful hands of seamstresses. His stubbly, weathered face and calloused hands were exposed and healthier than the rest of his lean but proportionally muscular frame wracked with red burning and itching, hot and always wet skin that seemed barely able.

The few months in the service had honed him and despite the filth were as dashing an emissary of home as any. Different muscles were required to kill than are used on the farm. Different expressions are needed that Jeb never knew before. Planting, harvesting, baling and feeding were the work he longed to return to—and would as soon as the strangers were made to leave.

He rested his elbows on his knees as he crouched. Between his hands the coffee was taken slowly so he could linger on each exquisite sip. As he sat, he wondered what the officers were doing and planning. The officers seemed to possess more energy and endurance between skirmishes. When Jeb and the rest of his company sat or lay exhausted, those of rank remained at work. Scurrying about and meeting in tents or riding off to meet others on a distant acre, the officers didn't seem to take rest. What they said when they must nevertheless feel the same would bear on him and they all had to wait.

He began thinking about the end of the war and a free Alabama. He conjured his recollection of fishing Duke's pond and capturing plenty of catfish to feed the family and neighbors and happily celebrate being together again. He smiled as he thought of Mary; maybe his chances were better now that he was a veteran and had grown up. He figured to become rich enough to earn a standing in Marshall County. *Maybe I'll be a judge... They may call me colonel... I'll have to be an upstanding citizen.*

"What are ye smiling about, Jeb? It does my heart good to see it, but share it with me if you will," the preacher said and smiled.

"I was only thinking of what to do after this here scrap."

"And what all will that be, reckon?"

"Oh, just to work hard and win the hand of Mary Hornsby. I want to be thought of as good."

"Well, I hope you take her sure enough and have a fine Christian home. Keep your faith, Jeb, and I'm sure you'll have a fine family."

"Thank you, preacher. But she is of class and I'm not, you know. There's also a sparker who is of the same. His name is Thomas Stamps."

"Don't give it a thought, young McCray! I tell you, if it meant to be, it will be and one should never consider class. Take only your heart to task and the rest will come surely if that is what your God wills."

"You must say those things, but I'll do what I can," Jeb smiled graciously.

"I'll tell you. A good union is one where it is true in heart. The man must be of a mind that all that matters is his wife, and in the wife all that matters is her husband."

"I know that's right, preacher."

"Yes, young McCray. And when you serve God, the two of you will enjoy the bounty reserved for the faithful."

"I worry that shooting a Yankee is not in keeping."

"I put such strain aside some time ago. I figure they're coming to us and we must do His will. He brought this test of faith upon us, and I don't really know why, but I suspect He is bringing the country to its knees for purpose."

"I don't know what the purpose could be, preacher."

"Maybe He sees the deprivation of some in our midst or the sin and is punishing us for our reckless lives. I don't know. But He puts us here and lets the killing. Now we are defending our lives."

"How are we to know?" Jeb asked.

"We won't know until the great beyond."

The order was near. The Eleventh Alabama was to move toward the northeastern land of Virginia. There was to be an offensive campaign to take the fight to the north. Captain Stewart had the men form up in column and begin the march toward Fredericksburg.

Jeb could only picture Mary's face in his mind and made her vision come to him at regular intervals when he could think. He thought of her voice and smile and watched her walk and move; every angle, every sight of her thrilled his heart. He loved her and wanted to be her husband; he thought of their gentleness with each other and how it could be for them. The march took them through the countryside on dusty roads, lined with both tall and scraggly trees, distant farms and occasional timber houses edged up to the path. It was well worn by wagon traffic to and from the city which was nearer than home.

The Confederates marched surely and confidently. They had been victorious at Bull Run twice and to a man, knew their commanders were better than what the north had to offer, at least as audacity and that meant victory. No one thought of any outcome except victory. The lucky ones and Jeb hoped and prayed he would be in that number, would return home to their farms and family or marry and begin one after securing freedom for the southern people.

Their trek left no man behind as the long gray column worked its way northerly to push the Yankees east of Fredericksburg and sue for peace, if it were in Lincoln's mind to do. He would have to be convinced before the cost of his folly became too great for the young nation to bear. Their road was chilled by autumn's cool air as they made their way to reinforce the poor fellows who withdrew to the high ground above the town. It was a matter of time when Burnside would attack with tens of thousands blue and silver appointed men to kill many and drive the rest south.

Jebediah reflected on his family and their struggle and fortune. He thought of his mother and could hardly imagine how he and John must be a worry to her now that rolls of dead were showing in the newspapers. How she must survey the lists and what that must do to her mind and heart! He knew from the moment Jim Payne was killed this was not the romantic adventure he bought; it was a horrid, ghastly, dead thing to be here. He wondered why it was he to take it up—and all the others, why was it to them to die so hideously and alone. Uncle Thomas could be wearing blue; he didn't know. Circumstances could be such that he joined to fight for his country, the same mind as he. Or he could be a conscript with no choice; how terrible and awful it would be if he fell fighting his enemies, a nephew and the Eleventh Alabama! He prayed to God none of his would never be in that number.

The town had been fired and General Burnside was putting pontoon bridges in place to cross the Rappahannock River. The attack would come surely and waves of blue were bound to try the heights and it was theirs to punish the invaders who vandalized and destroyed so much. It was theirs to repel the Yankee and push them back across the river.

"Ever been up here, Jeb?"

"Can't say that I have, preacher."

"Close to Washington. Be a lot of trouble here I'll tell you," he said as he peered across the horizon studying the lay and the river. He could envision where they would come.

"Reckon you're right."

"The Lord, He is with us."

"I hope you're right, preacher. This war's taking an awful toll."

"Try to stand with me, Jeb. I'll see you through."

The Confederate reinforcements camped just west of Fredericksburg and built quick breastworks. The trees, dead and alive, were stacked along with dirt and used as protective walls. The overnight garrison had the responsibility of stopping the Yankees from marching over and south.

Lincoln and his cabinet knew the pressure to get moving and quash the rebellion soon. It had cost much already and was interfering with commerce. Many felt this war should have been over quickly, before this year, and life should have resumed in the Republic prosperous again. The aristocrats considered it an overbearing distraction.

The heights overlooking Fredericksburg gave the southerners a panoramic view of American countryside. It was as beautiful of an area he'd seen in Alabama and reminded him of home. But Burnside had fired the town and the center had become an awful scene of ash and smoke. Undeserving it was, but the deed was done out of rage and hate by the hand of man.

Just out of range except long artillery, Jeb watched as the Yankees built pontoons to cross the river and come to them. It was clear now the means the blue would use to meet them. Having the high ground meant the men of the north below knew many would not live another day after they charged up the hills into the throat of shot and canister. For many this would be their last full day; tomorrow they would die.

More men would not return to their parents or wives and children. Many would not see their sons and daughters again. Sons would grow with no father and only heartache would partially and painfully fill the void left between the ribs of all those who knew them and cherished them and the remorse would fester and grow. More sons and daughters would never know life, as they will not be conceived. No one save God knows what the country will miss because of early deaths.

Chapter 6

In Boston, Thomas escorted his mother to Mass and asked the priest if the war was right. Mother McCray was getting on in years and becoming aged and slow. She listened to them and could hardly be committed to the subject. It wasn't that she was cold or passionless; it was that in her years she had already lived the saddest. The loss of her husband, one of her brothers so early, and so many friends who made the voyage with her had weakened her spirit. She resigned herself to this life—what was left of it for her—as an experience one has before heaven.

The men talking of war and whether it was right fell on her ears like a dead weight. It was something else trying to hurt her. She tugged on Thomas to take her to their pew and wait for the Holy Eucharist to unite her with Jesus. The church offered some warmth from the blustery autumn and made her feel closer to those who left her than any thought or dream she conjured.

"Father...I pray it ends soon," Thomas said.

"Me too, my son," the priest answered in Irish brogue. "The Lord is looking down on us and crying for humanity. I'm sure of it."

"Yes, Father. And it seems we're willing puppets of Satan himself in this God forsaken exercise of killing each other."

"Take heed, Thomas! The men who are dying for this cause will find His arms open for them in paradise. Now let us enter the house of Lord and pray for them."

After the two-hour service, Thomas returned to his home and Mabel, who had cooked some ham and beans over their hearth. Her warm smile warmed him and for a time had him in a mind to relish what he had. He watched Peter walk gingerly, a little unsteady still as his legs were growing to catch up to his wonderings. Their son was two years old now and speaking to them. The sound of his voice thrilled Thomas, old enough to be his grandfather but blessed instead with a son. He often thought of Abraham and Sarah and smiled knowing he was much younger than they when God blessed them with a child. Peter was a gift. Surely he would not see war, he prayed.

Mother McCray took up her chair in the front room and sipped tea watching Peter move about and making sure he didn't walk too close to the hearth. Mabel, a woman of beauty and grace, practically danced in the way she walked. When Thomas would watch her, he could hardly stop thinking carnally but he kept it to himself until they were alone and then expressed his desire through his hands by pulling her close to him. She was a willowy figure decorating their home with her every step. Her hair down and covering her shoulders while her form pressed against any dress she wore caused him to think of being with her constantly. He turned toward his mother and quickly put such thoughts aside.

"Are ye warm. Mother?"

"Yes, son…Thank you and Mabel. I will cook a pie today from the canned apples."

"That would be very good. You seem pensive, dear Mother. Are you feeling well?" he asked her.

"I heard you and the Father talking about the war, Thomas. I do so worry about Jacob and Jebediah. Do you think they're alive?"

"God, Mother! Surely. I feel for Lucious and Katy and for what they must be going through. I'm fortunate Peter is so young he can't think of such an adventure."

"Yes, son. I pray. God must surely allow our family to live."

"I know. Our losses have been most grievous already. But here we are and our family is growing. Mabel and I will try to have more children if it be His will."

"I hope, Thomas. I'll pray for you two." She thought for a moment. "You know we are blessed. I'm so very happy and proud of the McCrays. I wish your father was here to see it."

"I believe he's looking down on us and he must be smiling. "Thomas said as he took Peter by the hand to direct him toward the table room.

"Here, Peter. Let's put you up on this chair. Momma has your food coming."

In Alabama Katy and Lucious received several letters at once, the post service running into the mountain sporadically. Thus far it was good news—as far as Jacob and Jebediah being alive. Jeb wrote more than Jacob, Luscious knew it was the nature of fast moving cavalry causing the difference; still each letter from both of his sons was a special event.

"Jebediah lost a friend to a Yankee ball, Katy," he said knowing she would read it too. "I wish he were home with us. He's in fearful danger I perceive and there's no end to it." He watched her begin to cry quietly, tears running down the contours of her cheeks. "Oh, Katy…I'm sorry. He'll be safe. God will not let us lose him."

"Lucious! I pray you're right but I feel He may take him and Jacob too." She wept. "Does he say where he is?"

"No, dear wife. He could be anywhere. I don't know."

"And what of Jacob?"

"He writes he is riding through the Shenandoah. He got to see his brother for a spell in Virginia. That's good. They seem healthy and as happy as they can be, considering. Please smile dearest. We must be strong for Rachel, John and Carl. They are not accustomed to such fearful things."

"I know you speak well, husband. I struggle over what could happen. The lists are so long."

"We will not see our sons on that awful roll. I know we won't!" He felt himself fooling his mind and body. His words were not confident; it was not possible for them to be spoken with surety, and he heard himself. There was work to do to prepare for the winter and the work would keep his mind off the possibilities and help him find some happiness until the boys return.

Their farmhouse had been expanded to include four rooms now. Rachel had her own, the younger sons shared one and then Katy and Lucious had a door between their space and the hearth and kitchen area. He enjoyed seeing his wife naked with him and now could more often in privacy not afforded until this past year. She was still a beauty to him and he took her in with his eyes every day. She took him in with her eyes too and was still able to bear children.

John and Carl were help on the farm as there was always much to do. Mending fences, feeding livestock, tending crops and gathering were year-round chores every member of the family had to do. Katy continued to work as a seamstress between seasons. Lucious had fashioned a small cellar where the family kept canned fruits and vegetables and could hang salted meat for days. The work of the family helped them all live in peace.

The hell that was to be Fredericksburg was nearing all the men there. Burnside had the bridge finished and was planning the attack, taking his men across the river and then up the slopes to face the rebels. Jeb and Preacher saw it coming and checked their powder and inventoried their lead balls soon to be fired into them. It was duty to their country and their fellow troops. So many had been cut to pieces from shot or surgeons and those lucky enough to live were limping home not whole.

Arthur and Rebecca had settled near the Ohio River and were also keeping news of the conflict. They read posts from Lucious and knew Jacob and Jebediah had joined the cause. They were family they hardly knew other than the kinship of their brother. In her forties now, Rebecca had taken up with a River man between jobs as a soiled dove and lived with him off and on but bore no children. She began to lose her faith when her father died and allowed her mind to throw it away nearly completely by the time she was twenty-nine years old. She took money from men for the use of her body and suffered few pangs of conscious. There were plenty of houses she could work between the new city of Cincinnati, Cleveland and Ohio City.

Arthur had married twice and had a son from his first wife, Julia. She had taken their son and moved to Arkansas when he was very young with a merchant and lawyer she met at a farmers market in the square beside the River. He lost her to lust for a stranger in an instant and never heard or saw her again.

Brother Arthur came to love another, an Indian maiden named Willow Dove, and married her. They were happily engaged in farming and cattle for a few wonderful years before she died of influenza. He never married again and carried her memory with him the rest of his life. He loved her until the day he died.

Arthur and Rebecca came to share a sod farmhouse just before the war and tended a small garden and a few animals in their later years. Theirs had been a full circle not predicted or planned when they left Tennessee that year and now lived waiting to die.

"Sister. Lucious writes of our return. He wants us to come to Alabama and take up acreage next to them," Arthur announced to Rebecca.

"Yes? Well, I do hope they are well. Does he say anything about the rest?"

"He still has no news of Jacob and Jebediah. He writes they are on campaign in Virginia but are marching. And the other children are still with them."

"I don't know if I can return after what I've done, Arthur. I've been a disgrace and still have yet to care!"

"It would be a new start, sister. Maybe we should go."

"And have busy women talk about me? I don't know," she nearly whispered feeling ashamed for her past.

"And why should they know anything but what we say? That's long past and I see no reason to let it out—about my life too," he laughed. "I haven't been perfect, either. And truth is no one has in their life!"

"Maybe we should, dear brother. I could stand a gentler winter." She smiled one of her rare smiles. "Do you think we have safe passage?"

"If we decide, yes. We would go by river and rail but would have to go soon…before the war comes over this way."

"Let's sleep on it and decide tomorrow."

"Very well. I'll fetch some wood for the fire and we'll sleep on it. Lord, I hope the boys are safe and unhurt. It's a bloody mess and they have no business being in it. Maybe we can see them all soon."

"That is a nice thought, Arthur. We should also write Thomas and inquire of Mother, if she would speak to me again. I've had no news from them."

Captain Stewart had the company form a line behind the breastworks and take aim toward the river. They were the farthest part of the left flank as part of a large force readying to stop Burnside. The day was clear and the hour was close at hand. The Southern men had seen it all before and knew what was before them. Many of the Yankees were new to battle and would know after the day.

My Lord, be with me, Jeb prayed. *Let me return from this nightmare and wed Mary.* He whispered, "God help us in this fight and bless those souls wearing any uniform on this day."

"They be coming hard and fast! Men, ready yourselves!" the captain called out. "Remember your homes and your family! They're watching what we do here today!" As he said the last words any of them could hear, shots filled the air with their horrid noise and men began falling in front of them like chaff from sickle struck wheat. Smoke was rising, blood was laying and spewing, and human limbs and pieces of flesh were flying out of the contest. Jeb heard the familiar whistles passing over his head as many Yankees fired back in desperation paying little heed to aim.

The second wave of human flesh came toward them like the first and was struck by the flying lead with similar effects. *Burnside must be a fool!* Jeb thought as he watched his discharge undoubtedly find a target, they were bunched so close together shoulder to shoulder— the men falling back could have been hit by any one of them. He didn't know and at this point he had grown accustomed to the anonymous killing, unknown killing, doubtful killing, but killing nonetheless as it must be preordained. Surely he thought it had to be meant. He knew well that he must stop this or forever be a wretched curse wondering about the souls he helped fell. He thought they must all stop this for the sake of the country and mankind. *If they would only stop and leave us be,* he thought. This is the stuff terrible dreams are made of and he felt he would hardly sleep after so much. Only the grace of God would save him from the agony if it be His will. *My God! How do we come to this?* Dusk settled in and the attacks were thinning.

Cannon balls struck a hitched caisson behind him and exploded the powder, killing the poor horses instantly. Others came streaming in and took lives and equipment, but they could not stop. They must keep firing and repel the invaders lest they all be killed. He saw men in gray fall back from the line, struck hard by well-placed shots. A number of the Yankees had taken time to aim finally after so many fell. The time was on them to decide the battle and save all they could. Finally darkness came and gave them relief. The lines of blue stopped coming and the Confederates had some time to rest and pray.

Thousands of men in blue were trapped in the fields and many lay dying all night with no help for them. Jeb and the preacher listened to the wail and cry and waited for one after another to stop by the blessed relief of death.

"My, God, preacher. You hear them?"

"Aye, I do, Jeb. It is a sorrowful night."

"We treat horses better. I can hardly stand to hear them!" Jeb said.

"Just pray, but pray that those who may live will. And for those who are to die, to die quickly."

"I will do that, preacher. Pray for me too, will you?"

"Yea, Jebediah. We all need prayer."

The bloody slopes finally yielded change and their brothers walked back across the Rappahannock. It was a pitiful sight, men so sullen and drawn into themselves. They had lost the battle and twelve thousand men. The Rebels let them pass back into Fredericksburg unmolested to take countenance of their folly. Maybe this would help end it all and save more lives, Jeb thought and prayed.

Prisoners were taken and Jeb's Company was picked as one of the guards to usher them back to Richmond where they would be put on rail and transported to the prison at Belle Isle near Richmond. The day was cold and dreary, clouds weeping water on the hills and fields. Company B marched those who could walk toward Richmond. There were no wagons to use and the several days journey would be with little food.

"At least these fellows won't be shooting us."

"Their war is over, Jeb, for sure. They are luckier than we."

"Suppose you're right, Preacher, but they be along way from home," Jeb said and watched the scraggly line of nearly blue uniforms and saw his brothers save his family turning north instead of south a generation ago. He could have been in their number. They were like him, no differences except in address, he thought. He thought of Thomas and his grandmother and cousin Peter he heard about from his mother's letter. He thought how odd, how strange, how stupid this war is for certain, but how inevitable and necessary it seems. He scolded himself for thinking like a traitor. He would not be a coward or traitor; there is nothing worse to every man there.

"Where you from, Billy?" Jeb asked a Yankee who caught eye contact with him as he was being marched behind the lines to form up with other prisoners.

"Boston," he said. "And I mean to go back."

"You will see your home again, Billy Yank. No fear about that. I'm from Alabama and I will go home too," he said.

"I hope you makes it, Johnny Reb."

"I have family in Boston."

"I have family in South Carolina."

"I hope they fare well, Billy. I have some tobacco…Care for a snatch?"

"Thank you kindly. I would," the man in blue answered and gratefully took the pull of tobacco from Jebediah's pouch.

They arrived in Richmond, yet to be molested by any Northern aggressors. Jebediah knew better and knew his conscious would hurt, but he wanted the company of a lady. After delivering the prisoners to a makeshift compound that could hold them for Confederate wagons, Jeb went searching out the seamy part of the city. He didn't know for sure whether he would find such sin, but he was determined to try. It would be his first time and he wanted to live that before he was killed. A few dollars and eternal damnation didn't seem too high a price at the time.

"I heard you talking to Earl, Jebediah," the preacher said his eyes cast downward, concerned. "Need to consider that is not in keeping."

"I know, Preacher. Damn! I'm feared I will never know a woman."

"Aye. As much as I understand that, it doesn't make it right. You'd be going into sin purposeful. I pray you will not."

"I'm desperately close. I'm not able to keep from it," Jeb said, looking downward, embarrassed by his frailty.

"Think of Mary, Jeb. Do you think she would allow such?"

"I do think of Mary…a great amount, Preacher and no, she would have nothing to do with me if she knew how weak I am. I am weak."

"You're weak and so am I. Seeing boys lose everything in this life as we have so much makes a human being wonder. Maybe you doubt God's grace and guidance. Sometimes I do, but we mustn't give in to temptations lest we suffer more in battle than we do."

"Some boys never knew a woman. How awfully unfair, awfully not right, Preacher. Damn. I feel for them and it hurts me much to think of it," Jeb announced sternly.

"And so your answer is to buy a woman?"

"Yes, sir. I think so. If I'm to go to my grave, I would at least have this knowledge."

"It won't be worth it, and it won't be remembered except by God above. Think, Jebediah, and try to let the Lord take you away from sinning."

"Thank you, Preacher, but I am feared my mind is set on one course and won't rest until I do."

"I see. I love you any way, Jeb. And God does too. I'll pray for you so that maybe you'll have the strength at the moment of truth to walk away and return to us here."

"You are giving me much more than I deserve and for that I'm thankful. You're so much better than the rest of us. I'm sorrowful to let you down."

"Don't worry about yourself, Jeb. You don't let me down. The whole country let me down years ago, and there's more to come for certain."

Earl came and fetched his young friend and together with fourteen other troops walked toward the open bars section of Richmond. Their first order of business was a warm bath and shave, and they quickly found accommodations on River Street. Taking turns, they each cleaned their body and face using a large iron and tin tub and a straight razor dulled from use but sharp enough. The proprietor boiled fresh water to add as each man passed through. He thought of what the preacher said. He thought of Mary, seemingly unreachable and probably with Thomas Stamps letting him try to convince her. He continued to walk with the rest.

In Marshall County, Alabama, Mary Hornsby was waiting for Jebediah and writing him regularly. Her letters reached him sporadically, and it had been weeks since he read her last. It had been weeks since she read his last. Thomas Stamps had been trying to court the pretty, petite Mary, but she put him off. He lacked some quality hard to define but missing nonetheless, and she wasn't about to take him as he was. Her heart was on Jebediah, the fair-haired McCray boy from a family who worked hard, a good mother and father, loving brothers and the one shy sister. She admired their closeness and happiness from a view where her father kept distance and remained reserved as his dressing for position and status.

"I pray Jacob and Jebediah are safe, Thomas. Do you think of them?"

"I do, Mary. I believe what they have done is foolhardy and now the best they can encounter is returning alive," he said with a smirk.

"Many young boys and men went to fight because they believed in their country," she said as a teacher would say.

"Their country? It's my country too, but I am a man destined for high responsibilities here and will see to them," he said proudly.

Mary had a different thought. "And conscription, should it come here? What will you do then, Thomas?"

"I have already arranged payment for one to go in my place. See? I'll do that and we can be together! I can take care of you since I'm not leaving. I do wish you'd reconsider and let me court you and show you my affection and honorable intentions."

"Thomas... I think you should see someone who values status more than I. We can never be together; you and I can only be friends the way I see it." Hearing him reveal his intention to pay another to go to war in his stead satisfied her mind that she knew what it was about him she could never love.

"Well, Mary. You say that now, but I intend to keep trying. You're the one I want and in time, I'll convince you," he said as he walked briskly to his carriage and sped away from the church grounds.

Jebediah and Earl found the house early in their quest and walked in; Jeb entered timidly, embarrassed to be there as the keeper madam greeted the soldiers in her parlor. She was dressed in scarlet and white with her hair held upwards by ribbon. Her heavily made-up face could not hide her aged appearance before her years. The work seemed to take an early toll on most and as she and many others passed thirty, the lines and furrows became deeper.

"Gentlemen...do come in and enjoy the house. The girls will be out in a short time for you to pick one for company."

"Thank you, ma'am," Earl said.

"You are a handsome bunch. Glad to see some of our boys fighting the good fight!" she said. "Now don't be afraid. We'll treat you right and proper," she said and laughed.

Several of her charges suddenly walked into the parlor where the men were served drinks. Jeb took one and slowly sipped the strong brew, feeling his spine quiver as he swallowed. He saw the ladies and surveyed each of them. He didn't want to choose like choosing a pair of boots at a mercantile or a can of beans at dry goods. *How odd and cheapened this is,* he thought.

A soiled dove that called herself Julia stood in front of all of them wearing only a thin gown, her ample breasts hanging like overripe melons from the farm he remembered. She was still beautiful with her painted lips and long black hair falling to her round and firm-looking hips seen through the fabric. *I am to sin today with her,* Jeb thought. He shyly looked up to her and couldn't utter a word. She knowingly took him by the hand and led him upstairs past the gaudy organ, past the large paintings of women on inclines and in long seats, past the dangling bejeweled lamps, past the other Rebels who smiled as he went on his way for a few minutes of earthly paradise.

Tomorrow they would head back and into another battle sooner or later. There were skirmishes and bloodshed everywhere it seemed, reaching into Tennessee, Alabama, Georgia; all around there were other men with guns taking the lives of Southern defenders. It would be tomorrow though and until then they had their best chance now to know pleasure instead of pain, gentleness instead of hardship and heartache. After their sojourn Jebediah prayed for forgiveness in that he knowingly did this damnable thing and asked the Lord to let him be with the promise he would never sin this way again.

He now knew he was not yet good enough for Mary, and he would have to work on much that was him to be. He fretted whether he could. In this day it was back to the dirt and cold, blood and smoke with his fellows and back to the wallow that is war.

Chapter 7

Thomas and Mabel taught Peter to read and do some simple mathematics before he was school age. Having been made barren by his birth, the couple worked with him solely and loved him by showing him a great deal of what they knew early in his life. He was a well-mannered child and spent more time with adults than children his own age. He learned to play the violin before he was ten and could fairly do most music of the masters before he was twelve.

The war was now several years past Sumpter. The South was going through a slow death to defeat. Lincoln addressed the nation through print at Gettysburg, and the signs of an end became painfully clear as much of the South and many of her people were ruined or dead. Jebediah survived with slight wounds delivered over the past two years at Antietam, Gettysburg and Chickamauga near Chattanooga. The scars were on his face and shoulder. One wasn't healed yet but scabbing over sufficiently to return to duty. He hadn't heard from Jacob in over a year and figured he was buried somewhere in an unmarked grave shoveled in haste and no accounting or word from any officer or cavalryman.

Being weary of war and the continuous digging, waiting, then terror in hours did not matter. The Confederates still fought and defended with all their heart. It was Sherman running through Georgia like a sharp knife wielded by a vengeful God. His unit was nearly depleted. Earl and Sailor were left, but few others survived Gettysburg and afterwards from the original company. Enemy shot took some and disease took the rest.

Cousin Peter was learning fine living while the McCrays of Alabama were scratching a living more than ever. It was good that some part of the family McCray was improving their lot and prospering. Lucious bore no grudge; he turned to work harder and share crop two fields beside his own. Katy stood by him and kept the house, keeping John and Carl at ease with her plea how very much Father needed them to help at home and not in the war. Her youngest sons had grown and wanted to follow their brothers. Rachel reached sixteen and was preparing for her wedding to Benjamin O'Keefe, a teacher and bookkeeper in Marshall County.

"What for are we here, now?" Jeb asked Earl. "Poor Preacher. He breathed his last on that hill in Pennsylvania. He didn't see it coming at all! We should have never attacked up that slope. And we should not be here."

"I agree with you, Jebediah, but our bodies belong to the Army. We have no choice and even though it should be over, it isn't, and we're the last."

"The last to die."

"They are going to burn Atlanta, boy. Do you know what that means?"

"Not much I do ceptin' the poor people there will lose everything like the others. I think of killing every damn Yankee there is for what they do."

"We still have a chance to do that, Jeb. With a steady aim and dry powder, we do," Earl said in an especially surly voice. "If they burn Atlanta, I fear we've lost our freedom. We will lose this war and be at their mercy. That's what it means, Jeb."

"Well, maybe we'll be home soon. That's all I want now."

The long, dark-red hair adorning Rachel was cleaned and appointed with ribbons, tying most of it back where the bulk gathered. It was thick beauty of a young woman. She was planning to marry Benjamin in the small Catholic Church on the southern edge of the county. She was the youngest of this generation of McCrays and more independent minded than the rest had been owing to a loosening Lucious and Katy had toward her. She was graceful and not spoiled, but easily could be mistaken for a girl of more prosperous means who had to work few chores, more to prepare for socials.

Her brothers saw her as weak and precious and protected her in every way. When it stormed, they would fetch her inside, covering her face and body with their coats. When she would fall playing, one of them would carry her inside for Katy to clean gently and bandage. And no boy dared tease her at school or he would face one of the brothers in an encounter that was far less than friendly.

She looked like a small angel without wings in the wedding gown her mother cut and sewed for her out of while silk and cotton. Her veil reached the floor; cutting out of an angle formed by her hair bunch and made her appear to her intended as an apparition of a dream girl, a vision of white flow, small but overpowering by her presence. Lucious was dressed as fine as he could for the wedding as he was to escort her to the altar and give his daughter away to the groom.

She walked down the aisle with her father whose glassy eyes gave him away. He was proud of his daughter and happy that she was marrying a man of good character. He wasn't sure if he would ever see both of his oldest boys again in this lifetime and thoughts flooded his mind of his family. He and Katy were losing them as sure as time itself. The family would never be the same. But it must be because it is right for the children to step into the world as he had done many years ago after Boston, after Kentucky, after Tennessee. He glanced toward Katy and saw the same beautiful woman he met and married years ago.

"Who here gives this woman's hand in marriage?" the priest asked somberly. There was a soft flicker of candles and a subdued odor of incense throughout the chapel. The small windows let light in sparsely; the scene reminded Katy and Lucious of weddings in the old country. It was true life repeats life and nothing changes much in the spirit and heart of man and his love and loss.

"I do. I'm her father," Lucious barely spoke; broken by sobs he choked back and swallowed to hide them. *God, I wish my boys were all here on this day,* he prayed silently, giving in to his emotions. Having always been strong and fearless, he felt weaker by the hand of a God he was less sure answered his prayers. But he couldn't give up because Jacob and Jebediah were still away in the deadly contest, and he couldn't bear leaving them to chance. He knew other families prayed too and were answered with dire news. Many sons were buried a thousand miles from home; dirt farmers could never even visit them at their graves. *Why should my prayers be answered differently?* he thought.

The gathering afterward included men on strings, mouth harps, and fiddles along with an ample supply of hard cider to lessen the load of everyone there including the Priest. Lucious felt some relief. Somehow from somewhere he felt a calming and danced with his daughter to an Irish folk song, feeling her happiness with Benjamin. They were a fine couple and surely would blessed with fine children.

Jebediah and Earl took up their fighting positions once again. This time they were in the hills overlooking Atlanta following their withdrawal from Chickamauga. The ocean of troops that were soldiers of the United States came and came the flood so complete there were no lines to even slow the advance of many. Still where there were Confederates, they fought bravely and would not yield until ordered. The men had come from South Carolina,

Georgia, Alabama, Mississippi, Arkansas, North Carolina, Virginia, and Tennessee. There were remnants of units from Louisiana, Florida, Maryland and Texas as well who were willing to fight to the death should that be what they were asked to do.

Jacob had been captured during the previous year while in the Shenandoah and sent to Camp Chase. The prison was near Columbus, Ohio, and became severely overcrowded. He had little to eat each day as the commissary officer left the service to inexperienced replacements and malnutrition became the rule of the day. Jacob was slightly more than skeletal by the end of 1864, having lost fifty pounds off his mere one hundred and fifty pound body at the start. He survived an outbreak of smallpox in the camp by the grace of God and helped bury the dead and comfort the dying wearing a piece of shirt over his mouth.

He saw one after another pass into the next life—seemed every day there was someone's son, someone's husband who died alone inside a tent if he was lucky in the cold camp. Few buildings offered any form of shelter and most of the prisoners had to endure the weather with long coats and shelter halves made into skimpy dwellings as some days the snow covered them by half. Hunger caused constant pain in his stomach. He dreamt often of being home and having the fare laid out in front of him like he remembered on Sundays. He kept a modest portion of hope to live and return to those dinners. Here was time to pass in the cold, wet, stinking and crowded confines of earth that turned on him. He knew his strength would be tested, and he would know for certain whether he was strong enough as he thought. The winter had barely started, and time would pass slowly.

Paper was scarce and ink was scarcer. There were few letters to leave the confines of Camp Chase except for the charity of a new group of people who tried to help of the Red Cross. Jacob was finally able to write his father and mother late that year and tell him where he was. He spared him news of the hunger and disease. Instead, like the McCrays were compelled to do, he told them he was safe and looked forward to returning home. Lucious and Katy received the news and celebrated their son. He was alive and safer in prison! Now if Jebediah would live and come home, all would be well in the house.

Jebediah leveled his worn out muzzle toward the Yankees and fired into them as habit now and nothing to think odd of doing time and again. They held their ground, but most of the Yankees simply went around them and pillaged and burned as they did. He turned to Earl and saw in him a vision of Jim Payne and Preacher and many others, most he didn't even know their names, and he cried long streaming tears that only a man can cry. It was almost over and the future was uncertain. He clutched his left breast pocket and squeezed the letters from Mary.

"Dearest, Lucious...I see our children have grown. How wonderful they took the years. I am feeling truly whole but tired. Thank you, dear husband for our life," Katy said as she stood in the doorway gazing across the near field and breathing the fresh air of the mountain.

"I am as well, Katy. Your love made our home and the children are of you. I haven't done anything but made our life a labor I fear." He walked up behind her and wrapped his arms around his small wife. "We are blessed to be sure through them. Ours is the lot of God and America's promise." He stopped and thought, then said, "Let's take a ride to the lake and eat there, just the two of us."

"I will get it all together, Lucious. We have some chicken and a jar of fresh water. I can also bring a melon."

"And I will hitch the carriage, sweet Katy."

He loved her smile. Her years nearing sixty she still held youthful looks to his eyes and every time she smiled at him, his heart felt it. He enjoyed watching her and the sight stirred solid and faithful passion to love her forever.

She told John and Carl they may not return until sunset and to help themselves to the fresh chicken and potatoes she had made.. Afterwards they were to mind the cows and water the pen. John said they would and then intended to go into town with Creeless. He wanted to trade some wine, pepper and onions he worked for sweet meal and molasses and maybe a dime novel, for he had a passion to write one day and studied the work of others.

"Be mindful, son, and don't stray far. There are bushwhackers about."

Some men took to robbing during the war and employed their evil intent to take from anyone caught alone. Often their victims were furloughed soldiers they would kill for what was in their pockets and bag. People learned to stay on main roads and travel in groups when they could not. Even groups were not spared at times. It was a dangerous time in the more remote regions. It was rumored there were a group of them working near the mountains in Marshall County and north toward Tennessee. The body of a young man had washed up the river and found to have been shot with a fifty-caliber ball. They were like animal scavengers without a human conscience.

Lucious and Katy found a place to breathe and rest with each other alone. The rocks were formed as a sloping wall into a waterfall feeding the stream into the river a mile away. Trees—weeping willows and oaks crowded by pines—allowed one small patch of meadow near where the falls entered the stream. It was clear, clean spring water. For a time there were no worries, no war, no doubts about God's grace and the mature couple held each other and breathed. They kissed and thought nothing else. The sound of rushing water filled the edge of their senses as their souls embraced for all time.

"Dearest Katy…Are ye happy? Have we had a good life? I love you with all I am and want to know of you, us."

"Yes, dear Lucious. I love you dearly and wouldn't have wanted any more than you and our life as we had. You ask me often while you need never fear that, dear husband."

"You fill my heart, Katy. I deserve you not but take you as I would gladly take you again. If we were young and starting like our dear Rachel, I would take you again."

"And I would go with you willingly, dearest. I love you from the depths and can never think of not being with you."

"Do you think we dare go far here?"

"I am yours anywhere, Lucious," she said, shyly untying her hair and loosening his shirt.

Jebediah fell and broke his ankle. The hard tape and wooden splats use to immobilize his left foot hardly did the job and he was given a rough crutch. It happened as Captain Stewart had remnants of Company B left one fortified position to quickly flank the western edge of Sherman's troops in order to harass and slow. Jeb didn't see the indention in the ground as troops in front of him ran across and inadvertently hid it from his view until it was too late. Within days of the mishap, he was assigned to Andersonville near Atlanta where he would work as a stationary guard of the Yankees interned in the place.

He saw the guards were youngsters and old men except him, now a cripple. It was his lot he thought and he would hold his family's honor this way since it was ordained. He saw the conditions of the poor wretches kept there. His cause had become an evil result in this. The tents were shabby and men were dying every day for no reason other than being taken as honorable prisoners by his beloved Confederacy—now less so as this cannot be what it meant. He prayed their lot would change and President Davis would find the charity to feed them and protect them from the elements. The vast field of graves killed his affection for the cause.

He ambled through the space between the middle stockade posts of rough timbers placed into the ground and the outer walls, thinking and praying. Word was there were going to be massive transfers of prisoners as Sherman was taking Atlanta. He carefully negotiated across the creek that split the camp thinking surely these poor devils would get relief soon. Tens of thousands of men were crowded on nothing more than the space of a small farm. As Jeb wandered by himself, he saw many faces that looked familiar; perhaps they were aspirations of those he killed and they were here to haunt him. Suddenly, he knew he had seen one of them and stared into the man's eyes for long minutes before walking through the creek-bed toward him.

"Boston?" he asked, seeing through the torn rags covering a prisoner he had taken and delivered to Belle Isle that day. His face had become dulled by exposure and pockmarks covered part of his chin and neck, but it was he, lighter in weight and gaunt through the cheeks. It was the same man.

"Aye, Johnny Reb. Boston. You remember me?" his voice strained through intermittent coughs. "How ye been?"

"Good, Billy. How did you come to this place?" Jeb opened his eyes wide, scared for him.

"They transferred a bunch of us because Belle was gettin' crowded." He smiled; the closest he could manage to a laugh.

Jebediah retrieved a wrapped package from his butternut-decorated gray blouse and reached through the space. He handed him the biscuits and told him he would bring him more as soon as he could.

"This can get me kildt, Johnny. Must be mindful for there are some in here who…" he didn't finish as he quickly turned to see who was watching. Jeb knew what he meant and worried Jacob may suffer the same. "There are some who have killed in here and there's no stopping. They can do it and no one says anything, fearing they would be next," the Yankee explained.

"I'll take precautions, Billy. Meet me here at nightfall every third night."

"Thank you for your kindness, Johnny. I'll pray your leg mends properly and you get home."

"Thank you kindly. Tell me if anyone threatens. I can report that to Captain Wirz."

"Yea," he answered and paused. "I can't, Johnny. Please say nothing about what I have said. Please don't, Johnny. I fear that would mark me fatally."

Jebediah left him and felt dark about his assignment. It was even more horrible than the worse he thought upon arriving at the place. If there were one brother he could save, it would be Boston. *Lucky Peter and Uncle Thomas…some of our family I pray are lucky and safely living in Boston. Would it be they shall meet this man some day and he has seen me?* he thought as he gazed outside the walls into the fields and forest nearby. They were Southern fields and the place holding men in misery and death for no offense, for soldiering for their country as he.

Jeb met him at the same fence post the next night. Behind the bedraggled soldier was a mass of starving humanity in rags themselves; their uniforms long sinse failing them as worn fabric exposed patches of skin to the insects and heat in the hot summer and cold and frost in the winter. The stench of the living and the dead did not leave the air settled in the camp. It was heavier and lay just above the ground as testament to something strange and evil of his beloved South. Jeb deftly slipped him another biscuit and a small tin of tobacco.

"What's your name, Billy?"

"I'm Robert James. And you?" he coughed.

"Jebediah McCray. I'm honored to meet you again."

"Same for me…and thank you, Jebediah, for your charity."

"It's a shame what is happening here, but I fear we have no choice. I have learned the captain takes no pity. He's bitter from his wounds, I think, and is a miserable, pained creature. We are duty bound to keep his orders and keep you all hold up."

"I see no wrong in you, Jeb. And I blame you not. It is the war and our miserable failure to reconcile I suppose and…" he coughed the words. "Well, I am troubled making words," he said and smiled. "I hope you know what I'm trying to say to you."

"Worry not, Robert. I hope you become well."

"I hope to be home someday and will remember your kindness forever."

"I hope you are home soon too," he said and paused. "You know I have family up here in Boston. The McCrays—mother and uncle and his wife and a cousin." He smiled. "Maybe one day you can meet them and have a cup of brew to celebrate the war over."

"Aye. I can vision the meeting clearly and taste the cup. I would like to drink a cup to peace with you someday, Jebediah," he coughed. "In freedom outside a prison."

"Keep that, James. I would like that. Maybe soon we'll all be free."

He watched him swallow a large portion of the biscuit and hide the rest of it in an inside pocket of his blouse. Jeb returned to his barracks and prepared for a night watch that placed him in a tower until dawn. He was unsure whether he had the heart to shoot any one of them in an escape attempt and hoped none would. Once the test—the awful consequence of either would surely haunt him the rest of his life. It would be a price too high and so unnecessary.

Rachel and Benjamin settled in town where he could walk to the school. Their small frame house was covered with whitewash and surrounded by a small picket his father built as one of the wedding gifts for the young couple. He and Benjamin had cleared the ground surrounding it to dirt and packed it hard for sweeping. The one tree left standing was a tall oak growing at a front corner that gave shade across most of the wide porch. They had the room to start a family and grow a garden for food the next planting season—maybe by then, God willing, she would be expecting their first child.

Lucious helped the elder O'Keefe do the work for his daughter and son-in-law. He also gave them a large, heavily varnished clothes closet and several quilts cut and sewn by the deft hands of lovely Katy. The wedding was an aid to his worry about Jacob and Jebediah and eased the time some. The news from the war was sorrowful and the lists appeared every week and grew longer. He had not seen his son's names yet and worked to escape his thoughts of such by taking his mind away from such.

Soon there would be new sunshine throughout the South as men and women would be freed from work and shackles, from the humiliation of even being called property, and let alone to pursue the life they could. Soon the sunshine would bear more light on a South no longer at war and killing other Americans and being killed. Soon there would be some recompense suffered by many Southerners regardless of standing and intent, but survival assured.

Mabel took Peter's hand and held Thomas with the other and the family walked to Mass that Sunday. Mother McCray had taken ill and though infirmed insisted they go on and meet their obligation to the sacrament. When they returned, she was passed into the next world, peacefully leaving them with her lips upturned, smiling. Thomas cried and held Peter to his breast. His mother had joined his father finally, and it was sorrowful but right at the same time. He could think of her seeing his father and holding him in the sweet rapture of painless heaven, the ecstasy of paradise she earned by her faith and work on this pitiful earth, and he rejoiced for her behind the tears. She had never known luxury, but he knew she had it all and now, more.

It happened the day the bloody war ended as though she took all the fear she could and prayed all the prayers she could through the years for her family and country—finally taken when the work finished and peace covered the land as a new and bright dawn. It was a day of hope and the end of men facing each other shoulder to shoulder in open fields and forests, on the sea and in the mountains, blue and gray targets for hot lead fired out of fear and duty, taking its horrible toll and laying waste to a generation of men.

Arthur was busily selling his possessions and convincing Rebecca to move with him to the place where they had family for their late years. He thought of the son Julia took away from him and fed the part missing with whiskey at night. It took the pain away but had a way of returning every morning. He would be years past grown now, thirty-five and may be married with darling grandchildren, themselves testing adulthood. He didn't know. They were gone from him forever.

"I'm ready, sister. As I've planned, we can leave in the morning and be in Alabama before week is done. You must go with me for here there is nothing for you and it would cause me worry."

"I will, Arthur. I know it is best and time. I hope the climate will be helpful to my rheumatism," she said and managed a smile through the lines in her face. There was still beauty under them one could see even for her advancing years. The news of peace gave them more assurance they were doing what was right and could make a new life near other McCrays. They had yet to hear of their mother's passing. The morning was clear and crisp, as they set off on their trek southerly with enough hope to take a slow few miles each day.

The two passed through the countryside, leaving Ohio behind them, slowly merging with the distance and future until they were gone from sight. Alabama received them as she did anyone coming. As it was for most states, many of her young men did not return to live and build. She took all who came and embraced them in the bosom of earth and work that was in the mountains and farther south in her fields of pines then on to the ocean and Mobile Bay.

Chapter 8

"I'm Jacob McCray," he said when his turn finally came to report to the Union officer recording the prisoner release scheduled for Sunday. His taut frame leaned against the table as he began the process to freedom. His caved face and partially covered body in a ragged uniform would be on the way soon. He prayed he could eat soon and make the journey alive.

"Take your place over yonder, Mr. McCray. You'll be fed with them and given leave," the Yankee said handing him a piece of paper that was his pass home. The officials determined with the information at hand who should be tried on charges of crimes and who would not.

"Yes, sir. Thank you."

"You people will be on your way soon," he said.

The wagon was stopped nearby and several Union soldiers began taking out boxes of hard tack and passing it out to the prisoners who had their slips. Jacob put his hand out, clinched a piece and brought it to his mouth in one motion. He looked at the soldiers and smiled his thanks.

"You're hungry, Johnny Reb. Take it slow, man," a sergeant said. He was one of a small group who appeared kindly toward their charges and was happy to be of help. "The water is over there. One cup. Take turns."

The hundreds passed through in hours and made ready to walk through the gate that dusk. Then they were on their own to find their way from Ohio.

Jebediah left with Earl and began the journey walking. The idea he would not be killed became a truth for him the instant he turned from the Eleventh and headed west. He walked and kept his eyes ahead, not looking back at those who were left, those few and Captain Stewart who survived by the grace of God and no other way. He was empty of thoughts and emotions and barely bid Earl goodbye. He left him at a corral where Earl bargained with a group for a saddle and horse to begin his way to Rising Fawn, east of Marshall

County next to the Georgia state line. He walked a while, and then he rode on a passing wagon, as long as he could for various lengths, then walked again. He made camp on the edges in abundant tree stands near the well-worn thoroughfare.

Jeb found food along the way by the charity of farmers spotted throughout the countryside in longer intervals it seemed than was before. One woman made him a whole meal with beans, chicken and bread. She acted like she knew him and pampered the young man as though he was her child. He didn't ask out of fear but felt she saw him as a lost son—maybe one killed in a battle somewhere and left. He thought of Mary and how he may appear to her now. Knowing he was sullen, drawn, tired, angry, bloodied and scarred, he hardly was presentable yet, and it would take some doing to see her. He hoped he could get to his home and clean up before she laid eyes on him. His mother and father would see him and be preoccupied with the return. He thought of Jacob and hoped he would see him whole.

He left the old musket where the company disbanded in honor. The company had furled their flags, the Southern Cross and a worn battle flag of stars and bars. All he carried was a side knife Jim Payne had willed him the night before he was killed. His uniform was worn and the butternut well faded against a sun-bleached gray blouse, which was tattered and torn at the shoulders and front. Hastily stitched repair was beginning to fail him on his march. All he thought to do was let it be.

There were few nights he had to spend sleeping before he reached country he recognized. He felt the elevation change as he started up the grades of the foothills and came upon another kind farm family who put him up his last night before reaching Marshall County. They were the Hatches of Etowah, a blend of Cherokee and Scotch-Irish who sat the war out working their small space for vittles and little more. But what they had they shared with the soldier who had seen so much sadness and horror. He sat with them around the hearth in their small front room and listened to them talk of family and work. Much like the McCrays, he thought and was the same. He watched the parents fetch food and covers for him and their older children staring at this stranger in their midst who had been to war and returned. Their eyes were curious as to this fellow. The long black-haired daughter whose body was more mature for her age and not well confined in the clothing left from youth must be around fourteen he thought. She seemed to look at him with more interest than a curiosity toward a returning soldier. He felt uneasy about her, catching her eyes survey the whole of him and whether it was true or not, felt she may have an affliction of lust. It was in her eyes he remembered similar to his how his must have appeared during the foray into Richmond that day and the devil-may-care attitude about his body that cost him so much time in remorse and so much heart in repentance. He would have to leave them earlier and take out into the night after supper else face her if she was wont to wander and explore him more closely. He had to because he couldn't take the chance he was right about her.

Jacob came upon the kindness of dwellers the same as Jebediah, and he managed to eat and ride the length of his travels. He would arrive a month after Jebediah as it happened. As the younger brother came to the McCray farm, John was the first to see him and ran toward him, knowing it was Brother Jebediah. He jumped into him and embraced him tightly; the young men were strong as an ox and squeezed all the air out of Jeb. They laughed about it and ran to the front door where his mother Katy called for Lucious to come quickly and greet their son.

"Thank you for the letters, son. My God! How happy I am you are here and alive!" his father said on behalf of the whole family. "How wonderful to have you home!" He smiled as wide as anyone could remember him smiling before.

"Quick, Katy…fetch some drink for our beloved hero! Come, Jebediah, take a seat here and rest…rest as long as you need!"

"Jebediah. We missed you! We love you and are so thankful you have returned!" Katy said. "The boys are all grown now. Don't they look fine?"

"They surely do, Mother. I'm happy to be here with everyone. I'm so happy! I wished I had never left," he said as he smiled then turned his face down. She handed him a cup of hot tea and asked him what he would like to eat.

"We must get you out of that, Jebediah, and into something clean."

"Thank you, Mother. I know I'm dirty and offensive. You all are wonderful, and I'm a lucky son." He was afraid to ask about his brother Jacob but managed to out of need to be whole. "What have you heard from Jacob?"

"He is on his way!" As the words left his mother's mouth, he felt a consuming relief of worry. It vanished as quickly as a breadth. "He was held, you know, but has left the prison. We heard from Miss Winters of Etowah Red Cross last week."

"I pray he makes it safely."

"We do too—like we did for you, Jebediah. The bushwhackers have a nasty reputation as the snakes they are."

"Aye, son. But I'm sure his resourcefulness will see him through. We expect him soon," Lucious said.

"You taught us well, Father."

"You were men before your time."

"And what of Uncle Thomas and Uncle Arthur? How is Aunt Rebecca faring?"

"They are fine. Arthur and Rebecca are coming here soon. Son, I do have sad news about your Grandmother McCray."

"She has passed, hasn't she, Father?" he said and made it easy for his father.

"I'm afraid it's true, son. Month before last she went to the Lord. We heard she went in peace, Jebediah. I'm sorry."

"I'm sorry too, Father. She was a wonder."

"Thomas was with her and his wife Mabel. Peter is doing well these days as a scholar you know."

"That's good news. Thank you, sir, for everything and tonight! I have dreamed of homecoming, and it is better than my wonderful dreams."

They talked about the passing of old man Creeless, the new holding fence, and the men of Marshall County who were killed, the addition to the church and Rachel's marriage. Hours passed before they noticed. Jebediah asked about Mary and how she was. Judge Hornsby was still in place as the Justice and had grown fatter, but remained wise in his advancing years.

"Mary speaks to us often, Jebediah and talks of you," his father smiled. "She wants to see you, son. I think she has plans for you two."

Jebediah shyly looked out as he heard.

"She has shared her letters with us—but maybe not all," Lucious said and laughed. "I know you'll surely want to see her as soon as you can. Would you like to go tonight? You should use the carriage and call on her."

"Thank you, Father. But I must bathe. I have an inch on me I must take off before I see her. I'm sorry I'm in this condition for you too."

"We'll draw a bath for you, Jebediah. The water is already at boil. My straight razor and soap is ready too. Please help yourself as we finish." He called for John and Carl to go with him and see that all the animals are inside their pens and the gates securely held.

Jebediah slowly steered the carriage to the front of Judge Hornsby's four-column porch and tied it off at the rail. It was early morning and there was no movement heard or seen yet in the house. He quietly walked across the wood slats and used the brass doorknocker to announce a visitor. He waited for a long minute before the door was opened, she was standing there in a plain dress she used for working in the home, an apron slung across her front like a maid might wear, but it was Mary in her beauty. She saw him and at once leaped into his arms so hard he had to catch her to keep both of them from falling. She didn't say anything; she showered his face with kisses and held onto him as if she was holding life.

"Hello, Mary!" he wedged in words between their lips. "Thank you so much for writing me!"

"Oh, Jebediah…Oh, Jebediah. God!" she whispered between her kisses.

"Mary, sweet, adorable Mary. How I've missed you! I have missed you sorely!" he managed to say while almost choked by tears he hid from her.

"Come in, dear Jebediah. Please," the Judge said.

The couple entered the ornately decorated foyer and sitting room unwilling to part from each other's touch, holding hands tightly, and watching each other's every breadth.

"I was hoping you are free this afternoon to attend with me to see my sister."

"I am, Jebediah. Shall I bring some tea and cake? I have been seeing her with Benjamin in town and at church and would enjoy seeing them—and especially meaning I would be with you," she said.

Mary began talking fast and saying everything pent up and saved for him over the past three years. She knew now he was the man to be her lover. She told him of her father's garden and how it failed this year, of her learning to seamstress for his mother, her learning to ride from his brother John, how much she enjoyed his letters, and finally how very much she worried and prayed for his returning to her from war. "There were days, Jebediah, when almost gave up hope. That is terrible and one should never give up hope when you pray and listen to God."

"He saved me, dearest Mary. There were countless times when I asked him to let me live another day and let me see you again, dear heart."

"Thank you, Jebediah. That is so thoughtful that you would mind to think of me. I thought of you and," she hesitated. "Dear me, I'm going too far…"

"What's that, Mary?"

"Jebediah." She looked straight into his eyes; her mouth turned serious and stern. "I fell in love with you while you were gone," she said and turned her face away embarrassed. Her words took Jebediah by surprise and for a moment rendered him speechless. His heart felt like it would explode with joy and wonder how sweet and grand life is when he heard her say.

"Oh, Mary. I have loved you from school," he said and smiled sheepishly, turning his eyes upward through the eyebrows of a bowed head. "Mary. I desire that you to be my wife and I your husband—if you would have this poor boy." He heard himself say and was proud he managed.

He heard her say, "I do want this marriage," and that alone, softly, for his ears only. She made her mind to their joining while he was away and knew God would grant her favor in prayer for his safe return. This was the day He made for them to talk of commitment and record their love in the heavens.

She rose from the sitting chair, turned the lamps down to a flicker and kissed him in full as he wrapped his arms around her back. She was softer and more beautiful than he had even kept thoughts while on campaign. He took the delicacy of her feminine nature in with every sense. Her aroma was sweet and perfumed just enough, her touch was reassuring and gentle and warm, her mouth tasted better than the best sweet pie, and her voice pushed soft, loving music into his ears for his mind to wander into a place of delight.

"And when, Jebediah, would you think we should marry?" she asked.

"As soon as your father will give me your hand, I want to make you my dear wife, Mary." He kissed her again.

"I love you," she said softly. "And I will always be yours."

"I love you, too, and will always be yours."

They heard her father walking from the library, each step closer, to see the visitor. Her father was ambling in to greet him and welcome him home. He knew Jebediah to be a good, clean, God-fearing young man and approved his daughter's correspondence through the time and had thought it would come to this.

As he appeared in the double doorway, he saw them release from an innocent embrace and Jebediah stood and extended his hand toward him. The elder Judge Hornsby grabbed it and pulled him to him, squeezing him as a long away son or brother rather than as a young friend of his daughter.

"So good to see you home, young McCray! Welcome to our house!"

"Thank you, Judge. Thank you very much."

"I am indeed happy to see you, and I know Mary is. You're all she talks about anymore these days, and maybe now she'll quiet since you're here," he laughed.

"It is an honor and privilege for me to be accepted in your house, Judge."

"Is your family well? I see them from time to time, but hardly all together." He smiled. "There's many a fine stock from that farm."

"Yes, sir, they are well. We wait for Jacob still but know he's traveling home."

"That is grand. I won't keep you two. I just wanted to see you for a short while. One day maybe you will share your experiences with me. I believe it is important to chronicle the events of this war from our forebears to our descendants. They must know what men did and why so many died bravely."

"I'll gladly share what little part I know, Judge."

"Thank you, young man. I'll make no judgment on reason because it is done, but I will write of the men," he said. Jebediah thought he saw tears well up in his eyes. "Now I will take my leave and you two can have some time."

"It has been a pleasure to see you, Judge Hornsby. Thank you for seeing me."

"Now, Jebediah. Let's ride to Rachel and Benjamin. I would like to see them and tell them of our news. We should give Father tonight and tell him on the morrow," Mary said.

"Very well, dear heart."

Jacob was riding in the back of a merchant's wagon that had taken pity on him. Silas Muller was taking the journey from Cincinnati to New Orleans where he traded in fine cloths and linens. They were into western Tennessee and making good time. He would have him close to the Alabama line in a few nights and from there, Jacob would have but another few days to Marshall County. Taking more food now, he had gained back a few pounds he'd lost although they were still not visible. He felt stronger though and had hope once more. Along the way he dreamt of seeing his mother and father and brothers and Rachel, and how wonderful the reunion would be.

They rode on the front seat together and at dusk rounded a mountain where the rocks and trees turned closer, nearly swallowing them except for the path of a road that took them to a main thoroughfare seven miles past. Jacob felt them before he saw them and nudged Silas to take care.

"This does not seem safe," he said. "There are people about. I can hear them," he said, his senses still acute from his experience in the cavalry.

"This way will save us a day, Jacob. I don't hear anything."

"Maybe you're right, but I fear you're not."

"If there is someone near, they could be travelers like us. Do not worry, young soldier. We will make our way through this pass soon. I recall it will be clear ahead."

"Very well. In the event, I shall like to hold your Springfield at the ready, Silas."

"Do so, young man. It's under the sack behind our bench."

"Keep quiet, Silas. They mean harm," Jacob whispered as he brought the Springfield to his side low and took a long knife the driver had stored on the side of the bench. In the dark shadows he chanced whoever was close couldn't see his movement.

Suddenly there appeared a tall figure standing centered on the road just ahead of them. Jacob could see his long beard, a trademark of the bushwhacker, his large fitting clothing and floppy wide brim hat that nearly covered his eyes. He raised the rifle close to his side slow and easy and had it ready to their front.

Jacob heard about the scallywags and bushwhackers emerging from under their rocks to pillage people while many men were away. Some were Confederate veterans, most likely deserters, and others were not but seized the opportunity of a weakened society to rape, kill, and steal from anyone vulnerable. The vulgar, evil lot cared not a wit for anyone but themselves and feeding their greed.

Silas stopped his rig thirty feet away and called out, "What are you doing? Give way, stranger and let us pass!" he shouted. There was no answer. Jacob felt the presence of someone behind them. He whispered to Silas to make ready to jump quickly, leave the bench and take cover off the road.

"Ya'll stay where you'ns are, hear?" the man in front suddenly shouted.

"On me, Silas. Jump off."

"Very well, Jacob," he nervously answered. "If anything happens to me, take the wagon young man." He cried as if he suddenly saw his days ending.

"Go!"

The two jumped from Silas side, Jacob covering him as they rolled into the undergrowth. They heard the man shout out something and a loud muzzle sound from the 50-caliber rifle he brought up and fired at the instant. But he missed everything except a wood brace on the wagon shooting wildly. It would be a few seconds before he was reloaded, but just then Jacob heard the fast footsteps of another stranger who ran to the back of the wagon to find them. Jacob had seven shells and fired one of them toward the bushwhacker in back and then quickly readied the rifle toward the front. He didn't know whether he hit him and assumed he did not, but thought the sound may frighten the cowards away.

"Ya'll come out and we won't hurt you'uns," he lied.

Jacob fired his second shot toward the voice and shouted, "You must leave now or be killed!" He heard both of them laugh and was able to judge their approximate location. He turned Silas and led him farther back and to the rear. He could barely see one of them slowly coming toward them in a crouch, a weapon leading his path. He brought the rifle up to his shoulder and carefully held it to take aim the instant he had a chance. He remembered the same challenge while near a Yankee picket in the Shenandoah.

His mind was clear and focused. He felt the steel of battle hardened nerves and sharp eyes, and he waited. A good target would emerge and he would take him. He had but to wait. The bushwhackers figured they would have already been fired on in panic with all he had since that was how it happened before. And after the wasted shells were expended, they easily walked up and shot the man through the head. It happened that way once and this would be no different. Jacob heard the front killer say, "We got 'em, Clement! Go on in and finish them."

Jacob waited more. *Please God, help me aim true,* he prayed, bringing his eye to the rifle and sighting into the darkness. He thought of them as the animals he heard about—who killed wounded returning veterans for their purse during the war when they found them on the struggle home. The veterans only wanted peace and to see loved ones again, having made it through war, many with ghastly wounds and missing legs, arms or other pieces of flesh that would never heal. They were on their way toward the simplest of desires only to be killed by these devils before looking into their mothers' eyes.

He saw him enter the wood line and coming nearly toward them. Off by an angle he was listening for breaths or other sounds, searching for the witnesses to put a ball into their bodies so their fare could be taken with impudence. Jacob let him near and when he had, the shot was quick and deadly, felling him with a clean shot into his heart, and blowing out his life-blood in an instant. His partner had been wrong and a merciful God had given Jacob the shot.

"Move, Silas!" he said quietly, stroking his arm to follow him farther back but parallel with the road. Jacob knew the sound of his muzzle may bring attention and direction and fire from the other; he prayed there was only one left as he had few rounds to use in their defense. From the hidden position he found, he waited and watched, but there was no movement. *Perhaps he ran away and was no longer a threat,* he thought. Or he could be waiting for them and take devious shots. Jacob whispered for Silas to stay hidden in their cover and made his way to the edge of the road to take study of the new enemy.

He put himself down in prone on the parallel and watched. It seemed like hours, but it was hardly a few minutes as he surveyed the area in front of him.

Through the darkness he saw the wagon was there, the trees overlapped the road and were thick, and the road itself was nothing more than a lighter shadow than the rest of the view. He waited still as a statute for movement. As the minutes rolled slowly, he began to think the killer had fled when he saw a hint of a shadow change ahead. It was coming from the front of Silas' rig where he must be hiding to ambush them.

Jacob slid back into the woods and crawled forward through the brush until he was nearly beside the team. So far the bushwhacker hadn't heard him move, and it appeared the advantage might soon be his. He waited again. He saw the outline of the large hat move back and forth as his target must be looking from side to side past the wagon. *Patience now,* he told himself with his inner voice. *Still, Jacob!* He inched toward him silently and slowly until he could more clearly see the outline of a single man. *This is it. Steady, now,* he said to himself, bringing the Springfield up to a straight line into the figure. He had him sighted and fired, dropping his target as though a sack had been let loose from weak hands, a dulled sound of body striking the earth. He heard him moan and gurgle and knew it wasn't finished yet. Jumping out of his cover, he made his way to the foul smelling clump and put another round into his head.

His limbs began shaking as he walked back to Silas.

"It's done, Silas. Let's be on our way."

"Thank you so much, young Jacob. You did a great deed tonight. I'm sorry I brought this upon you."

"Not to worry. We must go on."

"I'm a taking you home, Jacob. You need not worry now about completing your journey. Old Silas will make sure of it."

"I'm indebted to you, sir. Thank you."

After removing the body that blocked the path of the wagon, they left and set out for the highway. Silas would take no more cross roads in an attempt to save time. They ambled on and came to Florence, Alabama, within a week and from there they would make Marshall County in three days of easy travel.

Arthur and Rebecca moved in with the McCrays the week before and were staying with family until they were able to make provision for themselves. Katy treated them as they were her own brother and sister and loved them as part of the family. She thought it odd but not evil that Rebecca did what she did for a living for a time, but would never bring the subject to the fore. She knew the woman had few options and selling her body was the one she took as others had done in the day. She was a peacekeeper as was Lucious who would endure the guests with patience and understanding. The house was more crowded now and the kitchen hearth area became unseemly with the number of people there at mealtime. But they could easily and happily make do for the sake of Arthur and Rebecca. It was not as bad as the boat had been so many years ago, he thought.

As the week passed, Jacob and Silas pulled up into the farm and he ran to his mother's door to embrace her. She wept when she saw him as she had done when Jebediah returned. Her family was home again and would not leave her. She thanked Silas for delivering the boy and invited him in to sup.
"I see my uncle and aunt are here. I'm happy to be home, Mother, and glad to see everyone," Jacob said as he and Silas sat by the hearth drinking hardy portion of cider to quench road thirst. His gaunt figure saddened Katy and she could hardly contain her tears of worry. She and Rebecca brought one dish of food after another for him and Silas.
"Thank you, ma'am, indeed. It was quite a fill," Silas said noticing Rebecca who still had some looks. "This fine lady your aunt, Jacob?"
"Yes, sir. Do not worry. She has no husband," he laughed.
"I wonder if she would allow me a visit sometime."
"Ask her, Silas. She might. But I warn you, she has only been here a while and may still be ornery from the trip!" he laughed.
"Ah, son. There's a cure for such a condition!" he laughed.
"I believe you two have had too much cider. Now behave!" Katy said, smiling.
Arthur took ill with influenza. He had been bringing a wagon load of wood up from the cut he was working and was caught in a cold rain. He didn't think anything of it at the time and kept going without taking cover. The next few days he was becoming sicker and finally had to be bedridden. The doctor came to see him after Lucious asked him against Arthur's wishes and diagnosed the elder with flu. Within a week he passed away and the pain of the sickness ended.
"Poor Arthur. He worked hard all his life and came to this place with practically nothing," Lucious said at his graveside the day of the burial. "But at least he was in his family's loving arms and we did love him. Now we honor him as an American McCray who came and built like his father did. Now the two are together in heaven."
The family retired to the farm and without asking each of them surveyed the blessing of each other. Arthur was gone, but before he left, he brought his

lost sister home—a final work not as glorious as war or building a city or railroad, but worthy of an American man in his element.

Silas decided to stay in Marshall County and marry Rebecca. They took up a residence next to Lucious and Katy, worked a few acres and began saving for a mercantile store he wanted to put downtown Guntersville. They were a loving couple and before their marriage when Rebecca told him of her past, he was as kind as Katy. It didn't worry him and he would never talk of it during their long marriage. They learned verses from Katy and attended church every Sunday, Rebecca finding her faith through Silas and prayer.

The day of the wedding was drawing near and Thomas Stamps made one last appeal to Mary to reconsider marrying such a one as Jebediah McCray whose standing was as low as one can get. And now that reconstruction had been foisted upon the South, it would be a while before he would have much. Thomas was an aristocrat from the area and could protect her from the overbearing Yankee district provost, who acted as though it was his personal mission to exact punishment from every secessionist. He couldn't convince her, and Mary told him she wouldn't share this conversation with Jebediah. Her intended, she assured, would take matters in his hands in such a way that Thomas would never do himself, and although he would surely survive, he would regret the day because of the pain. Mary wanted none of Thomas and planned her wedding to Jebediah. It was to be the happiest day of her life. It was to be the happiest day of his life.

Chapter 9

"Peter will be going to the Harvard College this fall, Thomas. Isn't it grand?"

"Yes, dear Mabel. We have a great deal to be proud of in our son. He has done well and thank you for your valuable help."

"It will lend him a great future, husband."

"I must go to the livery. Basel McGinity is to meet me there to discuss a proposition. He's a strange one with his ideas for a horseless carriage."

"And what of you?" she asked.

"He wants me to build a frame and a boiler. Not much different than what I've done, but for space to carry the steamer. I'll return in a few hours."

"Fine, dear. Take care, for it's thick with snow outside."

Jebediah and Mary had their first baby and named him Samuel. He had gone to work for the Judge, and while a law clerk, began studying to become a lawyer. Land deeds, divorcements, and contract law occupied him some, but the charges he could make did not provide the living he desired for Mary. He worked for Silas in the store some hours each day and Saturdays to make up the difference. Commissions were paid on the sales and his friend and aunt had built a business out of dry goods and cloth, becoming one of the few suppliers in the area and pricing fairly. They saw the business expand over the years by selling at a low mark-up and selling more.

Mary was a dutiful mother; she tended and suckled Samuel until he was two, not leaving him for any time. He started walking before he was one and running by the time he was two. They could see a healthy, strong boy emerging from infancy. When Jebediah returned from work, he always ran to his father for his attention and with Mary expecting their second, he would have more time with Samuel. The grandparents doted on Samuel and brought the young McCray gifts every time they visited their son.

Peter began his studies and lived at home, taking on the look of an educated young man early. He was tall and lean with dark blond hair that curled around his face and hid the spectacles at his temples that he wore to read. He met Maria at the café near campus and was talking to her some but had yet to call on her. He thought about it and worried he would lose time from the library where he needed hours to follow many classes. The professors took no pity and had no patience for any student falling behind and should he or she fail, most saw it as that which should happen.

When the McCrays of Boston heard of Lucious being ill, Thomas planned to see his brother. He was getting on in years and this may be the last time he would be able to see him and talk of the times. The rail lines had grown and made the trip a faster one than it was the last time he traveled south before the war. He thought he should make the trip, return within two weeks and have plenty of time with Lucious. A telegraph would confirm his arrival to Katy that day.

Jacob had worked as a deputy and was put up for sheriff of Marshall County by Judge Hornsby, now well retired but still heavily connected to the power brokers in north Alabama. Jebediah and Mary knew his time on earth was short as his breathing was labored and he was unable to walk any length at one time. They purposed to say to him all they needed to before he left them, words of love and appreciation, devotion to his principles and assurances his legacy of justice and kindness would survive. Mary worked with Rebecca in establishing an orphan's home they would name after Judge Hornsby. There were many youngsters and teenagers whose mothers were either dead or missing because they thought they could not care for them. Some had been orphaned by the war or influenza, and they were blessed to survive the outbreak but put out as lonely children.

The women began keeping two of the children in Rebecca and Silas' home who had been given over by the church. The older was a boy who was weakened by an affliction since birth; his small body barely carried him and he could hardly speak. When he did, he talked about how he would like to be a soldier like his adopted uncles were and wear the uniform. In his fourteen years there were few who loved him, but Rebecca and Mary did and had Jacob talk to him of the cavalry and Jebediah of the infantry. He praised the men and smiled a wide happy smile every time he saw one of them enter his room. Seeing them and dreaming of soldiering was his only pleasure in life as he merely survived day after painful day. His crippled body took its torturing toll and wracked him often with no relief. His limbs began folding around him and gradually became near useless. Jacob gave him one of his swords and the boy cried in appreciation of the affection and slept with it every night.

Rebecca watched him become more and more pained and weaker, and she cried every time she left his room. She tried to be good for him, but there was little she could do the make his life better. She prayed to the same God who took her father that surely He would spare this little fellow and give him a better life, even one year of playing with friends or riding a horse without fear, anything most boys do that he has never been able.

When the boy was finally free of pain, the sword was buried with him. He was put into a uniform the women sewed together from remnants Jebediah and Jacob had and could find from others and was interned as a full colonel of the Confederate States of America.

Thomas arrived midday and saw Lucious before night fell. He was alive, bedridden, and still lucid. He looked at Katy and nodded reassurance and smiled. "How have you been treated, brother?" he asked.

"Sulfa and steam, Thomas. I'm afraid there's little to do," he said and coughed.

"Your sons have done well, Lucious. John and Carl are on their way from Florida I hear."

"Yes. I wish not to trouble them, but they both are stubborn. I do not think my time is up, but I couldn't convince them."

"They want to see their father. And I hear Jacob is sheriff; Jebediah is a barrister, and Rachel a good mother of a son. My, have we seen the family grow!"

"Yes, it has."

"You must be pleased with them. And Katy, is she well?"

"Yes, she is," he said. "I'm afraid I trouble her greatly these days. I hope this goes, so I won't be her millstone."

"Dear brother, don't worry. I can help now and will stay as long as you need me," Thomas McCray said in a serious and low tone of voice.

"Peter is in college, isn't he? He's the first. Father would see it grand, wouldn't he?"

"He is watching us and I'm very sure he's proud. Mother too. They are both beaming from heaven; I know because there are times when I swear I can see their eyes on us and feel their hearts," Thomas said then smiled and reached for a clean cloth to wipe the sweat from his brother's brow. "Can I get you a glass?"

"Yes. Some cider please."

The two men visited at length and talked of the voyage to America, the time spent in the mines and how they wrestled in those days, the close call of war, the hardships and how easy they seemed to survive them and the families started. It had already been a journey and it was early. Soon this generation would pass into memory and their story would have to be told to survive the years.

"Jacob will be here soon, Father," Katy had entered and announced. "Mary is here and said he and Jebediah are coming early today."

Peter saw Maria and took a meal of fish that Friday. He watched her turn in the dress and the way her breasts swung around as she moved. Her breasts were the largest part of her body and he liked looking, hoping she wouldn't catch him staring. Her dark black hair she kept tied up gave way her Spanish heritage and her full lips seemed pursed even at rest. She was working class from the wharfs where her father worked the docks. Maria's mother had left them and ran away with a frontiersman.

The unmarried couple set out for California more than twenty-five years ago where he was promised a job if he came. They had begun their journey with the Snowshoe party which came to be known as the Donner party and were never heard from again. There were horrific stories published though her father tried in vain to shield away from her; they were everywhere and became widely read in newspapers and dime novels.

Her father provided for the infant and raised her well, accepting help from the ladies of the church with her through the years. She was now a grown woman in her late twenties, older than Peter, but as attractive to him as one could be. Her full hips and bountiful breasts were too much for the healthy Peter to put aside, and he began their courtship by asking her to attend a concert at Harvard with him. She hesitated but accepted, knowing their age difference was odd, but not so much as others have done man to woman or as in her case, woman to man.

"My father is presently in Alabama, Maria. He doesn't know of my interest in you yet."

"Do you think he may disapprove?"

"Only if you weren't Catholic," he said with a smile.

"I am worried some though. He does not know me."

"He'll be fine with it as Mother is. She adores you almost as much as I do!" he laughed. "I can hardly wait for him to meet you too."

"I will be honored. Father is holding a dinner for the Knights. Would you attend?"

"I would be honored, Maria."

Lucious turned toward his sons. They had all made it and were standing by his bedside. He no longer looked like the father they remembered. He was emaciated and weak. It was hard to look on him and not stream tears.

"Boys...I fear my time is short in this world. I feel life slipping from me. I love you all and want to say it clearly. Can you hear me?"

"Yes, sir." The sons answered partly in unison and then one after another until each had told him he loved him too.

"I'll pray for you all and your wives," he managed to say with a very weak voice. "It has been a good life because of you and your mother, boys. Do take heed to the Bible. It is your salvation."

Rachel entered the room and knelt with her brothers beside her father. He told her he loved her greatly and not to worry for if he is to pass, he will still know her and be with her. "I will be in heaven, daughter, for I have been saved by His grace years ago, and you children have made it right."

She was weeping. She could see that she was losing him and thought of her mother and how alone she would be when he goes. She ran to Katy's arms and held her, wiping away tears and trying to breathe between the chokes of a closing throat.

"Dear, Rachel. It will be all right."

"Oh, Mother. I am saddened to see him that way. Isn't there hope?"

"I don't know, dear. He is in God's hands and God always does for us what is best."

"Can't we have him with us a while longer?" she said, crying to her collar.

"Pray, child and maybe he will stay. But if he goes, he will be loosed from the sickness. There is no sickness in heaven," she said. She smiled at Rachel trying to reassure her. "This is part of living, child, and will be glorious for those who believe."

Maria's body was soft and brown, beautiful in his eyes; her chiseled figure was better naked than he saw her dressed. What they did was as natural as eating and drinking clear water to nourish the body, as keeping as the faith itself, and a spiritual joining as he lay with her and performed as a husband and she as a wife, unnoticed by a world outside the straw-filled portion of the McCray barn. The first time she let him they conceived. She would be with child and unmarried, a shame on her father and his family unless they set it right in front of God through a priest.

Peter learned of her pregnancy the month his father returned. Peter told him he intended to marry Maria as soon as the arrangements could be made. He loved her and would have her, with or without the blessing of Thomas or

Mabel or anyone for that matter. "This was preordained and fixed. We are blessed with a child. I have to know this soon," he said.

"Very well, son. If she is to be yours than I shall agree and bless the union."

"Thank you, Father."

"And I will ask Father Sheay to marry you."

Peter cast his eyes down in humility, not a common emotion for him as he could recall feeling. His life had been an easy one, full of the best life had to offer through the time. He had been protected from any hard elements all his life and learned to be master of those people and things around him. Maria taught him there was even more, and he took it too.

Maria and her father avoided the subject of her mother. Sensationalized stories were printed of the barbaric conclusion her party reached for some to survive. Her nightmares began to include visions of her mother's arms being hacked off to make a meal and her skull being opened for the brain used in a boiling pot. She saw these things in her sleep and worried it would cause harm to her unborn; she visited a pharmacist for a potion to relieve these awful dreams and was given an elixir with cocaine and opium as the main ingredients. She slept well but felt intoxicated by day. The movement she felt in her womb must have stopped some time during the night she thought when she noticed it late morning by which time she usually had felt many kicks and had not felt even one. She began crying hysterically and called out across the livery and at the house for Peter to come quick.

"My God, Peter! Something has happened to our baby!" she wept and screamed. "My God!"

Peter took her into his arms and held her, letting her tears fall on and past his shoulder as she laid her head down inconsolable and her emotions out of control. Flashes of her mother being eaten one piece at a time came and went, her sin, her age, her father, Peter, Peter's family...she cried she wasn't good enough and was being punished by God. "You must leave me, Peter! I'm no good! I'm no good! For God's sake, leave me and repent for your own soul!" she cried the words and dug her face into his shoulder harder.

The McCray heart is of strong vintage. Peter had it and finally knew on this day he was a true McCray. He wanted Maria and thought if the baby has died inside her, they must try again following the sacrament of matrimony. It happened the same night that took Lucious to his father in heaven. Peter loved her and wanted her whether there was a child or not.

"My dear, sweet, beautiful Maria! Try not to be sad. And please do not put me out. I love you and we will get through this together." The tears were coming, but he had to speak with a steady voice and strong.

Boston in the spring was the perfect setting for a wedding. The flowers were in full bloom with an array of colors gracing the cobblestone and the fields. The trees were full of life and enveloped all who saw them in peace and contentment of a surrounding beauty. The bay seemed even more beautiful and fresher somehow as waves glanced off pillars and rocks with its living waters, spray and foam. Birds filled the air and sang; animals of all sorts sang and talked to each other and their human keepers. The town was busy and filling with people walking about and doing business and doing no business but seeing and breathing. Carriages went up and down the boulevards, adding their rhythm to the sounds of nature. The town was rich. The people were enriched.

Father Hoban had retired and turned the business to his son-in-law. He enjoyed the rest of his life in comfort, as Thomas made good. He and Mabel were able to expand again and start a feed store next to the large livery and blacksmith shop where he had several of the newest bellows working six days a week, a laundry, and a trade in coal and iron ore for the new steel mills to the west.

Katy McCray moved into the home Jebediah and Mary made in the acres nearby the original plot. Jacob, Benjamin and Jebediah built two rooms, an outside door and a large porch for her comfort in little more than a week. As she had been, she was still loving class and a quiet woman, not given to interference in the affairs of her adult children. The pleasure of being with her grandchildren provided her with all the entertainment she needed to laugh and enjoy her waning years. She cooked and mended still and patched quilts for the children and generations to follow. She spent time with Rachel and Rebecca minding the unfortunate children in their charge every day as well and did the work even when her bones could hardly move without pain. She was close to the age of Rebecca and the two became close friends, beyond being in-laws.

The McCrays of Marshall County interred the father after the sons dug his grave in the church cemetery; the rain gently washed them as they took dutiful turns in the hole. He was gone and his work brought them to this place of good chance to make a life by his example of work and faith. Rachel placed a clutch of red roses on his grave and talked to him, thanking him for all he had done and being a good father and thanking God for all He has done for giving her the time she had him. Jacob turned to Jebediah, John and Carl and said it was up to them now and they must carry on the McCray legacy for their father's will had always been they be men of character and faith and do what their hearts knew what was right. He would be sorely missed. The years take the last toll.

"There's a group, Jebediah, that I need to know what they plan," Jacob said. "I fear they're a dangerous lot of bushwhackers and mean to do harm."

"I believe I know of whom you speak. Heard tell it was Bedford Forest himself at the head of this vigilante army and there's some good come out of it on the scallywags and all. They're up in Tennessee, not around these parts."

"There ain't any good, Jeb. Don't be fooled. Not now as they mean to do a great harm and many things that ain't right. They're killing innocent people."

"I didn't know…"

"And I read Forest resigned and asked them to disband. The news was that he helped start what he regrets. And I fear what they'll do. They say they mean to fight the carpetbagger provosts and keep the blacks down. We know there have been some killings up north of here by men wearing ghost clothes and we heard they are planning a meeting around these parts—so it's coming."

"Here?"

"Yes, Jeb. I'm feared that's true. Nothing good will come from it. Help me if you will and the county will pay you deputy wages."

"I don't need the wages," Jebediah said.

"I know, Jeb, but it keeps it straight. I'm enlisting others for the cause as we see them dangerous."

"Surely, Jacob. We don't need more war," he said and looked down, pensive and disheartened. "Damn fools! Don't they know?"

"They don't care, Jeb. It falls to us to keep them from doing their bidding in these parts."

"I'm with you, brother," he said. "This plight and scourge of men's minds must be met by men who know evil and right and are not confused."

"We'll meet after services Sunday in the Creeless house. I've had to ask many to come. Thank you, brother."

Peter and Maria's living quarters were attached to the McCray house and consisted of four rooms. He had a study to use and a small but growing library, there was a parlor-kitchen and hearth, a bath and their bedroom, complete with a nursery corner for the baby. He studied and did well enough to go on to his third and final year that fall while Maria kept the house and planned for their next child. Peter was offered a position in New York and it appeared they would have their own home soon.

The house had grown into a large estate and graced Thomas and Mabel's property from a rise in the center of their acreage. He had built a decorative rail to set off the front and kept pens in the back quarter near the barn. The family only kept horses these days and a few dogs that were more pets than able to watch and protect. Maria learned during the summer she was expecting again and prayed. Surely it would be good this time and she could deliver a son or daughter for Peter.

"You young folks must see the new cathedral they're building on the North Bay," her father said.

"I have seen the building early, Master Hoban…And I plan to return very soon. Will you attend with us?" Peter asked. "We thought to go there for early blessing and then again for the Christening. It would be an honor for you to attend."

"Certainly I will, Peter. You and my daughter are a blessed couple and have good hearts."

Maria's svelte body gave little hint she was expecting a second child and moved about as an angel set on earth especially for Peter. He tried to take notice and remember to say nice things to her. He tried to tell her he loved her by word and deed. She tried to return favor for favor. Both of them feared the results would be the same and could hardly bare the first and silently knew a second tragedy could mean their minds would slip into hopelessness and despair.

"But for you, Maria, where would I be?" he quietly breathed into her ears, feeling her hair against the skin of his face and lips.

"Oh, Peter, but for you!"

"Kiss me, dear heart, and love me forever."

"I will, dear husband. And I do love you so very much. This child must live as our hearts live."

"God is with us and we shall see the first steps of a new life, my dear, sweet, beautiful Maria," he said as he closed his eyes and as their lips met when she turned to him.

"Take me now, Peter, while it is early. I need you."

Over the next years the county sheriff's office confronted the Klan as many of them became known. They were the misguided and angry. They were shopkeepers, livery hands, farmers, and some restless types with no foundation or family, but were antagonizers for the sake of it alone. Jacob led his forces by quiet intimidation.

More than a few times his visits to each man alone he came to know attended Klan late night clusters put him on notice and stopped ideas of mischief because the consequences were severe. It wasn't that he was intimidating, but he was willing to speak out clearly and forcefully and the story of his cavalry days and what he did to bushwhackers was well known throughout the town—not by him. It was an advantage by reputation he used to keep them and his deputies safe. Often Jebediah, known too as a warrior, was with his brother making these calls.

There were still rallies and some activity outside the law. The acts seen as the meting of justice were allowed as a husband was threatened by a group of robed men warning him to never beat his wife again.

Jebediah and Mary were blessed with their second child, another boy they named Andrew. The next year she gave birth to John and the second year after to Tess, their first girl. Later they would have their last and named her Ruth. The oldest sons were by then eight and seven and old enough to work on their farm, learning the value of sweat and effort, building muscle and mind.

The city fathers pooled resources and built the first brick and stone orphanage that became a refuge for children who needed refuge and safety. Rachel and Benjamin taught the charges reading and arithmetic and loved them as their own. There were twenty-two children taking home behind the fences, ranging from two to sixteen years old. Nathan Hensley, a graduate of their efforts years before became their handyman and taught the children how to farm and care for animals. The home was able to sell jellies and meal, and traded in lamb and swine to meet the expenses.

Nathan was a small stature even for the time and barely passed five feet tall, but was a good-hearted young man who knew the children. He thought of them as himself a few years past and was as kind to each one as an older brother. His father had been lost to a Yankee canister shot that killed him with scraps of metal and nails the day of that fateful charge and his mother died from typhus before he was ten. Having no other family, he came to the O'Keefe home, a sad little boy who had lost his hope. He brought tea and cakes to Mistress Rebecca when she became infirmed during her last days before she passed peacefully during the night. He was ten when Mary gave birth to Tess, and had been given his spirit again by Miss Rebecca, as the children called her. He knew there was death and it was natural, but there was life too for a while and could be as good as he made it.

Her words to him came alive after she left the earthly bounds. He heard her tell him he was a good boy and that God tests us—all of us—so that we become strong and better. He could hear her gentle voice now telling him almost in a whisper to eat some of the cakes with her, how she enjoyed a handsome young man's attention. He remembered her smile; it seemed for him only as she approved of him. She told him she would not want him any different than he was and that God is the same way. *He wants you as you are, dear Nathan, and let Him have you,* she told him more than once. He heard her say he was her wonderful grandson and that Rachel his mother, Jebediah and Jacob, his uncles. He was to always hold onto the family God gave him no matter the blood; it was the heart that counts.

The day Rachel found her body still she was smiling. He remembered how it was sad, but didn't hurt him as losing his mother had hurt. She was in heaven as she told him and would look down on him from time to time to make sure he was smiling and the same sweet Nathan she loved. He talked to her inside himself every day when he wasn't praying as she taught him. Rebecca who had once moved so far away from God had returned to her faith to die in His arms.

Nathan was asked to watch the McCray children for a few extra coins and came to know Tess as a mischievous toddler doted on by her older brothers. Ruth was born and would grow to become a shy, sensitive girl, but smart in book learning. She watched her sister and tried to copy her, but the climbing and running didn't fit her as well. Nathan had to help get Tess out of hog pens, woodpiles and down from a tree more than once.

Mary fed him meals when they ate supper and took him to services with the family every Sunday. He was invited to live in the old McCray home rent free; he had to keep it up as payment. He could feel Lucious and Katy in the place and often felt they could see him there. Nathan never failed the McCrays and was to grow fonder of Tess than he knew when she was born. He watched her grow as he did, she from infancy to young womanhood and he from adolescence to manhood.

Maria gave birth to a son she and Peter named Isaac. They became parents of Matthew and Helen within a few years long after he graduated Harvard and began working on Wall Street for Mr. Hobson. Her beauty became known in his circle. Men desired her and a few tried, but she could not be convinced an affair was anything. His brokerage was growing as he new industries and businesses expanded in the country moving rapidly toward the twentieth century. Maria was working hard and busy with their children. She began to think the move south to New York moved her into a different world where frenzied lust seemed the rule. Peter worked with a bachelor named William Burger who was new to the firm and whose intentions toward Marie became dangerous.

Burger had tried with Marie too and was denied. He could not put the idea behind him though and a growing compulsion coupled with a violent but cowardly character, as it happened, led him to plan a forceful entry. He would wait, watch and seize the chance to take her when Peter was away. At work, he acted as though he was harried and confused as a cover, for fear she might have told him of his approach that day, but Peter never brought it up so he didn't know.

"I have so much to do, Peter. After I spend my hours here, I must write many company and trusts financials, you see," he said, appearing worried.

"I can help, William. It is our firm is it not?"

"No, Peter. I have been contracted by Simon Pedigrew and others who wish to keep the matters, private…you understand."

"I know of him."

"How could you know Simon?" Burger asked out of surprise and cowardice. If he knew him, he may learn of his lie and become curious as to why the ruse.

"Certainly. I met him at the ball when you helped my wife find her way to the powder room. I was talking to him and Matthew Dugger at the time. I recall he was thinking of selling his enterprise. I suppose he's having you prepare the finals for the buyers."

"I'm sorry, Peter. I thought you concentrated on rail and textiles."

"I do, indeed, but shipping and commodities are of interest. Pedigrew invited me to the port. I am not going to interfere with you, but to learn, you understand. I am happy to share any insights and ideas that may come of it."

"Thank you, Peter. I'm not worried. I am however, full, in terms of commitments and have so little time," he lied and thought of his plan. "And are you scheduled for this visit soon?"

"Yes. I will be at the port next Thursday. As you know, it will take hours to look at the books and discuss his business."

"You won't mention I have complained, Peter. It would hurt our partnership. Keep me out of your conversation if you will."

"You certainly can trust me, William. I have no envy or desire to take his account, but the industry may yield opportunity in export."

"I understand clearly. Good hunting, Peter!"

"Yes. And you too," Peter said feeling somewhat put off and confused. An ominous foreboding he couldn't define suddenly seemed more acute than slight mistrust he felt was probably in error in the months since meeting him. There was something unsettling as Peter thought of his narrow set and cold eyes and a mouth overfilled with tongue it seemed and pursed at the corners. He appeared as one who could not be trusted just on a few physical malformations, and he did sound nervous in speech that sounded as though he was hiding something. He didn't understand its origins so he put it out of his mind and planned the short trip of next week with his brokerage house, asking Sam Hudson to trade on the floor in his stead. He knew he could trust Sam, a studied man from an Arkansas farm family who made a growing fortune in cotton, silk and wool trading.

Maria was mending baby Helen's coddling sack used by her older brothers after feeding the young children that morning. She had seen Peter off to work from their brownstone home in Manhattan and bid him well and safety. He would take a train to the eastside and be gone for a long day as he told her. Their oldest child was six and in school a few blocks away Peter would take him in the carriage on his way to work.

That morning Burger showed at the brokerage firm and stayed for two hours to be certain Peter was well away from his home. Their home was only fifty steps in distance; Burger knew he could see her if she was home and leave in less than an hour. He pretended a sudden stomach ailment and left the office mid-morning, assuring Hudson and Dugger he could make the walk to Dr. Hearst without difficulty. Maria had just finished sewing and began to read to Matthew when she heard the rap on her front door.

"My! William? What are you doing here?" she asked him as she felt her hair stand on end. Her impulse was that this was no visit of normal and friendly consequence with Peter being absent and the nerves throughout her body suddenly rendered painful spasms. She felt the endings screaming forcefully to the end she could hardly manage words. He stepped in; there was no stopping or slowing him. Before she could stop him, he was inside the front room and closing the door behind him. He had yet to utter a word, but took her arm in both his hands and forced her deeper inside the home. She struck out at him, and he caught the swinging arm and pressed his body into hers. She tried to scream but his hands were fast. He covered her mouth and pushed her down.

"Be silent! If you do anything, I'll kill your babies!" he screeched in an evil, throaty, dangerous voice of a man-dog rather than a man. Her body and mind were seized with fear and for a while she was numb in shock. She felt the head swelling, suffocating wet like pain and dizzying of his fists time after time until she could not move by near unconsciousness. Her eyes were closing rapidly and her mind was fading into a black and spotted effort. She thought of Helen and Matthew and then Isaac innocently at school finding their mother in such a condition. She thought of Peter. She felt him force her legs open. She thought the fate of a woman who does not belong in this town. She knew what he must do and managed to put together the words she was driven to hope.

"If you kill me, please, do not take my babies too!" she cried. "You mustn't harm them! Please! They can say nothing of this and will not cause you…" she stopped.

He opened her up and had his way with her with the threat of a long knife and as he violated her, he stared through her with piercing, evil eyes. As he finished with her, she prayed a solemn request to God. *They are unable to tell anything of this. You must spare them. Please! My God you must spare the little ones!*

"My, God! Why must you do this, William?" she cried.

"Be mindful! Be quiet!" he gurgled from the depths. He fastened his trousers while pushing his foot down on her body for surety. She watched him withdraw a long knife from the leg harness attached around his right ankle, hidden under the trouser leg. She watched in horror as he quickly brought the blade to her chest. Her eyes suddenly were more open than there was room in her sockets to hold them as he plunged the steel into her heart and twisted the blade. She choked and cried, a single tear ran the course of her cheek and crossed her neck as she died. He looked for her children but was pulled from the house by fear before he found them.

Chapter 10

"Take it, Jacob!" Jebediah said. The two men were roping calves for branding. The dust rose up around them, nearly covered the animals and choking Jebediah, finding its way into his mouth and nose. He tasted the grit and heavy air it made and quickly spit it out. Jebediah readied the iron bringing it out of the fire.

Samuel helped his father and uncle control the animals from his safe seat on the fence rail. He smiled as the calf was caught and Jacob brought it toward his father. He had learned how to work and do the tasks of a fully functioning family farm in his early years so that he too could one day be a father. He was twenty-four and thinking of marrying soon, but was content to work the McCray acres for living in the house still.

"Come in, Samuel!" Mary called out to him. "It's time to eat, son."

"Best do what your mother says. We'll be in after finishing here and washing up, boy."

"Yes, sir," he said and jumped down.

"And fetch Andrew for me will you, Samuel? He and John are over by the barn shoeing the mule."

"Now sit down all of you," Mary told them. "After we finish, I will read to you and you to me."

She smiled toward her youngest, Tess and Ruth, young ladies of eighteen and sixteen now. All the children had enjoyed the reading time through the years and still enjoyed reading. There were stories of magic places and a little girl named Alice, adventures of young girls in *Little Women*, and Mark Twain's novels—from *Frogs* to *Roughing It* to *Tom Sawyer*. Their favorite was and still was the Bible; great true stories Mary read each year from Genesis to Revelations.

It was a nightly routine for the McCrays. Each child could read some before six years old, and Mary had them take turns reading aloud. Now the subjects were of politics and misery in the country compared to the rich, and true accounts of war, pioneers and adventurers of old who founded the land for Europe and Spain so many years past.

The boys were in their early adulthood and beginning to fully appreciate the young ladies, baseball and cider. There was no need to enter the military at the time as the still expanding country was at peace and venturing some in the Caribbean. When they were younger, they had played army, pretending attacking and falling. The weapons were wooden miniature Springfield rifles painted black. When the chores were done, they could also fish and hunt with their father, who taught them how to find the places on the river and sometimes the lake. Tess and Ruth learned of homemaking, shadowing their mother and doing every job—from cooking to making butter and candies. Mary learned the finer art of sewing from Katy and taught them how to create and mend clothing.

The farm was growing. Jebediah's law practice was growing. Jacob won the sheriff's office every four years unopposed, and the children's home was turning out good citizens. Marshall County was recovering from the war and becoming a prosperous place serving the many farms and industry that started nearby in every direction. America was growing.

Ruth was allowed to take the first piece of cake on her birthday. She was sixteen and had come of age as a young woman ready to marry. Since Nathan, who had remained in the community, was already courting Tess, Ruth's time was next for the right pick. Her birthday fell on the same day the news of the day was the Chicago fire, a great city lost and rebuilt twenty years past. Most of the cattle the sons grew fat were taken by the railroad to the city where brokers sold and slaughter companies prepared the important commodity for use by a growing population to all points east and west and some north to Canada.

A great reunion was held in Birmingham that year as many veterans of the Confederacy gathered to relive part of their youth and enjoy the fellowship of other men who had been part of the tragic enterprise and lived to recount the glory. Jebediah and Jacob made it and saw how much older they all appeared, but still were brave and humble men. The cooked meats, fresh produce, cold beer and ale were prepared by a grateful community recognizing the sacrifice each man made to fight for his country in such awful conditions and often with very little. The United States flag and the battle flag of the Confederacy were prominent decorations throughout the streets of the city as she welcomed her heroes one more time.

Five-year-old Isaac kept his brother and sister away from the room by hiding them in their parents' bedroom deep inside a dark closet. His stomach and legs were wet with urine. He was speechless and mindless. His mouth hung open and he stared in the dark toward the crack in the door where a sliver of light could let him see the bad man coming again. It would be hours before Father would return home. Mercifully, the younger ones finally fell asleep after the screaming and breathing and crying tears to the point of near dehydration. Isaac sat and stared in the dark, keeping vigil over his younger brother and sister as their only protector.

Peter finished with Pedigrew and secured a deal to trade shares of stock in the shipping company for it to expand with the new capitol selling shares would raise. He promised him that within a month there would be enough money raised to begin the build and purchase of the larger vessels that would make transatlantic deliveries and returns. He felt unusually anxious for a reason he couldn't figure as he waited for the train. It couldn't come fast enough to suit him and he began to compulsively walk back and forth along the gangway in front of the station. He had to get home quickly, he thought. At least his mind would ease when he saw his family.

The sky opened up and poured out a hard rain that sent Peter scurrying for cover. It had been overcast most of the day and windy. He saw the engine at a distance and felt his stomach turn. *Come on, damn it!* he thought feeling the nerves react impatiently through his spine. A man wearing a long coat pushed past him to the edge of the walkway under roof. He was tempted to pull him back but thought better of it and took a long, deep breath, staring at the boards under foot and counting the curves in the wood's grain.

As he neared their front door off the busy street, he suddenly felt a heavy, dark pressure fill him and thought he may pass out, the blood seemingly leaving his head. He opened the door and saw her. *My God!* he cried out and fell to the floor in a heap before going to her and trying to see what happened through the flood of tears that blinded him. *Oh, my God! Oh, my God! Maria! Maria! What is this? My poor, dear Maria! Oh, my God!*

Isaac heard his father crying out and ran out of the closet leaving the babies crying again. Peter could make out his son and took him quickly into his arms and ran into the bedroom. He composed himself just enough.

"Now, Isaac…Isaac," he cried. "Stay here for a minute. I'll be right back to you, sweet child. Stay here!" He hid him away from the ghastly, bloody scene as best he could and quickly returned to cover his wife with a blanket. He returned, took up the children and took them all outside, desperately looking for help. The passersby saw blood on each child and reeled in horror at the look of them. He took an older matron by her arm, pulling the children with one hand and cried out for help.

"Please, ma'am. You must help me! Please take my children and let me go to me wife. She's been killed!"

"Surely, sir," she said forcefully, taking up the job as a determined one, there to save and protect. "And what of the police?" she asked as she led them out of harm's way into a bakery at the corner of the block. "Don't you worry about the little ones, sir! I'll clean them and put them up safe!"

"Thank you so much, ma'am. Should you see an officer, please direct him to this door. Thank you!" he said painfully.

He wiped the water off his face and returned to Maria, leaving the door open behind him. He knelt beside her, pulled the blanket back and through his confused thoughts wondered what happened, why and who could have done such a horrible thing. He thought he should have been here to protect her and cried more, breathing between choking looking at her body. Her life-blood had left her heart; it was clear her chest had been cruelly pierced and she was left to die in pain and agony by a demon incarnate in human form, the worst creature God put on the earth. And this demon had taken from her, her life, and had taken from him, the woman he lived for. He thought he should be with her now and could take a knife and plunge it surely into his own chest to join her. His depression left as quickly as it came and his heart and mind turned to anger, a consuming, and total anger. He wanted to kill the demon slowly, take his life too and do it soon. He felt an energy he never had. He felt his teeth clinch almost breaking them. Several men appeared at the doorway and upon seeing the woman lying in blood, quickly entered the place. Peter turned and faced them while on his knees and stared into each of them, one at a time.

"Did one of you do this?" his first thought was to ask. "Tell me now, damn you! Did one of you do this?" he shouted. No one answered him or said anything for a while. He turned his face down and saw the bloody footprints for the first time. They could be his or they could be the killer's. He had no way of knowing immediately but gathered himself enough to ask them all to take care not to step on them. They brought him up and two of the strangers embraced him.

"Sir. No one here did this horrible thing. Was she your wife?" one gentle voice said.

"Yes."

"God, have mercy."

"Thank you, kind sir."

"Come with me and Tom and let us help you. The police will send someone here straight way. Let us cover her and wait on the steps and entry."

"Very well. I am sorry for shouting," he said.

"Please do not worry yourself with such. I saw you have children."

"Yes."

"I pray they are unharmed."

"Yes. They may have seen what happened though."

"The poor darlings. Well. Miss Maggie will look after them, sir. Do not worry."

"I am indebted. I..." he stopped and began crying uncontrollably again.

The man sent a runner to guide the police representatives to the scene of the murder. They stumbled together, holding the semi-conscious man and stepped outside after pulling the blanket over her again.

There were men who came and took her away from the place after the police surveyed the scene. The police helped him into the carriage and took Peter to the station where he was to be questioned at length as to his whereabouts that day. Miss Maggie left the bakery after reassuring them as best she could and took the children to her small home nearby.

"Peter McCray? Mr. McCray...When did you find your wife?" A stern, suspicious officer asked him. He was an Irishman named O'Malley who had helped quell the draft riots years ago when he was new to the force. The old policemen pointed his palsied, shaking finger at Peter and said he was going to find who did this.

"Whether it was yourself, Mr. McCray, or someone else, we will find the murderer. Now tell me so you may get a bed, did you do this act?"

"No, sir," he said.

He felt guilty from being there and spiritless. It was as though God had forsaken them for sins he committed during his life. A vengeful God punishes those who veer from the path, and he thought they both had before the marriage ceremony and that maybe that was why.

"Well, I tell you, Mr. McCray...If we don't find someone who saw you at the wharfs today, you've lied to us. No one lies unless they're guilty and whomever did this will hang. Now tell me, sir, who did you see there?"

Peter looked into his eyes through the mask of tears and told him it was Pedigrew. "Of the firm Coastal Shipping..." he paused to think. "Dock fourteen, down past the barber Cole's place."

"And what time will he confirm you concluded?"

"Five-thirty today, sir."

He felt his body had nearly given up and put him down—dying. Officer O'Malley sensed he was innocent. He could see it in his eyes and feel it in his Irish heart. The man had arrived home only to find his wife brutally murdered as he'd said and was suffering terribly. At least that seemed the most likely case to the sergeant who had seen a great deal during his years of policing the large city.

"You'll have to stay in the jail tonight, sir," he was required to say. Officer O'Malley was reluctant with Peter McCray and would rather have left him to return to collect himself and take countenance as to what was left in his life, such as the young ones, but he could not follow his instincts because of departmental protocol. The primary suspect was before them and had to be held indefinitely until evidence was sufficiently collected and studied to determine guilt or innocence. It would come about soon in this case, he thought, and let a patrolman escort him back to a cell.

Peter heard the bars close and sat listlessly on the edge of a wood-framed cot filled with a thin straw mattress, soiled and bare. He sat and held his face in his hands, trying to think about Maria and what she went through. He told his mind she was not suffering now, but the thought was little comfort. *What if her soul stays in the place it left?* he thought. *No. That's insane! The soul leaves the body of pain. She can't be suffering now!* he told himself over and over. He spent the night there and nibbled at the food he was brought, his stomach unable to take any intrusion except the water he was offered.

Burger went back to the office long enough to collect his pay and say he had a position with another firm. The idea of being close to Peter was more than he could bear and left the employer before he returned. He stopped working there without notice, an odd thing to do for anyone, but more than one associate was not unhappy he was leaving. There was something unsettling about him. Matthew and Sam heard about Peter's wife and knew he couldn't have done it—he always talked of her in such loving terms and complimentary ways. They were a beautiful, loving couple to show the way. It couldn't have been Peter.

Their confidence was confirmed when the police asked them for help in establishing his whereabouts on the day Maria McCray was killed, and they quickly were able to present Simon Pedigrew as a witness. The time and length of their meeting was confirmed, and the time it would have taken him to return to Manhattan was confirmed. He had not lied and he could not have killed his wife ostensibly in a jealous rage as was often the reason in such cases when the husband was the primary suspect. This man was clearly innocent and was set free within the hour O'Malley received all the reports. Walking out, he felt his teeth nearly breaking again.

In Marshall County, Samuel saw her first at the trading square where people brought their handiwork, crops, and whatever else they cared to sell or barter or receive cash in exchange. She was eating a candy apple at the stand hastily erected out of thin timbers and caused it to fall when she bumped into it as she tried to rejoin her family at the books. Miss Katy was bedridden, having lived a long, full life. She was bone weary and tired. It would not be long for her and all of the family knew she would rejoin Lucious soon.

Samuel approached her to help straighten the damage she'd done and took the opportunity to introduce himself to her. She said her name was Irene from Etowah and that her and her family come to Guntersville once each month or close to sample and buy fruits and vegetables. He became somewhat fixed on her long, thick mane of hair that circled her face and gently fell past her shoulders in waves and curls. Her family had come from Scotland too and arrived at the shores of America within twenty years of the McCrays.

Peter stayed out on the stoop for hours, searching with his reddened eyes back and for the and up the blocks, thinking as he watched the people which one did his wife in so cruelly. He was hoping somehow he would present himself, maybe brag of it; it was an absurdity to think anyone would of course and he knew that, but he remained locked to the front of his and Maria's home—the place filled with so much joy and hope because of her—and now it had turned into a hateful address. He ate nothing. He drank whiskey and numbed his brain for a while. It eased the pain some but did not take away the awful scent of despair and ruin. He thought it would not leave him—ever and taking revenge had to be his calling for the sake of it. Peter was a body and spirit of hate, loathing from the depths, and a searing hot knife in neverending agony on her behalf. There had to be an accounting regardless of consequences, but it was a large city, full of people and many coming and going. Were his task impossible, it would seal forever his plight and position of the mind, but it seemed to be just out of reach and made him be even more conquered.

He visited his children the next day and saw they were well cared for—a lucky thing from the kindness of a stranger. He insisted Maggie take payment and arranged with her to work as the children's nanny as he had no one else he could work with for them on such short notice. He had little time and felt the need to return to work as soon as the morrow came. Perhaps that would help him deal with what God had given him. Getting to it and putting his thoughts toward the valueless work may serve to occupy the hole ripped into his heart.

The next morning he showed at the brokerage house and surprised all who saw him he was back two days hence. He wandered at first and took into his mind the office and its people. He saw Matthew, who said all he could say and that was he was sorry for his loss. He saw Sam and asked him how he'd been. Sometime later in the morning, Peter heard about Burger quitting so abruptly. It was as though every nerve screamed at him from inside; there was a connection in front of him.

"That's odd, isn't it, gentlemen?"

"Yes, Peter. We thought so at the time, but no one desired to encourage him to stay. He's suspected of taking receipts you know."

"That could be the reason. Why now? Why would he not have left before or later? Why on the day after my dear wife was murdered?" he nearly whispered.

It came back to him in a rush of thought. He remembered how subdued Burger acted after the ball and heard someone say he had been on the terrace. He remembered Maria went to the terrace for some air after all the cigars in the place, but she hadn't gone there accompanied by anyone, including Burger. He must have followed her out. He must have worried Maria would tell him of his conversation out of earshot. He remembered he had asked him about the time and place of the meeting with Simon Pedigrew. He remembered Pedigrew saying he was not having William Burger work his financials as Burger told Peter. He thought nothing of it at the time other than a lying brag, but now knew he could have been planning to take Maria by force in his absence. He had to know for certain. He took to payroll records and found an address for William Burger. He could find his house; if he killed her, he had to find the proof.

"What did he say...exactly?" Peter demanded to the faces of both his associates in a loud tone.

"Now, Peter. You don't think..."

"Stop. He's got to answer to me some things, that's all!"

"I see. Well, he said he had another job and had to go."

"Did he say where it was?"

"No. And that's odd too. We know every house in the business. I suppose Chicago could have recruited him. Still, it doesn't seem likely he would move so abruptly, does it?"

"What else did he say?"

"Nothing. He wanted his commissions tallied through last week. Miss Killian said he didn't even leave instructions on what to do with anything he had coming for this week. Odd. Needless to say, old man Hobson was furious! But I think he was glad he left and saved him the trouble."

Peter left them with a scribbled note of an address across Manhattan on the lower east side.

"Will you return today, Peter?"

"I will not be able to, Matthew. I want to see his desk and then I must see about some business related to Maria's estate that cannot wait, you understand."

"Certainly. I'll tell Hobson should he asked."

"Thank you, Matthew," Peter said, as he touched his shoulder in humility, with a kind of pained seriousness Matthew could clearly detect. He sensed his friend was in trouble in his mind and didn't know what would result. Peter looked at the wood and opened the drawers Burger used for the short two months he was there. He made little out of it other than he must have been in a hurry as he left several photographs of animals he killed in exotic hunts behind he used to boast of in the office and his accounting guide from Princeton. He also left his reading spectacles. Peter gathered up the belongings and set out for the East Side.

It was still raining and there seemed no break in the clouds. He walked Burger's probable path and was soaked through the black and plaid suit he wore. *He could have done it! Surely I'm not running to nothing,* his thoughts expressed in self-talk loud enough for the people who passed close to him on the street could hear. *I must hurry!*

The streets were clearly squared and marked thanks to the city fathers who incorporated New York City some years ago and assured an efficient and safe design of her streets and boulevards. The east side was receiving many immigrants from Europe in these days and was dangerously close to becoming an un-kept tenement because of the rush and lack of immediate opportunity and resources of the new citizens. It was there Burger resided and the place Peter would have to confront him.

He found the number and quickly went to the door. He prayed, "Lord help me not harm an innocent man. Please help me have the strength to find the one. If it is this man, have mercy on his soul. I will not have mercy on his body, Lord. Forgive me for that." Sharp, crisp raps brought some movement inside. Peter was hidden from view so if it was Burger, he didn't know who was calling on his this afternoon. He slowly opened the door, carefully taking a look through the crack created. Peter didn't let him close it again and stepped inside, pushing the wood back and causing Burger to fold inside away from the visitor.

"Peter? What are you doing here?"

"I want to talk to you, William. Have you heard about Maria?"

"Yes I have. It was reported yesterday to everyone. I didn't expect to see you for a few days."

"And quitting, you wouldn't have seen me them either. I've brought these things of yours," he said, taking quick study of everything, his room, his clothing, and his shoes, the displaced papers and books for a clue, a single telling clue that would help him know.

"Why, thank you, Peter. It was entirely unnecessary you see. I didn't expect…"

"This is not why I am here, William, and I believe you know that!" his voice was forceful as if he tried to cause him to confess even knowing better of it.

"And just why are you here, Peter?" he asked coyly while also nervously moving back farther in the room and holding himself against the doorframe into the second room. Peter felt the distance and felt the message. Just as frustration set in at his lack of real knowledge and proof other than strange circumstances, he noticed a pair of shoes inside the doorway behind Burger with what appeared to be blood stains on the heels. Peter's eyesight was sharper than Burger's who must have been in a dreadful hurry to leave the firm and the city.

He stared at them for a long couple of minutes, past and through Burger, and onto the heels. His suspect was confused and waiting for Peter to explain the reason he showed up so forcefully in his home. His eyes twitched and turned around and around. His body showed nervous jumping; he knew why and what Peter was doing. He waited, easing slowly back to the second room where he had knives at hand he could use.

"Where are you going, William?" Peter asked him, his voice throaty with a spiritual quality from the depths of his being. His stare was unlike anything Burger had seen before too, and he convulsively let loose urine in front of him, wetting the trousers he wore.

"Tell me, Peter! I did nothing! What do you want?" he begged.

"I want the truth. I want you to tell me the truth, Burger," his voice sounding the same.

"On what?" he said and paused to think. "I did not steal from the firm," he began and then changed his mind. "Very well. I do owe Hobson. I had to use the money to care for my sick mother."

"And where is she?" Peter played. "Is she knifed as well?"

The men stood eye to eye and no words were spoken through several deep breaths. Peter felt the strength out of his resolve in control of his body. He took a step toward him.

"I did not do it!" he screamed.

"I want to see those shoes!"

"Shoes?"

"Out of my way, Burger!" Peter said and pushed his way past him. "Still!" he commanded. He picked up the shoes as Burger ran for a knife. He had noticed his suspicions were right in the instant he held one of the shoes and turned to block the killer from reaching a weapon. He had the right man. He confirmed it by going for a knife.

"Stop this!" Burger cried in a shout. "Leave me be!"

"You killed my wife, and now it's your time," his voice ringing like it had before. "You killed Maria and you must pay for that!" he shouted as he held Burger tightly around his middle and brought his hands up to his throat. Burger tried in vain to wrest away from the death grip that caused him to be able to only slightly breathe through a portion of his nose and labor through the compressed throat Peter was tightening slowly. He felt Burger strike him and fight back but felt no pain as he held him until he nearly stopped breathing. Having prayed to the Lord, he suddenly stopped and gave the man life.

"We are going to the police," he heard a voice come out of him say. It was though someone else spoke and merely used his vessel to form the words. "I should and would do it myself, Burger, but I am not. You will come with me now!" he said as he placed the shoes inside his coat and tied his hands behind him. Once there he would record the inconsistencies and lies he knew and present the police with the heels carrying part of his precious Maria.

O'Malley was impressed with the facts Peter offered. He had traces of prints from the scene that were matched by the shoes. He also had several people who could identify the face of a man seen running the block that day. A positive match and the killer could be convicted and sentenced to hang. The notes Peter offered on the inconsistencies and lies Burger told him and those around the office were helpful to seal his fate. It was all very neat and put together—a rare thing, but would remove a dangerous individual from civilization for which he has no place. He thanked Peter and told him he could be assured justice would be done in weeks.

Chapter 11

Jacob was the first to hear of his cousin's tragedy and grieved for him. Thomas had telegraphed the horrible news, and in the message Peter wrote, he said he and the children were returning to Boston. Jebediah thought of how he would feel if it had been his beautiful Mary, and how it must be hard to live. Of all the events in life one cannot imagine a worse result or a greater test of the spirit. He prayed with Mary and his children for the family in New York and asked the Lord to bless them now in more important ways.

It was Mary, so soft and gentle in her ways, who gave him life and means to stay the course. He loved her more than he had before, and it has been the deepest since he returned from the killing lines, smoke and shot and so much digging for burials. It was she who gave him life, being the reason he was spared he thought of as the truth central to his being. And it was truth. God had allowed a plan for him to father children and live in harmony and peace. The reason is God's province, not his. He is to do and teach what he knows that is right to pass to Samuel, Andrew, John, Tess, and Ruth. To have lost her the way Peter lost Maria would have to be the most awful thing to happen; it would surely have cost him his life too as he could not imagine living without her.

Burger was hung on the Thursday before Christmas that year and was put into the earth no more. His body would rot inside the thin wood, built cheap and quick, and his soul would burn for eternity. He had taken his lust and let it express his whole, selfishly using that which was not his and never would have been. No conscience stopped him from taking her that day absent a spirit of good and for the sake of his own; he killed her as one would an animal to eat. She was nothing more than a piece of refuse to him to use and discard to satisfy the dark craving of Satan.

Peter had left the city and moved the children to Boston in short time and set up with his father to provide arms to the American military coming of age as the new century was close and affairs in the world pressed the country to emulate Britain and France with notions of building an empire for its people to buy and sell rubber, exotic produce, spices, and raw materials needed for growing industry. He invested in the Maxim machine gun and a British firm Lee-Enfield. Isaac had not recovered and was haunted for years by what he witnessed as a child.

Interred to a mental institution, he remained on campus there as a creature locked inside himself and unable to speak for several years, until the day he saw a young girl in a runaway buggy, the harness coming loose and the reins and lanyard flying at the horse's feet. A bird had flown over the horse, and it was gravely spooked like it was whenever something was over its head. It seemed for years that Burger had taken a second victim past his own execution. The young girl had been left for a short time while the father sought out the building his brother was confined. They had brought a dim witted man some bread and jelly on their first visit from South Carolina when it happened. Isaac ran after the carriage and stopped it before the horse ran onto the roadway. He yelled at the horse, finding his voice, and then he asked her after if she was well.

Isaac remembered his father being asked the question when he was unable to form words and listened as he answered he was not. He saw that another human being was well before leaving her. Within a month he returned to Boston and began working as a clerk in his father and grandfather's business. A smile returned to his red cheeked, chubby, friendly face they hadn't seen since the day his mother was taken.

The years were quick. The work was steady and hard. Samuel had married Irene and began working on a family in the years before the century turned. Tess and Nathan Hensley had married and moved to Texas, a state in full bloom rich with oil and cattle. Rachel and Benjamin were parents to Jane who was near forty years and taught mathematics and English in the children's home. She had not married and had no plans to do anything other than keep herself in learned readiness and care for a dear companion, Annie who she had met at the library established by Katy and Mary years ago as part of the boarding home school grounds. Being the only one within miles, many people from the mountain and lakeside came to read there in as their only form of adventure beyond the Alabama landscape.

Ruth had gone to California with Jules Creeless a grandson of Zechariah to follow her husband to his job with a shipping company off the west coast.

They settled in a community called San Diego where she found the climate to her liking and happily began a café where she served Southern cooking up with a gracious smile. The couple learned of the beaches and became part of the social set, swimming the ocean, playing new games she enjoyed, tennis and golf with her husband his business associates and their wives. The life seemed freer than the strict discipline by expectations in Alabama, but still there was her character formed in those years that guided her as a faithful, loving and generous woman who never failed to help the destitute of the community.

She corresponded with her family back home by letter and kept them informed of their life. Every week she wrote a scribe expressing her love and telling Mary how she missed them even though her lot was to be next to her husband in their ventures. She wrote she would like them all to come to California some day to live—or see her and the growing family of Creeless-McCrays now on the west coast of America.

It is always sunny here and there's no cold! She wrote. *But we have the trouble in Hawaii which is of concern. It has cost Jules some, but I heard the Marines would help so perhaps all is not lost. Sugar is important as you know and the shipping has virtually stopped for a time. Meanwhile we play some and enjoy the place. I desire you to come greatly but understand. Your loving daughter, Ruth.*

She described the ship Jules and she took to the Islands and her visit there while he concluded a contract to transport sugar to the mainland. It was a place unlike anywhere she had been and let the family know of a different beauty she found there; the palms and volcanic rock, the flora and sand with large waves washing the beaches every minute. The constant gentle and warm breeze, a sensuous pleasure against the skin and how the air was as clean as the mountains in Alabama. The people who lived on the Islands were much like the Cherokee in appearances with sun-darkened skin and smooth bodies out of custom mostly, and beautiful in their own right. She wrote it had been a wonderful change from the routine for them, and their visit there resulted in her expecting a child come August.

Mary read the letter aloud to Jebediah and saw him smile. He was happy his daughter was happy. She had taken much of what she heard read to her as a child, the development of her curiosity and appetite for learning to appreciate the differences and was living a good life. To have his children, whether farmers, lawyers, mistresses of a household live as free Americans, happily, had been his and Mary's life task, and it was clear God had helped them succeed.

"It seems she has found her favorite," he said.

"I should say, dearest. In some ways I envy her, but do not wish to leave the rest."

"No, Mary. Certainly, I agree. Should we see her next year, it would be a grand thing. The rails carry the way now, and it's something we should do. It will be our first real holiday."

"I would in my heart, but I'm feeling too old!" she laughed.

"You are not too old to lay with me in the meadow!" he laughed, thinking of the sensual picnic they enjoyed last Saturday. "Oh, Mary! It is with great fondness I recall the event and do so desire to do it again, love."

"Hold those reins of yours, husband. It should be thought of as a fluke—don't expect the same often!" she laughed. "We must act our age."

"And who says that?"

"No one of account, but me. I'm not certain it's not unseemly. What if someone had happened by?"

"We were well away from the path, dear. Do not worry about such things. I shall want you next to me until I can do more than mumble and eat cold porridge with a spoon." He laughed. She turned away from him smiling, flaring her dress some.

"And I shall want you too, rascal!"

Julia had given birth to William in the center of Arkansas where the farm was being converted from cotton to rice. Having left Arthur generations ago, she died alone inside the small house on the edge of her property. She had left Arthur because she didn't want the life of a farmer's wife. The man she had for a while and fathered William had long since left and took off to Missouri where he drank himself to death. Keeping her married name, she remained a spinster after and cared for William on her own. William took a wife and fathered four girls and one boy in the span of ten years and put them to work in the fields for a few hours each day before he hung himself.

The Arkansas McCrays named the youngest child Phillip who would join the Army at seventeen, leaving home during the year of the roughrider's fame. They had no contact with any other part of the family McCray, never knew of the father's whereabouts and never talked to him by letter or any form. They didn't know when Arthur died.

Phillip had an eye for women and began drinking when he was thirteen. By sixteen he was stealing to buy moonshine and in the Army he was set to find amorous adventures and self-promoting mayhem. Some said he killed a man by shooting him in the back, but nothing was ever proven or done. The boy denied it and kept to himself, had a single on-and-off friend, and seemed destined for jail. He figured wherever he was sent there would be opportunity. It was good he left the small Arkansas town; the sheriff and residents thought he would amount to nothing but trouble for them.

Daughter Tess and Nathan became parents of Sarah and George when she learned she could have no more. Their ranch required a great deal of physical labor, and it was thought the strain had hurt her chances for more children. Now it was certain in the doctor's mind. She was told having another child could kill her, but it was unlikely she could conceive again. The couple made their happiness by remaining in the church and protecting Sarah and George fiercely from modern vices and sin that seemed to be taking hold of so many. Texas was not as far away as Boston or California, and they took a train to Marshall County every year, bringing Indian and Mexican goods and other gifts. Tess began painting and reflected the color and beauty of the flat desert, wildlife and people of the West. From the days of her listening to her mother read Twain, she enjoyed an active imagination and an acute skill to see as her sister.

Isaac returned home to Boston and his father, Peter, and resumed his studies. Although older than most in his class, he succeeded despite bites of word from unthinking, unkind children. He could have fought them but violence of any kind was an anathema to him over which he couldn't bear the thought without becoming sick in his stomach and losing the contents. Matthew and Helen were in the same class and did their work together with their older brother.

Peter lost his father-in-law the same year Isaac returned talking and remembered him as a man who carried on despite the turmoil of losing his wife to a wayfarer. He could do the same and make certain his children learned the word of God first and everything else second. Master Hoban would want that.

The eldest son of Jebediah and Mary, Samuel, and his wife Irene gave life to Daniel in 1887 and Paul the next year. Samuel remained in Marshall County and worked at the cotton mill to supplement his farm, a small patch of a few acres near his parents. The new machinery developed close to the end of the nineteenth century allowed the company to produce more cloth and sell it in volume at a lower price than before. The invention cycle was exciting to Samuel and he fashioned himself as a mechanic, learning all he could about how things worked. He began engineering in the nineties and was recognized as a proficient designer and fitter across the lake country, contracting to specify and set up new and strange equipment. Soon his reputation was such that other men sought him out to advise on their projects as far away as Atlanta.

Daniel was a runner and very strong, wrestling every boy in countywide schools and winning. He could run the mile and beat everyone who challenged him as well. Paul followed his brother and was also athletic. Together they began playing a new game invented in America from soccer and were asked to play football on a team formed at the University of Alabama seven years before and went when Daniel reached eighteen in 1905. Paul arrived on campus the next year. Quick and tough, they excelled in the sport and also passed in the classroom.

While Daniel and Paul attended school, a cousin unknown to them, Phillip, was in basic training, already stealing money from the pockets of his fellow recruits during the night. Cousin Isaac was within a year of finishing his studies at seminary in Boston and preparing himself to take the vows and assume the spiritual work of a priest. He did not know to what parish he would be sent or if he were to begin one as a missionary. Dedicated to teaching the peace and love of the Lord, he was willing to go wherever the church needed him most.

It was raining the day Peter attended the service. The middle-aged man sat in the first pew and heard his son commit his life in service of the Lord. He had grown to be a strong and upright adult who had the patience to work with people regardless of fault and save them in Christ. Isaac put everything away, had no desires for earthly treasures or vices that affect the common man and was set for a course of prayer and example walking in the spirit.

"Son. I'm very proud of you," Peter said.

"Thank you, Father."

"It is I who should call you father now." He smiled, the tears coming slightly, enough to redden his eyes.

"Never, dear Father. Thank you for everything. You saw me through to this and the Lord will surely bless you. I do love you, Father, and hold you in the highest esteem."

"Please, son, I...I love you too," he said.

"I will be readying for a move to Louisiana, Father. It seems there is a parish there whose priest has taken ill and I must fill for him."

"I will miss you, son. But God has far better plans for you than I do."

"Take care, Father. I will return once each year to see everyone. Matthew is doing well as an apprentice writer, and I wish to see him continue. And Helen! Do you see her as a brilliant actress as I?" he smiled.

"They are fine, aren't they?" He turned toward his other children who were waiting their turn to congratulate Isaac.

"Yes, they are indeed, Father. We have been blessed despite the tragedy."

"Yes, Isaac, despite the tragedy." His eyes were clear as he called Matthew and Helen over with a gesture of his hand.

"My, you're beautiful, Helen. Do take care, sister. I will pray for both of you."

"Thank you... Do I call you Father Isaac now?" she laughed.

"Congratulations, brother!" Matthew said.

"I shall miss you two." He smiled. "Remember the good times, will you? Like the time we sang at Christmas to the church as children and were treated as royalty for the effort. Remember Helen accidentally sipped on ale before someone grabbed the cup," he laughed. "Father was so afraid she would be sick and loose it all right there in the church vestibule! We ran around not knowing what to do, but we had to run!"

"I remember, Isaac," Matthew said. "And the time we wanted to cook Father a dinner and nearly ruined his appetite for all time. He was so kind he didn't say anything. I never told you, Father, but I found the contents in the trash pail after you left." He laughed.

"A father will do what he must to approve of his children," Peter laughed.

"So, it's Louisiana! I have read there are alligators there," Matthew said.

"I suppose that's true. And there are French-speaking people and Indians about as well—their souls are as valuable as ours."

"Of course. I envy you some, brother. You are leaving the snow. I imagine you will never be cold down there," Helen said. "Maybe one day I'll perform in New Orleans and can see you."

"That would be nice, sister. I do hope all goes well for you."

"It will. Old Turnbach has the troupe scheduled for a series of performances across New York, Pennsylvania and on to Ohio," She smiled excitedly. "I'm sure looking forward to the experience and seeing new places."

"And Matthew—stay to your writing, so you can influence people for the right."

"I will, dear brother. It's all I want to do. People need to know what is developing and happening in the world that seems to be closing around them of greed and corruption where it steals the food from babies and of good tidings as well. I plan to deliver it all!"

"And you'll do a fine job. Your essay on the mediation conducted by our president between Japan and Russia was brilliant!" Isaac said.

"Thanks to you and Father. Whatever I do have in the way of a talent, I do owe to you," he said.

"Talents are God-given, brother! He has blessed all of us in some way." He smiled.

Phillip was promoted to sergeant because he reenlisted then busted back to private for getting into a fistfight in a bar outside the base. He was in a card game and accused a player of cheating. The player didn't take the word kindly and exacted a toll for his use of it. Both being drunk at the time felt little pain during the exchange but a lot the next day. Phillip woke up in the brig and was summoned to see the captain early that morning, still smelling of alcohol and body sweat, blood and urine. He was also not in a proper uniform. The captain deliberated two minutes before administering justice and sent him back to the brig for seven days.

Samuel brought his father to their home, pushing the wheelchair in which he was now confined, Mary faithfully walking by his side. The gray line of the Confederacy was becoming old and more were dying each year, taking their memories of the lost brave, their voices and dreams with them. The South had survived and honored them with a simple respect and wrapped its arms around the ones who returned as best she could for the day. The reunions and dinners, the veterans clubs supported by governments and old soldiers' homes were some compensation for the total sacrifice made on behalf of freedom and their country. Had many seen the country now, before, and realized the freedom of all states, things could have been different and a half-million lives cut down young may not have been wasted. Their courage was the stuff of legend and was taught to every Southern boy from father to son to son. Daniel and Paul knew of their grandfather and great uncle's dedication and service and always thought of them as men—as men they wanted to be.

Irene had the table full for the entire family that Sunday. The O'Keefes came, Jane and Annie helping her parents walk, Andrew McCray and John came with theirs and Daniel and Paul. The trimmings on the three gooses included pineapple, celery, carrots and breads. She had cooked beans and plenty of pie for everyone. Samuel demonstrated a horseless carriage he built, giving rides to those who were willing, one at a time. The times had brought about changes. The rifles were more accurate and could fire faster, the clothing available was much more abundant and in newer styles affordable by the common man, and there was talk of flying machines. There were even indoor plumbing facilities available for those of sufficient means.

"Aye, family," Jebediah began. "It has been good. Thank you all and..." his voice stammered. "Thank you to our daughters and their husbands who could not attend. I wish you all well and I am thankful to the Lord too for giving Mary and me such a fine heritage," he felt his eyes filling. "I wish it were, so I could stay with you all longer, but I fear my time is short. I'm sorry, family."

They each knew what he meant and stood to honor him without a word.

"Please, dear...it's all right," Mary said, her voice cracking with emotion.

"Well I...I just want all of you to know how much," his voice failed him for a time. The family stood and waited patiently for him to resume. "I just wanted to say I love you dearly and wouldn't do any one thing different."

"Dearest...and I want you all to know I am of the same mind. I love you all with all my heart. And we may not have many days left, but Jebediah and I will be with you as our fathers and mothers are with us."

They were both gone before the spring and interred next to each other in the church cemetery. A single rose was etched on each stone to mark their hearts; the inscription reading the true hearts lived on. In fact they did live on, even though away now from their earthly binding; they were loving and watching from a different realm and would see and love every McCray who would follow them. It was theirs now, to take the challenge of the long voyage.

Ten years and three passed, and there was deadly trouble in the world—from the Middle East to France to Africa. In Boston, Matthew wrote of it as the Germans and French were in conflict. The English and their Allies were protecting their interest and soon the world seemed embroiled in a war of unlimited death and destruction. Some people in America were clamoring for war reading about the deeds of the evil Hun. They had massacred the Hereo tribe in Africa earlier and afterwards continued to bluster and intimidate other nations. From Morocco to Russia attacking Serbia, an Austrian protectorate, Germany declared war on France, an ally of Russia, without provocation. The world was purposefully falling headlong into an insane delirium of massive evil that would take millions to their death. A world-size demon of greed and hate had been let loose to consume people and the land.

Isaac was the first. He took leave from the church in Houma to join the Army as a chaplain. The troops would need many he feared as the weapons were such devastating things in this modern day. Many men were falling in France and now America was going. He wanted to attend with them. He spent the last days in Houma taking into account how happy he had been with the simple, hardworking Cajun group he had the pleasure of servicing. The bayou was filled with water oaks and cypress trees covered with massive shrouds of moss ghostly hanging, shifting softly with every faint breeze of air through the thickness of brown beauty as brackish water curled underneath to meet the ocean a few miles further south.

The place was warm as his sister told him it would be and warm to the spirit. The families of Broussard, Heb rt, Mouton, and Boudreaux had accepted him as their pastor and he administered the sacraments, baptizing their babies to Confirmations and First Communions to Last Rites. He came to love their humor, their foods, their faith—and them, with an intensity he never before experienced except with his own family. He allowed the Cajun music form to interpret hymns and came to love the music too. He found a home and would not leave for any reason he thought, but a war where young men would die was a calling he must attend. The soldiers need him more. The Army asked him to report to Camp Merritt in Dumont, New Jersey, where he would be trained in short order for deployment at the same time a large number of American youth was being trained for the infantry at camps across the east.

The train took him northeast toward the camp, and he had days to reflect on his work in Houma. Along the way he took coffee and ate sandwiches, lovingly prepared by the Cajun women of the Thibodeaus and Moutons. He remembered them and others traveling with him to the station and staying until the train left New Orleans—a difficult forty miles in those days—and how he saw some crying and wistfully waving goodbye as he was taken. He didn't know when he would return and prayed for their souls and Father Anthony who would travel from just south of New Orleans once a week to say Mass in his absence.

Daniel answered the call fresh out of the university and Paul went with him. The young men thought of their heritage and knew the country needed them; it seemed every man of ability was joining to fight the evil. News of the day captured the enormity of it all as causality figures of tens of thousands for each battle seemed normal. The McCray men felt the same as many—this was a grand cause and America was coming to beat the Hun and stop his killing innocent people. They also thought theirs was the only country strong enough to do the job and freedom was at stake for mankind. To march under the flag into the conflagration and take their due was the highest calling for every enlisted man and junior officer.

Father McCray reflected on his Cajun family and thought back to the happy times. He sampled the homebrew and watched the dance. As a people, they are sensual but grounded firmly in morals; the interpretation at times different than one expects in Boston, but as good in all accounts. There were fewer clothes worn, but it was hot. There were cases of fornication, but it was as natural as breathing to some and when of age, there was marriage. He heard it all in the confessional and absolved each one every time, knowing not all would resist the temptations. He was even tempted himself. There was the use of liquors and homebrew, wine or cider at every meal and after; still one not assume a loose and sinful society. The rules of behavior may be different but only in context and only for them. An outsider was gauged with suspicion and not readily accepted until they proved trust.

"Are you sure of this, Paul?"

"I'm as sure as you are!" he said.

"It'll take a while to get there. We may as well relax and enjoy the scenery. I'll miss Mother and Father. At least we saw them often enough when we were in Tuscaloosa."

"They weren't exactly thrilled with our decision, but I believe Father is proud of us. Don't you, Daniel?"

"Yes. I believe deep he is. He isn't sure about this war. The divergence of thought on it is wide, and he's read everything he could about it after we told him of our intentions."

"We'll finish this and be home before next spring," Paul proudly said and smiled confidently. "And being officers soon! I hope we do our men proud."

"Remember what Grandfather told us? He was convinced the officers who took every step he asked the men to do were far better and respected. Those who stayed back were held in contempt. We must be that," Daniel said solemnly, knowing little of the risks but knowing there would be some.

"I'll be. It wouldn't be right to have others do what we're unwilling. I don't fear that. This adventure will be the best!"

"The whole world is watching us," he said and stopped, noticing the mountains near Chattanooga. "They are beautiful here. The spring has brought all of nature's beauty hasn't it, Paul? It makes me think of women. Doesn't it you?" he laughed.

"Oh, yes! Are you still seeing Gerty?"

"I may when I return. We agreed to postpone our courtship until then. She has my best wishes to see others and I have hers, although I know she knows there are no women where we're going!" He laughed. "We're just close friends."

"I see. I am lucky to have no one woman who waits. When I return, I'll be more serious about finding the one of my dreams!" Paul said and forced a nervous laugh. "If I return."

"Don't talk like that, Paul. Damn! We're going to be fine and return home unscathed. I'm certain of it, because the McCrays have always been lucky!"

"You're right. I'm sorry, brother. Do you have any steak lean pieces left in the sack? I could use a bit of food to quell my stomach noises."

"We have another day before we reach Camp Greene. Best use only a little. I'm not certain we will have time to leave the train at any of the stops."

Isaac arrived first. He was escorted to supply, measured for a uniform and provided a full set of gear, from shelter half to canteen. His silver necklace and cross would figure as an important part of his attire until a chaplain major told him he would only wear a cross on his lapel else give the enemy a target from the reflection of so much polished metal. He knew his life was in God's hands, and that faith tested is faith restored. To be in a fight between desperate men as a mere counselor who is called upon to administer to all men including his enemies was to be God's witness, His agent in service to lonely death. But that the enemies of his countrymen would target him and must be stopped; he sighed and folded the large cross into a pocket. The world was a dangerous place. He prayed to allow him courage and strength to save souls before death.

Chapter 12

"Private McCray...for your offenses I will make it so you're one of the first to go to the front. You're lucky I don't court martial you for a dishonorable discharge!" the captain said grimly. "I don't understand how a young man of nineteen can be as you are. You're a ner-do-well, Private, and there's no future for you."

He stood at attention and listened, a sneer curling the corners of his mouth backwards toward his ears. A half smile from the soldier darted into the captain's opinion of him. He wanted this thief, this unruly bully who made enemies at home, out of his unit and quickly. Morale would rise the moment he left them, he thought, and he owed it to his men.

"I'm transferring you to Camp Mills where infantry is being prepared for deployment. We expect the president to declare war on Germany and send troops to France in support of our Allies. And Private McCray...you're to be one of them! I do hope you do not persist. You must find a character, sir. "

"Not for your pleasure, my Captain, will I gladly attend," he smirked defiantly.

"Take your leave, Private. See Lieutenant Miller for your orders and God help you."

"Yes, sir!" He snapped a salute and turned on his heels, smiling the way, leaving the Captain to conclude there was little hope the soldier would be a man before he was killed. And that was the way it should be for some, he pondered. Where there was no saving, there is waste. He was leading a wasted life and may as well shoot.

Arrival at Camp Greene by a thirty-mile transport in the back of a truck from the train station at Charlotte was a midnight sleepless, bumpy and wet one for the junior officers. They were out of food and hungry as the truck pulled inside the gate and parked in front of a small barracks. Sergeant Bell met them with a deep resonating voice forced from his diaphragm. The wide brimmed hat he wore covered his eyes or so it seemed, perched on top of the tall example of military discipline.

"Good evening, gentlemen! You've heard about the French at Verdun and how they charged into machine guns, losing 350,000 men to stop the Germans! You've heard about the English losing 400,000 men at the Somme, charging wave after wave into certain death—while killing a half million Germans and not accomplishing a G. D. thing! They did that without blinking, and I tell you now, the Americans are coming!" he said, monotone with a deadly seriousness in his voice. "Now get yourselves off the damn truck and stand fast! Move!" He began grabbing each man by the arm, quickly pulling each to the ground. Some fell out of the truck, others jumped.

Daniel looked at Paul in disbelief. "What have we gotten into?" he asked quietly. But it wasn't so quiet the sergeant couldn't hear it and turning his head and shoulders square, he snapped at the direction of the voice.

"Who is talking here if not I? You will not chatter like schoolgirls! You will form up and stand at attention!"

There were twenty men who came in from several states, mostly the South, standing in two lines of ten. Each stared straight ahead, following orders and waiting for the next one. Sergeant Bell had returned from Mexico where under General Pershing led a small force against Villa, and he had what he considered to be the honor of shooting to death more than twenty Mexicans himself. His job now was to prepare lieutenants as platoon commanders. Thoughts of what he said about the French and English seemed fixed in Daniel's mind. He could think of nothing else but the sheer numbers Bell mentioned. It was a staggering concept and he felt his body shaking uncontrollably under the weight of their suffering. *My, God!* he thought. *So many. Men like us who did what they were asked and that was to plainly die together. What is this?*

"Right face!" he commanded to turn the troop toward a nondescript wood building. "March!" he sounded out like a loud bellows.

He marched them inside and had them stand on either side of a long table that nearly ran the length and remain at attention. In front of each was a collection of tent and haversack equipment and a pail. A precise number of pegs and one trenching tool lay in the face of each man. A burlap sack was beside it all. At first the items confused the would-be officers. It seemed pretty base for them; after all, they were to lead the soldiers under command.

"Before you people can pin gold bars on your f'ing collars there's much you have to prove!" Sergeant Bell still sounded like a human heavy chain, his words coming out of him somehow in a manner they never heard before. "You put the government property in the sack—now!" he said. "Hurry! Hurry! I tell you, the Hun will kill you quicker than a single blink! You're not moving fast enough, people!" He raced around the room, pushing and shoving men at random, throwing his hands up and back and forth in exasperation. The troops understood quickly and shoved it all in place.

"Now! Pick it up to your shoulders and stand at attention! Right face! March!" He marched them to a larger building, illuminated by lanterns only and stopped them. "Hair cuts and uniform issue, gentlemen! You belong to the United States Army now and you will act accordingly! You are the property of the Army! You are nothing more than the duffle in my eyes and the President's! Take your ease for fitting here, people, and do it quick!"

Each man's head of hair was clipped close and then he was given a set of trousers and an Army blouse—one pair of boots and a campaign hat. There was nothing on the shirts except buttons and changing as soon as they received the uniform, they were formed up as a training squad and ordered to stand at attention until all of them were finished. They all looked the same. The musty odor of the blouses made them all smell the same. The night was giving way to dawn. The cadre was led to their huts and told to take a cot and stow the gear in the footlocker at the foot of each.

"Reveille at zero-five-thirty, gentlemen. That's a gift of one hour later than you'll get! Make use of it," the sergeant commanded and left them, each step taken by heel first, crisp and sharp.

"We have but one hour to sleep, Daniel. We're in something here, aren't we? That's not enough," Paul said with a hint of despondency.

"One night won't hurt. We've lost more than this." He smiled.

"Yea...but I do feel weary."

"Take a quick sleep, Paul and tonight we'll get more. Surely."

"Well. It's good to see North Carolina. Never been here," he snickered.

It would be two weeks before Samuel and Irene received a letter from their sons. In it Daniel and Paul both described the camp and training and new friends. Everything seemed good and the boys wrote all their needs were taken care of by the Army. Throughout the training cycle more reassuring words expressed their ease and care about being a part of the grand cause. Purposefully the boys held the physical and mental demands placed on them to themselves.

Precisely at the minute Sergeant Bell bellowed was their wake-up, he bellowed again, waking those who slept with a combination of his voice and the crashing sound of a large metal refuse can thrown down and across the middle of the ward. The men were bunked on thin cots lined up precisely on either side of the barracks and rose to their feet, not knowing what they were to do next.

"You're not moving fast enough, gentlemen!" he shouted. "Get up! Get up! Get your lazy good for nothing carcasses out of the sack!" He quick stepped through the bay. "You better stand at attention, gentlemen! I want you dressed and at the ready in front of your cot in two seconds!"

The movement of each became quicker and every man pulled on socks and trousers and stood, buttoning their blouse, their feet angled to the forty-five, backs erect, and heads looking straight out to nothing.

"We got a little activity planned, gentlemen. Fall out to the front and don't tarry!" he ordered.

Once the formation was outside, he had the squad take a right face.

"Double time march!" he shouted.

He took them on a mile run. Within a few weeks, he would have them running three miles and then follow with an hour of calisthenics in the yard, forcing the sweat from every pore.

"We only have a couple of months to turn you into soldiers, gentlemen!" he shouted. "You best get your behinds going or I will take your lazy carcasses and kick them so hard your mother will feel it!"

Their training and indoctrination had begun in earnest. Sergeant Bell was going to teach them everything the Army way and test them; he was to mold the small group of civilians into officers who could stand up to trench warfare and how to use the new mechanized artillery, tanks, and machine guns. Tactics had slowly evolved from the civil war to where now it was fire and movement, fire and movement, except for going over the top where it was charging into confusion if they did not lead and into the hot flying lead and bombs thrown or dropped into their path. They had to learn how to move their troops, how to take an objective and how to kill without a thought lest they be killed.

"This, gentlemen, is the method of the bayonet!" he said and stepped forward to thrust the weapon to his front, the point parallel to the ground. "You will do this and put some force behind it!" he stepped forward again; mimicking the movement of a rapier thrust used in fencing. This was an exercise not meant for sport.

The candidates learned how to shoot every weapon of theater and studied compass reading, tactics—grand to small—and Army language on command. They became fully indoctrinated in military discipline down to the cadence and every morning and afternoon there was the physical training, hour after hour of running, push-ups, sit-ups and others. Each man took turns leading the troop in drill and practice war. The eight weeks finally passed and it was graduation day where the bars would be pinned. Sergeant Bell gave them the news the last night before the pass in parade.

"Gentlemen. Congratulations, but your training has only begun. We will embark to Camp Mills in New Jersey for deployment. There you will still train. And I shall be attending with you as I am now to be the sergeant major of the 61st Combat Regiment bound for France."

"Now there's some news!" Paul whispered to Daniel, as usual it didn't escape the ears of Sergeant Bell.

"You may speak freely, gentlemen. I have done my charge and now must take you babies against the Hun. We will be responsible for over a thousand men under the command of General Griffin."

"When do we meet the men, Sergeant?" Daniel said, the first to speak up from the informal gathering, testing the waters. The group fear and psychology had been so pronounced that this was an unusual chance. Any words before meant a punch in the gut or worse.

"You'll meet up with the poor souls who have you people as lieutenants at Camp Mills where they are already formed," he said, his teeth clenched. "You may not be ready as far as I can see, but you will have to do."

Private Phillip McCray was steaming to Portsmouth, England, from where he would be deployed to the front in France within a week. He could feel the fear course throughout his limbs and body; when he thought of it, he felt his heart pounding hard. All he heard about the war was the futility of the charge. Many in England had to be conscripted these days as opposed to the start when plenty of young men volunteered for the adventure and honors. He found it difficult to have friends any way and thought of it from time to brief time, but quickly dismissed the idea. His mind was set on getting by as safely as he could figure and surviving this deadly assignment and letting someone else fall for him. He owed no one anything he told himself—and country and honor? Those notions were the notions of fools, he thought.

That May was especially beautiful in Boston and Matthew brought his father to the newsroom where he set an interview. The paper wanted a story about the arms trade and the impact it had on the weapons being used overseas against the Germans. It was to be an uplifting piece to provide some confidence of the effort for a citizenry whose doubts about our involvement still rang to Washington. Peter was hardly mobile and long since retired when he was asked for detail and comment. His last deal had been five years past when he brokered a delivery to England of engine parts that synchronized the firing of machine guns with the propellers of the craft known as aeroplanes.

He helped his father walk the long city block from the carriage park. Automobiles chugged past them, spewing smoke and causing the elder McCray to cough. He looked at the strange contraptions and thought they were a good investment since Henry Ford had developed the means of efficient production and repeat design that was selling well. Having converted to gasoline from oil instead of steam, the automobile was feasible to mass market especially with the abundance of oil old man Rockefeller had brought to the masses.

The trees were in full bloom with whites, reds, and crimson colors bursting in front and along the side of every old and new building in the city. The birds were flying in large groups and chirping in full chorus, as the breezes from the ocean were warmer and soothing to the skin. The city was beautiful and peaceful.

"Mr. McCray…thank you for coming," the editor said. "I want Matthew to take the story down and appreciate your help very much. We must give the people reason to take heart as our boys enter the Great War."

"I'll reflect as best I can," he answered. "Thank you for employing my son."

"Matthew is a good reporter and working on his stories of commerce and events. He's been very busy lately as you know."

"Yes. It seems the world has gone mad."

"I understand you have nephews in the service of our country?" the editor asked, making polite conversation.

"Yes I do…and I have a son who is a priest going over soon," he said in a worried tone. "The Lord is with him, and I pray he will return safe." The elder McCray knew the hazard because he knew the weapons. "Now if I may…I would like to proceed."

"Surely. You and your son take the office next to mine and make yourself comfortable. If there's anything you need, please do say, Mr. McCray."

Isaac looked at the group of men lounging on the ship's deck as they sat playing cards or talking away the hours. Many were drinking coffee again after an initial spell of sickness. They were a happy lot and completely unaware of anything but the moment. They enjoyed each other's company and were having plenty of laughs. He smiled with them and made sure each man knew he was available to meet their spiritual needs on call—confession or counseling, he would be happy to intercede on their behalf.

The food onboard was good. Navy cooks did a masterful job in turning bulk supplies of meats, potatoes, and fruits into wonderful meals for so many. The weather was cooperative and they passed the ocean without a storm. Coming close to the shore of England, the seagulls welcomed them by flying close for food scraps thrown up by the American men. The air had a clean smell and feel about it the men who were more observant took in and enjoyed its simple value. Soon the noise of a city once again became part of their landscape as the ship made its way into harbor. They had arrived safely; no phantom u-boat did them in. Some men thought the stories of such underwater vessels must surely be exaggerated like the stories of the German prowess in battle. Most of the younger ones didn't think of war as risk to themselves. Many figured confidently the worse they had to endure was the basic training behind them.

Phillip avoided the card games on ship because it was too close, and he couldn't escape easily or fight and get away with any designs he had to cheat. He cared not to risk money in something that wasn't a sure thing for him. He saved what he had and if he were to use it on anything, it would be a pass back to the States. He laughed. *Fat chance.*

Isaac heard there was a McCray onboard but put little to it. Someone remarked for a ship transporting only a couple of hundred men, it was a minor coincidence. He thought he would find him just for the sake of it sometime near.

"There be a lot of Irish in our ranks," a junior officer remarked to the priest.

"And don't forget the Scots!" he smiled in friendliness. "We're here too."

"Irish, Scottish, British... What's the difference?" he asked.

"Oh, young man!" He laughed. "The tales I could tell you!"

As the ship was brought to the moors and Navy men threw the lines, the order was passed to muster up on the deck. They were all told there would be taxis and a few trucks to take them to the camp a few miles north of the city. The commanders would be there and they were to become a fighting unit quickly. The ship's captain spoke eloquently of their grand quest as representatives of the world's greatest and largest democracy. He finished by saying, "Your brothers and sisters, mothers and fathers look to you, the towns look to you and the country looks to you to do the work we must do for the sake of freedom. I know you will fare well under God's infinite grace. You are men of America and no one can put you aside; no one can defeat you nor stop you from doing your duty! God speed, gentlemen!"

He left the deck to return to the wheelhouse and take up the supervision of securing the ship for two days of coal loading and foodstuffs courtesy of the English. Other ships would arrive within the week and add to the complement of troops gathering for their next sea voyage across the channel.

Daniel and Paul arrived at Camp Mills within the month and prepared with the troops who had come in following the initial deployment. They fell into leading easily and quickly as they marched them and guided the fresh and young men through their paces of exercise and training. Repeated dissembling and reassembling of weapons gave each man the knowledge and skill to take care of the weapons and with practice they became quicker and quicker. A firing range allowed them all to safely practice using them to hit targets. Classes were held on the use of the gas mask and there was first aid training provided simultaneously to volunteers for the medics. The regiment was nearly as ready as they could be. Daniel and Paul made sure each man in their platoon wrote a letter home before boarding the ship to cross he ocean that Thursday.

Major Sunday, the battalion commander spoke to the troops the night before and told them they were part of a grand exercise in the righteous cause of America and freedom.

"Tomorrow we will voyage to England and begin the work of returning peace throughout Europe!" he spoke, his voice raspy caused by a glancing bullet wound he took to the neck in China a few years before as American troops marched to Peking. "I tell you now, you will not fail! The boys who have gone before us are waiting and count on our division to arrive in a fortnight and take up arms to drive the Hun off French soil! We will not fail them!" he said, his voice pushed from the depths and breaking slightly as the sound captured every man. "We will know our mothers and fathers are watching what we do, and we will bring a quick victory! Sergeant Major," he turned toward Bell, "have the men fall out at zero-five-thirty with full gear! Until then gentlemen, rest easy tonight and I'll see you at the dock."

Isaac had crossed the channel with the 161st Regiment and was marching with the unit toward the Argonne. At twilight the men were walking in a sparse single file and saw figures at a distance coming toward them. They were the first battlefield casualties seen by the Americans as the lines closed toward each other. Isaac saw pitiful civilian mothers and children carrying a few belongings on their backs or pulling small carts, their heads covered in despair, faces turned down, watching their feet take steps away from their homes to the unknown—but away from the shells and fire. Then a staggering line of French soldiers slowly came on them, many wearing bandages over and across their heads. It seemed the eyes were especially vulnerable, the priest thought. He watched them pass, with only an occasional gesture made with weak hands.

Phillip was in the troop trying his hardest to think of what he could do to be removed from this risk. It was difficult for him to know how; the front was looming ahead and he was running quickly out of time. There was no place to go and no way home except by ship—he thought in a coffin or if he was lucky, on a hospital ship perhaps only grievously wounded. He had not joined for this, he thought, and he had to get away.

The Germans had built palatial underground respites in the Meuse-Argonne and furnished the rest area with the finest French beds and art. They had been leisurely using the space taken from the French and stored up plenty of food and wine, clothes and jewelry. They had been practically unmolested after taking the ground and built up strong defenses. The few attempts made by the Allies to retake even a few feet of the muddy woods had been easily repelled. The barbed wire and underbrush slowed them and then machine guns stopped them.

He watched them pass, bloodied and lucky to be alive. Many of their comrades were left where they fell to rot before the frost gave way to freeze and would suspend their bodies in a state of eternal posture of agony before the soul left them. The 161st stopped ten miles from the edge of the wood and set out forward observers while the regiment took to camp. Phillip McCray sat alone and slipped a flask out of his haversack and took a long drink. The next morning would take the replacements to the main body of the Fifth Corps.

The convoy bringing Daniel and Paul was on the way and it was smooth sailing the first day. The swells had been small and though they still caused many to be sick for a while, the boats easily negotiated through them bound easterly for the shores of England. They were to arrive at Portsmouth where a few weeks in camp for more training—this time on French weapons and artillery—would be their final preparation before joining the fight at Anould.

The brothers remained together with four other young lieutenants pacing the decks and reminiscing out loud about their homes and lady friends. They were proud to be wearing bars on their collars and still saw this as a grand adventure and opportunity to earn medals and return with more to them than was there before. The swirls and waves brought enough spray to their faces, they felt the pleasant touch of nature far out from land sooth them. So far the war was a fine thing.

Matthew McCray had been asked to take dispatches allowed from the front and form them up into encouraging reports of America's commitment. With fall approaching travel by automobile would become difficult to Camp Mills and Washington where he was allowed to talk to the Army's public relations group; the trains would do in winter, but much faster contact was made with the freedom an automobile gave him to come and go, and quickly arrive at any place where more information could be had from different commanders. The numbers of dead seemed unreal and his first objective was to verify what was fact and what was fiction on the front. He thought surely the stories must be wrong and exaggerated. For so many to willingly die in a contest where little has been gained or resolved didn't seem even remotely plausible. He thought of going over to attend the event and see first hand what was happening. This war to end all wars must be chronicled for the sake of the sacrifice made and posterity.

It was humankind's peak to dissolve conflict and after, because of the intellectualism of the day, will surely render peace for the world as it spread understanding and tolerance instead of distrust and hate. "That's the ticket," he thought confidently. He asked the editor, crusty old Earl Todefer, to let him go over there and wire dispatches.

"It will provide for first-hand accounts of the progress, sir."

"I know. I know. Reporters in uniform have done it before, but…I'll think on it, Matthew, and give an answer tomorrow."

"I think it will let our paper take a lead in the biggest story of our time! This is the biggest story of all time!" he said impatiently.

"Matthew!" Todefer said close to anger. "If I send you somewhere and get you killed, your father would never forgive me. Now, I've told you I would think on it. Let it be."

"Very well, sir. Thank you."

He left knowing it was unlikely he would be sent with this paper. Flashes of thought continued to put himself out for hire by someone who would come to him and send him over. This is the event of centuries and he must write of it, he thought. *There must be a way.*

Father McCray clutched he cross he carried in his vest and prayed for the souls of those this staggering line of men left behind. He tried to counsel as they passed and ask them what happened. His Cajun French was almost sufficient. In the dusk light he noticed through the shadows a tall figure whose uniform was nearly in rags staring at him for a few seconds as they past. His face was sunken and drawn down, skin exposed seemed to fall in ropes; his hair was wild in several directions. He looked as if he'd been sleepless for days and was managing to put one foot in front of another to make his way somewhere—somewhere behind Isaac, he observed.

"Mai je parl pour vous?" he asked him if he could speak to him. At first the stranger appeared confused or angry. The priest held his collar cross and pushed it toward him to show he was a minister.

"Dieux benissez vous," he answered in very fast French. Isaac knew just enough to understand the effort.

"Dieux benissez," he answered, "God Bless," back to him in broken French. "Quoi fait il devant?" he asked him.

"Mal. Vou á lochec... tre mort," he said and paused, struggling to speak to the death that lies ahead of the Americans. "Terrible...Devant terrible meutre. Il ný a vien de tel que Ils nous pr c daint "

"Mourant sortie?" Isaac tried to ask him if there were men still alive but dying. He must attend to them and give them last rites, he thought. *Surely God will help me get to the poor souls.*

"Oui." The French soldier looked deeply into his eyes and turned back to follow the one in front of him. The rest of their line passed in silence, no longer approachable as living human beings, returning to gray silhouettes melting into the background as ghostly apparitions of men. The 161st continued their march forward protected by mere iron and will. The French and English—and Germans—had already lost a generation while the Americans walked in untested and for a time, naïve. And the boys from North America, unmolested by the worse of technology man could devise to the day, marched toward their schooling only a little more wary.

They heard the sounds of distant guns and could clearly see the light from ordinance now as darkness wrapped the countryside and their path. Most had seen fireworks at home—whether in the towns of Alabama, Georgia, and Tennessee, the Cities of Massachusetts, New York or from the fields of Kansas and Texas. These lights were akin to their experience and appeared, as harmless but must be in fact killing lights; they knew that and had yet to feel that. Then foul odor overtook them in a wave and stayed as they marched onward. There was no escaping and no illusion as to the source of the sticky stench that seemed to attach itself to any exposed skin. Each breath became a heavy breath as the air was filled with it; most in their number had a faint recall of the smell from animals. Dead flesh was losing gases of decay and gradually eating itself to bone and mud.

The 161st cautiously took to the trenches they were to reinforce. They had been trained on the technique but aside from a short and clean example in New Jersey, this was their first. They learned the depths advised for safety, how to make and use quick ladders and dug steps to provide the security and the method to rush an attack on the enemy on line. The practice had been a fun exercise although with serious intentions, and no one was firing machine guns into their ranks stateside. These were not the same.

Phillip was one of the first to take shelter deep, quickly stepping and jumping in the divide. He felt a sudden and violent pain in his stomach as in a quick turn to survey, he glimpsed a torso barely illuminated by moonlight. It was the largest piece of what was left of some poor fellow, whose arms and head may be somewhere nearby. He wretched and lost the contents of his stomach. *What happened,* he thought, *to cause this in the deep protection?* And now he was in the same place. He quickly stepped away from it and felt the carnage followed him. Others joined and saw the same limbs and bodies; some bloated from the effects of time, some fresh and others partially eaten by rats. Many grabbed their mouths and tried to cover their noses too and look away. Father Isaac heard soft and distant moans outside the trench toward what must be the German lines.

"How close are they?" someone asked openly to anyone who had an answer.

"The German trench and fortifications are but fifty yards ahead. Stay down!" Captain Thomas called out to his company. Word was passed to them and the other companies the enemy was close, to face weapons out and to stay alert and ready.

Isaac crawled out toward the direction of the voice he heard in pain. There were barbed wire remnants that cut his clothes, bodies he had to crawl over that put some blood on him, holes filled with filthy water he swam, weapons of steel and other refuse left behind as the attack into the storm of shot went forward and jagged stumps left where trees stood before. He felt the slimy earth wet his clothing to the skin as he took one armload of earth after another and pulled himself toward the sound. He heard his own breathing during the struggle to reach the soul when the moans stopped. He stopped and listened while the dark consumed him as he lay there. Finally a faint sound out of a push of breath caused Isaac to pull onward when he saw him. Reaching out one arm after the other, he made the final yards and found him.

"Brother...rest easy. The Lord be with you," he said before he blessed him by making a cross sign toward his frozen contorted face.

The soldier brought a weak hand to his mouth gesturing for water.

"Yes, my son," he said as he took a tin of water trying to give the man some relief. He noticed he had been cut down at the knees and there was also blood on his stomach. The man's eyes were closing in pain and from the loss of blood. *He has little time left on this earth before he'll leave it,* Isaac thought, quickly anointing his forehead for last rites that were said in a language only the priest and God understood between the three. Only one of tens of thousands, but his wasn't quick like many. He had taken machine gun bullets the day before and had been lying there for hours, slowly losing his life's blood into the mud.

Suddenly a burst from a machine gun passed over his head. The war was on the man of God and his charge expired at that moment, no longer suffering on earth and absolved from his sins. Isaac cried for him and the countless others he thought of and prayed for them all. The priest slowly worked his way back to their trench where he was to be met by Captain Thomas and his anger over the chaplain taking such a chance. As he got the edge, Phillip pulled him in and helped him avoid falling to the water-filled bottom.

"Welcome to the war, courtesy of General Griffin, Father."

"Thank you, soldier." He gazed at the figure and watched him turn away and leave him into the darkness of the trench. In his place several large rats suddenly bolted out of crevices. They startled him. *Dreadful things these are!* he thought. There was nowhere for the men to put their feet but this—and him.

"Captain wants to see you, Father," the corporal said.

Isaac felt his pulse coarse through his head and stay. He rubbed his eyes and massaged both temples and heard the silence of the hundreds of men to both sides. "Very well, son. I'll be there directly."

"Thank you, Father."

He watched him taken by the black too. The walk to the covered shelter that served as a headquarters and mess area of sorts became a one step at a time struggle across an unknown and uneven bottom sporadically pocked with holes from mortar. Other steps were taken out of most of the water caused by bodies and human waste that rose above the water line. He held onto the braces of the breastworks and found the opening of a manmade cave. He raised the canvas flap and stepped inside the only dry space. A single candle was allowed inside where the men gathered around a small table left and ate tins of beef. The captain emerged from the shadows of the light.

"Thank you for coming, Father," he said.

"Yes, sir, of course."

"Take rest here if you will. And I want you to advise me when you feel the need to go over, if you will. If I cannot convince you not to risk it, I can provide some cover for you by riflemen."

"I understand, Captain. I'm sorry." He looked downward.

"No, Father. Please do not be sorry. We are in your debt for you bring God with you and my men need God. Now will you stay?"

"Thank you, Captain. But I must be where they are."

"I understand. How are you fixed for provisions? I see no sack."

"I have a communion set and a tin of chicken and rice. All I require." He smiled.

"Take this wine, Father, please," he said, handing him a bottle. "And have some food before you leave us." He paused. "Don't worry. All the men have been fed tonight." He returned the smile. He returned to the open trench where the rumor was an attack on the morrow across the salient. One of the soldiers ventured the objective was to take the right flank of the German line. If it were true, the first test of the regiment was on them and involved the suicide of going over the top.

In Boston Matthew asked his father to help finance his passage to England. He resigned his post at the paper to which Todefer said little at first, but stared through his furrowed brow into the eyes of a young man he knew must be a fool because of his age. He hoped the young McCray would survive but had little hope.

"I want you to reconsider," he said. "But I suppose if you're bound to the notion, I can't stop you, Matthew." He stopped and took a few labored breaths. "I believe you are a headstrong and impulsive man who does not know what he's asking for…It's more than a dangerous place, my boy, and plainly spoken, you shouldn't go."

Chapter 13

"Catch it!" Daniel yelled toward his brother as the football took a higher trajectory than expected. The waters had become flat and calm as they neared the English coast and several men were tossing it to each other on the wooden deck. Paul was unable to reach the ball, and it fell in the midst of several troopers sitting in a semi-circle cleaning their rifles, displacing parts with its soft crash. "Paul! You never could catch well!" he laughed.

"You never could hit a target, brother!" Paul smiled, imaging his hands in a spastic motion.

"All right, all right...fetch it back for us."

Paul slowly ran toward the group. "Excuse us, men. I must retrieve the ball my brother cannot control. I'm very sorry."

"That's fine, Lieutenant. No harm done. Do you know, sir, when we arrive?"

"In a matter of hours as I have been told. We're just off the coast and cruising in straightway, gentlemen." He took the ball and cradled it in one arm.

"What do you suppose it will be like, sir?" one of them asked.

"I don't know at all, but I imagine the Germans are beaten down pretty bad—just the sheer numbers of killed," he stopped abruptly. "We'll be fine. We have the best soldiers, the best aeroplanes and the best weapons in the world!" he forced a smile.

That evening the coast came into view and the captain of the ship began steering it slowly to dock. Smoke and movement on land meant they were soon to be still again as it made its way for mooring. Finally the order was heard to cast lines from the decks and tie up. Bell ordered the troops to secure their gear and bring it all topside and ready to disembark for the camp.

"Bring it all, gentlemen! Do not leave even so much as a cigarette wrap behind! Rifles on safety, people and slung!" he bellowed, the platoon sergeants repeating the orders in succession. The men gathered quickly and stood by with their bags at their side in full uniform and steel helmets, confident that since they arrived the war would be over soon and they would return as heroes.

The camp outside the city of Portsmouth was laid in the lush green of the English countryside. It would be their home for a month before the plan would come together taking them into the fight as soon as it was determined they were ready and suited for battle. Many English veterans were convalescing nearby as casualties produced during the last three years on the front. Some were mobile with missing limbs and would tell those who listened what it had been like—warnings of the minnies from the constant mortar attacks, whiz-bangs and heavy shelling from heavy artillery to the snipers and gas shells—none of which were as bad as the shrill of the whistle to go over the top and rush headlong into all of it and machine gun fire. Old Duke was his nickname and he preferred it. Daniel and Paul visited the hospital the most and spent the most time with the retired veteran and other wounded who would return to the front. Old Duke said he was appreciative of the new blankets they were given. "I used to pray to the Lord that if he would just give me a blanket to warm myself a little before I was killed, I would be as good a son as I cold be and attend the Sunday services for the time He left me. Just a little while with a blanket, dear God." They had come to be in little hurry except for their comrades still up there.

Life at camp was easy; the wooden floored tents were outfitted with all the comforts for the officers and nearly as good for the enlisted men. Between the cots, there was a coal stove in the center and footlockers on each end of the cots for storage of all the things brought with them or bought in England. Fresh coffee every morning and a hot breakfast was made by the local women instead of Army cooks as a show of appreciation to the forces who were finally there perhaps to save a few of their own. Daniel and Paul brought Old Duke back with them more than once so he could enjoy the rum and beer supplied by the officers. American cigarettes were a luxurious treat for him as well. The men enjoyed the way he talked and listened to what he said like children may listen to the stories read by loving parents. Most of their time together was a scene of men sitting around him to capture every word and imagine the story.

The training was completed within weeks with their learning artillery tactics and taking more practice with weapons of every country they may find and then be able to effectively use on the battlefield. Donning and removing the gas mask was part of their preparation in make believe gas conditions. Old Duke told them they wouldn't want to see the effects of chlorine or mustard as there was no helping the poor wretches who took it into their lungs. "It does not matter, ladies, as the human body being ripped apart by flying steel is even worse—only faster and you're sure to see that," he said grimly. "You need to stay down and watchful and still a German can find you." He took a well-mannered sip of the cup.

"And the minnies—oh, boy, I tell you. One minute after telling your chum of a woman you had in London, the next there's nothing of him—his leg will be here, maybe a sheet of bloody skin there, a piece of his head further and…you see you don't know when one is going to get you. It's hard waiting for it to happen, don't you know?"

On occasion he would leave them for a time, not physically, but his mind would leave them as he was thinking in himself. Old Duke lost his legs on an attack when he was tangled in barbed wire and was ripped by a machine gun. There was little connecting tissue left and having to wait hours before being helped and then more hours before a doctor saw him, the legs were lost to gangrene. Every night Daniel and Paul would take him back, pushing the wheelchair that held his legless body upright and they would help him to lie down once at his bed and cover the veteran in a warm blanket.

"We're shipping out for the front tomorrow, gentlemen," Daniel reported to his doughboys they would be joining the fight soon after along the Marne at Chateau-Thierry where the build up continues for an Allied thrust toward the Hindenburg line. "General Foch and General Pershing have more to say this time and we'll be the messenger!" The response was immediate; shouts of joy went up like an explosion itself from the excited men near Daniel.

Peter received letters from his sons Isaac and Matthew from England usually about two weeks after the post. Matthew arrived and attached himself to the First Division headquarters and enlisted to go with the next deployment as a military correspondent, the only way he had a ride, he jokingly thought. The father read of his son Matthew's growing fondness of an English woman he met at a theater. She worked as a nurse in the Londonderry hospital. Her name was Agnes Lewis and she had two brothers in the war. One had been killed at the battle of the Somme over a year past while the other was stationed with the First Battalion Artist Rifles near Aveluy Wood. She was a dark-haired beauty with a strong Welsh accent whom he began writing every day. He enjoyed listening to every word she spoke; the sound of her voice was like a joyous melody to his ears.

Peter wrote them back that he was coming out of retirement to take up the cause by working as a supervisor in the Sewell Company armaments factory. *It would be work that I will feel is important for the effort and maybe affect the gear used by our forces to win the war.* He strongly encouraged them both to be careful and said he would pray as that was all that was left for him to do on their behalf. He wrote he was proud and wanted them home as soon as this year.

Agnes went to the house where Daniel took up residence for the time he would be in country—courtesy of the Huckabees, an older British couple. They boarded several Americans, as many as they could afford to feed. There was Daniel, Tommy Baker, Jr., an engineer with the First Division, and Kenneth O'Leary, a large sergeant of the infantry at residence. The music from their piano livened up the place every evening with tunes played by Mrs. Huckabee. She learned while attending Oxford. Her smile warmed the hearts of the men; she had little knowledge of the war other than the toll of death and saw the Americans as friends before being Allies in battle. She was generous with happy music and English rum.

Samuel and Irene waited for word every day and took no measure of patience with the postal service. Both sons were at the edge of war and they desperately held their hearts for good news. So far it had been and nothing made them feel anything but proud. Having learned of the ship to England, the boys were close to deadly risk hard to bear. Samuel thought back to what he heard his father say about the savagery and waste of war and could do nothing but pray for his sons now that they had committed the same he did so many years ago. Jebediah McCray tried to convince all who would listen.

He thought, *the enemy is different but the vanity and consequences are the same.* His country had been reluctant as he was and stayed out of the fray until the Lusitania. *Damn ship!* he thought. *The insanity of the German military...Sinking a vessel with civilians, the contemptible bastards!*

"I had this feeling, Matthew, and wanted to see you immediately to know."

"I'm always glad to be with you, dear. Your face shows worry. Come in and tell me what it is."

"I was sleeping between shifts and was awakened by seeing you lying in France. Oh, darling, I'm so afraid," she began sobbing.

"Well, I can tell you, of course, it was only a dream. But I'm right here in front of you," he quietly said as they softly embraced each other. "Please do not cry for me, Agnes, my darling, beautiful lady."

"Can we go? Let's get away, Matthew," she said into his shoulder and squeezed him with enough force to nearly take his air. He was standing in slippers, wearing nothing but a pajama bottom and flannel housecoat he brought from Boston. The young reporter possessed a sculptured physique honed by the time he spent in a gym. He had visited the place to write a story on the bloody sport of boxing and became enthralled by the daily exercise regimen the men went through to toughen their bodies and strengthen their endurance. He softly held Agnes and assured her he would take her wherever she wished.

They stepped into the teahouse just before it closed for the night and took a booth. She looked down and away as she was distracted and worried. Having lost much already she knew she was to lose him, if not to German steel, to America. She had fallen in love with the McCray from Boston and felt she couldn't hold him from returning home some day without her. She looked up and took his wide forehead and blond hair in; she imagined his masculine formed and beautiful lips on hers and saw his shy eyes catch glimpses of her face between sips. How odd he was still shy in time when he had her and nothing to lose, she thought as she was on the verge of gathering back optimism and hope again. She wanted to feel the happiness she felt since meeting him the first time, how he made her laugh and how easily he caused her smile to return. Her smile graced her face and made her even prettier. He was unpretentious and simple, and talked in American, always polite and respectful to her as he shared the story of his family and as he talked about her and what she meant to *this poor lonely writer who cast away from his home to follow a foolish dream.* He thought he would chronicle the war and soldiers lives and instead met her and found a different future and a new frustration.

And she listened intently and understood his grief at times and his joy when he spoke of his father and brother and sister. Especially while with her, he smiled a great deal and seemed at peace with life. She liked that about him and she loved his honesty and caring attitude toward her. She thought she must have fallen in love with the man within the day. He had fallen in love before her. He told her he never expected to meet someone like her and that doing so across the ocean figures; the girls back home were far less enthusiastic about his company than she; she must be of a curious mind and a kind sort to meet with him—like that emotion the kindest people have toward stray dogs and puppies, they laughed.

The day she led him to the flora-covered meadow trapped in the bare center of the small plush forest of Londonderry and told him outright. She wanted to make love before the night had fallen to climax and seal their affection for each other—an affection that couldn't be undone by any force, consequence or other person. Maybe it was the war and the desperation, which flows out of it. She and Matthew knew only of each other for the time and cared not a bit for anything else. They came together, lost themselves in passion, took all of each other and planned to marry on his return. She said yes without hesitation, willing to give her family up to rare visits at the instant. After the war was over, he would surprise his father with news of her coming home with him to Boston.

"I believe the Lord has brought us together, Agnes. I love you with all my heart."

"I do know the Lord has done this as well, darling. Not the war but we were meant to be, don't you know, and His grace has brought us to each other, surely," she said and began to smile again. "I do so love you, Matthew. Shall we leave and attend to each other?" she asked, hungrily looking into his eyes.

"Yes, ma'am. I would love to be with you." They walked toward the meadow hand in hand, smiling, knowing. They had this precious time with only each other taken out of the world's loud, busy, and non-caring movement.

"Any word when the division is leaving?"

"No, Agnes. And if there were, I am not allowed to discuss it. Security you know."

"Not even with me?"

"It is not as I wish but as I am bound in oath, my dearest lady."

"So, I will not know until the day?"

"Until the day, sweet Agnes. It is coming soon I suspect as we are ready and your countrymen need relief, badly."

"Then let's make time now for our hearts sake."

Near the Argonne the Americans waited. Phillip had yet to devise a scheme he thought would be successful enough. Shooting himself in the foot was not an act that favored his intentions since it would cause pain. Desertion would give him no standing, and he couldn't speak the language. Feigning illness would not work either—the physicians would easily discover his fakery. He resigned himself to his fate for a time hoping this would end soon and he could return to the States and seize on his favored larcenous opportunities once again. He dreamed of such a scoring he would never have to work again and could have all the women and wine he wanted.

The days became weeks as the soldiers waited; rumors had become incredible and most of the troops came to pay little heed to what was passed. It seemed as if theirs was to be an agonizing routine with no stimulation save the occasional mortar fired from across the ugly divide. Only three had been lost and that happened on the first day when mortars found targets in the trench. One of the dead held an undamaged silk scarf between his fingers, obviously a last gesture he made thinking of nice things at home. The nametags were sloppily written, Morrow, Hopkins and Deevers and they were forgotten.

They did manage to cover the bodies and bury the fresh ones as well as those who had been lying a while underneath their feet enough to escape the worst of odors and the ghastly appearance of blackened and bloated faces, but the rats were busy nonetheless and every morning the surfacing of parts required more digging. They were simply there to keep the Germans in place and stall until the generals executed the plan of strategy.

"The English bloke said we were soon to attack," a soldier named Heady Evans mimicked the speech of the English who showed a week ago. Phillip heard him and frowned at another rumor being fostered. Mocking the English didn't bother him. He was known as a sour man devoid of friendliness; distracted it seemed by distant thoughts of other things most of the time.

"I wish you would keep it to yourself," Phillip said, an insistence in his voice. "We'll know when we know, damn it! Just do your job!"

"Brother. Do not charge them with such a demeanor. I pray you have patience. Every man is anxious and lonely," the priest said on hearing the exchange. Phillip looked at his collar and turned his face away without a word.

"You are one of the brave, Private. If ever I can be of assistance, I trust you will tell me."

"Yea…sure. I have little for the gossip. And I have little for these men who act like they are doing something worthwhile," he said as he turned away again.

"And you feel there is nothing here worthwhile?" Isaac asked.

"Nothing."

"Will you pray with me, my son? I humbly ask you for your favor and will not be against you no matter your answer," he said to the exasperated man from Arkansas. After a few breaths, he softened seeing the sincerity in the priest's eyes and feeling something for him. He thought here he was where he didn't have to be trying to put him at ease, and he would probably be killed just for doing that.

"Okay, Father. Go ahead," he relented and bowed his head.

Isaac started, "Father…bless this soul and all the men. Please see them through according to thy will and take care of them, Father, for they are young and brave men doing your work in this hell. Please see them home in your grace and if it be your will, let them all live. I pray you look after this man, Father, who is surely filled with good purpose and a good heart though he is presently angry. Let him know he is not alone for you walk with him. I ask this of you in the name of the Father, Son, and Holy Ghost. Amen."

Phillip felt his eyes produce tears, a rare thing for him and not repeated since he thought of his mother the day he left for basic training. He remembered her tears that day as he was all she had in the world and he left her standing there in nothing but under the leaking and rough roof of a tiny place in the middle of nowhere.

"Thank you, Father," he said, trying to hide his tears.

"You're welcome, son. I am here for you."

"I know you are and you shouldn't be! This place means death."

"What is your name? You're the one who saved me that night, aren't you? Do you recall?"

"I did nothing but pull you down. I'm Phillip McCray. Private Phillip McCray, busted from sergeant for misdeeds I cannot account for."

"Now that's interesting. My surname is McCray as well. Perhaps we're related." He smiled. "Tell me where you hail from."

"Arkansas originally, Father. But they want nothing to do with me there and desire me to stay out."

"Could it be? Tell me, son. Are you of Arthur McCray from Ohio? I have relations in Arkansas and know little of them."

"My father was William. He was gone when I was a baby. I didn't know him."

"Do you know what happened to him?"

"I heard later he hung himself. I don't know the truth for certain."

The weight of this glimpse of life suddenly caused a dizzying effect on the priest as he realized he knew of this pitiful man. It was true his father was a maternal McCray and had taken his own life, leaving his girls and one boy to suffer through more than hardship and sorrow. How a life can be so cursed to joyless existence by the hand of a man who had lost all hope and taken most of the children's lives along with his own was a mystery of selfishness. This tragic purpose should never happen to a human being child as it happened for Phillip and his sisters. *God save him from Satan's work*, he thought.

"Phillip...I am your cousin. We are family. Now that we have found you, all of us want to love you," he said to an open-mouthed soldier who never knew the peace of a loving family. For a moment he thought it possible but his condition was such he could not accept this love yet; it had never been something real, for him the idea of family was only imaginary in fleeting and weak moments. He couldn't help the tears though and they came; his hardened heart began to feel differently. Feeling ashamed, he quickly stepped away from the priest and buried his head into the folds of his arms. Isaac followed him at a distance. "Don't worry, Phillip. It is good. I must write my father and tell him I met you! And the folks in Alabama will surely want to know of you! Be not alone, son." He watched Phillip turn his head up toward him slowly, his eyes turned down at the corners.

"I have not been a good man, cousin," he murmured. "How can I...I am full of shame, awful shame. You don't know what I have done."

"The Lord forgives all. I know you must have heard of His mercy. And shall I not do the same?" he smiled. "What kind of priest would I be if I held anything against another man?"

"You say that, but I have been a scourge to other men."

"And now you're here! You have put yourself in this God-forsaken place to fight for other men's freedom. Don't you see all that means, Phillip? Such a personal and courageous sacrifice you make here!"

"It's not as it seems, I fear."

"No matter what brought you—or any here now. It is for all these fine men, and you too, Phillip. Take heart and believe Jesus Christ Himself is with you," he said smiling with confidence. He saw the man's face brighten with a humble smile of hope; he knew.

The 61st was ordered to make the crossing and make their way to the Marne at Chateau-Thierry where they were to secure a bridge and hold it for the divisions to use in a massive push toward German soil. They would be taking on a battalion of Marines and some French troops in the Fifth Division and go to war.

"This is it, gentlemen!" Sergeant Bell let out forcefully. "Do your country proud over there and come back in one piece!" He led them to the boats that would ferry the troops to France. "No stopping once we arrive, gentlemen. There's no time to talk to French maidens." He smiled. "And no time to taste their wine! We have work to do first and then we can drink together and get properly drunk!"

After they landed and began the march toward the western side of the Marne, they saw the first evidence of the war. The trek was void of men it seemed; perhaps they had all been lost already except for the occasional sighting of men without limbs, there seemed few along the way. As the approach took them closer to the village, they saw more. Tank machines and other vehicles, mostly destroyed, stopped haphazardly by shot and shell wherever they took it, were still smoldering, broken aeroplane parts, trash heaps and the smell of smoke and gunpowder and acrid residues of gas or rotting flesh—most were not sure what all it was but the stench filled every nostril.

"Lieutenant. Take your group and approach the town from the high left flank," Major Sunday told Daniel. "You need to protect our flank as we move into town." He then directed another lieutenant to do the same on the right flank. Paul's group and the main body were to enter head on, using fire and movement should there be resistance. The division proudly carried the stars and stripes and each battalion had their own battle flag waving to the French breeze—each one flying high with pride and showing determination. They had yet to see a German or receive any incoming fire.

The Marine detachment met them at the crossroads where they had taken rest and moved the wounded to the rear. Battle veterans willing to share a little of what they were in for, joined grimly and marched alongside the new targets as they thought of them. "You'll have plenty killed," one of the ragged Marines said to the man next to him. "Don't get too close to anyone, boy." His face was frozen in the fearsome look of a killer who could do it with no hesitation, quick and easy.

"The Second has left. We're bound to be next and soon, Agnes. There are but few units left in England, so I fear I will be leaving you any day for a while," he said. Matthew saw her face drop. It was inevitable she knew, but each day of postponement gave her hope for another. She suddenly felt empty as he was taking himself and her heart with him.

"Matthew…What can I say to cause you to not go? I'm sorry…I know that's foolish talk. I'm so sorry," she sobbed, hardly able to speak through her breaths.

"I'll be back soon. I'm certain of it! No war can cause us to fail each other!"

"Now, Matthew…I will pray that's true. It's…" she began to say then stopped and cried. He handed her a cloth and took her into his arms.

"Just love me, Agnes."

"I will always love you," she labored the words between the choking effects of overwhelming emotion.

"And look in on the Huckabees, for I know they have grown fond of our company. Will you, darling?" he said, hoping the job would tie her to him some.

"I will."

She tucked her head toward her breasts; a long and steady stream of tears ran onto her clothes. She had some knowledge of war, having seen its effects and heard the awful story of each patient she attended—at times to maimed recovery and at other times only forestalling their death. She could not help but think Matthew could be one of that gruesome number and only lucky to return and not be left in one of the trenches somewhere in an unmarked grave and no more to be heard or seen.

The men of the 161st were manning their posts as they had day after day when suddenly there was more happening on the German side. As soon as they noticed and started to report, several blasts and explosions enveloped the trench. Some bombs had struck nearby but outside the protection the deep cuts provided. A few landed directly in the trench and took all who had the misfortune of standing in the spot. The screams were a sudden wake-up call that the war was on them. Isaac ran the length from the shelter and saw several mangled bodies of men who had been in the path and others lying about, semiconscious, confused and nearly out of their minds. The smoke rose from the points of impact, leaving body parts and blood mixed with water, gravel and the few strands of grass in the mud beneath their feet.

"Man the breastworks, men! Do it now! Ready yourselves!" the captain screamed at the top of his lungs, using all the capacity he had to make sound. The Germans could be seen out or their trenches and rushing toward them on line, staggered and quick. In a few minutes they could be on them.

"Fire at will!" the captain called out again, desperation clearly in his voice. "Bring the machine guns up and let loose, damn it!" he yelled to get the whole line of men firing into the enemy charge. As soon as they began shooting, Germans started dropping like weighted sacks in the place they took the bullets.

"Private McCray! Take these men and circle to the right!" he ordered.

"Keep firing, men. All of you!" he shouted as he put coordinates for the mortar crews. "Now blow them to hell! Get it going!"

Across the field there were men falling from being shot when the explosions of the mortars began taking more in loud retorts of smoke and ripping hot shrapnel into every body nearby. The whistle of bullets flying into the front of them and overhead came to be ignored but the mortar shells couldn't. There were more and more, some missing direct hits while others found their mark and took more of the unknowing in an instant. Phillip was leading the squad of men when a mortar round fell close and knocked him to his back in an instant. He quickly got up and resumed running and firing at the figures running toward him and his charge. A hand-thrown bomb landed behind him near a soldier, and he turned and dove headfirst, picked it up and threw it out of harm's way, saving a life of one he didn't know. They were able to set up and put fire from the slight height the right flank afforded them until there were no more targets.

The screaming, noise, smoke and explosions were horrific for a very long ten minutes, and then sudden quiet finally rested across the field except for some late shots from the American side. They were fired out of fear or because spasms of impulsive nerves caused fingers to convulsively pull triggers and fire into the skyline where enemies once appeared as the very angels of death engaged in an orgy of violence.

The field was quiet and the soldiers of the 161st kept vigil for more through the night and next morning. Isaac attended to those he could, and blessed the dead as he found them. He brought first aid packets and helped the medic use them along the mile long stretch of trench. The priest wondered about Phillip and asked where he was. He watched one of the troopers close to the shelter point out to the right with an arm still shaking to signify he was out there somewhere. The McCrays, it came to him, have found themselves in the midst of many struggles and fury for the sake of the country, and do not ask anything of it except to live in peace.

He thought of Uncles Andrew, John and Samuel—who gave up sons to this effort and of his father and Aunt Tess, Aunt Ruth and the rest. He was happy the family living and working in the United States was practically unaffected. He knew they were supportive and hopeful this violence would end for all time, but he also knew it was not likely given mankind's condition. He thought of how many others and from what generation would take up a fight and die for the principle of freedom the McCrays cherished so much.

He found Phillip on the field surrounded by dead Germans who came up on them and used bayonets. There were seven dead Americans nearby and only two still alive besides Phillip who was bloodied but conscious. He bent down to him to check his wounds.

"Hello, cousin. Best you not stay here…" he pushed the warning out of his diaphragm. "They know we're here and will come back to finish us. Please go back without me for I cannot move. And take the two fellows with you, Isaac."

"We will all return, Phillip. Where are you hit?"

"I've taken a blade into the side of my stomach I'm afraid and a bullet into the leg," he managed to say. "I know it's broken." He looked toward his left leg where the bullet fractured the large bone as it went straight and square into his thigh. "That's why I can't go with you," he said becoming impatient with him. "Now. You must go!"

"Let me set it, Phillip, and then we will, damn it!"

"Such language from a priest!" he said as he found a laugh. "Since you're so angry today I suppose I'll try, but let's be quick about it!"

Isaac got the other soldiers to help him. After tearing his tunic in strips and using the pieces to tie them to rifles he had fashioned a splint tightly around his cousin's leg. The three of them then drug him by holding his blouse and pulling him back to the shelter. Phillip had second thoughts and tried to insist they leave him and save themselves. He sensed the Germans were coming again. "Be quiet, Phillip! Just don't try to talk!" The priest said in an exasperated and angry tone.

The group made it back to Captain Thomas and reported what happened. He had thought Phillip could be a leader because from the first day in France he was more serious and mature—he heard him forcefully tell a soldier to do his job. He handled the trenches well and was a sharp eye. He was the first to see the German movement before the last advance. He would have to decide to lead, however, and he came through on the flank. His actions far exceeded the expectations the officer corps had for a private with a sordid past. Captain Thomas saw something more in him.

The small force had stopped a German advance that could have flanked them and allowed them to fire and move into the trench to their right where the French had left it open for egress. Being forced to assume the mantel of leadership when the time required had brought it out of him. He didn't say anything to him that day, but the captain would put Phillip up for a battlefield commission to regiment, and if allowed, would tell him when he had the bars to pin. He needed replacement officers as two were killed that day.

The lull was caused by the German high command deciding to launch a major offensive along the Somme once more—this time with more than sixty divisions. Word had been received to simply stay and hold until the strength along the western front was complete. The command wanted every unit intact for the offensive. Word came late for ninety Germans who had to be killed in the Argonne. At the same time the 61st was moving cautiously into Chateau-Thierry.

"Lieutenant McCray!" Major Sunday called for Daniel to start his flanking maneuver. "Get going now! Mark seventeen-thirty hours to meet at the front edge of town."

"Yes, sir!" he replied and took his troops behind him to the left flank in a single file with weapons at the ready. It was their first time to ready weapons in earnest and many wondered what they would do when the time came they were to use them against another human being.

The main body of the force slowly marched toward the entrance to the town, still a few miles away. The Major had them split to use both sides of the road and maintain as low of a profile possible by blending with the background from which the road was cut. Ahead they could see the lights were explosions over the city and surrounding area. Paul kept his men behind him and was one third of the way back in the regiment march. The platoon would be one of the first to intersect the German infantry.

"Take cover!" the command was called out as one went down, shot through the chest by a sniper. Men in the back of the line didn't hear a shot and didn't know what was happening. Ducking into the ditch one side of the road and the brush on the other, they waited in the twilight for further word. Daniel and the forty men in his charge did not see or hear the order and kept moving upward and around the northern edges of Chateau-Thierry, feeling the ground beneath them give way through the soft leaf-covered, velvet-like ground they weren't touching directly. The peat cushion almost caused a bounce as they took each step. Daniel came to a step-up in the dark and nearly fell over it to the other side, making too much noise in the silent spot of wood.

He passed the word to the men behind him of the obstacle, and as he did, he heard the discharge of weapons and fast scream of bullets flying into their position, landing in front, to their sides and passing overhead like a lightening storm in miniature. There was a perimeter the Germans established between them and the town; enemy troops were dug in and had machine guns placed on both ends and troops in a shallow trench with rifles at the ready.

"Fix bayonets!" he ordered. "Sergeant Harris! Sergeant Harris!" he called out. The Sergeant ran to him and fell down in a crash at his side.

He felt the sweat pour from the back of his head thinking for a moment he'd been hit from the dampness he felt with his hand. He asked the Sergeant to take half of the men and form a line to his left while he took the other half and pushed and prodded them on line to the right. There he had them wait as the sound of crackling limbs and branches as if there was a conflagration of fire on top of them. It was machine gun bullets fired generally in their direction. The minutes passed slowly as Daniel was thinking what to do. They seemed pinned and had become unseen targets in the blackness. He heard the first one come in and explode behind the line, then another and another. The Germans were shooting artillery rounds toward their position from placements behind their own lines and the bombs were falling too close. Inches and speed could make the difference of life or death to the man. Explosions rocked them, tearing trees out of the earth and putting dirt and rock into the air. Several Americans were in the wrong spot on all of earth.

"On my order move forward!" he said. "Pass the word!" With that he rose up on his elbows and then stood, waving his pistol to follow him. It was much like he had been trained to do but safely in a camp in North Carolina.

Matthew was one of the last to board the paddleboat that would ferry them to France where trains and cattle trucks would take them to the front. He stared at Agnes as he boarded, relying on Tommy Baker in front of him to guide his steps along the gangplank. She stood there wistfully, her thin frame draped in dark purple and wearing a wide brimmed hat that fell to both sides of her drooping shoulders. He noticed her punctuated lips and longed to kiss them more than he had time as they were directed to step up to the boat. He already thought of their feel as a memory and could taste her. They slowly waved to each other as he walked up and once at the guardrail, he looked on her and she him until the boat moved out of harbor.

As Daniel began his charge into the night, he heard a sudden burst of weaponry, furiously firing to his right and advancing through the draw. The fight was fast and loud and he could hear battle screams from deep determined voices as the German guns were silenced in a matter of minutes. The Marines had linked with his left flank and took the field, leaving no German sentry alive.

"Boys...take it up with us," the Marine Sergeant said, smiling when he found Lieutenant McCray. "We must pass through their lines, now!" Daniel waved his pistol for the men to advance through the lines with the Marine detachment. As he approached the cut where the enemy had set up, he saw a Marine sticking one of them with his bayonet, a final and fatal blow into the German's chest, plunged deep and hard to the ground underneath.

Daniel heard a noise up ahead and saw one of the Germans running back toward the town; a Marine put several rapid shots into his head and back. His men had fired while walking toward the direction of the incoming fire but couldn't know whether they hit any of them. This was up close now, and it was clear they may have stopped some, but on this occasion it was the Marines who killed most of the men who were defending the enemy perimeter. He observed most of the veteran Marines seemed to delight in putting the enemy out of earthly consciousness. *Now...We should learn from those who've been,* he thought. *I need their experience and expertise to make it out of this alive.* It was clear he was in a contest that demanded life and his ability to save as many of his men as he could given the orders would be his most important objective throughout campaign. The Marines seemed to lose fewer by being as aggressive as a human being can be and fast to kill before being killed.

The main body took the town as only light resistance was left as the Germans took up positions across the bridge on the other side of the river. It would fall to them that this was the enemy they would fight. Luckily not a man was lost who had been on the road.

Daniel lost half of the forty men he chose; eleven killed by artillery or machine gunfire and nine were immobilized by varying seriousness of wounds. One more would die in hospital later. Their orientation was complete and awful, and it was theirs to gather for an offensive and protect the bridge the Allies needed to cross the river to march east and free the people from this German aggression.

Chapter 14

It'll be okay…you'll live and be home to apple pie and pretty nurses in just a short time!" Isaac comforted the soldier who had quick stepped to Phillip's right into the path of a burst from a German machine gun that took both his legs. One bullet pierced a deep artery; the constant bleeding required a tourniquet placed on the hip joint of his thigh. His bayonet had been used for the turn and tied back to the rag strip as tight as it could be without ripping it away. He lost a great deal of blood and was still seeping through some and Isaac knew he may not live even the length of the trip to Sanitary Train—a field hospital set up eight miles behind them.

The priest saw the suffering in his eyes and could hardly tell him bad news in the dire condition he saw. In moments of delirium he heard him ask his mother not to switch him. "Please, Mother, I won't do it again," his voice sounded like that of a little boy then trailed off to a faint whisper under his breath. When he was more awake, as aware as he could be, Isaac heard him simply ask for his mother, wanting her to attend him—to take the hurt away. Isaac hoped his words of hope got through some. When the young soldier returned to a kind of sleep, he administered last rites.

The stretcher bearers came and took him away in an ambulance and would not be seen by his company again. The priest thought he had lied to the man but was compelled out of humanness and couldn't bring his will to say otherwise. Isaac turned his face down and prayed for him and all of them. *Please, Lord, be with them. Do not let my weakness cause them to suffer. What that I would do, I do not. What I cannot do, I try. I can't stop the bloodletting, Father. You can if it were your will. I am nothing and I know in your eyes I have no standing to make this plea. Please help me be your humble servant and do the good work although I am most imperfect. Please take this from all men.* He opened his eyes when he finished but was void of hope the death would end by man's hand and except for a divine intervention would not—an intervention not known since the days of old and scripture. He knew there would be none as man's foolishness is not of His making. Isaac went back to the men who were living.

Matthew boarded the train that would take him near the front. From there he would be riding a truck the rest of the way with the last of the engineers and clerks. He would finally see the glory these men were earning for themselves! He thought he would write their story and the record would remain for generations. And he would have the material to write about soon so people back home would know their sons were fighting bravely and winning the war. No one he knew could boast of such a chance as he had, and no one could deliver what he could.

"Take it, Isaac. You must eat too," Phillip said to his cousin, handing a tin of pears and some wrapped beef to him. "The captain said he wanted to see me first thing, so I should report."

"God speed, Phillip. Thank you," he said, feeling his stomach hurting and rolling from hunger. He sat deep in the cut of the trench and ate, taking a seat in more shallow mud now from several days of dry weather. His father was reporting to work and getting the employees lined up on what their tasks would be that day. He sweated the details because he wanted the production to be perfect and the weapons' parts perfect for the American boys fighting in France. Every rifle and pistol frame he handled he thought of Isaac and Matthew, sons of whom he was immensely proud and both who had put themselves into the theater out of dedication to the troops—although in different ways. *Any one of these pieces could be the piece that protects them,* he thought, *and it must work the first time and every time it's needed.*

Helen was traveling with her theatrical troupe across Wisconsin on the way to finish in Minneapolis the next week. Turnbach wanted them to add a month and go south to perform in Des Moines, Kansas City and the St. Louis before returning to Boston. She wanted none of the extended tour, as she had to return home. There were many letters to write and plans to make.

He had them practice and learn several plays and song and dance routines to draw and was taking receipts. While on the overnight train trip to Milwaukee Turnbach had propositioned her—an interaction for which she had become accustomed owing to her beauty and at times her less than modest appearance on and off stage. Her freedom spurred some men to make assumptions. But she thought being chaste may be best and would rather wait for marriage to the right man. Helen had given some thought to having relations with a soldier she met in Albany early in their schedule because he was about to report to Camp Mills. He didn't press her and she didn't press him. Instead they decided to write to each other and remain open to meet and take up where they had left it after three intense days of seeing each other. Every day before her show, they would swoon and neck, and every evening after the show, they would lie together in beautiful affection. Although a few years older than he, she saw a man she would happily marry and begin a family. She loved Harry Hopkins for the time, and her heart was filled with hope. He was in love with her too and desired her as much as any man. He must come home, she thought, because they were meant to be.

Her interest in the suffrage movement did not define her as such a free spirit either but instead of her knowing from her father that she had a say as learned and as important as her brothers had in the affairs of the country. She thought Wilson was slow to enter the war because she felt the death caused by evil alliances must be stopped for the sake of peace. Those who argued against going over there left her cold; *how could anyone not want to support freedom?* But with Harry going into the war, her ideas became confused and muted—she recognized them as being selfish and wanted him where he was.

Her perfectly proportioned body, curvaceous and smooth, graced by long dark-red hair, perched thick lips, and large oval eyes attracted a great deal of attention and admiration. Harry had seen into her heart though and knew more than the beauty the world could see. He carried the embroidered scarf she gave him on their last night together; the large rose was as deep red as her hair centered the silk. He took it overseas and kept it close to his heart, guarding her memory—a simple expression in cloth he would remove from his breast pocket and think on when he was lonely. She left letters in each city to be sent through the Army to Harry. *After the war! After the war we'll be together forever!* she thought every day, enjoying the new dreams he gave her that filed her heart with a wonderful anticipation.

Matthew got to the front as the German offensive along the Somme commenced. He was immediately thrown into a unit the Second Division left at a valley near Fricourt; the trenches had already been used for several years and still bore the frantic and desperate evidence of the first battle of the Somme. He was pushed into one and allowed little leave to venture except through the trench. On occasions, mostly unexpected, remains of those fallen would make an appearance as if they still owned the place they died, the last dirt they saw. Uniform-covered skeletal remains were in the trench and underneath, the skulls seemed most likely to pop up and scare the soldiers nearly out of their boots at first. There were rats, feces, urine, and other forms of filth he had to live with in that trench. He thought of being with the Huckabees and sitting in their parlor—a clean, quiet, and safe place. This was horror which could hardly be described by words. The hell of the trench became less and less of an unknown—fewer gruesome surprises confronted him after a few days.

The Germans began by using a heavy artillery barrage making the men think it would never end and surely they had gotten themselves into something they never should have. It was most likely they would be killed outright before even firing a shot in defense. Then Matthew detected a faint odor of chlorine and tear gas until it became stronger causing the Americans to don their gas masks. The next duty the German Army had to follow the plan was moving tanks into the field, followed closely by the infantry. Matthew could hear it all. He saw the movement of dark machines in the distance and lost his water out of fright. They were coming into them and there was little they could do to stop them, he thought. He had been able to get little of the story put together and this was their first real test—which he may not live through. He knew he had been foolish and prayed to God he would live to see the next morning.

"My God!" he heard one cry and looked to see a blackened and smoldering figure stumble toward them; it appeared as if the left side of his face was gone and his left arm blown away to nothing. "Gripes, man!" another shouted as he went to him to rest what was left of his body. Two soldiers eased him down into the floor of the trench near Matthew. Another man ran screaming in agony to his right but away from them and ran up the parapet to the divide between the German advance and the defenders. He wanted to be shot and taken as quickly as he could be to end the misery.

The confusion and hell and deafening noises from machines, explosions and voices caused Matthew to quiver and lose the ability to move for a while.

He was shaking uncontrollably and couldn't seem to regain any sort of self-directed action to his parts. He slumped into the pit of the trench and tried to pull his whole body into the steel helmet the Army issued and ordered him to use while he was still in England. While he was ducking small more explosions and falling pieces of human beings rained around and on him. He wiped some brain matter off his face and picked off a foot, separated from its leg and blown out of its boot. Suddenly there was a lull in the noise and after a few dreadful minutes, he raised up expecting to see the tanks nearly on top of them by this time. His eyes went to the sky as he climbed, and he saw the British and American bi-planes in a pitched frenzy of dives and take-offs, flying hard and fast, grimly pointed toward the enemy and steadily making their bravery and risk count. They were dropping bombs on the advance and using their machine guns to strafe the German vehicles and infantry. Behind him he heard someone shout, "They're coming from 'round!"

The Second Division was flanking the action and a thousand troops were on the attack to pinch the Germans. Matthew watched between dropping his head down and up again to gather what was happening. He felt his body under his control again and a flash thought raced through his mind that this could be the moist dangerous time for him, but he couldn't resist the look and watched them stop the Germans, answering his prayer. The aeroplanes kept coming— it appeared hundreds but was only forty courageous pilots were taking and flooding the sky with steel, doing the job on the Germans. Should he live he knew his reports would be more and different than what he thought they would be. Agnes came to mind and her face drove him to take up a rifle of one of the fallen and fire it as part of the American Army defending itself now for a victory later. They had to win he thought, for the sake of every man there.

At the Argonne Isaac and Phillip watched the replacements arrive in their fresh and clean uniforms, weapons new and polished and faces still able to smile. Phillip was a lieutenant now and took the commission knowing the life expectancy was short for a company officer. He didn't know why or how, but somehow he was very comfortable being responsible for fifty men and took to it easy. Behind the first arrivals, they were told, there were more trucks on the way as part of the buildup. Phillip watched the new ones become acquainted with the trench and following their vomiting, watched their faces turn. "Easy, men," he said, the serious tone in his voice welcoming most to adulthood as men. "Take care to keep your weapons dry. Use the pegs on the sides," he instructed them. "And you must keep your feet dry. If you don't the trench foot will start eating away at flesh. And it's always hungry!" he smiled. "Stay down at all times. If you do not stay down, you will be shot. Should you have any other questions, ask me directly," he said matter-of-factly. He then made his way to Isaac to introduce him as the chaplain of the regiment.

"You people will need to know Father McCray. He can save your soul and your hide in a fight! Take heed to him and take care of him," he said to the young crowd of men in awe of the hard and dangerous-looking veterans. "Many of you are going to meet the Lord sooner than you wished."

The force was being built up and the 161st would lead the way when the order came. Phillip and Isaac would be among the first to go over the top to lead the way and keep going until the division had moved the stakes deep into the wood and driven the Germans out. The 61st occupied the Souilly area near Verdun and enjoyed what was left of the food and wine. The regiment would keep vigil on the western side of the Marne and the bridge for several weeks in quiet anticipation of a German counterattack that seemed less likely as the days passed and prepare for the Meuse-Argonne campaign.

"I miss Alabama, Daniel."
"Me too. It seems a mighty long way from here."
"Yes. I wonder how Mother and Father are doing and if they're well."
"Surely, Paul. We will have to take them out for the biggest dinner when we return. I can taste it now—and the ale! Oh my, the wonderful combination of a fat, juicy steak and ale! I hope it's soon for my stomach can take little more of this hardtack, canned roast beef or salmon," he laughed. "I'm withering to nothing here...haven't been this small since before high school!"
"We could hardly take a strong tackle anymore. That's certain. I miss the game."
"You never fail to miss the catch!" he laughed. "It'll be soon, I suspect. Germany is beat and they know it. Now that we have so many more men committed to the field, they'll give it up soon."
"I do hope you're right. I want to feel the red clay and see the magnolias in bloom and Mother and Father and Uncle John and Andrew—wonder what they're doing right this moment."
"I suspect they're working the mills still...trying for women. Maybe wishing they were in California with Aunt Ruth and making all that money out there."
"I'd like to see it someday."

"Me too. She thinks it's near paradise. They have palm trees and ocean breeze," he said wistfully. "It's beginning to seem to me that where palm trees are, that's the place I should be. I can see it now. Sitting on the beach with a bevy of lovelies, sipping ale and eating lobster and crab and breathing in all the fresh air you can possibly take," he laughed. "I can see it easy."

"Hope we get there..." He paused. "But I miss Alabama more and if I should never see the coast of the Pacific, that's all right by me. I just want to go home."

"Yea. We will. I don't think Jerry is coming and all we'll do is wait by this stinking bridge until our teeth fall out—seems that way."

"It's better than getting shot, I suppose," Paul said. "Ever think about the men we lost?"

"Yea. We have lost very few compared though."

"What do you think it was like for them?"

"I don't know, Paul, and I'm not wanting to find out for myself."

"It seemed like a bad dream in slow motion, those men taking it like they did. For some it seemed painless. For others we know. We just don't know how bad it hurt."

"I would very much like to get off the subject. What's done is over, and they're gone. That's all I can say."

"Sorry, brother. I'll put my mind into something else. Maybe I should inspect the men's weapons."

"Good idea. I will too. We can give Major Sunday a good accounting for our readiness anyway. That's something worthwhile."

"Gentlemen!" they heard Sergeant Major Bell's voice as he walked up on them. "We must clear the buildings now! The Major figures Jerry will target these dwellings with artillery to try to trap us in them and we will not be caught asleep!"

"Very well, Sergeant, Bell. And our positions?"

"We'll take the Marne and march to Foret-de-Hesse at the coordinates inside the town of Boisse-de-la-Puliter and set up a base of fire easterly toward all points. He is talking to the Marines and the rest of regiment now to spread as much outside the town possible. Let's get 'em moving, Lieutenant!"

"Best get the palm trees out of your mind, Daniel!" Paul said after the sergeant major left to find the other lieutenants.

"Be careful, Paul. Don't let a sniper get you."

"You too," Paul said. He didn't tell his brother of recurring dreams he saw himself in a losing battle. He saw and felt the spectacle of being overpowered by a German with a saw-cut bayonet in hand-to-hand combat and would awaken because of the sweat saturating his bedroll. The other dream that caused such torment was getting hit in the square and center of his forehead with a jagged piece of steel shrapnel like he saw happen to one of the replacements. He remembered his gurgling shouts, *Mother of God! Jesus Christ!* before he died in agonizing pain. He wondered what it would be like to be wounded or killed and shouted daily, silently, *Good Lord! What have I done? Why am I here?* And he would scold himself for being such a fool; it could easily have been another in his place—someone with more skill to fight.

He could not accept he may be a coward and steeled himself for the duration; he would stay and fight and die if he must for the honor of the McCrays. If he weren't skilled enough to kill his enemy before a bayonet put him through, then the Lord meant this to be his end. He tried to remember his life past, the schools and football and the plans for courting to get his mind off the war.

Peter saw her on his first shift on the job and took little notice until she walked up to him and plunged her hand out like a man to introduce herself. He shook her hand and saw her eyes fixed, seemingly peering into his very heart. Her name was Gladys, and she was younger than he, but he was taken by her looks and spirit. She was a full-bodied, strong-looking woman and pretty, everything in its place very neatly and her fresh-looking face sported a modest amount of makeup. She held his hand for the longest minute, and he sensed she might have more than a passing interest in this new man who showed up to run the machining shift.

"We're so glad you came, Mr. McCray. I've heard a lot about you and am glad to finally meet you."

"The pleasure is mine, miss."

"It's Gladys. Please! I heard you worked in New York."

"Yes, some years ago. I returned to Boston twenty-seven years ago and took up brokering."

"I know. I was working here in the main office when you were selling."

"I see. Well...I..."

"Maybe some time we can have a coffee, Mr. McCray."

"I would like that very much, Gladys."

He thought of it as a possibility and knew he should tell her soon he was fifty-one years old; it appeared some number of years her senior. He had been alone for twenty-seven years, possibly since she was born and was intimidated at the thought of a courtship. He decided to let it be what it would be as he was running out of time and his children were gone. Loneliness can lead to a man's thoughts of fancy and opportunity to seize, appearing out of unexpected places and at unexpected times as a woman destined to meet him walks the same path. He could miss it if he's not open to the possibility. *Could this happen for me after all the years?*

The Fifth Division was ordered to take the offensive across the Marne as more than sixty other divisions would move east at the same time. Major Sunday split the regiment and prepared the line to move on his order as the Allies were staged from north of Brielles and past Chateau-Thierry. The crossing of the Meuse had to be made to advance. It was November and the regiment had escaped the German artillery with few casualties during their first crossing. This one would be different and promised to be a bloody exercise; the Germans were as determined to stop them in this, their last chance to stem the tide of war and sue for peace before a catastrophic loss.

The air had become crisp and cold, biting through their clothing like a constant pincher of discomfort. The German guns fired sporadically and kept them uneasy during the wait; some were on the verge of giving up hope they would live and thought they would as soon attack and get it over as to wait for an unseen shell to squash the life from them while sitting and doing nothing. At least they would be trying to kill the enemy front on and could see what was ahead of them.

Daniel checked his men and made sure they each had 120 rounds of ammunition, extra bandoliers, a good rifle and repaired boots. Paul did the same for his group. Both men had received replacements to make up a full complement of fifty-plus men as they started with a few months ago. Their losses had been light but steady. It was as if the enemy tormented the Americans, picking off one, one day, three on another, and was waiting to finish them all. Taking the fight to them across the Marne made a difference, and this magnificent push should make the final difference.

Everything Old Duke told them was true only it was far more and far worse than he described with words. Perhaps if it was possible to have looked inside of his mind, the picture of their future could have been seen for what it has been. The veteran Marines helped them learn quickly the value of not hesitating even a fraction of a second. To hesitate meant getting killed. They also learned the value of aggressive action, taking the fight to and through the enemy and as quickly as humanly possible.

Within a month she no longer received letters from him; she thought early it must be that he is unable due to the Army marching forward and a lack of postal service but after four long weeks, she became worried, and was not able to learn directly where he was or what was happening with him. It would be another month before his mother told her when she finally wrote to ask her of his status out of desperate fear. She thought of losing her faith because of it and could have easily given up on the divine; at the very least, she regretted not making love with him during his last days in Albany. *Helen McCray... you're such a fool! How dare you think happiness can find you! You're of suffering and loss and you'll surely die that way!* She scolded herself. The theater gave vent to her melancholy as she could act the drama naturally for it had always been a subdued part of her, but now it was clear and she would never forget again.

The attack resumed—it was a month-long advance punctuated by periods of quiet. Their next objective was the Meuse River and canal. Daniel was as seasoned of a platoon leader the Americans had, as was his brother. The artillery would barrage the east first as the Army Air Corps strafed and bombed. Then engineers would quickly add bridges for the troops to race across the water divide toward the enemy. The Germans had pulled up every tank and division of infantry to face the expected attack and were fortifying their positions with dirt, sand bags and machine guns as the Allies were massing. Beads of water appeared on Paul's forehead after he left the troops to wait for the order. He now had the dream while awake and was unable to think past it.

Phillip took the remainder of his company to the rear for rest and cleaning. They had a week and then it was back for the offensive as the French and English were gathering logistics for the attack across and through the Argonne with the First Division. He walked with Isaac and took a hot meal of baked bread, roast beef and fried tomatoes—their first cooked meal in weeks. He sipped the clean water slowly at first and then faster, taking large gulps that didn't carry the taste of tin. He sat with Captain Thomas who narrowly escaped death being wounded in the chest by glancing shots as he turned slightly in the instant from the machine gun they attacked and destroyed.

"I guess this is it, Daniel," Paul said.

"Yes, you may be right. This push should do it. I heard they're already talking, but nothing is done yet."

"If anything happens to me, Daniel, take this for Mother and Father. Will you?"

"Nothing is going to happen to you that doesn't happen to me," he said softly. "I pray to God we make it through. We'll be home in no time."

"I fear I won't be, and it's time I owned up to it, Daniel," he said as he handed his brother a thick letter to deliver in the event he cannot.

"I'll put it up for you. It'll get home. Do not worry, brother."

"You know when we first came I gave no thought of dying. It just didn't seem possible with my life in front of me. This was like just an adventure we would enjoy until it was over. It's really odd how so many men think they're not the ones. So many think it'll happen to someone else. They, nor I, don't think about losing all. We just go along for the sights and action, not thinking we're others someone else, don't we?"

"You have a strong point of fact, Paul. Can't do anything about it now. We must go and hope."

"I have little. I feel my time is up, and that's why you must take this letter of respect and affection to the family. I want them to know I did my best and thought of them all the time and missed them. I want them to know it's all right with me regardless of what happens for it was God's will. I'm certainly lucky to have had them as parents and I shall remain happy in heaven. I put it all in there."

"I shall write them too and give it to you," Daniel said to a solemn and plain-faced Paul who while nodding acceptance of the responsibility knew that would not be. It would be him to get it this time; he felt the future in his heart and soul. Paul thought he was fortunate to know before and have the time to talk to God about his life and ask for forgiveness before he saw Him—

in this he knew privilege not bestowed on every man. He thought, *It is all I can do now to pray and look after my men.*

The barrage began and continued for an hour, pulverizing the other side in smoke and shot. It kept Jerry's head down as the pounding, so familiar, rained down on other men with deadly intent. Looking across the river it was difficult to imagine anyone living through it, but they somehow do—it seems they always do. And they rise up to kill the ones coming—it seems every time. The hour was close. The minute would come. The men of the division would rush into battle as lonely men except for their comrades rushing the same direction and not talking, not visiting or laughing, but dying instead. In that dreaded instant, they would be alone again and take it and fall and know no more. Each man is a mother's son, a father's son, and has someone who loves him. Soon many will be left a corpse, a body busted through, some headless, others torn apart from neck to crotch, and left to become only part of French dirt and mud.

Liberté

All along the line the order was heard and the men responded in concert at once. The engineers successfully put in a floating bridge for Daniel and Paul's regiment and those to follow losing five men to rifle fire from Germans who had the courage and tenacity to rise and shoot during the bombardment. Along the river there were several spans hastily put in and the Allies began to cross each one and at each one were met by a furious hail of gunfire. There was so much artillery being used for kill effectiveness the Germans could fire and send exploding shells close to them, beside them, over them, behind them and in front of them. Some bridges allowed only space for a single-file crossing and one after another each made it some distance across before being shot or blown off and falling into the cold water beneath them.

The men made a dash across and kept running until they were over and able to fire back, finally bringing pressure on the remaining Germans. The division on this day became known as the Red Devils by the Germans because their advance continued despite doing all they could do to stop them, throwing everything at them to kill as many as they could, and yet they kept coming. They wore a red diamond patch with a "five" prominently centered, marking their brotherhood.

It was Paul's platoon before Daniel's and he led his men on a fast run to the river and then to the bridge. They made it halfway before the first fell.

Another few steps and several more fell, bullets whizzing by and explosions rocking the footholds. The platoon was nearly at the other side and about to run the bank when Paul got it from a hand-thrown bomb that landed just in front of him. The explosion put iron into his face and neck and knocked him back, dead before his body landed straddling the side of the bridge and the river surface.

They poured into the valley and made it their day by taking it to Jerry, killing every one of them they could see with eyes and more they couldn't by laying in fire on a thick plane and throwing bombs into the fortifications. Daniel took his men across last and cleaned up any threat behind the depleted division. He didn't see his brother down; there were so many bundles of khaki all around and he couldn't take time to stop even for an instant. The enemy side was in desperate confusion laced with shooting and explosions as the men of the Fifth Division fought for every inch with steeled determination and heartless rendering to the Germans. It was because of them the Americans left home, got into the awful trenches and had so many good men killed. They had to pay dearly for it and between the Marines and the soldiers of the Fifth they made certain a high price was exacted.

Daniel came upon a wounded German and without a thought, put a shot through his skull. His men were doing the same as they secured the sector. Germany reeled. The nation had lost over a million of its young men and more today, nine days before the armistice was finally signed by fat, comfortable German men well away from the fighting and dying, sitting in fat plush chairs smoking fat cigars.

Along the Somme and through the Argonne the results were the same. Matthew got his stories and set sail for England and Agnes, shaking the dread off his heart. Phillip and Isaac lived to ponder the war and what it had cost. Houma beckoned the priest back. Arkansas looked better to Phillip and he thought to make a home there. France was free. England was free to retire and take back those men who were left after four years of misery. America was free to come home though light of many she took over the Atlantic the year before.

Daniel didn't see Paul the first day and found out what happened to him when Major Sunday summoned him to his headquarters. "He died bravely, Daniel. I'm proud to have served with him." The major said.

"Me too, Major," Daniel said, wasted of tears and emotion. That would strike him later when he was alone and looked across the night sky to see the twinkling stars—a silly childhood thing, but not so much anymore. It was easy to think Paul was looking down to him and with him still. He would never forget his brother, his best friend, and his partner in everything—from wrestling calves to football games and in the Army. He could not take it back; they had joined to fight in the grand cause, the righteous chance to adventure and be men holding to the family tradition of courage. He volunteered to write the telegram for his parents and wired the message of his death. He wrote that their son, his brother, loved them with all his heart and he died as one of the finest and that there was more to follow. He left the message, clutching the letter Paul had entrusted to him. It would not be sent by post, but delivered by him alone. The spontaneous celebrations at home left Helen quietly happy for the sake of all the soldiers, but cold as hers would not return. She had read the Bible through twice since learning of Harry and started at the beginning again the day the Armistice was announced on the streets and in all the papers.

Chapter 15

"Tell us all about it, nephew!" Andrew said, he and John walking alone with Daniel in the front yard of the old home place. The family had gathered for a large Sunday dinner put on for all the returning veterans of Marshall County in the house Jebediah had built with Mary forty years ago. He smiled kindly toward them and said he would on another day. "It is a story to be told, uncles, but today I am favoring Paul." He saw a veteran slowly moving toward the front porch on crutches wearing his uniform, walking toward them attended by a young woman whose appearance received a great deal of attention from everyone she passed. "Who is that?" he asked.

"He's Hobart Bailey," Andrew said.

"And the lady? Do you know if she's his wife?" Daniel asked.

"She's Katherine, his sister from Etowah. Are you interested in her, young man? She's mighty pretty," John smiled. "She's been helping him since he left the hospital last month."

"I might be," he said quietly. "I just might be."

Irene and John's wife, Lillie Ferguson, had cooked several turkeys, pies, and plenty of biscuits, green beans, and cranberries to feed the veterans and their families. Children from the home were paid to attend and serve, their smiling faces a welcome sight to every man who returned from Europe and saw children in dire circumstance. Lillie was the daughter of Ennis Ferguson who worked the Creeless farm and ranch, which stretched from Marshall and into Etowah, as the foreman of several hands who raised the cattle and swine. The operation had grown over the years and now supplied much of the beef and pork bought in north Alabama. A brief flirtation with the Klan brought him to the attention of the McCrays years ago, and he learned he had nothing at stake with the secret group. One arrest in his youth and the months in jail were all he needed to be spurred into a better work.

The ladies beckoned everyone inside where Samuel sat at the head of the table. He smiled at each of them as they took their chairs; there were six men and one woman, a nurse, who came home. A single chair was decorated with a pillow holding the medals, rank, and photographs circled by roses of the one who could not attend. Samuel had put in a large flag hanging on the wide wall.

"Welcome friends!" he began. "This is in your honor. Your courage and spirit have won the day! The county clerk's office, the church, and my family wish to thank you in a small way and tell each of you how proud we are and how much you're in our esteem! Now, please sit and rest easy."

Katherine helped her brother take a seat and then sat beside him, across from Daniel as it happened, and smiled toward him. The ladies served the dishes and filled the glasses. Daniel could hardly keep from staring toward the dark-red hair and curvaceous body causing the dress to tighten at her hips and breasts, and he knew she would find it odd—disquieting. He smiled and said he was sorry for looking on her so much; it had been a while since he's been able to notice a lady. She said she understood and was flattered.

"I understand you're here with a brother," he said as he reached across and shook the man's hand. "Hello, Hobart. I'm Daniel McCray. It's good to meet you, sir. Glad you're home."

"Yes. And thank you all for doing this. This is wonderful," he said.

"Yes, thank you very much," he said. "Where were you?"

"I was at the Meuse. Left a brother there. That's his place you see."

"I'm sorry," he said. He looked away with a sad expression and turned toward him, his mouth turned down toward his chest and eyes wide open, his bottom eyelids drooping.

"Splendid job, Mr. McCray."

"But do not be sad. He was a great man and now he's in heaven," Daniel smiled. "And where were you, friend?"

"Kriemhilde."

"Kriemhilde? I heard about it. That was rough."

"Yea. Lost part of my leg there; gangrene you know. Jerry must have had a rusty bayonet," he managed a smile. Daniel knew the place was where there had been close fighting and men used anything and everything to kill each other, from bare hands to knives to point-blank shooting.

"I'm sorry. I hope you fare well. Have some turkey," he said as he handed him a plateful. "And I understand this is your sister? Will you kindly properly introduce me?"

"This is Katherine. She's twenty-two and unmarried." He smiled.

"Nice to meet you, Miss Bailey. I'm surprised."
"Surprised at what, Mr. McCray?" she asked.
"That you are not taken. You're very pleasing to the eyes," he laughed. "I'm sorry for being so forward."
"You are a flirt indeed, Mr. McCray."
"Please call me Daniel. May I call you Katherine?"
"Yes, Daniel. You may. Now you'd best eat before it goes cold."
"Okay…and may I call on you?" he blushed, looking down shyly.
"I'll think on it," she laughed.

Matthew and Agnes were together during the last days before he returned to America. He had taken his field notes and finished several articles on the conditions in the field and had plenty to fill a paper every day for a month. He asked her to marry him again and come home with him.

"I know I want a life with you, Matthew, and I'm sure I shall like it there because I'm with you."

"I believe you will, darling. Boston is a great town and there's the beauty of the harbor and country, a wide girth of land as far as the eye can see! We also have spectacular winters that are picture postcard quality, dearest. And my family—you'll love them as they'll love you!"

"I am so much looking forward to the life! I've heard it's good and so large with all that room to breathe!" she laughed. "Let's seal our bond to each other and to a safe journey," she said as she handed him the large wine glass.

"And to God who has seen fit to let us be together!"

"It is forever and as it should be between a man and a woman."

Peter and Gladys met them at the docks and drove them into town where he had arranged a fully furnished home for his son. The fire was made and hot to greet them inside the stone dwelling that rose three floors, more room than Agnes had ever had. She was in awe at the seemingly richness of the place that stood out prominently amid the January snow. It was like a new London, street lamps, perfect buildings, manicured hedges and cobblestone streets, set in a busy atmosphere as many people drove past them and walked to and fro. The place was alive.

"Son…this is Gladys. She works with me and is going to be my wife."

"I'm very happy for you, Father. Hello, Gladys. It is good to meet you. This is Agnes I wrote about," he beamed.

"Welcome home, both of you!" she said. "I'm so glad to meet you, Agnes. I've already made plans for you to dine with us tonight. Do you like crab and lobster?" she said to the surprised woman who had become accustomed to sparse helpings of chicken or beef and more greens with little more of anything else because of the war. "I understand you're a nurse."

"Yes I am. I've liked my work a great deal."

"There's a post for you at Boston General if you want it, but not to rush!" The well-endowed and youthful woman said as she took Peter's arm. Matthew saw his father was happy and was happy for him. "And what of Isaac and Helen?"

"They're fine. Isaac is the parish priest in Houma and has just been honored by the Archbishop for his service. Helen is home and will be at dinner with us. Speak easy to her. She lost her intended in the war, Daniel."

Matthew went silent and felt uneasy. He and Agnes were alive and here and Helen, his dear sister, had lost her love. He thought it an unfair, strange turn that such a tragedy would interfere in her life when she was home while he suffered only memories of others he didn't know when he tasted war and death all around him for a time. He prayed she would hold up and go on to a good life though not the one she planned and that she could find happiness to match his.

"Glad to meet you, Agnes. I do hope you come to love Boston," Helen introduced herself to the Englishwoman. "I'm happy for my brother." She smiled.

"Thank you, Helen. I have met the love of my life to be sure."

"You make him happy and that's important to me. We'll have to meet sometime and do shopping. I know all the best shops and where to get the best values," she said. "You have the prettiest hair! The long waves and such a nice color brown. I can understand why he was attracted to you." She smiled.

"Thank you. And yours—the fullness and color—such lightness very much set your pretty lips. I understand you're an actress. That must be a challenging vocation—to play so many parts. I'm amazed you can put yourself in the mind and words of other people."

"It's something I have found suits me I suppose. Maybe I care little for who I am," she laughed.

"I would like to see you on stage sometime. I admire that ability and enjoy the theater. Don't you find it difficult?"

"Only the memorization—once that's done it's not hard to add my particular flavor to the dialogue. And then there's plays that require quick changes of costume!" she laughed. "Sometimes that gets rather harried—and there are men around. I still feel uncomfortable with them near. Isn't that being a silly girl?"

"I don't know." She smiled. "What's next for you?"

"I'm thinking about going to California and to find work. They are beginning to make these films out there and the money is good—so they say. If I'm lucky, I'll land some parts. If I'm not, I'll return," she sighed, suddenly becoming distant.

"I do wish you well. It's so far!"

"It may help me forget Harry." She turned her head downward then looked up again into Agnes's eyes. "But I don't wish to bring sadness into an event that is supposed to be a happy one. I'm sorry."

"I heard of your tragedy. I'm so sorry," Agnes said.

"It's life. I suppose some of us know nothing but bliss one day and the end of a whole world the next. But I am fine with it. I have to be. Thank God for my father."

"He is a fine man."

"Be quiet! He may hear you!" She found a laugh. Matthew entered the room and placed his arm around Agnes. "Well, sister. Isn't she grand? Dinner is served and I have been dispatched to bring you." He smiled.

"She and I were getting to know each other and I know you have met a wonderful woman, Matthew. I'm happy for you," Helen said.

"Did she tell you she was expecting?"

"No! Well, congratulations! I'll finally be an Aunt! How wonderful!"

Helen would meet James Riker her first day in California; he fashioned himself as a writer but worked as a stagehand and met her at a screen call. She didn't get the part but acceded dinner with him that night. After that encounter, they were never apart.

The twenties would become a raucous time with prohibition starting the decade and flapper skirts providing men with more to see that pleased the eyes than they had before. Life was loosening a great deal, and it seemed to take many people into a kind of confusion of morals. It seemed many put aside the church and God and turned to illegal drink and hedonism, casting aside most strictures that had become routine and expected. All around Peter and Gladys, Matthew and Agnes and to a lesser extent, the family in Alabama, there seemed to be a drive toward an American form of a kind of paganism and to most, immoral forms of freedom expressed inspired by something in the air, perhaps.

Daniel thought it was society gone mad by passing prohibition. Liquors and beer had been helpful in the war and innocent divergence from tedium after. Those who became addicted should not have caused the rule of the day that the government outlawed drink that had been acceptable through the ages, including the marriage ceremony attended to by Jesus Himself. But he could do nothing to stop it. And people had gone mad he thought because of the necessary undercover acts of defiance, and had allowed an excuse for other, darker, human desires to suddenly flaunt themselves. He did think Katherine looked good in a flapper though, and he did take a little shine occasionally he bought from Red Higgins, a black bootlegger who brewed the best.

That summer was a hot one. He had been back in the States for a couple of years and remained in Marshall County to attend to his father's affairs, as the man became infirm. His father died in June, and he thought best to run the farm and stay in contact with his uncles and the rest of the family until it sold. His love, Katherine, married him last year and moved into the family home. They were still trying to have children.

Irene lived with them and became like Katherine's mother, full of love and grace, and not wishing to be an interference or burden. She stayed mindful of the couple, did the garden and quilting, read her Bible and wrote letters to everyone she had. Through her nineties she wrote and expressed every detail and offered recipes and other household hints to all her children. Mass was important to her and she took the sacrament every day except Saturdays.

The old cedar chest had rarely been opened and during the weeks following the service and grieving when his mother passed away, Daniel finally lifted the top to sort out all the family heirlooms and memories before moving to Texas to work for Standard Oil in Houston. The farm was profitable one year and a loss the next, and it had come the time when he thought he should apply his education to a field in which a steady income could be generated for the family. He had been hired to supervise accounting for the firm in the general office and had the opportunity to provide a good living for Katherine. Andrew and John had helped with the farm but were no longer able to do the work of their youth. Tess and Nathan were still in Texas where they were parents of adult children, Sarah and George, born before the turn of the century. He would find them once he moved to Houston; the occasional visit between years had been good visits, but it had been six years since their last. The children were establishing their own lives, and Tess and Nathan were older and not able to travel well anymore.

He opened the top wide. Inside were papers and garlands gently laid on top of photographs and books. He peeled one layer at a time until he found Jebediah McCray's uniform of the Confederate Army. It had been years. Daniel stopped and read some of the papers his grandfather kept and was struck by how much alike he and his grandfather were. He thought he could have written the same words dealing with the war and its aftermath on the mind. It seemed they had come full circle and learned of honor and God and the respect for the fellow next to you from the same teacher but in a class separated by more than fifty years.

The words of his grandfather were words he heard before from him and his father; they were loving tributes to family and the country for life itself. The depth of his appreciation had easily become the depth of his appreciation for everything. It was the act of taking nothing for granted and understanding the Lord sees one through if asked with a sincere and clean heart. There can be no hidden human agenda; it must be truth. It was as if a ghost lived with his family and told them and must have been every generation back to the days in Scotland. And he was a convincing ghost, he thought, for the McCray men to have stayed the course.

He knew he would take the chest with him intact. Nothing was to be disturbed or taken. It had to be left as it was packed—a life's story, a man's deepest convictions that drove him every day, in every work, springing every joy. Everything was there, the love and triumphs, the joy and sadness of each family member as life rolled on toward the day. And he knew he was but another and God willing would pass it to his sons and daughters. He left the room after gently closing the top and replacing the blanket that covered it for years and found Katherine working in the kitchen and suddenly looking powerfully appealing. He wanted to make love to her now and although he didn't ask her gently, she enjoyed the attention.

"What's gotten into you, Daniel?" she asked as he was kissing her blushing face hard and finding her lips, cutting off words in mid-sentence. He began tearing away at her dress as she held her arms around him. The raven-haired beauty stood with him and helped him past the buttons and zippers. The next deep moments they both had no thoughts but were totally immersed in mind and reacting with their bodies to the heat of human passion and natural contact. Each movement brought quick desperate exhales of breath and more intensity than either had ever known until finally the release blessed them and so it was to be, also were blessed with a child in nine months.

"Oh, Daniel! I must say…never have I felt that way. You are wonderful!"

"You are wonderful, dear Katherine. I love you so much!" he breathed.

"Should I..." she stopped and nestled into his side putting her head into the gap between his arm and shoulder. She sighed.

"Yes, dear. Me too," he breathed. After another restful few moments, he asked her about Texas. "Are you happy to leave?"

"I'm happy with you, darling. I'll go wherever you go, you know."

"I want you to love where it is."

"I will, dear. As long as I'm with you, I will love it."

He visited Red Higgins to stock several of the illegal gallons for their move—he didn't need the government to tell him what was right and wrong. He knew that from priests and the good book, and he knew the intrusion on his freedom could not stand, at least as far as he could take it as one man.

"You won't be seeing me, Red, as we're moving to Houston."

"Well, Mr. Daniel. It's been good to know you. Come back if ever you come close to Etowah, you hear?"

"I will, Red. You be careful and don't get caught."

"I will, Daniel. Old Red here is always careful and won't let 'em gets me." He laughed. "If they does, I be headed for Orleans."

"Well, I hear it's mighty nice down there," Daniel smiled. "I'll be closer than you, and I will miss this." He shook one of the jugs. "It's kept us warm at night!"

"It'll do that for sure," he said as he laughed. "And it'll fire up for you too if'n you need it."

"You know, Red. I'm sad about leaving home. Haven't been away from the state but once, and I am already regretting it."

"There's not much here for a smart man like yourself, Daniel. I knows a smart man when I see one."

"That's kind, Red. I'm not nearly as smart as you," he said as he smiled. "You have your feet firmly planted and are an institution around these parts. Just stay out of trouble. God forbid you wind up in prison. They won't have a bed big enough for you!" He laughed. "Take care and tell your family hello for me."

"Yea..." He looked squarely in his eyes. "You, too. I know what your grandfather did, Daniel. Your good people."

That night they started. He was jolted awake by the vision of the last German he shot; he stared at him with hollow eyes asking him over and over, *why*, when he was no threat—only lying wounded by the side of that bridge fate took him to die young. Only a soldier in a different uniform he answered his country's call too and left parents and friends forever because he shot the man again. His eyes were wide with fear and pleading in those last few seconds and Daniel had none of it. Mercilessly he took him from them and now it was on him as his face haunted him now; details he hadn't noticed in the rush had now vividly, forcefully replaced peace in his mind as he saw the youthful look of a boy who entered the world only to fall on his first venture. He awoke in a sweat pouring from his forehead.

In California Ruth and Jules were in their mid-fifties and enjoying the life. The several cruises they made to Hawaii had been romantic escapes from a romantic San Diego—at least it was always that way for them. The Creeless name had become known in the circle of friendly and generous society that included property owners, business people and newspaper owners. There were three dailies being printed and each had their own pet political and social agenda—but each also sold as much ad space as they could.

Ruth was childless and volunteered in the hospital on the pediatric ward where she met children with varying seriousness of illness, wounds and burns owing to terrible accidents at home. One case in particular took her eyes. The boy was sick with pneumonia and had come from a cotton mill where the dust had contributed to his lung full and probably fatal condition. His name was Tommy, and he came from a fatherless home where his mother worked as a laundress and housekeeper for one of the editors of the *San Diego News Journal*. Only fourteen he had worked ten-hour days since he was ten, and the sight of his thin, sickly body that made his head appear oversized hurt her heart. She wanted to take his pain away, to make him well, to make him happy and to live a childhood many were not.

Blissfully unaware until Tommy, she saw it first hand finally and knew. The *Journal* railed against child labor but was closer than it would have it said to the problem. The editor knew of the woman's child and held her wages as low as he could. It was the way and he couldn't be faulted; the prevailing wage was set by the market and fair. Tommy's mother didn't want him in the mills; she wanted him in school. They needed the few dollars he made each week to buy food. Had they needed heat, they would have surely starved, she thought.

"How are you today, Tommy?" she asked him. He was sitting halfway up on the single, small bed in the ward. There was a bowl next to him and a pitcher of water on the table that was between two beds. The boy next to him was lying with set fractures to both legs, done by his cruel stepfather in a fit of rage. On the other side of him, a boy of eleven was sick with a cancer that slowly and painfully consumed him—only the opium kept him from going insane with pain. His time was short and his pain would end for all time soon. Ruth tried to avoid crying but couldn't.

"Take this towel, Miss Ruth," Tommy said. "It's okay to cry. My mother told me so."

"And how are you?"

"I'm fine," he wheezed. "I got this letter from Colonel Abrams today! He was in the war you know."

"That's good, Tommy. Colonel Abrams must be a nice man."

"Yes, ma'am. He says here that he wants to come and see me. He heard about me and..." He stopped and coughed for several minutes. "I told him I wanted to be in the Navy, but he says the Army is best. He likes when they play football." She let the water flow down her cheeks keeping her eyes on him. "I would like to play football some day."

"I'm sure you would, Tommy. Maybe soon you can," she whimpered.

"Will you take the towel, Miss Ruth? Don't cry, ma'am. Try not to be sad," he wheezed. "I get pie today. You can have some too."

She glanced around and explained to Tommy she needed to visit others and would return to him soon. "There are some boys and girls here who also hurt, Tommy. I should see to them a while."

"Yes, ma'am! I'm glad you do that. They like company. Davey over there don't get much." He pointed to the boy whose legs were set with boards and wraps and roped still. "I feel sorry for him. His mother can't come and his stepfather won't ever come."

"I see. I'm sure his mother comes as much as she can."

"Yes, ma'am."

"I'll be right over there, Tommy. Now rest easy and read this." She handed him a book she had brought. It was a collection of western novels bound together in one volume. "There are a lot of exciting stories in this, Tommy."

"Thank you, ma'am."

"I could think of no one else who would enjoy it more!" she said to a broad smile. She gently moved his hair to the side of his head and then left him for a while.

"Hello, Davey. I said your name right, didn't I?"

"Yes, ma'am."

"It's no fun right now not to run, is it? I bet you can run fast!" she said.

"I'm a fair runner, ma'am." He paused. "I can't run now."

"You will again. I'm Ruth Creeless and I work around here…when did you come?"

"Last night."

"What happened, Davey?"

"He was mad at me and mother. He broke my nose and hit my legs with a poker."

"I'm sorry, Davey."

"That's why I'm here…he lied too when the police came to get him."

"He lied to the police?"

"Yes, ma'am. And said if we told on him he would do worse next time." He stopped. "Please don't say I told on him." She looked on the little figure, his face wrapped and covered with white concealing his nose and tied around the back of his head. "Please?"

"Don't worry, Davey. I won't cause him to hurt you or your mother anymore," she said, reaching deep for courage not to cry again. She knew he was almost certainly going to be hurt again and again unless he was removed from the house. *How many more suffer like this?* She wondered and cried sick inside herself. She had to do something about it. This one little boy must be saved from the cruelty and allowed to grow up and enjoy a happy and safe childhood. *Surely to God there's a way!* she screamed inside herself.

"I want to ask you about Tommy and Davey in the ward, miss."

"What can I do for you?" the nurse asked.

"I want to know how I can take them to live with me and my husband for a while."

"I don't know. You'll have to see the police I suspect and learn if there is a way. I haven't seen it done before myself. Good luck! It is sad what happens to them, isn't it?"

"Yes. It cannot be. There must be a way, surely."

"Maybe their parents will allow it. They may not have the money to keep them you see. I know that's true in many cases."

"Thank you, ma'am. Can I get their names?"

"Certainly. See the head nurse at the desk."

Ruth used the telephone at the nurse's station to call Jules and tell him of her plans. He didn't say a word as she went on about how they must do this. He knew they must take the children too for the sake of having a good conscious. She said she would call their friend Judge Johnson and tell him he must prepare the legal arrangements and that he had no choice. The parents had no number so she set off for each address in her automobile driving fast and determined. She would plead if she had to, pay them if she had to, or commit to whatever they needed for the privilege boarding their sons.

The first door she found was that of Tommy's mother. It was an address that took her to a row of cheap hotels and boarding houses in the city's seamier side she had hardly ever seen before—but read about in one of the papers crusading by their will the plight of the homeless and near homeless. She was not answering and was probably not at home so she drove to Davey's address, a small whitewashed frame on the same side of town. She heard the footsteps come toward her and for a moment felt a queasy stomach. She pushed inward to rest it and steeled her gaze and her spirit on the objective. And that was to save a little boy.

"Mrs. Foster?"

"Yes."

"Mrs. Foster...I am Ruth Creeless and I do work at the hospital where your son is being treated. May I come in?"

"Yes...of course. How is my Davey?"

"He's able to talk and doing fairly well."

"Good. For a minute I thought something had happened. I don't get to see him as much as I want to, you understand...busy around here."

"I see. Well, the reason I'm here is that I would like to take Davey home and care for him. I've got the time and can see that he gets all he needs," she said, watching for the woman's reaction. "I mean no disrespect, but I have grown fond of him and just feel I can do things for him you want to do but can't," she said in a businesslike, rapid-fire set of words. "Of course, you would be welcome to come and spend as much time as you can with him. I'll even arrange for your transport." She could see this was a lot for the woman to grasp at once. She also knew the mother knew the boy was in danger if he returned to the home.

Her new husband was an angry drunk and showed that after their marriage last year. He turned on them both and allowed a hateful, violent side to emerge. She wanted to leave him but felt she had nowhere to go and be safe. She knew this was an opportunity for one of them to be safe and decided to let it happen for his sake.

"You're kind, Mrs. Creeless. I guess it would be good for Davey to stay with you for a while...understand I must sort some things out here, and he'll be better off if he didn't have to be around for a time."

"I understand completely. I will be his guardian only, I can assure you, and will take good care of him," she said, noticing the woman staring at her new automobile. "I will make the arrangements and here," she paused, "let me write down the address. I'll have a taxi pick you up any day you wish."

"Yes. Thank you, Mrs. Creeless."

One done and one to go—this day, she thought as she headed back to Tommy's apartment. This time she found the boy's mother in the company of a man she thought she recognized but couldn't quite place. He didn't seem of the neighborhood as he was finely appointed and dressed in a fine wool suit and acted embarrassed when she introduced herself and interrupted their hastily arranged liaison. Ruth knew what was going on before her eyes right away. *Poor Tommy,* she thought. *It has come to this for his mother.* She was a plain-looking and thin woman, whose eye shadow and lipstick seemed to have been used hurriedly and out of place for her. She quickly agreed to let her tend to Tommy for an unspecified period of time.

Strange events were shaping a future that no one could expect. An obscure German rant was capturing some headlines in the papers, and its spokesman, a former corporal in the German army named Adolph Hitler, had been arrested and put into prison. More at home that gave rise to some optimism was the arrest of the Ku Klux Klan Grand Wizard on murder charges.

Agnes gave birth to a girl, and they named her Claire. Matthew received an offer for the *Boston Globe* and went to work for the paper again. He was no longer reporting local events and human-interest stories. Todefer assigned him to follow the political landscape and report from Washington D.C. He, Agnes and Claire moved to Georgetown that summer as events were unfolding that began to wedge their way into Congress and the public's eye. The treaty was universally recognized as a failure, but there was little momentum in America to push for some revisions to enable Germany to become a viable economic power—and there remained more than distrust of the German government and its penchant for warring against France and England.

Claire was born with a headful of black hair that lightened during her first year. Not one who met her said she was anything but the most beautiful baby they've seen. She was walking by one and talking by two. Everything was in order for the Boston McCrays, and life held much promise. Across the nation, new industry blossomed as rubber, textiles, steel, automobile manufacturing and parts suppliers figured prominently, providing an explosion of jobs available for people to augment farm income. The service industry bloomed too as a new phenomenon of service stations, motels, and department stores showed on the landscape in every city and most towns. The telephone began to be used by most households, and every home had at least one radio.

The wild twenties allowed a market for the speakeasy, dance clubs, burlesque and movie theaters. There were alcohol-driven parties and Hollywood parties to read about. Scandal and avarice held interest, as many people were curious about hedonism let loose in parts of America. Amongst it all there were the McCrays and the Creeless family, the Hensleys and the Rikers. As generations passed, new ones began living and working in America.

Chapter 16

He went about his business when he noticed them. He turned his head away to escape a confrontation. He hoped they wouldn't draw him into it, as he had no patience for foolishness. *People who don't act right will answer for it with their eternal souls,* he reassured himself. The young women walked away and into the club. They were flappers who wore makeup, bobbed hair and smoked cigarettes.

He heard about them and thought it shocking many began acting out this way—and the dances were wild and energetic, often showing too much leg to suit him if she were his sister, daughter or wife—but he enjoyed the sights more than he would let on in "polite company" as he put it. He heard about them and their smoking and petting parties and the jazz and drinking. He thought this was the devil's work bringing the country down. Things were changing.

Daniel and Katherine had four children born between 1920 and 1925. David was the first, then Rachel, Victoria, and Thomas in 1925. He made a life for them in Houston and took his job seriously, often spending ten to twelve hours a day downtown. Standard Oil paid him well enough for the family to live in a seven-room house built in the Pasadena section of the growing city where he could easily drive the twenty minutes. Katherine worked hard in the home and cared for their babies twenty-four hours a day. Once each reached nine months of age, she could relax some, knowing she would not lose them in their sleep. The family managed a trip back to Alabama once each year to visit the aging family who remained in Marshall County. The couple spent most of the time with just each other out of necessity and would take the children out for strolls and an occasional visit to Galveston where they would walk the beach and collect seashells.

"Katherine…I love you so much. Are you happy, dear?"

"Why, yes, dearest. You've given me a wonderful life. Are you happy as well?" she said with a slight Irish brogue still present in her voice.

"Yes, of course. I am a lucky man!" he said with a smile, but the routine was a burden and the weeks passed with little change or excitement. "I would like us to take a trip and visit a cousin near New Orleans. He's a priest and I have hardly seen him over the years."

"I would like that. I've heard New Orleans is very pretty."

"Yes, it is. There are some of the first buildings ever built still standing and full of history."

"And your cousin? This is Isaac—the chaplain?"

"Yes, the same I told you about. Hails from Boston where he has a brother. His sister is in California. I believe she's still married to a Riker. Anyway, we can learn how everyone is doing by seeing him, I'm sure. And while we're there, we can enjoy the food and wine a good amount."

"I would like us to go, Daniel. We need to get away a bit."

"Very well. I'll make arrangements at work to take a long holiday soon."

"Thank you, dear." She smiled.

Helen and James Riker were married in the early twenties and worked in the film industry. He landed a job as a technical assistant with United Artists, and she became a costume and makeup specialist although she still dreamed of acting on set. The studio's most prolific producer, Harwick, liked the couple and trusted them. They were fresh and full of energy; she was attractive in his eyes and having her even this close improved the looks of the place, he thought. He had enough projects to bring them into the organization in minor capacities. In her time she took parts offered to her in downtown stage plays—just enough to have a few lines to say that others wrote. It allowed her to be someone else for a while.

The couple had heir first baby, Luke, in 1923, then John in 1925 and Matthew in 1928. They managed by living in a tenant home near the bus stop for a direct route to the studios. At first she took the baby with her and cared for him in the makeup room; later they were able to afford a nanny part time during the week. The strains began to show in the marriage because of his wondering eye and her work with the children when they were not at work. They held on though because in the times that is what most couples did for the sake of the children.

"You're late again, James," she said.

"Yes...there was a lot more to do on the set today. Why?"

"It just seems you're late often since last month. Are they working that many hours?"

"You know how it goes. They'll stay until a scene is finished, and sometimes that takes several tries. We're getting close though, and I can see an end to it."

"I know the United Group wasn't filming today, James. I called Joanie, and she said everyone had left. I believe you're hiding something from me. Now, where were you?" she asked, as she watched him turn away from her and wring his hands in angst. "Well? Tell me, James. Who were you with?"

"No one, Helen. I was working, and I don't care what Joanie says. She wasn't there." He looked down and away and began to step out of the room.

"I don't know, James. It doesn't seem right."

"Are you saying you don't believe me? I work very hard to provide for you and the children, and you don't give me credit....All I get are suspicions from you, and I'm getting sick of it!"

"I know you work hard. So do I! I work all day too and then all night with diapers and feedings and...You don't care, do you? You say one thing and no one else ever says the same thing. Are you cheating on me, James?"

"Of course not!" he lied. "Now I want a drink, and I'd like to try to relax! Do you mind?" He began cursing her, his first time, and took several hard and fast swallows of a mixed drink poured in haste to ease his conscious.

"What are you doing, James?"

"I'm drinking a little to forget your damn questions! Just leave me be, woman!" he said angrily and took another gulp, swiping the few books lying on the table off to make room for his ashtray and drink. "I can't stand your constant nagging! Leave me alone!"

"Alright, James. I'll leave you alone. But this is not over! I'll find out who she is and what you've been doing!" She went into the room next to where he was sitting and picked up Matthew, the smallest and held him to her chest. She thought back to when they first met and found each other's company to be all they wanted at the time. There had been a change since the days when he spent every minute he could with her and she with him. He had become distant since the children were born, and she couldn't help but envision some would-be actress or hanger-on taking his time and affection to play him. He was not the man she met.

She thought back to their time in the park and how they used to swoon and talk softly to each other all the while shutting out the world around them as if they were alone and meant to cling to each other. She remembered their quiet walks, how they held each other until the last moment before going their separate ways to work and how much joy there was when they saw each other again in the evenings. Small celebrations for having work during a week with inexpensive champagne would highlight the success of reaching for the status that seemed important in the studios. She remembered their toasting each other on the beach where the red, blue and gray sunset from a dark artist covered the California coast on several Saturday nights and feeling drawn to him in body and mind. She thought he was drawn to her the same way. She remembered the evening they made love one night on the sand while surrounded by the rhythms of the sea and its gentle concert and how sweet it was and how long they stayed after, sleeping under bright and distinctive stars in each other's arms. She remembered her mother, barely, and how she thought she would be happy for her.

She began to cry and pulled two-year-old Matthew closer to her, tucking his little head into her shoulder. The namesake of her brother was the smallest baby and had been born the earliest. It was God telling her enough—that James wasn't what he seemed, she thought, and this baby would be her last. She didn't know and her mind was spinning in confusion and worry, not letting her see through the fog clearly, but constantly telling her all was not right in their home. *Could it be me?* she thought, feeling as if she may have done something or ignored him to the point of driving him away. *Maybe it's my figure?* she worried.

But her figure was still pretty good. She knew she had worked very hard to lose the weight after each birth and was within ten pounds of her weight when she first met him. She told herself that these things couldn't be—that all she had done is work hard and mind the children and did all she could for him. And the way he returned her faithfulness and effort was to become a stranger. It didn't seem right or fair, but it was happening before her eyes.

James had noticed her on the set when the studio hired several extras to play flapper girls in the background of a bar scene. She seemed to look at him with more than a passing interest, and he took no caution but made his way to flirt with her, acting shy and reserved at first and then asking her to have a drink with him after the shoot. She was a very young-looking woman—easily passing for fourteen—and part of her personality was a constant giggle when she was around others. Her bobbed hair, small face and petite body seemed to shout, *Take me now!* They were unspoken words he heard only in his mind—a weak man open to straying—and he did take her the first opportunity he had. He took all of her in the back room of the equipment storage area. That was weeks ago and had become a habit every day since then. He enjoyed her girlish body and had to have it as often as he could manage. He also had to keep his affair from Helen; a break-up of their marriage would be disastrous for his finances and possibly his career, even in Hollywood. The most popular actors and actresses could do a lot, but the employees were subject to intense scrutiny in those days. Producers and directors didn't need the distraction of low-level employees bringing any confusion or scandal to their studios.

Luke was six now and as a two-year-old would stand quietly beside their bed and look at his parents as they turned in, James often with a book, cookies and milk to read himself to sleep while snacking. There was a wonder in his eyes and he must have been taking it all in, standing there and looking expressionless—a beautiful baby boy whose presence was sweet and humbling as he looked on them. Helen watched him and loved him deeply. She smiled at her son and the others every moment she was with them. She knew she should be home with them, but it seemed the family needed the money she could earn since James' job wasn't paying enough to provide the food and rent for the family.

That evening she left him sitting alone, drinking the blended whiskey he preferred and didn't know what to do. Her mind was tired even thinking about it. She prayed herself to sleep with Matthew and Luke in her arms, trying to hide the tears. James was not the man he had to be for his sons, and she felt she was not the woman. *Show me, God, what to do. Please, I ask you from the bottom of my heart! I must have Your divine guidance in this...Only You can help us. Please help us,* she sobbed and held her babies tight.

The weeks passed slowly and James came home more often on time. He was still seeing her, but unknown to him she was also seeing an assistant director—a studious man, also married, who could help her get more parts. She began the withdrawal from James as she took another step toward her hopes of achieving a measure of fame and fortune. He asked her what's wrong and she said that since he was married, she felt they should move on for the sake of his wife and family.

Peter and Gladys were boating alone off the coast and enjoying the sun that summer on the small craft. The waves were modest to begin the day, that Sunday, and they were having a good time breathing the salt air and feeling the breeze against their skin as the boat rocked gently back and forth and forward into whitecaps. He took her farther out and was caught up in a stream that pulled the craft even farther out to sea. But it was nice still, although the swells were becoming larger and larger. Finally they became frighteningly large, and Peter told her they must turn back.

"We'll be in some trouble if we don't, dear."

"I want to go back, too, Peter. I'm feeling a little nausea—these waves are pretty rough!"

He turned to and powered the engine as fast as it would take them, but it seemed they were making no progress. "I must be in a rip!" he shouted as the wind picked up velocity and became louder past their ears. "I must turn and run with it! Hold on, Gladys!" He angled the boat toward the sea again to pick up the diagonal direction home and let off the gas some to ride. The fuel would only last them another hour, so he figured on conserving as much as he could. He looked up and saw the gulls quickly flying inland as the sea seemed to want to belch them out of its gut and was becoming angry looking. The boat was being tossed like a rag doll, easily without effort and without regard to consequence. He looked at Gladys and feared for her life and secondly his own. They were in trouble and may be lost, he thought.

Suddenly the engine stopped, flooded with seawater spray and cold to any sort of ignition attempt. He turned it over a few times and could hear the battery weaken each time. He tried the pull rope, but that didn't work either. "Hold on, Gladys!" he shouted.

"I'm scared, Peter!" she shouted back, the fear in her voice obvious and chilling to Peter. He was scared too and had little he could do about their drifting farther out to sea and being tossed by the waves and swells and feeling the wind carry in a storm. He looked into the horizon and saw the wall of darkness descending toward them in a fury of nature.

"We're going to be hit hard, Gladys! Let me lash you to the cabin!" he shouted and tied her at the waist to a gaff rig on one side and a bow cleat from the other. He lashed himself to the steering post just as they were hit the first time by an overpowering swell from the angry squall that shook, rose and tossed the craft like the insignificant speck it was. Thrown into the air, the boat turned and landed upright. Peter looked at Gladys and saw water streaming from her wet figure, her head down, her hair hanging lifelessly, her body tied in nearly a spread-eagle fashion, and he knew their time was nearly over. She raised her head slightly and looked at him without trying to say a word. He saw her eyes and the fear. A sea in rage was taking them, and they were helpless to do anything to stop it. He loved her and prayed this would not be their end.

The second swell took the small wooden boat down deep and then upward, throwing the craft over and under the water; it rose again and bobbed with the rhythm for a few minutes, the bottom visible as a last testament before it sank out of sight and took Peter and Gladys with it. He couldn't close his mouth. He knew the same was happening to her. A power was such that he was forced to swallow; the sudden and overwhelming strength of heavy sea pushed water into his lungs, and before he lost consciousness, he felt a strange warmth and contentment—a beautiful, pleasing dream he was seeing and feeling. He saw Maria, Isaac, Matthew, and Helen—in their younger years when she was his beauty and the children were toddlers in a happy home—and he was there with them. The water entered his lungs easy and took him without a whimper. He felt an unexpected, pleasant sensation as if he'd been drugged though he knew this was drowning. He saw Gladys in a glimpse just before the eternal sleep took him and knew the same was happening for her; she must feel the same ease. He felt his heart smile then, followed the bright hollow light and nothing more.

The family heard nothing of them. It was as if the couple were swallowed up and taken away forever. Helen sensed they were gone from this earth, but had no proof. Isaac prayed for his father and stepmother and knew he Lord had control of everything. Matthew tried in vain to find them by tracking every lead he could find through friends and others as he searched records and their home for any clue to their whereabouts. Finally he checked the docks and confirmed they had taken the boat out and never returned. There was no radio, no signal, nothing. Only the faint recollection of the manager of the Harbor Marina gave him the answer most probable as to where his father was.

Matthew looked out to the sea and prayed for the man who taught him everything of value and worth, the man who allowed him to go to Europe even against his better judgment but for the sake of seeing a child through as he saw each of them through. He remembered the gentle man who took them as little ones and brought them to a new home after losing their mother and did the best job one could do in providing everything—from spiritual awareness and appreciation to understanding their place in the world as curious observers and motivated contributors to society in the ways of their choosing. He remembered a loving father who left himself with each of them. He remembered his father telling them of Thomas and Mabel and how they carved out a good life and remained faithful throughout their lives to each other, their child and to work. He came gently and must have surely left gently regardless of the swampy muck of violence that penetrated his life.

Soon, as Matthew wrote of the resurgence of German militarism, the stock market collapsed as though fakery must have held it all together until truth finally wielded a mighty fist and struck the economy a fatal blow. People were ruined financially and many were also ruined lives because they let it. The roaring twenties drew to a depressed close as though God Himself was punishing the brash new country—and the world—for its puffery and dedication to riches rather than that which was important. In its wake, starvation became a real possibility for millions and the soup lines became the lifeline back to the church for most.

"You lost your job?" Helen said to James who stood at the arched doorway into the small parlor room of their home. The children were in elementary school and oblivious to what had happened that October other than some mention by a teacher that the markets were correcting themselves. Not understanding anything about what she meant, they looked forward to the Thanksgiving holiday coming soon and all the turkey and dressing and trimmings.

"They cut back and told me they no longer required my services. Damn! Now I don't know what I'm going to do." He looked down and contained the beginnings of tears.

"We will get by, James. Don't worry," she said while wondering herself what they were going to do. Each payday was spent before it was received and one missed meant bills unpaid.

"It will be alright," she said, not knowing how. "The children will be home soon, and I think we should plan what we are to do before telling them."

"You're right, Helen. They wouldn't understand, and we shouldn't worry them with this until we see."

She began to think of all she could sell to make ends meet for a while—if she could find buyers. She also thought of leaving Los Angeles if neither could find work soon. It was a large city and their chances were good, she thought, to try here first before moving back to Boston for the charity of her family. Surely things weren't as bad as the papers reported, but she knew they probably were. She thought of Isaac and Houma and the possibility of working the fish camps there but knew the chances were slim and the money very little.

"Where are you going?" she asked him as he left the house.

"Nowhere."

"I wish you would stay home and help figure this out, James."

"Here." He laid a few dollars on the table in the kitchen. "Take this and use the savings we have to buy food. I may be gone for a while."

"What do you mean?" she asked.

"I'm going away, Helen. I can't stay here any longer."

"You're going to leave me and the children here alone?" she asked as he walked out. "James!" she shouted after him. "James! Come back, James! We need you!" But he walked on and didn't turn back toward her. "Damn you, James!" she shouted, the fear gripping her to a reality that seemed the worst.

She cried loudly and couldn't stop. Her tears ran—a continuous stream of frustration and confusion. She hated him. She felt the heaviest weight she ever felt; worse than losing Harry, worse than giving birth, worse than anything she had been through.

"Why, God? Why are You punishing me?" she cried out. "What would You have me do, Lord?"

The children would be home soon, and she didn't know what she could or would tell them. She had to have some answers, but they didn't come quickly. She buried her head into a pillow and cried out the last tears before rising in anger and let it take her for a time to put an end to the crying. She suddenly felt strength, enough strength to see them through anything, she resolved. She hadn't married well and was going to fix it! And her children would eat!

Helen thought it right for her to wait for James to return; perhaps he would come around to being a man. She returned to United and offered to work any number of hours free, doing anything the company needed. Harwick paid her wages out of his own pocket to start. Gone was the nanny, but she was allowed to bring the children with her as the producer wanted to do what he could to keep her. Harwick died before two years passed—a sudden death from a stroke while on the set, and her job was over. James had not even called them. She was well over him and thought again about moving the children away from the city that seemed to evolve into a cold, distant, and cruel place.

The first call she made was to Matthew. Her brother would bring her home and help them until she could make it on her own again. He did tell her he would wire a transfer of funds so she and the children could take the train to Washington. "And we have plenty of room, sister! Don't worry about anything; you'll be fine here!" he told her confidently. "I'm so looking forward to seeing you and my nephews! And Claire will be so excited to finally see the cousins she's heard so much about! Please come!"

"Thank you so much, Matthew! You're so kind. I will repay you."

"Please, Helen," he said into the mouthpiece. "Please don't even think about that! My gracious I won't have it! Now how soon can you make the trip?"

"I don't know, but I'll find out as soon as we are finished."

"Call the station now. I can have the wire done in an hour," he said in an excited and happy voice.

"You're as good as Father, Matthew," she cried with joy.

"No, I'm not, but we're lucky to have each other—all of us. Isaac will be happy to hear of your move, too. He thinks California was too far." He laughed. "I know he'll come see you and the children here soon. Please go ahead and find the next train, and I'll call you at five."

She hurriedly got the departure times and arrivals. Within a week she would be gone. Leaving everything was easy as she gathered up her children and a few clothes and boarded the train. There was nothing from James. He was gone and would never see the children again. He had left the house that afternoon and went straight out and bought the first fifth of whiskey of what would become for him a fatal habit.

Winter brought her cold air and snow, laying the beautiful white blanket across the countryside; the thick quilt of crystals caused it all to slow down. Agnes helped the victims of flu and falls as many came to the emergency rooms during the weather. The snow kept falling steadily and slowly and within days, there were eighteen inches laying siege with drifts up to over four feet high accumulating at corners of houses and fences, against parked automobiles, and in large concrete drains, angled walls converging to the bottom straight pathways that were stopped. As she came closer to Washington, the train was slower, plowing through the fresh snow toward Washington, and the scenery was art appreciated again. She had not seen such beauty for several years, and it made her feel she was home.

"Luke, John..." she spoke to her oldest. "We're almost there. Time to get our bags put back together." She reached for Matthew and cleaned his mouth and face with a damp cloth. "Hold still. You're going to see your uncle. You want to be clean, don't you?" she asked the youngster. The older boys put everything back in its place quickly and zipped the bags. The contents were all they had now.

"Look out the window, boys."

Luke and John were fixed to snow they had never seen before. As the train was leaving Virginia, they could see some other children in the distance outside playing, running, jumping and sliding down small hills. "That looks fun, Momma!" John said. "Can we play like that?"

"Surely. It'll only be a little while. I'm sure Uncle Matthew will know where you can go. But you'll have to dress warm." She smiled.

Matthew waited at the station with Agnes and Claire and saw them step off onto the platform, each holding one bag. He rushed toward them and embraced his sister. "Hello, Helen! So good to see you!" he said.

"Hello, Matthew, Agnes. And this is Claire?"

"Yes," he said as the little girl curtseyed as she had been properly trained.

"She's beautiful! Meet your cousins, Claire. Luke, John and Matthew are happy to meet you!"

"What have you heard from Isaac?" she smiled toward her brother.

"He's fine. He managed to make the trip for the memorial service last year," he said. "He'll be visiting this spring and wants to see you and the boys. He's growing fat he says on all the cooking the ladies do down there. No…Things are well with him and he is part of their family. He said the people are great and earthy, full of humor and wine," he laughed. "So is he."

"I do so much appreciate your help, Matthew! I don't want to be a burden and will take care of everything as soon as I can, you know."

"Please, Helen. Don't feel that way." He smiled.

"You are welcome here, Helen, and we want you to stay," Agnes said and smiled.

"Thank you."

They went to the Georgetown home and remembered their father. "I miss him, Matthew. I wished I hadn't been away for so long."

"He was a great man. I know he's in heaven with Mother." He looked down. "I miss him, too."

"I wonder what happened."

"I don't know any more than what I said on the telephone. He and Gladys were lost at sea and have not been found. You know—at least he didn't linger in a bed before he died. I would have hated that for him."

"I suppose," she said. "Dear Father. He should not be gone. I'm so sorry I couldn't be here." She wept.

"We all understand, Helen. Please don't feel that way! He wasn't here after all. It was simply something for us—not him." He smiled at his sister. "Agnes has a pot of soup and cornbread for everyone—have something to eat while I put your things in the rooms you'll have."

"Thank you, Matthew. Now…tomorrow I wish to find employment."

"You don't waste any time do you, Helen?" He smiled. "Can't you relax for even a little while?"

"No. I must get our lives back together and take care of these boys. It's up to me and me alone."

"I suspect it's always been."

"I should like to look at your paper and read the employment ads."

"I have something for you to look at, sister. The *Times* needs a secretary and I told Smith about you. Do you think that would be something you'd consider?"

"Times are so bad. I would consider anything! Thank you again, Matthew."

"You never know, it could lead into more if you like it over there. They're competitors but nice people." He laughed. "Watch out for Greenlee though! As soon as he sees you, he'll try to buy you a drink!"

"Oh, one of those?" She laughed.

"Yea…he has a habit when it comes to the ladies."

"I'll watch out for him." She laughed.

"Good!" He poured the soup and served each of them. "This will warm you, young men," he said and watched her cool Matthew's bowl by gently blowing across the rim. "Old Greenlee will hire you, Helen. Be gentle." He laughed. "The poor old Hoover Republican is still reeling from the election of Roosevelt. But he says he needs someone."

"I look forward to meeting him."

"I want you and the boys to plan on living here for as long as you want. Agnes has already contacted the school and we're all set. I'll take them Monday."

"Thank you, brother. I'm supposed to see him at nine?"

"Yes, but he is often late so you may have to wait."

"I have the time," she chortled. "That's all I have."

Helen arrived early and was shown to a seat in the lobby. She watched people pass her and enter the large, busy office where many sat in front of typewriters and began their morning by sipping coffee and smoking cigarettes, flipping through pages of something and chatting with each other. There were many stories to write from the Roosevelt New Deal initiatives to Japan's blustering and continued aggression in Asia and the *Night of the Long Knives* in Germany. There were profiles of world leaders to share with the public from Stalin to Hitler and Chamberlain, and there were the isolationists, the communist, and Nazi movements in America, which sprung up to capture the interests of people inclined to seek some security on the edges for themselves. It helped many to forget their lot and think on things outside themselves. And there was the routine; stories of bazaars and graduations, house fires and accidents, and the latest fashions in men's and women's clothing.

She watched them from the lobby as she waited and thought she could write too if given the chance—and it would pay more than typing what someone handed her often in handwriting difficult to decipher. Impulsively she turned the front of her hair farther down the lines of her forehead and across her cheeks. She redid her lipstick and checked her eye shadow. Greenlee would see her at her best, she thought. She had nothing to lose. He hired her on sight after a twenty-minute interview. On her second day he asked her to have coffee with him at lunch.

She would remain with the paper for over thirty years, breaking into writing and editing. She was smart and imaginative, able to use words to describe detail to the readers, which captured their interest. Greenlee did invite her to see him socially, and they became a couple within a month. She thought of her father and what he would think, but also thought of her boys and what they needed. He wouldn't object to her doing the job and the manner she used to open the opportunity was resourcefulness, she thought, nothing different. And Greenlee was a nice man. His potbelly, receding hairline, and cigar habit didn't turn her away from his warm and sincere smile; she enjoyed his company and his wit. She realized after the first few dates she would have seen him in any circumstance had they been brought together.

Within a year a new German leader would emerge from relative obscurity and become chancellor of the nation. The Unites States government had set in the Stinson Doctrine, which formally declared that Japan's efforts to have the world recognize their encroachment into Manchuria was merely an unacceptable aggression into China. The world was slowly and surely inching its way toward another catastrophic conflict while many Americans were asleep. Helen worked hard to provide for her boys and prayed Hitler's rhetoric of hate would somehow change. The idea that eventually her sons may be in a war with Germany came to her one night in a dream and shook her awake. It was an awful thought, and she put it out of her mind. *Surely, not again,* she thought.

She didn't think of Japan as being a danger—it seemed far removed from her daily life. The lives of many men and women were improving; those who worked on government-sponsored projects were paid even if artificially, and the manufacturing sector was finally coming back. It appeared there was a turn in the economy as market forces caused orders to factories, and more start-ups and expansions provided more jobs. Phillip had started his construction company in Arkansas after the Great War built up the firm's capability and reputation to the point where he serviced contracts to build plants and other large-scale buildings for industry in Little Rock and Memphis. The bulk of his wealth was invested in hospitals and utilities. He knew there would be an ever-growing reliance on the innovations in health care, an increasing use of electrical energy, telephones and natural gas. Well established by the mid nineteen-thirties, he married Theresa Waring, a fifty-year-old widow thirteen years his senior who captured his attention in the Little Rock Café while serving him dinner one evening. Stiff and reserved but a pretty brunette when he first met her, she loosened up when he took her to dance clubs and courted her with picnics and canoe trips along the Alabama River.

In San Diego, Ruth and Jules called them Tommy and Davey; everyone else called them Tom and Dave now. They had all grown very close over the years and the Creeless couple were the surrogate parents of young adult men. Tom and Dave spent most of their time together in sports, and during the school year, working part time at the marina where Jules docked his boat. They began as dock hands, cleaning and tending boats, helping move them under cover for protection and washing hulls and performing simple tasks. As they grew older and more experienced, they both gravitated to more complex maintenance on engines and sails. Tom was the first to tell Ruth he was thinking of going into the Navy. Dave listened that night and decided he wanted to stay with the boy who had been his brother since that time in the hospital.

"If that's what you want to do, Tommy, I support you. We don't want you to go because we'll miss you terribly," she sighed. "I understand a young man must explore and do…. We had thought you would go to college. This is a big step."

"I would like that, Mom. I guess I was thinking it would make sense for me to go to school after I've had some time in the Navy."

"Well, I'm sure you can get in. You're smart and seem at home around the water." She smiled. "Are you sure? When?"

"Yes, ma'am. I'm sure. It'll be good for us. I'll see the recruiter tomorrow and find out."

"Very well. I'll tell Jules. I don't think he'll be surprised. You all have talked about this for a year. And I heard you say, 'us'…both of you?" she said.

"No, ma'am…not surprised," Tom said at the same time Dave said he was also joining up.

"I see." She frowned. "Well, you're both over eighteen so I suppose all we can do is wish you God speed and hope you get out of it all you expect. Just always be careful! I hope you get stationed here."

"Yes, ma'am."

Claire was a serious student and preparing herself for college. She caused Helen's boys to be more interested in learning by her example as they came to look up to her. She would start attending after her eleventh year in school and take classes beginning the fall of 1936 at Harvard University where ivy had literally grown for years up the walls insulating the old brick and mortar of the institution. The vines and green were decorative covers validating authority of the place where higher learning was man's noblest quest toward understanding, prosperity and peace through intellectual application.

Chapter 17

"I can't see anything, Tom. Can you?" He held his arms out in the smoke, calling for his brother. It was Sunday morning and the chief petty officers didn't know what happened yet. There was the violent noise of an earthquake around them below decks on the ship where they had planned to sleep late, as their watch was not scheduled until five that evening. Smoke filled the galley and poured with a gale force through every portal. The brothers had been in the Navy for six years and were on sea duty on board the *USS West Virginia*, a battleship moored at Pearl Harbor. Ruth and Jules had shared Hawaii with them a few times, and the place offered a home they were already familiar with. Tom and Dave both used most of their liberty time showing other sailors the finer sights of the islands. Instantly more and louder explosions rocked them again and put in more smoke, this time followed by spitting fire and tossed steel.

"What the hell...?" Tom shouted as he fell against the bulkhead and hit it hard. "Damn! We gotta go topside and see what the..." He was interrupted by another explosion.

"I'm here, Tom! Where are you?" Dave shouted, feeling his way on his knees deep in the hold.

"Over here! Watch your..." Dave heard his shout. They were the last words Dave would hear Tom say forever as a second round of deafening explosions blackened everything. He was suddenly taken into a painful unconsciousness, violent, complete, and total blackness as he felt his whole body slammed to blood. Dave didn't know how long he'd been out when he felt one of his eyes open. He stirred slightly, feeling wet and hurt. He slowly reached to his head and felt the unevenness of the skin and hairline. Then found the first gash. There was gunfire and explosions he could still hear as he withdrew his hand and saw the blood. The bulkhead had been opened enough by the bombs that he could also hear aircraft.

Must get moving, he thought. *We're being attacked. Oh, God...* He rolled over and raised himself as much as he could manage. *We're being attacked.*

The acrid odor of fuel oil and smoke combined filled his nostrils and choked him. He opened both eyes to a slit to see and tried to find Tom. He searched the whole area, peeling back unrecognizable objects and remained there for what seemed like an hour. There was no sign of him or anything that belonged to him. *Maybe he made it out,* he thought, as he slowly made his way topside by holding and pulling himself along the jagged steel. He tried calling out his name but the escaping steam and water, the explosions and gunfire kept him from being heard. He couldn't hear any voices except the screams from above. As he reached the breech above, planes were still flying past, firing sharp deposits of lead that struck around him, nearly taking him; the unseen lead struck close to his side and overhead, his instincts saved him as nerves jerked him back and forth and down to escape being hit. He raised his head to see the devastation.

Everything was unrecognizable and being systematically destroyed by an enemy which came in to deliver a deadly and awful sucker punch. The fire in jagged metal, smoke, screams, and bodies were covering the deck, what was left of it, and the ship began listing. His ship was being strafed and bombed and sinking in the harbor where it was supposed to be safe. He didn't see and couldn't find his brother. He had nothing against these people, but they had violently come to take them.

He and Tom had done what they were expected to do in San Diego; they had gone to school, studied and worked and never hurt anyone, but here others were trying to kill them just for being. They were simply Americans—two of millions—doing a job in the Navy and now for this they were to die! "God, what is happening?" he cried out, tears of rage reaching his chest. His eyes furiously strained and pointed to spot this enemy. He knew there was nothing he could do to fight these bastards, but the passion to do so could not be put away. He wanted to stop them, kill those who took his ship; he wanted revenge now but knew he was powerless. He felt the inside of his stomach convulse with contractions sending waves of anger inside that seared his chest with heat.

He saw several sailors, clothes torn and burnt lying about, some in grotesque positions and some dismembered. One sailor, someone's son, was left headless on the deck. No one was moving. He moved on some and saw burnt corpses, at least he thought that's what they must be, and he heard the screaming closer. He saw someone running past him and called out, "What happened? Where are you going?" But there was no answer as the figure left the field of his vision. Suddenly another came up to him on his blind side and grabbed him by the arm to help him move faster. "Come on, Chief! We gotta get out of here!" he said. Dave glanced up and saw it was a young ensign, his uniform half torn and burnt off, but the bar on one collar still visible.

"Yea…" he muttered as another pass of the aircraft struck the ship. One after another the planes came in toward the burning hulk and sprayed it with machine-gunfire. "Damn!"

"Stay with me, Chief!" the officer shouted as he walked both of them to the port side where there was no fire. "She's going to sink. We've got to get off!" he said, straining to pull them. The next moment Dave knew was waking in a busy and crowded hospital ward where men filled the place beyond capacity. He looked to both sides of the bed he had and saw them put everywhere—even in small five foot spaces squeezed out of corners and aisles, on beds and makeshift cots; some who could sit upright were in chairs while taking intravenous fluids. Most had been burned; arms and faces were nearly destroyed and the youth had suddenly been taken from them. Many looked past their years now with a fixed hurt. The most serious cases took morphine until their semi-conscious state finally yielded to the relief of death. Tom closed his eyes and thought of Tom. Ruth and Jules couldn't know what just happened to the boy they took in and provided a loving home, he thought, and when they did, it would surely devastate them. He cried at the thought of their loss—such an undeserved loss, such a waste of a young life who only meant to do what was right.

President Roosevelt spoke to the nation the next day and declared war on Japan. Dave was resting the next few hours when he heard a radio report that Germany declared war on the United States; he sighed loudly and turned his sore body over to hide his face from the awful sights on the ward. There seemed no end to misery. He felt himself about to cry for them and Tom, and he buried his head into the pillow.

Daniel knew what it would be and as he listened to the President he felt beads of sweat quickly form on his forehead. David was finishing school and only twenty-one, about his age when America sent him to France. He found Katherine tending a flower arrangement as an apparent diversion but noticed she was crying behind the façade of focus on a project. He looked on her still-girlish form and felt frustrated he could do nothing to ease the sudden onset of worry that had her in its strong grip caused by the prospects of war.

"Darling," he said quietly. "Try not to worry. I'm sure everything will be fine, just fine."

"How can you say that, Daniel? David is of age and Thomas will be soon…I just fear the worse," she wept.

"We've been attacked, Katherine."

"Why, Daniel? Why?"

"I don't know." He looked down. "But that's the worse thing that has ever happened and we've got to do something."

"Leave me be, Daniel. I need some time," she said and left him to work the flowers on the back porch. The flowers were almost dead due to an unexpected frost in Houston. During the day the weather warmed to eighty still in December, but last night it had dropped to near freezing and cleaned the air.

He called his son to ask him how he was thinking about Pearl Harbor and the event pushed on the country. The phone rang several times before anyone on the senior floor picked up the receiver. Finally a cadet answered it, and Daniel asked to speak to David McCray.

"Yes, sir!" the young man said. "I'll have him here directly."

"Thank you, young man." He realized he had said that to one who would probably be in battle before the year was out and it was difficult to imagine the young voice would soon be defending the country in such a way. *Damn!* he thought.

"Hello?" He heard David's voice, now a disciplined and manly one, over the phone lines. He thought, w*hat can I say to him? What can I possibly say?*

"Yes, David. It's me. I guess you've heard by now."

"Yes, sir! We're around the radio for hours these days trying to catch up on what is happening. A lot of the fellows are pretty excited." He smiled. "Some are scared, I think, but they won't let on." He laughed, confident in himself.

"Well, son. I suspect the cadet class from A&M will be in the lead on this thing and go when they start sending."

"We are already being briefed on the possibilities. It seems they have been planning for a while."

"Is your commissioning still set for May eighteenth?"

"Yes, sir. No plans to move it up as far as I know yet."

"Good. That'll be another few months. Your mother is worried."

"I'm sorry to hear that. Tell her I'm not."

"I will do that, son. Now how is everything going for you in classes?" he said in a weak attempt to deflect his true purpose—to try and somehow be reassured his son would be safe.

"I'm having an easier time of it than I did last semester. I know it's winding down and the professors are treating us better. The classes seem easier."

"That's good. It's a great school, son, and you must know I'm very proud of you," he said dryly. "You're a good young man. Watch out for the beer parties, will you?"

"Sure, Dad. I know how to handle it." He laughed. "You and Mother take care, too."

"Okay, son..."

He couldn't tell David this coming war was anything to be even a little excited about and didn't want to cause him to think he didn't approve of his going if it came to that—and it was almost a certainty it would. The memories of all the blood, pain and agony in war hit him, and he couldn't continue. He thought of the rats, the gore, and shooting that German; he was breathing deeply and unable to think of what to say. He thought of Paul, nothing more than dust and skeleton by now, but still ridiculously dressed in his uniform although to be forever unseen in a coffin.

"And tell Rachel, Virginia and Thomas to behave!" David laughed.

"I'll tell them you're doing fine and miss them."

"Okay. Thanks, Dad." He wanted to tell his father about Sarah McCoughlin, a senior at the teacher's college nearby, but it didn't seem to be the right time. He met her at a Texas A&M formal military dance last month when she visited with several friends on the general invitation sent to the women's college. Since then he had seen her several times and had a good time taking her to the movies and dining with her at soda fountains. She had a lot in common with him, only she was from Arkansas. She had three sisters and her father had joined the service during the Great War although he spent his time in garrison as an instructor in demolitions. His job on the Boulder Dam had given him the experience to handle explosives and the Army needed him to transfer that knowledge to engineering recruits that summer of 1917. Since he was doing a good job, the Army kept him there for the duration. She was learning to teach mathematics, and he was soon to be a graduate mechanical engineer.

Her athletic body and long legs set off Sarah's dark hair and green eyes. She always outran David in the distance runs and could do more pull ups than he. She could also dance like there was no tomorrow, encouraging David to stay on the floor with her long past his endurance for keeping a rhythm. When she heard the news of Pearl, she took a taxi to his dormitory and walked straight into the wide double doors, spending only a second at the front desk before raising eyebrows by walking up the stairs to his room. A voice called out toward her saying she couldn't go up there. She turned for a few seconds and calmly said, "Oh yes, I can! And I will!" No one stopped her.

When he saw her at his door, he knew she loved him that instant. He wanted to tell his mother and father about his fiancée soon. It would be the first wedding of one of the children of Daniel and Katherine.

"So! What is going to happen now, David?" she asked him; the curt turn of her lip on one side communicating to him that she was not pleased.

"I don't know, Sarah. What are you doing here? You're not supposed to be up here." He smiled.

"Oh, I don't know…I guess the fact that you're about to do five years in the Army and we're at war has something to do with it. David! I love you! I don't want to lose you before we're even had a chance together!" she said, staring fiercely through him. "Well?"

"I'm speechless, Sarah…I love you, too," he said shyly. "I hope you'll understand. We don't know where we're going except for Toccoa, Georgia, where some of us are headed this summer."

"I guess you're one of them, right?"

"Yes, I am, Sarah. I must do it. The best training is there for my chosen field."

"And what is that, David?" She cocked her arm on her hip.

"Airborne school. I am joining the paratroopers."

"I should have known you'd do something like that. Well, I'm going to Georgia, too. I'm going to stay as close to you as I can."

He knew better than to argue the point with her and loved the fact she was willing to do that and that she loved him that much. He smiled a wide smile and felt the tingling of life inside of every part of him. This was good, damn good! "Sarah," he said as he embraced her, pulled her tightly against his body and kissed her lips, his tongue dancing with hers. He held her until they were both tired.

"I do love you so much. It's all my heart and mind and everything I am that I love you with and never want anything or anyone else," he murmured pushing the words under his breath, feeling her pulse through his heart and his pulse rising hot inside his skin.

Sarah and George Hensley prayed goodbye and buried their mother in Houston and had Nathan move in to live with them. The graduate of the Marshall County Children's Home was in his seventies and still lucid and smart. He lost a step because of his age but was still active and able to work on the ranch. He missed Tess and was never the same engaging personality after her passing; she was his heart and spirit.

Sarah had married twice and finally lived as a single. George never married and rose through the acquisition of properties until he owned several tenants and a cattle ranch. The time the family was together in Texas with Daniel and Katherine McCray was sweet and centered on food and talk. George had a good recollection of their history—with Jebediah and Jacob figuring prominently—and he shared with the grandson the life and times of his ancestors, filling in all that Daniel didn't carry with him from Samuel and Irene. At different times, trips to Alabama to see the rest tied them together—although every visit was a painful one still for Daniel because his brother Paul wasn't there.

Greenlee had retired with emphysema and was being cared for by Helen, who now worked as an editor for the *Times* and approved and turned copy for typeset late at night to early dawn, just in time to make the morning run of deliveries. When it was war again, she thought back to when she was thirty and young and the excitement and fervor of the time, but also the heartbreak of the events as men were killed. She knew what Isaac had seen, and she remembered what she had seen. In Los Angeles there was a man who would march up and down the coastal roadway calling out orders to invisible troops like he had done in the Great War. They said he was shell-shocked and his mind remained somewhere in France for the rest of his life. She thought of Harry, too, and how different her life might have been had he returned home and she married him instead of meeting James in Hollywood. It would have been better—at least during those bad years with James, she thought, but she would not change anything because of Luke, John and Matthew. They had been a true blessing for which she was thankful and remembered them every day that way.

Isaac had his congregation pray in unison for peace every Sunday, and after war was declared they prayed for a quick end to the hostilities. Day to day he was baptizing babies, rendering comfort to widows and widowers, teaching pupils in the small school he started mathematics and reading, and making sure the destitute in Houma had food. The Parish had grown enough because of the new chemical industry in the area and refinery that brought jobs close enough to the bayou for the children to stay, work and live.

Matthew was a senior editor for the *Times* and covered Congress and the President—his fascination with government still intact. He enjoyed doing the analysis of its good and bad effects on the populace. He was credited with a major run of stories when Roosevelt attempted to change the Supreme Court to allow for him to have more control toward an American brand of socialism. But that was not to be as the public window of information proved too much for the administration to overcome and even brought out a discussion of impeachment for an intended violation of the separation of powers set out in the Constitution.

Matthew and Agnes attended Claire's graduation from Harvard and helped her move to the dormitory at Georgetown where she was admitted to law school. Luke entered the Marine Corps at eighteen and John followed him at the onset of World War II.

Matthew Riker was still in high school and designed to join the Army Air Corps as soon as he could if his eyes were good enough. There was an excitement in the air and most men of age wanted to do something against the evil Nazis and Japanese imperialists. They were signing up for hitches in every branch of the services. Factories began a quick conversion to wartime goods and supplies, and women entered the workforce in droves.

Midway had been a successful repulse of the Japanese Navy, and Wake Island, where a few hundred Marines beat back a Japanese naval invasion, inspired many men to join the Marines. Although Helen worried herself sick about their decision, Luke felt this service would be a good one because the men with you were trained well and knew what they were doing, and John would never stand by and watch his brother do the fighting without him, as it had been in school. There wasn't anything she could say to dissuade them as the young men had watched and listened to all that was around them and spent their hearts toward the great patriotic mood of America, which captured men's minds. The country put out the call, and it was the manly thing to do rather than stay at home to answer why they did nothing. Being attacked as it were must cause men to rise up and exact the heavy toll, punish those who killed innocent countrymen; it was a fight a bully started and had to be met and put down, disgraced into humility for the gall.

Luke and John reported to Parris Island, South Carolina, to begin training as American Marines who would come after those who bloodied the country in such an evil way and with so little provocation. David finished the paratroop school after the physical training staged in Toccoa and the jump school at Fort Benning then was temporarily assigned to Camp Mackall,

North Carolina. There the Army was amassing a new capability to engage the enemy deeper behind its lines, and Sarah set up herself and David in a room. He was promoted to first lieutenant and had under his command a group of one hundred and forty physically fit men; young ones with ideas of medals and stopping the Germans and Japanese quickly. His older sergeants knew better.

David received a letter every week from his parents and treasured holding them in his hands. Each page brought him to back to the sanity of Houston and away from the constant drilling and physical training, the spit and polish routine he was to oversee—a kind of game, and the preparations for war. Rereading them time and again made him feel he was comfortable and safe at home for a few minutes.

Seeing Thomas hurl a baseball while pitching for the school team, watching Victoria perform a recital on her piano as Rachel served coffee and tea while teasing him about the times—the mischievous and funny things they acted out together. He remembered them fishing together; he set a hook in a stump and pulled hard fixing the steel underwater forever while she caught a five-pound catfish at the same time. She and David would take turns and pretend to be a priest holding Mass, doing communion with half a saltine cracker and using grape juice as the wine.

He remembered her first date, and how afterwards she didn't want to see the suitor anymore and asked David to tell him. He remembered helping her with math and her helping him with English. He remembered they were washing Father's car and how he got her good with the hose making her scream—and how she got him back when he was washing the tires, making him holler; the water was cold. He remembered her laugh and smile and how he enjoyed seeing his sisters happy. He hoped his service would spare the rest of them, especially Thomas, from the chance of war.

Following a field exercise in Kentucky where the men lived in pup tents and endured endless night marches and tactical practice, setting perimeters, digging foxholes and fighting a pretend enemy, the unit received word of their transfer to Fort Bragg, North Carolina. David had been in the active Army for a year and remained stateside the whole time as he watched newsreels of the fighting in Russia, Italy, Africa and the British victory at Al Alamein. He wondered when they were going; they seemed to be ready but were held in training between Kentucky, Tennessee and Indiana. Fort Bragg was better; there were hot showers and good food. His men also received new uniforms and rifles and began spending every day on the firing range. It became apparent they were getting closer to meeting the enemy and could get the call any time. Sarah made the trip and stayed just off base in a small apartment she rented. She went to work as a cashier for the largest grocery store in Fayetteville.

"I believe we're shipping out soon, Sarah. Things are too good here," he said to her that evening, his longing for her still firmly set in his eyes.

"I see. Well, it was bound to happen. I don't know what I'll do.... When do you think you'll have to leave?"

"I don't know, darling." He looked down and felt her approach him closer. "Maybe you can return to Houston and teach for a while. Once we're overseas, it may be a while before I can see you again. I'm so sorry."

"You know I'll wait for you. Damn war! It isn't fair! We haven't even begun to live and start a family."

"Yea...it isn't what I want."

"It's not what I want either. Can't you get a job here? Don't they need instructors or something?"

"No, ma'am. I'm committed to the guys in my company and have to stay with them, you know." He stopped and looked into her eyes. "Sarah, will you marry me before I leave? I know it's not what we planned but there may not be time for a large wedding in Houston," he said then quickly added, "Besides, I won't have the time on leave to make it down there and all."

"I think we should do that. Mother will be disappointed, but I know she'll understand." Her eyes were filling with tears. "We have to do this...Oh, David! I don't want you to go! I don't want to lose you!"

He held her warmly and tightly. "Honey...I want you to be my wife. Today is none too soon. I'll talk to the Major and use the day for us to get the license."

"Okay, David."

"Thank you, dear. Thank you so much. I love you."

Chief Petty Officer Foster spent three months in San Diego convalescing before being reassigned to the *USS Alabama*. James and Ruth Creeless were able to see him often and brought him love and cookies, visiting their son and listening. Months later the crews raised the *West Virginia* off where she settled upright on the bottom of the shallow port and found seventy more bodies and a calendar one of them crossed through each day to December 23rd, the last day of a son's life after being trapped in her hull for two weeks underwater. Dave knew at least his brother was spared the agony of waiting for a slow death, for his end was quick, but took grim solace, and he had to kill as many Japanese as he could. The best way for him to do that was to volunteer for battleship duty again.

"Davey, Jules and I want you to know we love you. We don't like the war, but we know we have no choice but to fight them."

"I'm getting out next week, and I'll be so glad!"

"If I could, I would take your place, sweet Davey."

"I bet you would!" He laughed. "I'll be fine. I've got orders for the *Alabama* and she's brand new—going through her tests off Maine now."

"So you're headed east?"

"Yes, ma'am. I've got several days to get to Norfolk."

"Lord, help us, the war." She looked down. "There's nothing that can stop it—we'll just have to pray for your safety. When do you leave?"

"I figure next Tuesday, Mother." He thought for a moment. "I'll need to see Mrs. Foster before I ship out."

"Of course. Jules and I can bring her."

"That would be nice. And Mother, I'm sorry about Tom," he said, looking away from her.

"We are too. It hurts."

"It does hurt a lot." Her face reddened and her eyes swelled with water. "He had a life, didn't he?"

"He did. He loved you and Jules and did have a good life, Mother. I wished I could have got to him." He looked down, tears forming in his eyes.

"You did all you could, dear. Please don't blame yourself. It was the Japanese. I believe it was God's will to take Tommy, and he's looking down on us now with no more weak lungs, no more sorrow—only happiness and love for his true family."

"Yes, ma'am. I believe that."

"I must go, Davey. Jules is getting everything ready for your going-away party. We'll have your favorites! And all the neighbors want to show their support. Be brave!" She managed a laugh.

Luke and John were ordered to the activated Third Marine Division organizing at Camp Elliott in Sand Diego as part of the Western Pacific landing forces in training and preparations for action in the South Pacific. The Marines began massing and overflowed the capacity of barracks to house them. Large side-walled tents were put up in orderly rows; some with wooden slat floors and these were home to the division until they boarded the LST's

(Landing Ship-Troops) bound for points in the Pacific as part of Halsey's fleet. The fleet's purpose was to deliver to the Japanese expansionists just payment for their exercise in murder and defeat the militarists.

Each boy wrote Helen and Greenlee of their routine and redundant training. They wrote about how proficient they had become on the firing range with the M-1 and of their fellow Marines, who they were becoming close as true friends united by the passion of the Corps and their mission. They wrote their mother about the beauty of Sand Diego and how much they were enjoying the weather and the place. They left out references to their mission and the bars and women in Tijuana, Mexico, where their diversions by a quick taxi ride on the weekends usually ended with both of them out of money. They had their share of beer and card games and were having the time of their lives.

Colonel Shepard was the commander of the Ninth Marines and reported to General Barrett who was the first commander of the new division. His job was to get them ready, to instill the fact that every Marine was a rifleman and must be able to perform, whether he was a cook or a clerk. The vast majority were being trained to face the enemy as an amphibious assault force. Time after time, they practiced offloading from the sides of a ship into landing craft and hitting the beach on the attack. Col. Shepard was a tough one; he knew the level of difficulty and physical preparation of his Marines would be reflected as a proportion to the number of Marine bodies he would bury. He knew the harder he had them train, the fewer would be lost to an enemy who already had a reputation of being savage to the Chinese and British.

The rumors of the Japanese army included executing civilians and torturing prisoners; they meant to win and suppress, and so it seemed would do anything required to terrorize people into submission. Men, women, and children who were not Japanese were considered inferior beings who were expendable and merely feeders who could and should be disposed of like nuisance animals. The Marines heard all of this and could hardly wait to kill them and stop the pillage. Luke and John were motivated and ready and when the order came would do exactly what they were ordered without hesitation, without a thought, as every Marine.

Killing another human being was still a foggy idea to the innocents at Camp Elliott who came from across America. News of their brothers being killed at Pearl Harbor and the Marines' courageous fight on Wake Island were stories that, although real, were somehow distant in their minds. Each worried how he would react under fire when the time came, but held fast to the exercises Col. Shepherd had them engage. Being with each other was just enough to feed them confidence that as they learned about booby traps, Japanese tactics, weapons and armor, they would prevail and live. Day to day, their routine seemed to take on a normalcy, a safe time of being.

"We have liberty Saturday night, John. Let's go to Luigi's for some spaghetti," Luke offered. "I'll buy."

"Sounds good, Luke. I have to pull firewatch at ten Saturday night, so I've got to get back that early."

"No problem. The bus makes their runs every hour, and we'll be done long before. I want to keep it in anyhow."

"Me too. I think I just want to rest this weekend as much as I can. That forced march yesterday still has me breathing hard and sore."

"That was a long one—and the people in front made it harder."

"Yea. We oughta give the first platoon a taste of what it's like to be in the rear." He laughed.

"I bet they'll be the ones who'll dance tonight! The low down…"

"They make us run back there so they are fresher for the ladies. Reckon that's true, for sure." He laughed.

Dave made his way to Norfolk and boarded the *Alabama*. The battleship was about to become part of the British Home Fleet and cover the island of Spitzbergen, which lay in the path of the northern convoy route to Russia. Germany had Russia reeling from the blitzkrieg Hitler ordered and Leningrad was under siege; her citizens beginning to starve and die. He was as far away from home he could be and not fighting the enemy he may prefer, still Germany was an enemy aligned with Japan and it would have to do for him to kill them until he could kill Japanese. His heart was in it for Tommy, the lost sailors—any of which could easily have been himself, the sailors around him, and his country. The year 1943 was drawing near and America was turning its eye toward the work.

Chapter 18

That morning David felt the crisp air on his face and breathed deeply taking in the fresh air of the mountains to his west from a blue sky, clean and vast over the horizon that tasted like peace. Turning his face east the sea was beyond sight, but he knew it was the divide between his country and France where men were dying at the hands of Germans whose leaders had convinced people they were a master race. He at once wanted to be in the fight and did not want to be in the fight. Sarah was waiting for him to return Sunday when they would have a quiet midday meal and then make love until the evening shadows brought them sleep. Then for him it was back to the base in the early morning.

His father had been to France and beyond a mere twenty-four years earlier and did the same. He lived and brought him and his sisters and brother into the world. David thought that a fraction of an inch difference for any shot of lead would have ended their life before it had begun. But for destiny, he would not be there. He thought of men who took that lead and didn't father children whose unknown talents and contributions would never be known; no one would know the children not born. *Some women would never meet the husband—some the one they should have had, others the one they shouldn't, but still the hearts were gone and buried on foreign soil. They fought the last war, the Great War to end all wars, but it was not to be and now much worse for humanity. Was it a tease by the unseen spirit of Satan working to fool men in the deadliest and most horrible exercise of free will? Was it man's doing alone? Had the Great War been only a stall, a ruse, and a temporary respite to grow babies into men and women so more of them could die? This time the world had to surely finish the Germans and their allies and end it,* he thought. But it could only be another chance and not the last.

His parents were making the trip to Fayetteville next week to see him before he was sent to England. Daniel knew he might not see his son again for a long while, if he ever saw him again. He thought there were things he could tell him about how to survive but telling him of dropping flat on the ground and curling inside his helmet when he heard artillery coming in on top of him and somehow explaining how to run toward the enemy in sporadic spurts and volleys of movement and being unseen would not protect him as a certainty—would not even come close.

The boy would learn about combat the same way he did; it was something he, or no man who had, ever wanted to do again, and he would never ask to. But his son would soon feel the vibrations, hear the deafening retorts and see the most awful sights of his young life and that he would ever see again—sights that would haunt him forever. And it would be worse in these years as even more advanced and deadly methods of killing other human beings had been researched and built. Only by the grace of God would he live. Daniel felt the tears begin flowing. He dried them as best he could. He found Victoria and embraced her, found Rachel and embraced her, and found Thomas and embraced him. He then embraced Katherine, sweet innocent, hardworking Katherine, the love of his life, the mother of these beautiful children and who was so wonderful he could hardly believe he was as lucky as this, having her and didn't want her to lose one they loved together. God, there would be nothing he could say if they did lose him and nothing he could do to ease more pain than a human being can imagine and could only know if it happened.

In Houma, Isaac was saying a Mass for the troops leaving the state to report for duty. He had twelve in the parish. Some had left and there were seven to leave soon. Every one of them was young and brave and taking up the fight as they saw it on behalf of their mothers and fathers. The air held heat and so much water it seemed to ooze and cover everything without raining. Rain would discharge it in sweet relief. The young soldiers kneeling in the pews were prepared, and after Mass they would enjoy a large dinner, courtesy of the church.

The band played favorite Cajun tunes, and for a time, there were plenty of smiles and hearty laughter heard around the tables set out in shade under the moss and large oaks. The girls were wearing their one piece dresses and happily skipping and dancing, teasing the young men a little with the promise of a kiss and a little flirting. Each girl older than fourteen went to each of the seven and kissed him, each one on the mouth, who was bound to leave soon.

Isaac looked on them and smiled for the time and prayed silently for each of them to come back home in one piece soon. There was Jack Broussard, an eighteen-year-old Marine and nephew of the Broussards who had been members of his parish since he arrived in Louisiana, and John Justin Smith whose mother married a millwright from Meridian and settled near Houma to work the refineries. He was only seventeen but lied about his age to enter the Navy. One of the Boudreaux twins had joined the Army and the other was qualified from the Navy to work as a corpsman for the Marines. Raymond and Eddie were due to ship out across the country and then almost certainly overseas to some destination where there would be no family nearby and no Father Isaac to patch them up after a baseball game and serve them communion on Sundays.

The moss gently moved to the rhythm of the sea breeze as a quiet dusk settled in around them all. There were not many days left for the boys to take in what was their home and its unique beauty. They were centered in what most Americans considered the worst area—swampy and infested with insects and larger species, which carried no attraction other than some curiosity and wonder. There were the alligators and snakes, minks and muskrats, and an untold number of other, different creatures living in harmony with the people of Houma.

They all shared the beauty in the eye that could see, and Isaac saw the grasses, the bobbing heads of turtles, the birds, the flowers, the rustic handbuilt homes so comfortably airy and accommodating to strangers in need of shelter for a night, and there was the chicken, fish, shrimp, frogs, deer, rabbits, and many other fruits, vegetables, and rice making up a wonderful smorgasbord. The hot wind would blow through Houma and fix it as the place for a special people. Not everyone would love it as Isaac came to love it so much. He studied each of the young faces and wondered what would be the fate. *Would Jack—the pimply faced fellow with the broad smile and black hair the color of coal—would Jack meet some Japanese boy and not be quick enough?* He looked at John and wondered what sights he would see so far from home and near such strange coasts; there was nothing like them in Houma. He knew Eddie had one of the toughest jobs a young man could have. To be a medic—a corpsman in the Marine Corps—would require him to do twice the running back and forth and be twice as close to shots fired at him. He would be doing his job without a firearm. He studied Raymond. He had never been away from his brother and now he would be in a different theater all the way across the world away from him. *How would he do? He's such a gentle soul,* he thought. Now was a time of celebration though and Father Isaac kept his thoughts private and just smiled.

Luke and John spent their last night stateside eating dinner at Luigi's in San Diego, and they shared a bottle of wine to drink with their spaghetti dinner.

"What do you think about it, John?"

"Think about going? I don't know. I'm ready to go because I'm sure tired of this stuff here. I'm more than ready!" he smiled. "What do you think?"

"I think I'm ready to kill me some Japs…and we're going to finally get the chance," Luke said.

"Be careful what you wish for! They are some nasty little S.O.B.'s who don't care if they live or die. Remember what the Cap said." He took a long pull from the goblet Luigi's provides with each bottle.

"I know. All it does for me to hear that is motivate me." He smiled, showing the teeth of a warrior.

"I think about Uncle Matthew. You know he saw some action in France and never talked about it much." John looked into his brother's eyes.

"I don't intend to talk much either, John. After this is done, I'm going to get my butt back to D.C. and never leave again."

"You mean you don't like it here in California?"

"I like California fine—but not where we've been!" He laughed. Just then more Marines walked into Luigi's and nodded to the brothers. "Appears the guys are taking it easy on their last night," one of them said. He smiled at each Marine as Dan and Tiny passed them first, then Rusty and Killer Ben, James, and Shorty O'Connor. Someone suggested they pull tables together and be as one as they are every day.

"Here's to the United States Marine Corps!" John offered a toast. "The most dangerous green machine in the world!" He smiled. The whole group raised glasses in unison.

"And here's to ole Shep! By God, he got us ready and we're going where he's going!" another one of them said. Again the glasses were raised uniformly as if it was another close order drill command.

The next day the Marines boarded ships and left for New Zealand to prepare for stationing on Guadalcanal and then the Bougainville operation against the Japanese. None of the men knew or could foresee with certainty anything ahead of them—mostly only the next day they knew. The battalion would hit Bougainville then Guam and finally finish their fighting on Iwo

Jima. Many would be replaced through the course of the campaign in the Pacific and the battalion would only resemble its original make-up of men as a shell with the unit designation.

    David marched to the front of the men's formation. "At ease!" he commanded. "I have some news. Stand fast!" He picked a piece of paper out of the front pocket of his blouse and began reading. "Our orders are to board trains for Camp Shanks in New York." He looked down at his notes. "There we'll be processed for oversea's duty. You are to remove the screaming eagle patch from your shoulders and un-blouse your trousers." The reason was to prevent any German spies from noting there was movement of an Army airborne unit, he would explain later when the grumbling threatened unit morale. They had worked extremely hard for the right to wear that patch and paratroop boots and did not want to give them up. David had to say goodbye to Sarah, this time longer than the few days for training exercises. This time it was final, and he would have to leave her until he returned or the war was over.

    When he walked in that evening, she knew before he said a word. "This is it, isn't it, David?" She looked at him, her eyes wide and red, and her hands trembling. She slowly walked toward him and he took her into his arms.

    "Yes, honey. I am leaving in the morning," he said softly and squeezed her harder. "I'm so sorry."

    "We knew it would come," she whispered. "It's alright, dear."

    Helen found Greenlee that morning peacefully reclined in the living room. He had moved to his favorite chair sometime during the night and passed away quietly. She wept softly; it was something both had expected but it was still hard to accept when it did. He had been a good father to Luke, John and Matthew and taught them how to treat a wife with tenderness. Always considerate and loyal to them, he had turned his life around and lived settled. Matthew was still in high school and Greenlee was the only father he had known. He didn't remember California and didn't remember James except as an obscure figure he saw once in a while before he knew what was around him.

    She reached Luke and John through HAM radio operators connecting to New Zealand several days after that morning and told them. Greenlee had been good to them as well and helped them stay focused on school and church. He taught them both how to fish and hunt when he was able and stayed with them at every scout meeting and baseball practice. He taught them to be patriots and love the freedom of their country, never to abuse it and always to protect it jealously. He drove them to the bus station bound for Charleston and Parris Island. When he left them, he shook each hand firmly and after returning to his car where neither could see him and he began crying. He thought he would take their place and leave them at home with their mother if it were only possible.

A few months later Helen visited her brother Matthew and Agnes and took her Matthew with her. They had been invited to a dinner to celebrate Claire's engagement to Henry Lee, a recent graduate of Princeton who worked in the law office she clerked as an intern. He was twenty-four and claiming a back injury to keep him out of the armed services. He lied when he told others he was 4-F and that he had been rejected.

His father had been a legal partner to the junior Senator from Massachusetts and had influence enough to cause the legislator to make a call to the draft board on his son's behalf. Helen arrived at the brownstone with Matthew who didn't like the idea he had to dress in a suit for a family dinner, but he obliged his mother.

"Hello, Agnes," she said. "I do hope we're not late."

"Not at all, Helen. Please come in. My, you are quite handsome, Matthew," Agnes said.

"I understand there's to be an addition to the family. Congratulations, Agnes," Helen said.

"Yes. He's crazy about our Claire and she's crazy about him. That's the way it is for young people these days." She smiled. "He's in the library with Matthew...my Matthew." She laughed.

"I look forward to meeting him. I'm sure he's a fine fellow."

"What do you hear from Luke and John?"

"They're fine. I receive a letter from them every week. At least they have time to write. They can no longer tell me where they're going though. All I know is they are no longer in pretty New Zealand. I should share what they told me about the place sometime." She smiled graciously.

"You must worry so. I'm sorry. They are the finest young men, doing the job for freedom. I admire your boys and pray for their safety."

"Yes. I pray every day. Thank you, Agnes." She stopped. "I would rather them be at home, but I have to understand I suppose. There are millions of mothers who wait as I do, no different. I wish the war would end now of course."

"Me too, dear Helen. Let me introduce you to the groom." She smiled again. "This is Henry Lee. Henry, this is Matthew's sister, Helen, and her son, Matthew."

"Glad to meet you, ma'am." He shook her hand weakly and glanced toward Matthew for a few seconds and nodded. Her brother was in the room and embraced Helen.

"Glad to see you outside the office, sis. You should come over more often."

"I know, Matthew. I've been busy after the funeral with everything imaginable and unimaginable." She laughed. "Matthew here is a senior next year. Hard to imagine, isn't it?"

"Yes. It seems like only yesterday when he came here as a little one. He's sure growing up fine like his brothers." He smiled.

"I'm proud of them. I hope when he finishes he won't have to go." She patted her son on his back; his expression was a youthful sour.

"I would go if I were old enough, Mom."

"I know, dear. I know." She looked around the room and noticed a disinterested Henry fiddling with the tumbler of tea he was holding. She suppressed an instinctive feeling about him that was negative. After all, she had only just met Claire's intended and hoped first impressions proved incorrect. Still there was something about him she didn't like.

Luke and John were now in Guadalcanal training for the Bougainville operation with intensity such that many thought their encounter with the Japanese would finally bring relief to their bodies. No one in the battalion had faced enemy fire yet though and heard and felt the lead and iron passing in and around them—the waves of concussion and heat from which there would seem no escape except by the grace of God. The exercises had them on large marches and tactical maneuvers that tested their endurance. They marched until they could march no more; they ran until they could run no more. Every man in the battalion knew his body's limits on the canal, as the heat sapped every ounce of water out of them first and then their legs would begin to shut down. With a quick take from a canteen, they could do a few more miles.

They practiced in squads, fire teams, taking imaginary machine-gun bunkers, infantry lines and armored formations. Each team had in its make-up specialists who each carried weapons they were trained on—one man with a flamethrower, another with a machine gun and his sighter, a grenadier and several riflemen. Four fire teams made up a platoon. The ninety to one hundred and twenty men making up a company of four platoons was a complete small unit fighting force, but only as effective as the degree which they worked together as a coordinated team. There was a Navy corpsman assigned to each company and a radio operator.

Helen proudly hung the banner with two stars next to the front door of her home. She used her opportunity as an editor to write of coordinating and sending troops soft items, not that people needed any encouragement. America was sacrificing and working to make the lives of her soldiers as close to home as they could. New razors, shaving cream, cookies, pictures, letters, candy, tissues, toothpaste, canned milk, coffee, sugar—most of home was sent to her boys to keep them closer. Her warehouse was only one of many across the country that collected and packaged for shipment to the many men who were only children in high school not too many months ago.

David led his men up the gangplank and onto the deck of the *Samaria*, a converted Indian passenger liner bound for England. The 101st Airborne was on the move again, and he wrote Sarah of his love and his missing her. She was expecting their first child in six months and treasured each letter. She poured her heart into the ones she wrote him, often two or more each day. During the week she would carry the bundle of letters to the postal office at Fort Bragg where she returned and took up her old job at Bailey's Grocery. Letters were all she had and she pressed each one to her heart before and after reading it over and over again then gently put it in the cedar drawer where she could retrieve any of them during the loneliest moments.

On the *Samaria* there were more troops than she was designed to keep and many men suffered seasickness in claustrophobic conditions that would in turn cause other men to become sick. It seemed a neverending cycle with little relief in sight as the green and bluish ocean surrounded the convoy making them small and insignificant specs on nature's vast reservoir of salt water—used for cold showers on board. During the day when the sea was calm, the Airborne cleaned weapons and gear, played cards, sang, and made the best of their voyage. For most it was their first journey outside the United States and for many the Army brought them out of their counties and towns for the first time.

They were bound for Liverpool where they would finally step back on dry ground to be met by truck convoy for transport to Aldbourne, a small English village near Swindon. The *Alabama* was steaming back to Norfolk by August of 1943 for an overhaul and repairs. She would transit the Panama Canal to assume her role in the Pacific theater as part of operation Galvanic—the assault on the Japanese Gilbert Islands. Dave Foster, a member of the Creeless family, was on board and finally heading toward the people who killed Tom. He loved his mother and father, Ruth and Jules Creeless, and wrote them to request adoption so he cold bear their surname into battle. The Creeless-McCray joining were overjoyed at the prospect and happily set out to finally recognize what they had felt for years for both him and Tom. It was the highest honor Ruth and Jules ever received.

The landing was quiet after the Naval guns stopped hitting the island with a great barrage, sending rock, dirt and trees exploding in the air and leaving pillars of black and gray smoke lifting the sky. Soft waves being pounced by rain brought the Higgins troop transports, an open-air boat built in New Orleans, close to the beach where they left the ramps at as much of a double time possible in water up to their chests to start. *So far, this isn't bad,* Luke thought, as he went to the right and took up a fighting position on the flank.

Suddenly he felt his pulse quicken and couldn't control it, he felt his eyes convulsively squinting like a grain of sand was lodged by the Japanese to make him a more susceptible target. He couldn't see the sun in the overcast envelope and didn't see anyone ahead of him, but knew they were there somewhere waiting for them. He felt lonely though there were Marines to his left and like him were on the ground as low as he thought he could get—later he would be able to get lower, nearly burrowing into the earth as his only protection. The sand and dirt stuck to his heavy uniform, and he felt it cover his face. John was somewhere to his left, he thought, as he was on a different Higgins, but he knew he landed safely as part of the first wave of Marines. Finally the gunny ordered the line to move toward the jungle edge, and every man rose up enough to run toward the tree line. He could hear shots through the sheets of rain, and they were coming at them. Instinctively his training took control, and he dodged, weaved and found cover to return fire.

"Get going, Marines!" He heard the command. It was the unmistakable voice of his gunnery sergeant leading the company on line into the canopy of palms and brush. Luke fired as much as he could toward the unseen enemy as he ran forward, not knowing what he would encounter through the next mound, the next tree cluster, or rock formation—whatever was ahead. The line stopped and took up positions inside the foliage just in front of a mounded clearing pocked with craters and formations that resembled sand dunes only they were mostly rock. The opening expanded nearly across their entire front and Luke took the opportunity to glance to his left in an effort to see John, but most of the men were not in view and he couldn't see his brother. Suddenly the firing stopped for a minute from each side.

He watched the captain motion with his arm undoubtedly toward a squad on his left flank and then picked up the mouthpiece of the radio again. Luke stared out in front of him trying to catch a glimpse of the enemy when the firing resumed, this time the loud explosions of grenades added concussion to the sounds of war and seemed close. Behind them were more Marines to land so it was their job to clear the way.

"Move!" He heard the command and saw the gunny wave his arm to bring the men toward the clearing, and they jumped and attacked. Beside Luke, Tiny was cut in half by a burst from a machine gun, but the rest were able to get to the edge of the clearing. That's when he saw his first Japanese soldier, but it was only a body now, not moving and lying in a distorted posture he thought must be uncomfortable even in death. Half the man's face was gone and his legs were broken back, bending opposite of his knees. His uniform was ripped, torn and covered, soaked with blood and water from the rain. He stopped for a second at the shocking sight; it was the first dead man he had ever seen. At that second he felt he was knocked backwards by a force like that which must be like getting kicked by a horse. The next conscious thing he knew he was lying on his back, unprotected, until he rolled over to take up a prone firing position. He didn't think to check himself for injury until later.

You have to squeeze the trigger, gentlemen. You don't jerk it...you don't pull it! You squeeze it slowly! he remembered the monotone voice of the officer on the firing range in training. They had been taught to line up the target by sighting the bottom of the black with the front sight aligned with the rear sight and to adjust the windage and elevation. It was very clinical and became easy for both him and his brother. The kick of the weapon was enough to cause a swollen lip or a black eye, so he learned to pull the rifle into his shoulder tight. They both qualified as experts since they were able to hit the bull's-eye with every shot after setting the *dope*. On the range one sighted his rifle in and wrote down the number of clicks for elevation and windage at the various distances. This allowed them to know exactly how to adjust the sights to hit the target—as long as they held a still rifle on line with the target, pushed all the air out of their lungs, and squeezed the trigger at the right time. He remembered that and how different that was from this new reality. He was firing toward the front, paying little attention to proper sighting and squeezing. His only reaction was to fire as much as he could load toward the enemy and sight in his general direction. Still targets were hard to come by.

The Japanese were staying dug in and had a line of lightly fortified defensive positions all along the coast. It would take some doing to dislodge them and win this fight. They were a tough bunch, a seasoned and experienced army of men dedicated to their emperor and mostly living the Bushido creed, which was foreign to the Americans. To a man they were willing to die on command if ordered to die, whether by suicidal *banzai* attacks at the hand of an enemy or their own hand to protect their honor in the samurai tradition.

John was with a fire team, which was given the task to take out a machine-gun nest covered with a mound of grass beyond the mounds. The men moved up in starts and spurts, quickly flanking the knoll where several Japanese soldiers were laying a base of fire toward the Americans. He threw a grenade first and as it exploded, they sprayed the low lying hut with machine gun fire, then jumped closer and hit it with a flamethrower. The screams didn't last long. Instantly the stench of burning flesh overtook their sense of smell and the awful but sweetish odor stayed low to the ground. Not a breeze or a puff of wind was enough to take the heavy residue away. The constant rain seemed to help it remain as a telling of doing a horrible thing to other human beings—who had the intentions of doing those things to the Americans as they had Tiny. Still it was a powerful, soul-searching eyeful of pain inflicted on purpose.

At the same time Luke and his squad took a shallow trench filled with Japanese on line. Some had been killed by the naval bombardment and those who were left dug in were dispatched by the Marine rifle squads. Luke saw Shorty finish one with a bayonet, plunging it deep into the neck of what appeared to be an officer. Killer Ben stood over the top of the trench and sprayed the ditch filled with bodies with Thompson rounds, one clip after another until the barrel overheated while other Marines moved up and did the same with their M-1s. The first line of defense was finished, but the Japanese were on the island in numbers farther inland and the Third Marines were in for a long fight with a dangerous enemy who desired death before surrender.

The perimeter was set as reinforcements moved onto the island. The Marines took some time to quickly chow down and take a little water before the next order. Luke remembered his mother and knew he wouldn't share this with her; she had no need to know. He thought of his grandfather and all that he went through long before he was born. He would have loved to have known Grandmother; she must have been a woman full of heart and passion, dutiful to her family until the family missed her forever. Maybe he would meet her someday in heaven, he hoped. He remembered the tragedy that took his grandfather and Gladys at the same sitting and prayed for them and himself and John. *One of us must survive this,* he prayed inside himself, *for the sake of the Riker name. We've got to make it for the sake of the McCrays, for the sake of mother's heart. If there must be one taken in this, Lord, let it be me and let John return to mother and live a life.*

At that moment he sensed someone watching him and felt uneasy. He moved behind a sloping mound farther away, hidden from the interior of the island. He saw John walking toward him when the sniper took the shot and caused John to dive head first toward his position. Afraid his brother was hit; he scrambled to him to see for himself.

"Are you hit, John?" he asked in a panic as he heard the raking other Marines cut into the tree with 45- and 50-caliber rounds where the sniper was hiding until he fired. The Japanese warrior fell with a dull thump, a heavy bag of flesh and bone covered entirely with blood red hit the ground fifty yards to their front. The guys on the perimeter did the job very efficiently once he revealed himself.

"I...I don't know!" John said as he felt around his body trying to find whether he was bleeding through his wet uniform. Sweat crusted blouse seeped through the web gear and rucksack each wore into the beach. "I don't feel anything. Do you see anything?" he asked.

"No. Turn over and let me see your back."

John did as he was asked and rolled toward Luke. "Well? Am I hit?"

"Don't see a thing but a torn place on your pack. Damn! That was close! We're going to have to watch out for those guys!"

"Thanks, Luke." He looked into his brother's eyes. "War. Damn. You don't know what it is until you're in it."

"That's right. No one knows unless they've been there."

"What do you think Shep will have us do now? There's a lot of Bougainville left out there," John said.

"I think that as soon as the rest of the division comes up, we'll start moving inland. There's where most of the Japs are," he said pointing toward the vast land area to his front. A squadron of Hellcats suddenly flew overhead, low and fast toward the interior. "There they go! They're clearing the way!"

"You know, it's too bad this place is being torn to pieces. It is a beautiful—or it was." John paused, appearing distant in thought. *I've just got into the fight and I'm tired of it already. Wouldn't it be something nice to be here and just enjoy the scenery?* He smiled as he heard the aircraft begin strafing and bombing nearby, making low runs up ahead out of sight of the waiting Marines. "Guess we're mucking it up pretty much."

"Here comes the Captain, John. Maybe we'll get the word."

"Yea. Check your weapon, Luke. It looks pretty sandy. We don't need any jams." Streams of sweat began rolling down the sides of his face and mixed with the dirt, sand and small pebbles imbedded into his skin. "Jesus, be with us," he uttered out loud as he fingered his rifle and blew into the chamber in a vain attempt to clean the heavy mixture of oil and sand out of the breech. "I bet it'll be soon, Luke." He tore a piece of cloth in half and handed one to John. He used the other to dab out the residue of his weapon. "Got your rod out? Let me borrow it after you're done."

"Sure, John."

"Riker! We're moving out. Take the point with Jones and Miller," the Captain ordered looking at Luke. Move north by northeast toward the village. It's three clicks that way." He pointed ahead and reached for the radio receiver. "Move out in five." The unmistakable sounds of tanks were chugging up to support the company.

"Aye, aye, sir!" Luke said.

The quiet which settled along the horizon would soon change; the Japanese were waiting and the Marines knew they were. Their next contact could come at any time. Luke took one step at a time not knowing when he would be a target from the unseen enemy. He led the small squad taking the company deeper into Bougainville and firmly fixed his eyes and mind to looking for any movement and subtle changes on the ground that would give the enemy away when they attempted to kill and stop the Marine advance.

He suddenly stopped and held his arm up to pause the march inland. "Pass the word!" He quietly forced enough air through and pushed the words to Jones who was behind him to relay the target to the armor unit driving beside and behind them. "There's something up there! Get down!" He heard the tanks stop in idle.

Helen and Matthew strolled Pennsylvania Avenue that morning. The November air had a cool bite to it and most of the leaves were gone. Her brother Matthew was asked to cover the war in Europe and travel to Italy for the *Globe*. Daniel and Katherine read a letter from David about the sights in England and the cozy pubs he enjoyed. Sarah and George Hensley had dinner with their father, Nathan, in Houston. Nathan was nearly too old to walk at all and had to be taken by wheelchair. Chief Petty Officer Dave Creeless was on board the battleship *Alabama* sailing toward the Gilbert Islands. The year of 1943 was drawing to a close, many American men had been lost. Many men, women and children of the world had been killed and the killing continued. In many parts of the United States there seemed a lull in spirit and a still air, leading toward a climactic period—something, somewhere had to give for the sake of any life on earth, it seemed.

Eddy Howard, Lawrence Welk, Benny Goodman. Harry James and Glenn Miller brought music of the big bands to America; and the Andrews sisters, Ella Fitzgerald, and Kay Kyser sang the salty, uniquely American-styled lyrics fast and loose. Free and hard hitting rhythms on records filled the airwaves with sound over radio. Dancing became a rage again. The beer and wine flowed freely and in ever-growing volume. Romance was where one could find it—whether in Hawaii, Norfolk, Virginia, Australia, Italy, London bomb shelters, and everywhere else men and women came together. There were many tens of thousands short-and-fast courting periods and as quick marriages, pouring out of this unknown and desperate time. As it has been through the ages, women looked good to the men and men looked good to the women—and most wanted to share life as partners.

Tin and iron were being collected from donations for recycling in the mills to make military vehicles and ammunition. Rationed gas, rubber, nylons and other goods helped the country gather resources needed for the war effort. The eagle was mature and making tools to overwhelm Satan's minions in short order under the leadership of Dwight David Eisenhower. At home, there were baseball and football games being played, hot dogs and hamburgers being cooked and served with Coca-Cola, and cars being modified to run faster. Looney Tunes cartoons and movies brought some escape as the picture shows were filled every weekend.

People were being brutalized and tortured, systematically slaughtered, buried or burnt in camps like animals for the reasons of religion, race and national origin—and for no definition. Fear was the governing force and the skull and crossbones its symbol. The killing would not stop until the world raised up to defeat the evil Nazi vultures and their proxies. Whole towns and entire families were disappearing; the German SS and army pushing them into churches and locking the doors, Satan's joy, and burning the people alive. Lands from Russia to France and the Balkans were being raped of decency and replaced with merciless evil.

Father Isaac was performing confirmations, first communions and hearing confessions. He prayed every day, several times a day, for the salvation of a bruised mankind. The year was drawing to a close; the world was losing its humanity. It was up to America and her Allies to salvage something and bring back love and kindness out of the horrid, insane venture of man's doing. He was older now and had seen the madness, the neverending pain of loss, and felt the suffering of fathers and mothers losing sons and daughters because other men followed greed to its ultimate conclusion. *Oh, dear God... Save us from ourselves,* he prayed. *Take the beast and destroy it for the love of your children.*

On Bougainville, Luke waited for the company to form up on line for the advance. Once in position the order was given to double time and attack in starts and stops to cover and take the land past the clusters of trees and low-lying mounds simulating undergrowth. The Japanese let loose with a stream of fire and took out several the first few seconds and then took a barrage of rifle and machine-gun fire followed by exploding grenades until most could not find a target, having to hide to avoid being killed. The fighter aircraft hadn't killed them all. The armor, which drove onto the beach and took the lead, was slowly advancing over them as the Marine base of fire and flamethrowers cleaned up the holes and pits full of enemy. Luke watched screaming and burning men run out for the relief of a fast bullet to end it as a trail of fire was put into one grass-covered foxhole after another. And they quickly got their wish.

It would be one enemy line after another for the next two months. A stubborn enemy, the Japanese did not concede early to spare lives and minds. Marines were lost at every encounter and left a trail of dead grunts, each breeched and broken body recovered and taken to the rear for identification, tagging, and burial. Bougainville was never in doubt as America poured her men and machines into the first fight for the division of many to come in the Pacific.

Luke and John survived the operation but knew their number could come at any time in another place with war fought like this one. Save luck or some divine providence, each man knew he could be one of the pale bundles of dead weight, lying close next to each other, who would feel no more pain and would never feel more pleasure. The stack of rifles collected would be checked and inspected for reissue to another mother's son. Following a couple of missed starts, planned attacks on Emirau and Kavien, New Ireland, which were cancelled, the battalion was off the coast at Saipan two weeks after David made his first combat jump with the 101st in Normandy on June 6, 1944.

Lieutenant David McCray survived and got his first German kills in the first days of Operation Overlord but didn't understand why he lived when so many died. He didn't know how except by some luck or divine oversight. Thinking back to the flight over Normandy and the planes being struck by so much shrapnel from exploding flack and the sudden fire ripping through aircraft inside of which there were men like himself and the awful sight from inside the jump door of one violently going down with all her paratroopers was more than he needed to want to kill. Men were being pushed into a conflagration of technology with one purpose; human skin would be ripped and burned up at an alarming rate.

Visions of Sarah stayed with him during those moments he didn't have to think about what was happening and what he had to do. He thought of her having their babies after the war and wondered what they would look like and be like. Hearing of the awful toll taken for Omaha was more than he needed to anxiously see the state of his soul. He hoped Sarah would find happiness if he didn't return. And if his number was called, he prayed it would be quick.

Dave was on the *USS Alabama* at Saipan firing her batteries and saw the troop ship holding some of his relatives as a reserve fighting force if needed. Luke and his division would sail toward and hit the beach on Guam to again fight Japanese within the month. The battleship *Alabama* would also be there and a few of the McCrays watched the same sky and water a world away from one more. David would march his company into the thick roots and vines of the hedgerows and into the quaint and what must have been pretty towns before to face the soldiers of the evil-incarnate Hitler doing his bidding; German soldiers fought out of love for each other, but they were terribly misguided and misled, terribly brave and effective, taking many American, French, Polish and English men before being killed or surrendering when all hope was lost they could defend what wasn't theirs.

Isaac McCray prayed for the chaplains and all of the soldiers and sailors as the newsreels revealed so many climactic meetings between good and evil. He knew though that many people on both sides would have to fare in heaven as it was war again because of the continuing effort of mankind to rule the earth when the only truth, the only ruler was God. Father Isaac knew He would let the world be in free will and so the consequences were of man's asking and judgment was quick.

Chapter 19

*T**herefore it shall come to pass, that as all good things are come upon you, which the Lord your God promised you; so shall the Lord bring upon you all evil things, until He have destroyed you from off this good land which the Lord your God hath given you.*

When ye have transgressed the covenant of the Lord your God, which He commanded you, and have gone and served other gods, and bowed yourselves to them; then shall the anger of the Lord be kindled against you, and ye shall perish quickly from off the good land which He hath given you. Joshua 23; 15&16.

To reach Carentan David led his company across a marsh and over a bridge where the men were exposed to enemy snipers and machine-gun fire; it was difficult to negotiate through the swampy areas and hedgerows at night, but they had to push ahead, often one man at a time, through the tiniest breech in thick brush and undergrowth and across knee to chest-deep marshlands. When they reached a path and then the road, there were bodies of men and livestock along the way at every turn. Across a hill they would find bloated carcasses staring straight. Germans were ahead and the first contacts were the shots from snipers, their shots penetrating a still night slowly and sporadically as fear consumed the front line of defenders who shot toward the shadows of their enemies.

"Don't look into their faces!" the Major told them as they could see the bodies from previous attempts clearer now in the light. He had been to France before, years before, and wanted to spare the younger men what he learned—that looking into the faces of the dead was a vision that stays with a man for the rest of his life. Though they were all combat veterans, he wanted to spare the new ones the nightmarish involuntary habit of reliving the scenes during the night when sleep is suddenly disturbed by the results of doing the violent job required to live themselves.

The 101st had taken refuge in the ditches on either side of the main road into Carentan and waited for the order of the day. The troopers had a few hours to rest their bodies before the advance into the small village. David got the word and led his men behind Easy Company as German machine guns began firing and German mortars began pouring down on them. As they rushed, some were knocked off their feet as if hit by an unseen truck; those close to the relatively small aerial explosions were killed instantly by deadly shrapnel from the blasts.

The companies of the 506th Regiment of the 101st Airborne took Carentan by moving in combat starts, using covering fire until lead elements blasted out one German objective at a time, losing a few men as they killed the Germans. They attacked and destroyed machine-gun nests with a fury and rooted out infantry one building at a time using grenades and bullets made in America. The troopers secured the town quickly as the German defenders who were still alive escaped, leaving their dead behind.

Germany had brought the eagle to her doorstep; the Lord was taking from them what they had heartlessly taken, squandered, and killed to acquire. The wrath of God, through America, was slowly advancing to destroy those who had worshiped Hitler, Goebels, Goering and Nazism. It was the beginning of the end for the black-hearted, evil heathens, but it would be a stubborn boil to lance.

"Major Garrett...permission to speak, sir," David said.

"Yes, Lieutenant?"

"Sir...the men have been in the field for two weeks and need some rest. Is there any way I can get them a night's sleep?" he asked him.

"The Germans will launch a counterattack, Lieutenant, and we must hold Carentan. See that your company is ready on the left flank of Easy. Put an outside perimeter along that line and wait."

"Yes, sir."

"The Second Armored and Twenty-Nineth will relieve us, Lieutenant, and we'll get them back in reserve then."

"Yes, sir!" David said as he surveyed the remainder of his men; each was caked with dirt and blood, filth and dried sweat. They were a ragged-looking few now but still very dangerous for the enemy. He prayed no more would be lost and the ones left would all live—those who were killed between the jump and this day would be forever missed by their families, their fellow troopers, and him. In nearly two years of training and living together, they had become like brothers and beloved friends who, before the invasion, were never seen as men who would be lost—and no one knew who would or could be killed; the idea didn't seem real until it began happening. David could call up their faces and clearly see each one. He could hear each one's voice as if he were still alive but only as faint echoes now; sad echoes of men who worked so hard to earn and have the honor to wear that eagle patch.

They weathered the counterattack, which was sniper fire and more mortars, but the Germans did not attack in strength and within a couple of days, the 101st was relieved and made its way to Utah Beach. From there they were taken back to Aldbourne for refitting, rest, and to plan the next jumps. David got his surviving men back intact and was surprised by a package sent from his father, Daniel. The contents were the cavalry sword Jacob McCray used and a Bible that belonged to Jebediah McCray. His father wrote him that there was no better time to deliver this heritage. The letters, postmarked June 8, arrived at the base camp by July 21, 1944. He said the family was strong and whole and had made its way from peasants for the Fergusson clan in Scotland to leaders in America, and they were each the forebears of a proud name—it was his time now to defend his country, and he was. Daniel closed saying he loved him and prayed for his safe return to America and Sarah.

David looked at the last, long, slightly curved blade of the family, finely polished and meticulously inscribed and the 1860 leather handle still intact and hard. He carefully lifted one page after another in the Bible and felt their presence as though both McCrays were watching him. The weight of honor and faith caused him to go down to the floor where he gripped the sword tightly and pressed the Bible against his heart. He determined he would never let them down and fastened the scabbard to his web belt.

They were nearing Guam where the Japanese were once better placed and dug in to defend the large body of land surrounded by the beautiful South Pacific ocean. Luke checked his watch and noticed it had stopped working. He was standing in the middle of the Higgins boat, pressed on each side and front and back by other loaded-down and well-armed Marines. The life of a grunt is such that one follows and does, kills or dies, and somehow makes his legs work to keep up with the unit. Without thinking and without hesitation, they must move. He thought of his brother Matthew and wished he were with him in Washington; he would not want to exchange places however; he would never have his brother see this.

The *USS Alabama* was part of the fleet to conduct pre-invasion attacks on the island and Dave and his crew worked the shells and guns and fired the batteries in a chorus of loud and smoky reports, blasting away at the landing area and behind it fifty times. The ship then blasted the interior with another fifty firing the 16-inch barrels hot. They worked until the last bit of sweat seeped from their bodies, never slowing down or stopping. The LSTs begun their turn toward the western beach of Guam and began deploying Marines over their sides and into landing craft.

"Jump out on landing, Marines, and cover the beach!" the command was heard from Lieutenant Crosby, a mustang replacement officer who had been promoted just last month. At least he had been where they were, Luke thought, and rated to wear the red stripe down the outside seams of the enlisted man's dress blue trousers. He checked and rechecked his M-1. He felt his grenades hooked by the levers on his combat utility blouse. He said a prayer for him and John. It was time to do this work before them and not let any of his friends down, nor his mother, nor his country.

As the bow swung open and down and hit the shallow surf beneath them, mortars and machine guns began ripping through the landing craft and beach front, causing concussion and flying dirt and rock. The Marines ran off the ramp and took up low positions on the beachhead, firing for cover into the thick jungle ahead of them at mostly unseen targets. There was some resistance here, but each man knew much more were waiting for him farther into Guam. "Let's go! Let's go!" someone shouted as Luke's platoon and the platoons next to him rose up and ran toward the jungle canopy. En masse they moved toward the enemy fire.

"Sniper at three o'clock!" Lieutenant Crosby shouted and was followed by a volley of fire into the treetop, causing a limp body to twist through branches and fall to the ground. Making their way five hundred yards to set a perimeter, tanks began arriving and moving up with them, taking target direction and coordinates from the spotters. There would be twenty days of desperate fighting, a repeat of Bougainville in every way with a determined enemy. He would have to be routed out and burnt or shot every day as he took all the Americans he could before dying himself. John took a piece of shrapnel in his shoulder and was hurt to the extent he required surgery to reset the bone, muscle and tissue and sew it back together. Luke saw it happen when they attacked a machine-gun nest and was held up in cover for a few minutes by grenades and mortars. Other Marines were killed outright and fell as they rushed forward. They rushed out of the path quickly after a survey of everything being thrown at them.

The flamethrower put his flame into the slit and burnt them out. As the Japanese soldiers who survived rushed out of the back between sandbags, the fast fire of angry Marines immediately took out each one. Luke was sent on patrol with nine other Marines flanking the main body to spot enemies when he suddenly felt a wave of something different inside of himself. His mind was clear, he recognized. His steps were the same; his weapon was ready and pointed to his left, as he needed it. It seemed everything was in order. He felt he was watching himself from outside his head, trunk and legs—as thought he was a spirit waiting. He shook his head violently back and forth to regain his sense of real time and what he was doing. But it wouldn't leave him; he watched the man take each step toward the field they marched across at an agonizingly slow pace and heard his mother's voice firmly tell James he must stop drinking and that she would help him if he let her.

He heard her say she would work, too, if he just tried something different, just tried. He saw it not affect his father and saw him leaving. He saw his mother's tears and felt her hold him close before she held John and baby Matthew. He remembered the beat of her heart. He saw them on the train bound for the east without his father and tasted the peanut butter and jelly sandwiches they ate on the way. He saw her humbly walk up the steps to the door of his uncle's house and stand there stooped, her head fixed down in shame. He saw himself unable to make it go away for her and remembered not even trying to say something to make her pain leave her.

Luke thought this must be it for him. This feeling of being outside may be what a man feels just before he is killed. He heard the stories of people dying and having flashbacks of their life projected inside their minds before that was all and this was vivid, clear, and definite. He walked onward toward the fatal shot whenever it would happen, from whatever source. It was for the brothers in Marine green he had to go on and not dread the expected event. His soul was as right as he could make it. His brothers needed him; if he were not there, one of them would be taken in his place. It was as if a toll had to paid for every inch of ground and the price was determined beforehand. He marched onward, afraid and unafraid at the same time, looking for Japanese sons.

"We are bound to run into the bastards! Stay alert!" the Lieutenant said.

"Aye, aye, sir!"

"Luke... Do you see it? Hold up!" Lieutenant Crosby glanced toward Riker and knelt beside him.

"Yes, sir. I think I do."

"Let's fan out on line and move...Wait for my signal. Duck and cover." He raised his arm up and pumped up and down to get the Marines moving and fanned his arms to spread them out.

"Aye, sir," Luke said and moved to the left with James, Rusty, Killer Ben and Dan. The rest went to the right and quickly the line of eleven Marines was poised for the attack. The Lieutenant looked at the objective one last time. It appeared to be a pillbox waiting for the Marines to close where they could mow them all down with machine gun. He noticed a ravine cut that ran at an angle close to the enemy position and waved the group on the right to take it and move in closer. He pointed to the left for Luke and his squad to flank it from the left side. There was an open part of the field they would have to run across.

"Ready?" his deep voice came from his diaphragm. "Move out!" As quickly as he said it, the Marines ran to their positions and began advancing. He threw a smoke grenade to his left and in front of the line of fire. The Japanese fired their machine guns at the same time and were pulling up the fire when the first grenade hit and exploded twenty yards to their front. The fire continued through the puff of smoke. Then another exploded closer, then another. Fire was put toward the pillbox causing a brief interruption in their aim. Luke made it, but James did not. He was cut nearly in half by a volley placed at one point—through him. Killer Ben put fire from his BAR toward the slit to hold them down for the right flank to take them. Luke joined and left the field to run toward the box, seeing they were firing wildly, possibly blinded by the smoke and forced to take cover by Ben's fire. He had a very few seconds, made it to the side of the enemy position and lobbed a grenade through the slit. His aim was perfect and the Japanese inside were either dazed or killed. Rusty finished the job with his flamethrower. As soon as they finished, more shots blasted into them and Killer Ben was hit along with Rusty who took one to the stomach and reeled backward to the ground.

"Can't rest, gentlemen! Damn it! Stay down!" Lieutenant Crosby shouted. "Corpsman!" he called out. "We've got wounded here!" He then turned behind him and shouted, "Radio man! Radio man!"

"This is Crosby! I need a tank up here, Major!" he said as he shouted to the men to dig in.

Helen was a mature professional woman of fifty-seven years and had experienced a love soured and a love of convenience and comfort. James had begun as a true and exciting partner and lover but lost his way. Greenlee began as a dear friend, brought her into the business where her talent blossomed and remained the closet friend one could until his death. Her blond hair had turned to mostly gray, but she remained fit because of the schedule the paper required. Many nights were spent on re-writes and editing final copy to get the stories correct; objectivity and truth fastened her heart to her work. The still-attractive woman worried over Luke and John constantly and thought that lighting candles with prayer in the cathedral would spare them. She thought her sons were all that were left to her and gave no thought of romance. Matthew saw her work many hours and had a different idea for his sister. He brought her and Greenlee together; he could help her in this though she neither wanted nor asked for any help.

He met him in South Carolina while doing a story on the aftermath of a killer hurricane and came to know him well enough to know he was also a widower because of his wife's cancer; he was a good man. There had been several boats lost at sea and a number of people killed on shore. Horace Greene, a distant relative of Gen. Nathanael Greene of the American Revolutionary forces, wrote for the *Atlanta Journal* and was covering the aftermath at the same time. The men found their work on the South Carolina coast to be more efficient by sharing notes and anecdotes. Families who lost were interviewed and their memories and grief brought to life as a testament to agony on earth and ecstasy in heaven. Matthew shared meals and beer with him, and Horace shared fine Cuban cigars.

They were on the assignment for two weeks and became fast friends. He mentioned Helen to him as she was about his age, and he said he would like to meet her. Horace was particularly interested in the upbringing that produced two such brave sons who volunteered and because of her work with them knew she was a true patriot, a true teacher of what is right. They agreed he would travel to Washington in the summer, and if she were available, he would meet her then.

Horace remained by his wife's side until she died. She was bedridden off and on for over five years, but he never strayed or even thought about it. He was short and stocky; a balding and gray man with a country-oriented personality, he possessed a gregarious kind of humor and charm. He could mingle with anyone. He spent time with factory workers drinking beer and with the people from the boardrooms drinking wine. He easily found both as enjoyable to socialize with in their own comfortable setting. They had one daughter, now married to a doctor in Chicago. She rarely called anymore, but he loved her and his grandchildren.

It was in July he made the trip and fell in love with her the first time he met her. He knew she was the woman he wanted if she would have him, and she thought he was too good to be true. They began to know each other their first night together. Neither thought it odd as they came together in human passion and deliverance from loneliness, and neither talked of ideas and convictions, which led them all their lives until the meeting. They were pulled together as if by providence without time being a factor, as if they had known each other for years. She happily surrendered to his smile and loved his warmth and honesty—he was a transparent man with no agenda other than showing her attention. He wanted her lips to touch his and feel the wonderful affection between a man and woman he remembered.

"It was good of you to come to Washington, Horace. I never…"

He stopped her by pushing a shush sound between his lips. "I'm glad I did. I met you, Helen," he said somberly, looking down.

"You're something!" she said smiling. "Look up, will you?" she laughed. "I'm not going to bite."

"I hope you don't think of me as bad," he said.

"You mean your Russian hands and Roman fingers?" she laughed. "Not as long as you don't think of me as easy!" She smiled. He took in the contour of her beautiful lips and fresh, open eyes on him and felt childhood butterflies in his stomach. He hadn't felt this way in a very long time. She was the most wonderful thing to happen to him since he met his wife years before.

"Yes, ma'am. That's exactly what I mean."

"I think it happened quite naturally. I couldn't help myself and I'm glad you are loving." She smiled. "Most unusual. Most unusual indeed!" She paused. "Do you think two old people like us can have such a time?"

"We did and it's wonderful, Helen. Besides, we're only as old as we let ourselves be." He chuckled. "You sure don't act past your prime!"

"And you could teach the youngsters a thing or two about making love, Horace! Thank you," she said and put her arm around him; she saw he was thinking deeply. "Something on your mind?"

"Helen…this may sound crazy, but I want you to return to Atlanta with me. Is there a way you would chance it?"

"I wouldn't be taking a chance, dear." She smiled. "This war has caused some stranger things to happen than us! I wondered where you were and now I know! You've been down South!" She laughed, her heart full of joy.

"What do you think Matthew would think? He'd be losing a star editor."

"He is happy for me. I've already told him he's done it again!" She laughed.

"I want you, dearest Helen, with all my heart I want you."

"And I want you! I love my work, but I love you more. Besides I'm sure I can find something to do down there, can't I?"

"Yes, ma'am. I hope you would consider the *Journal*. We have some good people and a pretty relaxed atmosphere...but only if you think you can stand being that close to me." He smiled.

"I want you too," she said looking straight into his eyes, her tone serious and unmistakably firm, sober, and willing. "Maybe it's crazy, but so is everything these days...my boys in a war so far away and I'm not sure I'll see them again." She began to sob gently, quietly. "I worry about them so. God, I want them home!"

"I know, dear. I'll pray for them as this mess draws to a close. Surely they'll come home soon."

"It seems it will never end. What's wrong with people that causes them to want to kill other human beings? Damn," her voice tailed off to a whisper. "Do you think God will take them for what I've done?" She looked upward through her brows to his eyes.

"I know God is a loving God. I believe He has brought us together for the purpose of loving each other and nothing more."

"I feel that's true. And I do love you, Horace."

"I will wait for however how long it takes. I know there is a great deal you have to do and of course, I'll help in any way. God, Helen! You have made me so happy! Everything will be right in the world when Luke and John return whole and I have a chance to meet them and they have a chance to start their lives."

"It will happen, won't it? We will be all together some day, won't we?"

"Yes, dear. I can see it now! Maybe they'll come to Atlanta too!"

"I'm sure of it. And Matthew is finished high school and ready for college. He'll be fine with me moving. They'll all be fine with me moving!"

David McCray survived Bastogne but lost seven of his original platoon. The 101st were leaving for Haguenau that February to make certain the Germans would not break through again as they had done in December during the Battle of the Bulge. An eighty-eight round nearly got him while he was in those woods surrounding the small French town, and he carried deeply imbedded iron as a result in his neck and back. Small pieces lodged in his skin and missed his vital organs; they were like splinters that were difficult to remove without risking more serious consequences. He grew comfortable with them and didn't feel them except when he ran his hand across the spots where he was hit, and he could feel the hard bulges. He carried the sword during the campaign and would keep it on him until he was killed or the war was over. The Allies were advancing toward Germany and in a matter of weeks would step onto Hitler's earth in the drive to finish him and his servants of destruction.

The *USS Alabama* was in dry dock at Puget Sound being repaired and refitted for the next Pacific cruise. She had been through a typhoon and attacks by the Japanese desperate resort of Kamikaze aircraft. Chief Creeless used several days of his liberty to explore the channels and estuaries feeding the inlet and the countryside near Seattle. He saw his breath in the cold and thanked God for every one of them. He had a breather before returning to duty and made his way to beautiful snow-painted forests and cold-water lakes. He spent most of the time alone to contemplate and relax after the strain of many months at sea and the next attack, which could come at any time—whether by submarine, Kamikaze, or Japanese battleship. At the same time, Luke and John Riker were moving off reserve and beginning their landing on Iwo Jima as Marine forces had taken ferocious losses during the first stage of the battle for the lava rock patch of nearly uninhabitable earth in the Pacific. They were quickly joining the fight in the hell and heat that was Iwo.

During his second week in the Sound, Dave went to the bars with some sailors of the *Alabama*. The beer tasted great, and he was in the warmth provided by busy proprietors along the strip near the docks. It was a seamier area but one comfortable and welcoming to Navy personnel. He thought of Tom and wished he could have been there. It had been three years since that awful day at Pearl Harbor, and he had seen a great deal of the East and West Coast and the South Pacific without his brother in heart.

"Here's to Tom Creeless, my brother! He left us at the Pearl and was a good man!" He raised a mug of beer, joined by every man at his table. The bartender heard it and told Joan to let them have all the beer they wanted on the house.

"The owner said you guys are welcome to help yourself—on him!" She smiled, showing one tooth missing from the right side. Dave noticed her and wondered what her story was. She kept her head turned so low he thought she must be mighty bashful or something. He watched her walk away and felt an urge to know her if she would allow.

She was thin and homely, plain with no makeup and appeared as a stereotype leftover from the depression. Her humble nature often made it difficult to make a living this way when a customer became belligerent, but she got by. Indeed she had traveled west with her father who took the youngster and her sister to California in search of work during the late twenties. He settled north where he worked timber in Oregon and finally moved to Washington where he died in a logging accident. Joan stayed in the state; her sister left for Los Angeles in vain hope. She found she could make a handsome living doing what was her last resort—selling her body to lonely men—and was still surviving in the occupation working out of a house near the courthouse in Oakland.

Joan had married badly. He was an abuser and had a habit of getting drunk and returning home to beat her. She felt she had no recourse but to stay and turn over tips to him she made at Clancey's bar and grill. Life was a slow hell for Joan. The one child she conceived was stillborn, she thought because of any one of the numbers of beatings she took. It was easy for her to hate him and she did when he was home, sometimes forcing himself on her for a very fast conclusion, all for his own satisfaction.

"Excuse me, ma'am…" Dave raised his hand. "I know you must hear a lot of junk from sailors who come here, but I must have a few minutes—nothing bad, just a coffee?" he asked her, his hat in his hand. At first she left him without saying a word and returned with a platter of full mugs for the table.

"I'm sorry. I'm very busy. You understand."

"I understand. Quickly, what is your name?" He leaned forward.

"Joan. Joan Clay." She smiled. "Yours?" she asked one of them for the first time, but he seemed innocent enough.

"Dave Creeless, Joan. Glad to make your acquaintance."

"Yes, well…I must go now."

"I understand. Maybe in a while…"

"Leave her alone, Chief!" a sailor, feeling several beers spoke up. "She's not your type!" He laughed. "You need to meet someone who can be around the smell!" He laughed heartily at the chief who smiled back at him and nodded then turned back toward Joan and saw her smiling.

"I'm sure you smell fine, Dave," she said and then asked the men if they wanted anything to eat. She took their orders and walked back to the bar.

"Listen guys…you all remember what you stand for, the *Alabama*," he cautioned his men. "Have a good time but don't get too rowdy, okay?"

"Got ya, Chief!"

"Now excuse me, I'm going over there to talk to her."

Three of them raised their mugs to wish him happy hunting. "No…it's not that!" he said and smiled. "Believe me. It's not like that!" He left his chair and walked toward the bar where she was writing tickets. "Excuse me again, ma'am. But may I have just a moment?"

"Go ahead, Dave. I don't mind talking to you, but you should know I'm married."

"Well...when I saw you, I felt I should talk to you. That's all, just talk. What are you doing here, Joan?"

"Working. Can't you see that?" She smiled.

"Yea. You seem out of place down here. Don't you find it kinda rough?"

"No...mostly its guys like you all. They come and go, and cause no harm. They just want a little while to relax I suppose."

"Well, there's a war on, so I guess it's the way it is."

"Yea. I wonder what happens to them when they ship out. Have you been in the war or is that a silly question?"

"No, ma'am. It's not a silly question, but yes, these fellows and I have seen action, but I'm sure glad to be here." He smiled and as she was finishing the tickets, asked her. "So, you're married. Husband in the service? I hope he's okay and all."

"No, he's not and never would be." She frowned, her face changed right before him to a contorted expression he didn't fully understand but sensed there was something amiss. He wasn't sure what to say to that. He just looked at her frazzled brown hair hanging low with a slight wave taking each strand to each own direction. He watched her walk to other tables and noticed she had a slight limp. He also saw a kind of haze surround her, a haze of sorrow and agony he had seen before. Only he could see it; he saw it when he was a child and it left him when Mrs. Creeless took him to stay with her and Jules.

Most men would turn away and not make it any of their business, but Dave was not like most men. He had been given a life and knew what love was and was not. He knew this family as his, who took them in and cared for them and cried with them when they hurt and mended their hearts every time a boyhood disappointment struck them in mid-stream. He knew his adopted parents loved him and Tom. He knew Joan needed a better chance at life. *Am I man enough?* he thought.

Dave reflected he was man enough to face the Japanese Imperial Navy and Kamikazes, the shot and shell and Navy life of hard work and many hours. He was man enough to handle Tom's death and seek revenge. He was man enough to handle anything, even a protracted problem of this married woman and all that would mean with his stepping forward. He would not turn and run away leaving this poor woman to suffer. His brow furrowed with strength and his mind set determined to make this right too. Ruth taught him and made him this way and he could never let her down; knowing or unknowing, it did not matter. She raised a man.

"Joan...I'm not leaving until we can talk more." He looked directly into her eyes. She knew he was serious and it confused her.

"What do you want from me? I'm just a waitress and I told you I was married."

"Why are you limping, Joan? And what happened to your tooth?" he asked her; she knew he wanted to know. He was the first to ask and show this much concern. He caught her off guard, and unexpectedly she felt safe talking to him and telling him the truth. He was strong and young and a leader. That was obvious.

"Let me tell Jim I need a break, Dave, and I'll talk to you a little while. We must meet outside though because it's against the house rules. You understand." He nodded.

"I'll be outside, Joan."

He waited outside in the cold, snowy night and began to feel anticipation not unlike that of how he felt before he knew a battle was about to begin. He felt his face perspire, putting out tiny dots of water across his cool skin, and he felt his stomach rise inside. She suddenly popped out of the front door and walked quickly to him.

"Where can we go? I don't have a car here," he said.

"How about down the street at the diner."

"Sounds fine, Joan."

"You know if I'm seen talking to you, I'll be in a lot of trouble."

"Trouble...yes. I don't want that for you," he said. "We'll have two coffees, ma'am." He told the waitress who had appeared at their table. "And do you have somewhere more private?" She pointed toward the back of the diner where the last booth had been vacated but still needed cleaning.

"You can go there. I'll get to it as soon as I can, deary."

"Thank you, ma'am."

"So, Joan, you didn't answer my question. Am I getting too personal?"

"No, I don't guess, but why do you want to know my husband hurts me? You knew, didn't you?"

"I suspected as much. I'm sorry he does that. I can't understand men like him. What are you going to do about it? Can you tell the police?"

"If I do that, it would be worse." She ducked her head, crossed her arms and began crying. "I don't know what to do," she sobbed. "Thank you for caring a little, Dave."

He was silent and sat across from her and looked at her. He felt a moving inside his heart and wanted to kiss her to make her sadness go away. Her soft features, small nearly malnourished frame, and hurting eyes caused him to want to reach her and protect her. He was attracted to her simple and humble nature and her very nice, wide smile, imperfect even as it was. He wanted to hold her in his arms and make her feel loved.

"I would like to see you, Joan," he finally said. "I want to spend time with you. I will be here for at least a month."

"Are you asking me to have an affair with you?"

"I only want to be a friend and I will solve your problem," he said. She thought for a moment.

"Hogwash! Why would you want to help me? You don't know me at all and you're saying you're going to help? All I'll get is beat up for any minute I spend with you! I think I need to get back to work! Don't ask me again," she cried and looked at him. He was staring straight into her heart; his eyes were like darts, focused not moving.

"I will solve your problem, Joan. Believe me. I won't let you down," he said calmly. "Give me a chance. The proof is in the pudding, and you'll see I'm a man of my word."

He sat there and would not interfere if she wanted to leave. He wouldn't try to hold her or stop her, and his offer was an earnest one that once made he was willing to die in the effort rather than go back on his word. But she would have to take it and trust this stranger with her very life—a proposition he knew was the largest and most dangerous she ever had.

"And what can you do?" She sobbed. "You don't know me either and you don't know him! I'm afraid, very afraid."

"Let me say…he's beaten you and did that to your mouth and will again, won't he? You're so pretty. You should never be treated that way!"

"I have marks all over, Dave. Yes, he hurts me."

"That's all I need to know. The first thing is to get you into a room away from here, and then we'll get him out of your life."

"I want to leave, you know that, Dave…but I don't have anywhere to go."

"Yes, you do. I would like you to first take a room on us in Tacoma and in a few weeks, I'll arrange a bus trip to San Diego. My family will put you up and take care of you."

"Tacoma? San Diego?"

"Yea. I need time to tell my parents. You can't tell him where you are or there'll be trouble and someone's going to get hurt. Will you do this for me?" he said, noticing her worried smile. He detected doubt in her eyes and face. "I am what I speak and can make this happen for you, Joan."

"And you don't expect anything from me? That sounds strange."

"No, ma'am, I don't. I'm not like that and you'll see. Now—give me your address and his name, will you? You don't even want to say goodbye to him, please." He paused. "Are you ready for this?"

Joan saw he was a strong man of character like her father was, and she sensed he was genuine. She looked at his square jaw and curly brown hair; his tattooed forearms and the neatly pressed uniform and knew she would make love with him if he asked her. She put aside her fear, said yes and handed him a note she wrote with an address and name.

"Don't get into trouble....Stay away from him," she said. "I have to get back now, Dave. I'll do what you tell me, okay?" She reached for his hands and held them; he squeezed them slightly but with strength and felt his heart sing.

"You'll see, Joan. I'll take you away tonight. At the last moment, tell Jim you won't be back and I'll be waiting." He sat with her in the taxi to Tacoma and put her up in a room at a hotel. "You keep your tips, Joan and here's a few bucks for food tomorrow. I'll see you tomorrow evening."

The next day Dave went to the address to get her things. Several sailors insisted he not go alone and were standing with him. The coward Eddie Clay had just awakened and had a hangover. He let them in and sat in a different room, smoking one cigarette after another while nursing coffee. He hardly said a word at first; he knew she had finally left him and only cared because of his loss of the money she made. He hadn't counted on her having the strength to actually do it; he figured he beat the idea out of her after the time she shouted at him.

"Where is she?" Clay asked at one point, standing in the doorway to their bedroom, leaning against the frame. "She oughta come home." He saw the sailors putting her clothes and other items in a suitcase and canvas bags they brought with them.

"She's gone and won't be back here," Dave said.

"And how long has she been cheating and working on this B.S.?"

"Your wife is no cheater and she's safe now. I'd advise you to go on with your sorry life and forget her."

"You can't talk to me like that! Who the hell do you think you are? I oughta kick your ass!" he mumbled, looking at Dave's powerful forearms.

"Don't start anything you'll regret, Clay."

"I would if she was worth it, but hell, she's a sorry excuse for a woman."

"Say your peace, but don't come after her," Dave said clearly as a matter of fact. "If you do, we'll stop you."

"Yea. You and your friends there." He forced a smirking laugh and returned to the kitchen.

"Mac...Make sure he doesn't grab a knife or something."

"Aye, Chief."

"The bitch can have you!" he shouted from the next room as the men from the *USS Alabama* loaded her things in the trunk of the taxi. It was one of their missions while in port and they performed it well.

She spent a couple of weeks in Tacoma where Dave visited her and began a relationship. She began to radiate beauty to him and found a genuine smile, something she didn't have for a time, and she loved him. When he had to ship out, she left Tacoma for the Creeless home over a thousand miles south. Dave sent letters with her for his parents and said he would be home in a few months. He also wired money to them, which they didn't expect or want for Joan's care and expenses. She never heard from her husband—if he tried he couldn't find her. Dave had been right and true to his word and helped her make it happen—a life of freedom, happiness and true love.

Luke and John began their search and destroy patrol that morning on Iwo Jima and found rotting bodies in the way where Marines who came before them rooted out enemy soldiers hidden in surface caves and holes. They were putting up fierce resistance and sacrificing their lives for every inch of ground. At any moment there could be shots into their unit from suicidal Japanese soldiers suddenly appearing as if from nowhere. America brought her aircraft fighters, bombers and Navy and pulverized the airfield and surrounding areas. The Marines were slowly taking the day on the ground, one dangerous step at a time. It was the end for Japan.

After Iwo, they would prepare for Operation Olympic, a planned invasion of the Japanese island of Kyushu—where Nagasaki is located as a port city. Before the invasion which Luke heard would have cost many lives of Marines and soldiers because the word was that in addition to her army, every Japanese civilian would fight; two atomic bombs caused Japan's capitulation and the end of the Pacific war. The brothers were on their way home, two of the lucky ones who had a chance to live.

David McCray was one of the very few surviving original airborne platoon leaders in Germany as the 101st made its way to Berchtesgaden where his men found the liquors and champagnes Hitler stored and used for his retreat and rest time from the work of planning devilry, plunder, killing and pillaging of all of Europe and most of Russia. His promotion to captain was anticlimactic and of little use to him when he remembered the men he came to love and lost in the war in so many ways devised by an enemy. The troopers had been through hell fighting for justice and freedom. They lived and won every battle against the Vermacht and the SS.

The war was over and the noble, moral nations finally won it; late for millions, but on time for millions. The world had seen the most horrid and evil expressions of humanness, all the paths with no God, and the most vile and wicked inclinations allowed venting to indescribably evil actions. Finally it was done, over. Pockets of freedom were safe; opportunities for a better world had been earned. A generation of men was no more and the rebuilding of civilization itself had to start yet again in earnest and in truth. The fact that millions of people were lost was an incomprehensible thing for most to imagine; the number was so large it seemed unreal, but it was true. Man is a dangerous beast. Those who had no close relatives killed in the concentration camps saw the pictures; in their mind they could only imagine what it was like for them and for the ones left behind to have suffered such loss.

David returned to Sarah at Fort Bragg and embraced her for an hour before letting both of them up for air. Daniel and Katherine met their son there and celebrated with them his return. It was time to start a family and come to live the life they dreamed and planned. She didn't say anything; she just cried in happiness and held onto him as if she would lose him if she let her grip fail.

"Are you happy, Sarah?" he slowly said each word, looking deeply into her beautiful brown eyes.

"Oh, yes, David! You're home and I love you so much!"

"And you know I love you, Sarah—with all my heart!"

Chapter 20

"It is mighty clear today, Sarah," David said as he looked toward the horizon; the summer day offered a full landscape for the eye with every tree in bloom, flowers and deeply rich grasses. The birds were busy and loud as nature played in the sunshine. The sun put heat on him and made him feel overdressed for the occasion. They planned to move back to Houston for a start and after a few weeks of time off, would set about to make a life together.

Dave Creeless returned to San Diego, married Joan and promptly took her to Hawaii for their honeymoon. Jules and Ruth had brought her in as part of the family, and although now in their seventies, they were very able and active. Ruth told her of her mother, Mary, and Jebediah and of the farm in Alabama that was her heritage. It was now part of Joan's if she would have it. Luke and John returned to Washington and enrolled in college on the G.I. Bill. Being veterans and older than most students, they felt undeservedly revered by most in the day.

Isaac was in his sixties and managed to remain the parish priest in Houma. Promotions in the church meant nothing to him compared to the families he loved. Two of his boys didn't make it back whole. One was killed outright somewhere in the Pacific and was buried at sea. Another had been confined in the Veterans Administration Hospital mental ward in Norfolk. The young, Southern men were two more casualties who would hardly be remembered after a few years, but had done more than their share. His brother Matthew had retired and moved to Florida with Agnes, who still spoke with a wonderful British accent that delighted everyone she met in the retirement village. Helen was happily living just outside Atlanta with Horace, beginning to become a local presence with her renewed interest in theater where she convincingly played roles of the older woman who has seen life in its best and worst.

"Joan, let's leave and have dinner," Dave said while taking in the sight of her in the black one-piece bathing suit she bought for the trip. She had picked up a healthy weight while living with Ruth and Jules and had blossomed to her natural beauty. No longer was she afraid and never again would she be beaten.

"Yes, dear. I'm getting hungry." She smiled. "What do you feel like?"

"Would the Pineapple Cove suit you?"

"Yes, of course. And after I think I would like to go to our room." She winked.

"I sure am glad to have you, Joan. I'm happier than I ever felt!"

"Me too, Dave. I don't know where you came from, but I'm glad you came. If there is anything you ever want from me, all you have to do is say so." She smiled.

"I just want you to be my partner forever!" He smiled. "You're the best thing to happen to me, and I want to give you everything your heart desires."

"Just give me you!" She laughed. "That's plenty!"

"This is a nice place. I love the ocean and these beaches. You can see for miles and feel the rhythms of waves and breathe the finest air. I didn't appreciate it before." He looked out to the horizon. "You know, I wouldn't mind staying here." He turned, took her in with his eyes, embraced her and felt her embrace him in return. "You know, I've always thought that where there are palm trees, that's the place for us," he said softly.

"I don't care where we are, dear. As long as I'm with you, it doesn't matter a bit. I love you!"

"Oh, Joan. I love you! It must have been God that brought us together in the Sound. That's all I can figure."

"It must have been! I thank Him every day!" She smiled gracefully, showing her full set of teeth Jules took upon himself to help her repair. "And if you want to stay, I can get a job and help a little I'm sure."

"I know you would. But since we want to start a family, I could work it out with my father. He still knows some people here and maybe something will turn up for me to do." He paused in thought. "Let's talk about it later, honey. Right now, we have a dinner date with Jim Collins and broiled fish!" He smiled and stared at her body; her rich brown hair fell to her waist and she looked every bit like a princess, he thought; her milky skin had turned a deep brown and her blue eyes were wider now, showing beauty, innocence, love and affection for her Dave. They stepped through the sand and walked back to the beachfront room where they fell into natural passion, convulsive and expected, deeply unaware of anything outside themselves, lost in each other.

He was named David S—the "S" short for Samuel and was born in 1948 with a headful of curly black hair. David and Sarah were in Houston where he worked as an engineer for a design firm. He decided buildings and bridges were more interesting and fun than oil wells and derricks, and he added flair to his concepts by using glass, full richly manicured shrubs and small trees to surround his ideas. Sarah remained home to care for the baby and before 1952 had three more. There came Katy, born in 1949, James in 1950, then Jesse, another girl. The couple and their four children made a home near Galveston where the surf and sand were close enough for a day visit anytime they took a mind to go. It was therapy for David; when he gazed out to sea, he could forget the war for a time and feel happy and secure.

Luke finished a degree in biology and began working as a teacher in Richmond, Virginia. John followed him through school and got a job as a football coach for Fairfax High School near Washington D.C. Claire and Henry Lee established their own law firm in the Washington metro area and were plaintiff lawyers working for those they described as the "little people." The earnings were taken from companies and individuals however and only a portion was shared with the plaintiffs who brought suit for issues ranging from workplace injuries to torts out of slips and falls, defective merchandise and breech of contract. Some were actually damaged and recovered only a percentage of their loss. The couple was not happy even though they made a good living. Claire had stayed home with the children until they started school and then returned to the firm last year. Henry looked at every attractive woman he saw as a possible affair, and Claire came to know him as selfish with his time and income. He rarely returned home at an early hour and usually spent everything he had—she didn't know on what or whom. She was unhappy, frustrated and thought of the day when she could end this; her life had become a routine set of lonely hours, some few with a man who was not her husband or lover but instead a distant and a cold presence.

"Henry...I've had enough. You are spending most of your time away from me and when you're here, you're not," she said flatly.

"I don't know what you're talking about, dear," he said, emphasizing the word *dear* in a smarmy way. His eyes squinted narrow to frighten her out of anger for being questioned.

"It just seems you don't love me at all!" she raised her voice. "I don't see you and you spend all your time away from me with Lord knows who! I know you're not working so I don't know what you're doing!"

"It's my business! Are you leaving me? Just go ahead! You won't get a damn penny from me!" he began shouting.

"If that's what you want, I will! And I don't want anything from you!"

"Fine, then. You go ahead! I work hard for us and do all I can to provide everything and this is what I get?" he shouted. "Damn it woman...if you don't trust me, you're not worth it!"

"I don't see you're doing much around here and you're so cold...why can't you be like you were when we started this marriage?"

"I guess I'm grown up now! And I don't need lectures from you...All I get is trash from you, Claire!" he shouted angrily. "Ever since the kids were born, you've spent all your time with them and forgot you had a husband!" he lied.

"I had to do all the work, Henry! You never helped, and they need me. Why did we have children if that's how you feel?"

"You didn't have to put me aside like a piece of furniture! Don't give me that crap about helping; I've done plenty! You just forget. I don't think you love me!"

"You're not being honest. I can't think of hardly any time when you were even here to help. You'd better think of them—they're both our kids!" She paused and saw him sullen and looking away and down from her. "Tell me where you go after work!"

He didn't answer. She waited for several minutes and his face didn't move or change. He stared at the floor and remained silent. Claire had followed him from the office without being noticed last week and saw him take a woman by the hand and escort her into the lobby of the Grand Hotel before she turned away and went home.

"So that's the way it is...Okay then. I'm going to think about where this marriage is and decide what to do soon. I suggest you do the same if you don't want to lose the children." She looked toward him and didn't get any reaction or response. He didn't admit anything to her; she began to ask herself what she had done to cause him to find another woman. It was a feeling she couldn't stop and blamed herself. Maybe there had been too much time spent on the children and not enough on him. His admission would have at least been the start, she thought. If he would be honest, maybe there would be a chance, but it was not to be.

She hurt inside. She cried inside. She felt guilty about something she should never feel guilty for, but no one was there to tell her that, and she could not shake her doubt. She was confused and her world had suddenly and dramatically come apart that day when she saw them together. She quietly left him sitting in the room and found Henry Jr. and Elizabeth in their backyard playing with toys while Mary was sleeping in the basinet near the large kitchen. Claire felt the weight of an unseen trap of misery without escape, without relief. She cried and tried to hide her tears from Henry Jr. and Elizabeth who were old enough to notice.

The months went by and no other words could be exchanged between them without the words leading to the same argument and silent treatment. He still came home late most nights and still had no money left to pay the bills or buy the groceries. She knew what he must have been doing with his earnings. The responsibilities fell to her; he weakly lied and explained it by saying he hadn't had settlements come through. She felt worthless and needed some out, some attention, some love—even a little, even for a few moments—to feel alive.

Matthew and Agnes were happily living in the warm climes of Clearwater, Florida, in a small frame home near the city. Being on the gulf side of the state, he worried less about hurricanes. The couple spent many hours sitting on the bay watching sailboats slowly move and an occasional small school of dolphins smoothly gliding just under the surface and taking in nature's light and beauty painted on the Florida coast. He became an expert in outside cooking and served up shrimp, fish, and chicken to his wife nearly every day on their slightly elevated, white and covered, comfortable porch; just the two of them taking their time and enjoying each other's company in the relaxed ambiance they made together. Twice each year, Claire would bring the grandchildren to stay for a couple of weeks and the time finally arrived for their next vacation. This year Henry didn't come.

Agnes doted on the children and taught them to snorkel at an early age in the clear blue water just off the beach. She showed them how to tend to jellyfish stings, to swim freely and see and appreciate the coral, fish and underwater plants that graced the bottom. There were many colors the children could only see when they were with Grandmother. She bought them ice cream and gifts, took them to the park to swing and went with the children to see occasional movies at the theater. They watched the new entertainment forum, television, together and didn't care as much about was being broadcast as watching every new show being produced. The grandchildren's favorites were *Howdy-Doody*, *Captain Kangaroo*, and *The Milton Berle Show*, which allowed them to laugh together.

She noticed that each seemed to become more anxious about going home after the last few visits. She saw more stress in their eyes—they didn't want to leave. Claire finally shared her growing suspicions of Henry and her unhappiness with her mother one evening after dinner when the children were asleep and the two women were sitting alone on the porch.

Matthew walked out and saw his daughter crying. He turned and noticed Agnes was sobbing. "What is it?" he asked them quietly.

"There's a problem with Henry, Matthew...I don't know if we should even talk about it."

"What is it?" he asked.

"It's a woman thing," Agnes said, as she looked toward Claire asking her with her eyes if she had already gone too far.

"It's okay, Mom," she sobbed. "I'll tell him."

He heard her say how Henry treated them mentally and that it was getting worse every week. She told him how he was squandering money, ignoring the children and her and having an affair. Matthew heard enough and quickly said he wanted them to move to Clearwater to live. "If he doesn't like that, he will have to deal with it, dear. I hesitate to make it my business, but I know it would be best for these children."

"But, Dad...I don't know. It's not that he beats me or drinks or anything—he's just nothing. He's never home and doesn't care."

"Would you like me to talk to him?"

"No, sir. I don't think so; it would only make it worse," she sobbed.

"Then you have to take care of this. These children need to live in peace and harmony, don't you think?"

"Yes...of course, but I..." She stopped and hid her face. "I'm so ashamed!"

"It's not your fault, angel," Agnes said softly and held her. "He is doing this to you. You did everything you were supposed to, dear."

"You don't know...I have been busy, so busy. Maybe I didn't treat him like I should have." She stared toward the small bay and into the horizon, her eyes half closed and wet.

"Claire, please! You are a mother and a professional woman who has worked very hard for him. Don't feel like you had anything at all to do with what he's doing. My, God! He has to understand and he doesn't!"

"There's something else, Mother...I don't know," she pushed out in a whisper. "I haven't been perfect."

"No one is, dear daughter." She tried to look her in the eye, but Claire wouldn't allow the contact. "What is it, honey?"

"This is hard for me, but I can't stand it any longer. Last month I let...I let a man from the firm... it was at lunch. We had a long lunch," she slowly said quietly and turned toward her mother's eyes. She noticed her expression was fixed and stern. She couldn't believe what she was hearing her daughter tell her and felt her nerves begin to rage in anger and frustration. She couldn't think of any words. She struggled to work through all of this in her mind; the family was falling apart and she was powerless to undo what had been done by both of them.

She recalled from deep inside her memory Helen's warning. Her husband's sister had been right about Henry, but no one else saw it before the marriage. She felt like cursing herself. Finally she spoke to Claire, the gifted student who led the way for Luke, John and young Matthew. "Dear…it's okay. Come live here and forget him. If he can't find himself, you're better off to leave him to his own." She looked at her daughter with loving, understanding, and grace-filled eyes. "Do come, dear." She smiled. "And I won't mention your desperate act to your father…let's keep that between you and me. Now, do come!" Claire heard her and knew she was sincere.

"Oh, Mother…I would love to! Thank you so much! We won't get in your and Dad's way…I promise. And as soon as I can, we'll be on our own!"

"Don't you worry about it one little bit. It's a bloody sad world full of ups and downs, but we'll be so happy to have you close!"

John Riker led the football team to the District of Columbia Championship after six years of steadily improving seasons by teaching discipline and hardening the boys' bodies with rigorous physical training to make them stronger and tougher. It became well known that if a youngster desired to play football for him, the former Marine would test his endurance and require maximum effort. Luke attended a few games each year, driving the few miles across the state line to stand next to John on the sidelines. Their younger brother Matthew was in Atlanta working for the Georgia Power Company after attending Georgia Tech and finishing a degree program in electrical engineering. He married before the end of his senior year in 1949 to Marlene Gruver, a student from South Carolina.

Marlene was in the student center one day, and while raising a sheet of notes to hand to a friend sitting at the same table, she struck her glass of coke and spilt it over the table surface. Matthew went over to help and met her. She had light brown hair and wore glasses, and she was attractive in a way that caused him to be curious. Her sweater was pink and decorated with a monogram of a duck, It didn't fit tightly over the long flair skirt she wore. Her hair was straight and cropped just below her shoulders. But her lips were full and puffy under a slightly upturned nose. Her eyes were large blue opals behind the frames and as clear as a summer day. She seemed nervous when he met her and fidgety, handling her pocketbook clumsily and fingering her notebook several times as if she didn't know what to do with it. And she didn't move out of the way of the spilled drink fast enough to keep it from staining her skirt.

Matthew didn't know she had seen him first and was interested in meeting the local before. He was of medium height and brown haired, very motivated in his classes and never missed a session. They had been in the same calculus class last year, but he didn't remember; she did. This is not how she wanted to meet him but was the first time she had a chance to say more than good morning.

"I'm so clumsy!" she said and smiled, finally rising from her chair.

"That's alright. Let me help you with these." He reached for her notebook. "I'll get the towels." He smiled.

"Why, thank you. But really, you don't have to do that. It's my mess and I'll clean it." She laughed. "I guess I can't handle doing more than one thing at a time." She stood and looked at him as he wiped her table. "You're mighty nice."

He noticed her and said she was too. "I'm Matthew Riker. Aren't you Marlene…Marlene Gruver?"

"Yes, I am. You remember me? We have been in a class together, but you sat in the front away from me." She smiled. "I wouldn't have thought you noticed."

"Well…I like to make sure I can hear he professor and see the board, you know, in class. But I noticed you."

"How are you doing? I guess you're a senior…are you leaving after the year is over?"

"I still have a few courses I can only get this summer. I'll be here for a few more months. You?"

"I'm graduating in May. I'll be interviewing this spring to try to find a job."

"That's great! Congratulations! I sometimes think it'll never end." He laughed. "Can I replace your drink? It's coke, isn't it?"

"No, thank you, Matthew. I've had plenty. But I would like you to join us if you can." She smiled.

"I'd like to. Maybe you can give me some tips on old Stewart. I'll have him next term for Strength of Materials. I've heard he's tough." He saw her nipples through the fabric of her sweater; she was very large in front and couldn't dress enough to disguise her endowment. He caught himself lingering below her chin. "Sorry for staring."

"I know...let's go to the Coffeehouse. Maybe we can talk there. Stewart is okay as long as you ask him to explain. He has a tendency to talk to the blackboard and leave out a few details. I think it's just an age factor." She laughed.

"Let's go! I'd like to get away for a little while," he said.

She told the two young women she was with to keep her notes until tonight and excused herself from the table to walk with Matthew off campus. A copy of an English teahouse was adjacent to the campus downtown Atlanta and served coffee and items from a small menu to students wanting a quick wake-up blend and snack. The establishment arranged wooden booths like the booths the owner saw in England when he was stationed there in a supply regiment during World War II. They became a couple that day and saw each other every day after. Soon they both desired to be more intimate and decided to elope. They left Atlanta together one weekend and were married quickly in the first wedding chapel they found in Gatlinburg, Tennessee, a new business starting to take root in the beautiful mountain community nestled between running springs and green, full slopes north of Knoxville.

Their marriage was now in its ninth year, and they were as best friends as they had become following the day in the student center. The couple had three children and was expecting a fourth in the early fall season. They lived happily near Helen and Horace on the east side of Atlanta where he could drive to the main office of the power company in less than thirty minutes. Every summer they would drive the few hours to Marshall County, Alabama, and stay at Lake Guntersville to picnic and fish. The water and air, mountains and trees, deer and birds allowed for a peaceful escape for vacation. There were relatives still living nearby as relatives of Samuel and Irene and descendants of Andrew and John McCray had lived in the county to still help at the children's school and keep the small farm in the family where now all they had were horses and mules grazing on the forty-acre patch. The Rikers found them and visited every year so the children would know and incidentally learn what it took for their original family to make a living. It was later when they learned of the McCrays in Arkansas and set out one year to find Phillip and his family.

Phillip and Theresa had five children who were adults now. Two worked in the construction company founded after the Great War by their father. One had moved to North Dakota and two were married, living and working in Dallas, Texas. When Matthew found the elder McCray, he told him of what his brothers had done in the Pacific and could see the tears come to his eyes.

Phillip knew the risks that so many in his family had undertaken for the sake of duty to one's country and was both proud and humbled by the strength of character and fullness of the heart passed down by Lucious and Katy, he thought. He almost took the wrong path but was put right by a cousin who was not a fighter, but a priest. He shared himself with Matthew and Marlene—the path that some in families may take may not the best. He almost stayed in the quagmire but was saved by the grace of God and family.

He asked them to always remember and teach their children so they may know the sacrifice and work and that so many had died. "They should never be forgotten as their life was as important as any. They wanted to live like us and be happy, but were taken from our family, and many families the same as ours, much too early," he thought aloud sadly and proudly at the same time. He determined to find Isaac once more before the shade turned dark and his life was over. He had to thank him. He turned to his Theresa and embraced her tightly in his arms, feeling her breath. Being the warm woman she had been for nearly forty years now, it was not over for them. She embraced him back; she didn't know all he felt because she couldn't have been there to see the deaths, but she knew him to be a kind and thoughtful man since she knew him. The war had educated him and taught him to never take anyone or anything good for granted or himself as anything other than a man, but a whole man. "Louisiana would be nice," he said.

John Riker began a relationship with the school's senior English teacher, Debra Jones, and they married the same day peace was declared in Korea and the thirty-eighth parallel was established as the dividing line between two radically different political ideas. He reflected on the men who had been lost in this conflict so soon after so many gave their lives as a price for America to be safe and guard the freedoms she must for all her people. He wondered how it was he was spared while many just like him, no better, no worse, were taken. He never wanted any of his children to be in a war.

Luke was still single. He came close to marrying once, but his constant nightmares had taken a toll and put him into depression. Long regarded as the tougher of the two, it was he who couldn't forget and go on with a clear mind. He finally had to be committed to the Veterans Administration Hospital, a late casualty of Germany and Japan's demons. One day in class he broke down, cried and began screaming incoherently, frightening the students so they ran out of his classroom in panic. There was no medicine for him, no words, no treatment or surgery that could fix him again. Maybe in time he would come back; no doctor knew, no priest knew, no brother or mother knew. His mind had become locked somewhere no one else could enter and find him.

When Matthew heard, he rushed to him. When John heard, he rushed to him and took his mother, who cried uncontrollably over her boy. Helen couldn't reach him, this different person than her son, and her tears couldn't bring him back. It was as if a bomb exploded between him and her she couldn't deflect or shield him from and had to look on him as a lost man, a soul that had done too much, seen too much, and broke under the weight of it all. Blood and bone without thought were pumped out and broken in those years; jaws and heads were ripped open, spilling the contents of a man's life. There were rifles and machine guns, artillery rounds and mines, and the marching into killing zones for all of it and all of it came back to him as the present he lived every minute of every day. His pale face, unruly hair his mother tried to groom and couldn't, and his sitting so alone in a dangerous place kept him from them. His sullen, faraway stare had him facing Iwo Jima again, and there was no leave, no discharge in sight. All she had left was prayer.

"Mother...let us leave him now," John said. He took her hand and nudged her to come with him. "He doesn't know we're here." She looked into his eyes, saw his tears and knew he was telling the truth. Matthew stood in the doorway to the ward and waited for them. He had seen his brother in a state he wanted to forget and couldn't understand why it was happening like this and what Luke was seeing and feeling that they couldn't see. His mind was blank. He wanted to hold Marlene and forget Luke for a time. This was not suppose to happen to his big brother—a big brother he always looked up to and admired, It wasn't right or fair, he thought.

"Let's make sure the doctors do everything they can for him."

"Yes, of course. And pray for him, boys," she told both and let them escort her out of the sight of him. Helen felt her age for the first time and left her oldest son, watching the floor with each step, not thinking, just feeling.

Dave found work in a fruit-packing house and made love to Joan every night under the warm glow of ocean stars, their light brighter than they seemed on the mainland. Ocean breezes and the mingled sound of traffic and ocean waves made the calm nights a little busier and exciting for the couple. He loved Hawaii since the visits he made with Jules, Ruth and the Navy had him pass through for more time on the islands. This was home for him and she grew to love it as much. He read newspaper reports of Hawaii and Alaska becoming states with the pen of President Eisenhower, and that fact made him feel even more at home.

He and Joan saved as much as they could to start a small bar and grill which would let them plan an apartment in the same building, saving more from expenses they could use to build the business and work independently. It was a dream they shared, knowing it was their future. Tourism had taken hold and there was plenty to do that would earn them a living catering to visitors.

The place was named "Tom's" after his brother. They built a second floor overlook where the couple would burn candles, sip mixed drinks and gaze into the evening sky, colored in shades of blues and reds when it was theirs. During the day, the couple worked their place and served up hamburgers and fruity drinks in a homey atmosphere, the dark-stained woods interspersed with bamboo dividers and native decorations making it an attraction for those who desired a quieter place. Dave and Joan found peace.

"This is my dad's hat from the airborne," ten-year-old David told a group of friends in the Pasadena neighborhood, which was one of the new-style subdivisions built following World War II. The sidewalks were uniform and the houses looked pretty much the same block after block. Children played freely and ran and rode bicycles everywhere they could reach by asphalt roads. There was a lot of sun in south Texas and the pavement would run hot most days except when it rained. The children would gather at one or another house for home-baked donuts or Kool-Aid drinks made by loving mothers most of whom kept house during the day.

"Pull me in the wagon, David!" Katy asked, putting her whole body into the bed of the Red Ryder David had bought them for Christmas last year.

The doors were left unlocked even at night. Every night David checked on his children to make certain they were sleeping well and covered. Every Sunday the family went to Mass and heard the priest say the sacrament of the Host and offer the people Jesus' blood and body in the symbolic form of grape juice and round bread wafer. At church and home the children were taught right from wrong, righteousness and sin, and how to behave with manners. At school the pledge of allegiance was recited following the morning prayer broadcast over the school's intercom. There was the inevitable paddling to be earned for bad behavior of any kind while attending school with other children who were watching and learning. And homework was assigned and tests were given to motivate every child to learn in order to pass to the next grade. Summer vacations were long, a full three months, and parents of most all the children came to all the P.T.A. meetings and teacher's conferences to help the school and track how their child was doing and what he or she needed to improve.

David S. played peewee football and little league baseball where effort and sportsmanship was valued and winning was a good thing to accomplish but not quite as important as how the game was played. His father watched him run fast and tackle hard at every practice and game. He taught him how to shoot and treat the rifle or pistol as if it were loaded and never to point it at someone. He led his Boy Scout troop and taught him how to camp and hike using a compass for direction and how to build footbridges, tie knots, fish and hunt. David worked with his son on every project he had, from first aid practice to carving and making shelters with few resources other than what nature provided naturally. He taught him to always treat girls with respect, to remove his cap in front of them and indoors and to open doors for them and say *yes ma'am* when asked. He taught him how to be a gentleman after his own father, Daniel's, strict enforcement and advice. The boy was growing up to be like him. And Katy was being raised to be like her mother and work in the home as an efficient homemaker. James and Jesse were following their brother and sister and being taught the same things. They were subject to the same spankings for lying about anything, showing temper toward one another or showing bad manners to an adult.

The fifties were prosperous in every way to America and her people. As the younger children learned, some older ones were drag racing between stop lights and cruising new hamburger stands while listening to rock and roll with Buddy Holly, the Tams, Johnny Cash, Elvis, Little Richard, and the Teenagers. The '57 Chevy with a large block V-8 and a four-barrel carburetor was the most popular car to take one's girl on a date, and many tires had to be replaced more often than parents had to replace them. White socks and tight jeans became the young men's rage in fashion while it was tightly fitting skirts for the young women. Letter jackets were to be earned and worn as a boast you were good enough to make the team. Soda fountains and sock-hops, skating rinks and amusement parks drew every teenager for miles where their mission in life was to go with a good-looking member of the opposite sex and make out in the dark—whether it was in a car on a date or stolen moments inside a house when parents were not home. Cigarettes and beer were the most nearly inescapable temptations many could not resist. There was James Dean, Jane Mansfield, and Marilyn Monroe in the movies along with foot-long hotdogs, ice cream sodas, and Green Stamps at the grocery stores. There was fast, loud, whopping freedom of thought and acts—as long as one didn't encroach or leave the boundaries of the polite, church-influenced society—and even then the consequences were more often only social rather than sanction. There was enough money for those who would earn it.

France had a fighting presence in Viet Nam, and Russia blustered and threatened because they too had nuclear weapons and ran their news as propaganda as everyone with even a little common sense could see. There was fear about communism spreading and the immeasurable destruction the next war would mean to mankind. Practice drills were scheduled *in the event of a nuclear attack.* But there was peace in the country and barbeques were fired up in backyards across every state. The beer was flowing, now available in kegs men kept in the second refrigerator in the garage. Parents held teenage parties in their homes and provided the music, chips and soda and only occasionally entered the same rooms where the young men and women were getting to know how to socialize with each other.

During the next ten years, John and Darla, a woman he met in church who also volunteered as the church secretary, were married. He stayed at Fairfax and coached every year while he taught history and mechanical drawing. She was a secretary at an insurance firm and was studying to become a claims agent and in some of her off time, she typed and copied the church bulletin for St. James Catholic Church. By the time John Kennedy was elected President, they had become parents for the first time and named their daughter Kelly. When Kelly was five years old, they learned of Darla's inoperable brain cancer that left her with a year to live according to the panel of physicians assigned to her oncology at St. Peter's Hospital. Her primary doctor was Dr. Jane Bray, who was established as an expert and was also a qualified brain surgeon.

"Life has its ups and downs, I suppose, John, dear," she said as she lay in the hospital bed; her latest episode of pain had caused them to rush her there once more. Now the staff knew her problem and quickly administered the morphine in a sufficient dosage without wasting a lot of time and causing her more suffering.

"I still expect you to get better, angel. You just have to! Stranger things have happened."

"I don't think so, honey. I can tell. I'm so sorry." She sobbed for them. "I don't want this either and would give anything to make it go away."

"You know, since I met you at St. James, I knew you were special," he said to change the subject onto something more pleasant for both of them. "Have

I ever told you that the first thing I noticed was your looks?" He smiled. "You were so gorgeous I couldn't keep my eyes off you."

"Oh, John!" she slurred. "You're such a bad boy!" She smiled through her hurt toward him. "Where's Kelly?"

"She's with your mother, dearest. She's fine."

"You know, next fall she is starting the first grade and I so looked forward to helping at the school in her class. Miss Crumley invited me, you know."

"Let's think that you'll be there, honey." He felt tears forming, tears he didn't want her to see, but tears he could not stop. "God can do this, Darla...He can..." he stammered out one word at a time and was finally unable to speak because his throat closed tight on him.

"Don't let me upset you, angel. Please," she said clearly, suddenly as sober as if she hadn't had any drugs. "It'll be fine. Now why don't you go home for some rest? And, John...pray for me, please."

He nodded yes. He leaned over to her head and kissed her gently, using his hands to embrace her shoulders and squeeze them out of affection. "I'll be back tomorrow afternoon, honey. I'll bring Kelly."

Chapter 21

"Get out! Get out! Get out!" the Marine drill sergeant shouted from the depths of his diaphragm inside the door of the bus where its sixty or so passengers boarded in the Charleston Airport forty miles north for the trip scheduled to arrive at Parris Island at 1:00 a.m. "Get your ass on the footprints, ladies!" he directed them with untouched violence. There was violence, syllables and words that sounded like hatred in his voice used to train Marines. But there was no hatred; there was a commonality of confidence that with the right regimentation these civilians could be transformed into fighting men who would jump and attack without hesitation on the order. This is how it had to be for the recruits, a lowly assignment, to assure more of them would survive and do their country's bidding whatever and wherever that may be.

It had been five years since President Kennedy was assassinated and President Johnson had the United States committed deeply in Viet Nam. He would choose not to run again during 1968 and Richard Nixon would be elected to the Presidency largely on the promise of resolving the conflict that had become very unpopular. The issue split families and destroyed friendships, caused fights and ultimately mass demonstrations against American policy as it was currently being carried by young troops sent for thirteen-month tours of duty. For the McCrays it was the family's sixth generation involved whether in the military service or as young adults questioning the direction of the country. David S. signed up for the Marines after a less-than-successful high school experience and a longing in his heart to be the man his dad had been. It was as simple as that for him. The Marine Corps offered him a chance to prove he was an able man and not a boy. He signed up and left the summer after he finished high school and turned eighteen.

From the instant the drill instructor herded them off the bus, there was not a moment of true peace of mind without worry for eight weeks. He told himself it would be over some day and kept his mind in a state for the duration. There was one small goal after another to look forward to that meant the time was drawing nearer to the day when he was no longer under the constant barrage of verbal assaults and gut-wrenching exercise and group runs led by the sergeants. The first goal was to be allowed slightly more hair and a starched cap. The second milestone was finishing qualification at the rifle range, and finally the third was graduation when parents would come and he could proudly march in front of them as part of a well-disciplined group of young men who were now part of a known dangerous military fighting force. He thought to himself during those weeks how great it was going to be to march smartly for his dad to see. He thought how great an accomplishment it would be for him to have earned the title, Marine.

It was true in most of the South, from Texas to North Carolina; able young men finishing high school generally supported the war and thought it was the thing to do to enlist in one of the armed services. Those who heard and knew the reputation and desired to become one of the "best trained" signed up for the Marine Corps, Army Airborne, and, for the ones with an education, the Army Special Forces. Viet Nam seemed distant, and dying didn't seem real. Besides, many thought, their training was such that they would be one of the best.

The movement was a way for some to meet girls, chicks—women. The party atmosphere and opportunities to get stoned on new drugs for a price were unparalleled as was the freedom to have sex with a willing partner and say and do all that came from one's darkest desires, expressed these days and accepted by most in the movement. Psychedelic art, heavy metal and acid rock music, and a sense the individual was god led them. Their badges of desirable youth, acceptance and defiance were long hair, beads, and bell-bottom jeans—and a pocketful of grass or patches of acid. Their mantra was peace. Their way was protest, where there were plenty of females to talk to if you looked like one of the enlightened children of flower power. Thousands upon thousands of the younger David's generation wanted to be accepted and showed themselves in cookie-cutter uniform while at the same time wanting to be regarded as rebels against a repressive society and its requirements of behavior and dress.

Having become accustomed to comfortable living, convenient and easy, with plenty of entertainment, food and material advantages, there were many who didn't want a regimen of military life to interfere in their life of leisure. There were some who legitimately wanted to stay in school and pursue their education. Many were simply enrolled to escape the draft because they were cowards. The war was an excuse for some, the bane of those who were afraid, and a real reason to revolt to most who thought of the United States' involvement as outrageous examples of greed of their overused phrase, *military-industrial complex,* and American colonialism in a country for which we had no business interfering. Communism didn't matter to the Vietnamese who lived in mud and grass huts and scraped a living out of the earth the same way, anyway, they figured. The country wasn't defending herself; she was making war in a foreign land for no good reason; so went the rationale. Many young men thought differently and knew in their hearts the people wanted the freedom of democracy and needed help to fend off tyrants.

In the center of the storm taking the nation were young men like David S. who knew America would never do anything not right. Having grown up in a patriotic family and only been influenced in a Southern high school by the thoughts of other young people that were generally the same, he saw the movement as against him and wanted no part of it.

To him it was a simple question of right versus wrong—and who could object to helping another people have freedom except those so selfish they would sacrifice those of a different race. They would also sacrifice him, his brothers and sisters who are doing the fighting. *Screw the sons of bitches!* he thought and said as he sneaked beer and cigarettes with his friends. There was a lot he liked though; the driving rhythms of some of the music got him moving and tapping his hands to the beat and the braless look and short skirts many girls wore were fine to look at. He enjoyed the idea of sexual freedom although he wouldn't join the movement just to indulge himself with that. And he liked to slow dance at parties and dances and make out in the small backseat of his Mustang. Doing the right thing and being proud only required a two-year enlistment and was a small price to pay.

They were marched single file into the cutting room where a seat in the barber chair for a two minute haircut made them all look the same. They were *"boots," "recruits," "scumbag civilians."* The mental and physical training began that early morning in earnest and each had to keep up or face the dreaded condition of being *set back,* which meant more time on the island or a stay with a motivation platoon for even more punishing harassment and torturous physical training, shortened to *P.T.* for use in drill instructor speak. Every one of them was issued uniforms, field gear and an eight inch flip book with basic Marine lessons, including general orders they were to memorize.

The weeks did pass and David learned close order drill, how to disassemble an M-14 and fire it on target, how to use a coordinate map and compass, pitch a shelter half, dress as a Marine, salute and posture as a Marine, the dignified and fierce history of the Corps and how to attack an enemy and kill him with any means. He learned to jump on command and how to work with others who were like him in concert to accomplish the one and only objective—killing the enemy.

At the graduation ceremony, he did march for his dad in the square where there was a large duplicate statue of the Iwo Jima flag-raising event that so beautifully and poignantly defined the Corps. He was then bussed with his platoon to Camp Geiger, Stone Bay, near Camp Lejuene for advanced training in his specialty—military occupation number 0311, Marine Rifleman—the infantry. He was made a *grunt* and now was a part of an elite fighting force like his dad had been. David the father knew more and didn't want his son to go to Viet Nam, but he knew it was his duty and honor was at stake. He couldn't and wouldn't try to stop him as his father, Samuel, hadn't stopped him. All he could do was pray to the unseen Father in heaven for his son's safe return. It was almost a sure thing the boy would go to Viet Nam and fight.

It was a cold day in northern Virginia when the family buried Darla. She had lived another year beyond what had been suggested by Dr. Bray. She attended the funeral as well and remembered Darla as a mother who used as much of the time she had left as she could to be a source of happiness and strength to children admitted to the pediatric oncology floor. She was able to use hand puppets to bring a smile to their faces, from those who were bound to die soon to those going through the torture of chemotherapy assaulting their small bodies and taking a good part of their hearts at the same time it took their hair.

She remembered Darla made her voice like that of a child when talking with her hands and told them jokes on herself through the characters she created with the puppets. Her favorite was a purple alligator that was always hungry and wanted to eat the fingers of each child. Another she used often was a large, multi-colored toucan that had a penchant for small noses and ears. Jane Bray loved her. She placed the puppets on the casket during the memorial service and wept as she heard John tell of his wife and how she was a faithful servant to their church, a wonderful, loving mother, and a dedicated spouse who stayed the course to constantly learn so she could rise in her job. He said she took her work seriously and didn't miss a day of work or study and did so with a ready smile and warm, friendly words always for her family.

The doctor became close to John and Kelly as well and visited their home often during Darla's last year and had the family come to hers for visits and to let Kelly use her pool during the summer. She visited their church and became a faithful member with Darla's example and encouragement—not a fake kind, but true and real. She patiently taught her and brought her to the faith out of love, admiration and understanding of human shortcomings. She never lectured the doctor and never even thought to scold her for her human desires, which she shared with her out of concern as to whether she was good enough.

Jane shared her love interests of the past, the lovemaking involved and her latest, a married man who seemed sincere and truthful when he talked of being emotionally abused and financially taken by a self-centered wife. She was waiting for the divorce when he suddenly broke up with her, having met someone else who could satisfy his wandering, lustful eye for a time. Darla quickly put her at ease and explained those who would deny others and put them down for slips and falls are not being Christian at all—and are, in fact, like the Pharisees, hypocritical and worse. She remembered the lesson.

In the months following, David S. did report to Camp Pendleton for final preparation to follow his orders to Viet Nam. The manila envelope held his orders, and he opened it with eighty others who received them the same hour, outside the barracks at Geiger; most of them received the same duty assignment. The First Marine Division was involved in Southeast Asia and took young Marines into a war. This one though was not like those before and everyone could feel it. So many American people were against what they were doing they felt at odds within themselves, confused, hung out to die without so much love and appreciation their father's knew in World War II and Korea. It was a discouraging thing to many and came from the corner of the coward.

John called Dr. Bray that evening out of the desperation that flows from grief to have someone to talk to and take his mind to a better place.

"Hello?" she answered and he heard her voice, wondering if he was interfering with her work or plans; he hesitated at first and thought he should just say he'd dialed a wrong number and leave her alone. "Hello?" she repeated her voice quicker this time.

"Hello, Jane?" He owed her so much; he knew he must be honest.

"Yes?"

"Jane, this is John Riker and I'm sorry to call you…"

"Why? Don't be! I'm glad to hear from you!"

"Well, I wanted to talk to you. After we lost Darla, I thought I should leave you alone…but I know you were her friend and mine…and it was just an end and all."

"I was wondering about calling you myself to check in with Kelly and see how you were doing, John. But honestly didn't know if I should because…well," she said and paused. "Because it was the saddest day of my life when she left. And I know it was the saddest day of yours."

"Yea." She heard him pull air up through his nose and could sense his angst on the other end of the line.

"Well! I'm so glad you called! So, tell me how have you been the last few months?"

"I've been making it one day at a time as the song says. But I miss her terribly and can't understand why she was taken."

"I know, John. How's Kelly?"

"She's in school but doesn't laugh much these days. She misses you."

"Oh, the poor dear. I must see her! Can I visit soon?"

"That would be nice," he said.

"I can come tonight…if it's not too much trouble. Do you think she can handle seeing me?"

"Yes, ma'am…that would be nice."

"It's settled then. I'll see you two in a half hour," she said and then quickly freshened her face, put on a pair of three-quarter length pants that fit her tightly, naturally, and threw a plain top on over her head. She found herself primping her hair some and wondered what she was doing at first, and then as she applied mascara and lipstick, it was clear. *It's for Kelly,* she told herself; even though she knew it was also for John, a good man she found attractive and honest.

At his door she embraced him and gently asked for Kelly.

"She's in here. I'll get her," he said and turned to call for his daughter. "There's someone to see you, punkin'!"

The little girl came and stooped momentarily in the doorway to their living room and as soon as she caught a glimpse of Jane she rushed to her. "My! Well! Aren't you fine?" Jane said as she warmly hugged the child against her breast and kissed her head. "You know, Kelly…I'm so glad to see you! I've missed you!" she said thinking of how foolish she'd been for wondering how she would react. "Let's sit down and you tell me all about school! Do you like it?" she smiled.

"Yes. It's fun," Kelly said in the sweetest little girl voice, which brought a tear to her dad's eye.

"Well, I'm so glad! You will do well. I know it!"

"Would you like to see my picture?"

"I'd love to see it."

John watched the woman lead his daughter by the hand toward the den where she had her schoolwork spread out near some board games he played with her. He wondered if she would see him, if she could possibly find him good enough to date. She had been a wonderful and loving companion to Darla and Kelly through the past year, and she had a beautiful heart. But he was a mere teacher and thought he had the life with Darla, never expected to lose it, and hadn't considered dating anyone. He was ready in a surreal way to feel the touch and warmth of a caring woman, but Dr. Bray was much more. He watched them together and saw the love in her eyes for Kelly as she attended to her and marveled at her work, slowly and carefully handling the page and studying each line the little girl made on the paper.

"This is wonderful, Kelly!" she said.

"And I got this from the teacher for all my pictures!" Kelly said, showing Jane a page she used to paste stars in a crooked line across the top of the page.

He watched them from the doorway. "May I get you something to drink?"

"No, thank you, John. But I was thinking we could all go to McDonalds if she's hungry." She smiled. "Would you like that, Kelly?" The girl nodded she would. "How about it, Dad? Can we?"

"Yes, ma'am. I'd like that." He walked into the room and told Kelly to put her shoes on. The girl jumped up and ran into her bedroom to find her small sneakers and quickly returned as though she was afraid to be left behind.

"Good girl! Okay, let's go!"

It was hell-hot when David stepped off the plane following a large enough number of Marines. He wasn't sure how many were in line in front of him. And there were as many behind him as he was about half way between them. The airport in Da Nang was busy and cheap looking; the flies were everywhere and descended on every man, often massing on the back of their necks in large black and green groups. Most of the men stretched their legs and were happy to be out of the confining seat on the aircraft. Vietnamese men, women, and children were everywhere, working various jobs inside and outside the terminal and scurrying about in nearly double-time, oblivious to the new arrivals. They had seen many come to the place and many leave, often not as whole as they had arrived and with a different look in their eyes.

David was still highly sensitive to anyone wearing more than one stripe. Even lance corporals (one stripe with crossed rifles underneath) were like masters to him. The Parris Island experience still had him jumpy. There were one hundred and twenty Marines new in country and were held outside the terminal in a group by the noncommissioned officers in charge. They had to wait for orders from the lieutenant and captain. David sat on the concrete next to Kannawaa, an American Indian who joined them in Pendleton after a delay because of his contracting pneumonia following one particularly long forced march. On the other side was Peter Harris, an Englishman who joined the Corps last year and went through recruit training in San Diego. David liked his accent.

"So, what's going on with this shit?" he asked.

"Don't know. We'll find out soon enough, don't worry," Peter answered.

"I am happy here, just fine," Kannawaa said. David noticed the Indian was a large man with a wide, strong nose and jet-black hair. He wasn't more muscled than David for his size, but he had plenty of power, he thought, plenty.

"Damn, it's hot!" he said. "Can I get you guys a coke?" he volunteered to fetch the drinks from inside the building.

"Gentlemen. This is Lieutenant Rapier," Captain Hollis, their C.O. since Pendleton introduced the lean, dark, and dangerous-looking individual whose unstarched utility cap hid his eyes. A prominent silver bar centered on its front decorated the cap. "He's been in country for over one-and-a-half years and is serving his second tour. He has been transferred to Lima Company. He'll brief you here before we load up."

David and the rest heard Lieutenant Rapier tell them in a raspy and deep voice of their beginning their tour by working out of Phu Bai. They would be executing patrols and watch duty. "You will live on C-rations but we'll get you hot chow as often as we can," he said. Then he described more about how things were in Nam. He reminded them of booby traps and ambushes— "Like you heard about in jungle training, it is real here and they're loaded. Ain't no empty casings to hunt like an Easter egg… these will kill you!" He turned toward the group, now all sitting on hot concrete.

"Come in closer, Marines," the lieutenant called out. "We'll be taken there in 6-bys today. Keep your head down when I say. You'll have to keep your gear with you at all times and do what I tell you, when I tell you, and don't hesitate. If you hesitate, you die." He stopped and scanned the young faces. "Charlie is a smart and ruthless fighter. He is brave and will let you walk right on top of him before he lets loose. You've got to be quicker and more deadly than he. He's been doing this for twenty years and knows the ropes. Keep that in mind, gentlemen."

David adjusted the helmet he was using as a seat. The lieutenant finished and walked away with Captain Hollis to a group of sergeants and second lieutenants standing nearby to wait for motor transport. He watched them talk as though they were at some office somewhere in Texas and not armed and in a war. His tour of duty was to be thirteen months before he could return home, and he began to figure the date he would be finished here in his head. Kannawaa offered him a cigarette and he took it and began smoking that day. Peter smoked one with them.

"Reckon they'll be here soon," David said. "Are you ready for this?" He smiled.

"It doesn't matter. While I'm here I intend to thoroughly kick Charlie's ass!" Peter said, sounding strange with his cockney accent. He laughed.

"Well, at least we're done with Pendleton and the island! And after a little while here, we'll all go home!"

"And what, mate, would you do at home? This is your home!" He laughed.

"Buy a new silver Corvette!"

"Oh yes, the grandiose plans of the youthful mind! And I suppose you'll have your pick of birds when that happens!" Peter paused and hummed, then said, "Maybe I should do the same! I should get along quite nicely in jolly old New York! Yes, I can see myself driving her in a convertible model—red, I think!" he laughed.

The battalion had been reinforced for less than a week when the first patrols were ordered. Two companies were sent into the mission, First Platoon of India included David as they set out on foot for an area between Highway 1 and the city of Hai Van near a peninsula stretch of beach to the south were Da Nang and mountains and most of the time friendly villages had to be checked for Viet Cong and NVA infiltration regularly. As they made their sweeps, the Marines were keen to watch for booby traps and ambushes. David was in the middle of the line this time; Peter was *Tail-End Charlie* and Kannawaa was the next man behind the point. When the platoon reached a rice field, it began raining hard and soaked everyone to the bone. Lieutenant Rapier had the men spread out in line to advance across the shallow marsh and walk steadily onward toward a line of jungle on the other side where they were to search and destroy any VC they drew contact. India was to make first contact, Golf Company followed about a half click (500 meters) back.

They moved in silence, the slow walk toward an unseen enemy, each step causing a wake behind a wet and hungry Marine, able footsteps treasured by thoughtful ones as they still made them. Like the first steps for Mom and Dad, now they were taking him to defend principles taken for granted in the States and put to use in this place to stop the enslavement of another people. No one heard it until the mortar hit and exploded. To be so suddenly thrown backward and into the dark reed and paddy punctuated water with burning sensations across the body was so quick the pain didn't catch until he woke up on the chopper. For Bill Martin, an Alabama boy from Bessemer, he never knew what hit him and took his life.

The supersonic bees flew past them as they hunkered down and low, some laying, some sitting up to their waist and trying to fire back toward the tree line. Contact had been made and the fight was on! David emptied his first magazine on full automatic and felt the fear for the first time, but there was no time to worry with it, only to react as a Marine. Within seconds the platoon had enough fire going in the direction, the VC who were there to ambush were being quickly killed by the hail of M-60 and M-14 fire. The lieutenant had them rise up and move toward the edge to start putting grenades on the enemy as second and third platoons ran up to flank their sides and bring a crossfire into the origin of enemy fire. The heavy moisture in the air still squeezed out rain between them, fogging the senses and blurring eyes as they rushed, laying in fire and hell in platoon strength, cutting trees and men who were in front of them. They were each angry beyond words, angry because of what they did to Bill, angry they were shot at, and angry at being here because one group of the same people wished to enslave another.

"Son of bitch!" Short bursts and long bursts filled the jungle.

"Get down! Get your ass down!"

"Over there! Get him!" Shots rang out en masse, deafening everyone.

"For you, Charlie!" A long burst followed, followed by a long, strong almost mental laugh from a Marine on the right flank.

Suddenly they were gone, either killed or stolen away into the shrouds and blackness of the jungle thick. Sgt. Gunnels, a veteran Marine from Jackson, Mississippi, began the recovery. David saw the bodies of the ambushers, dressed in pajamas and lying scattered. Some were disemboweled and others were laid with large cavities opening their chest to the flies that came so quickly as if they had been perched nearby watching and waiting for a good meal. One was nearly cut in half and his guts had spilled out, rolled out like too much material bursting a cheap paper bag between his hips and chest. He felt nauseated and walked away to throw up the meager contents in his stomach and then heave with nothing left to lose.

He heard a voice from behind him as he was bending over, trying to catch his breath. "You okay, David?" He turned to Ronny Brooks, a lance corporal squad leader.

"Yea. I'm sorry...shit!"

"That's okay. Take some water, man. But hurry. We've got to get medivac for a couple of guys and pick Billy up... and then take our shit farther in," he said, quickly turning to sight the lieutenant. "Let's go!"

"No problem. I'm right with you!" David said as he re-slung his weapon, put his helmet on and quickly adjusted his web gear.

It stopped raining and as abruptly as the rain came, the heat inside the jungle canopy began baking them. It seemed they were stepping around an oven, but this heat was a wet heat and water poured from every pore. David felt his forehead melting, every spec of dirt and mud flowing with his sweat into his eyes.

The utilities he wore stuck to him like a second unruly skin that must have been designed to make him uncomfortable and chafe spots on his skin from his chest to his thighs. He tore open a C-ration and ate the chicken and fruitcake.

The lieutenant was organizing a patrol ahead to recon the village, a squad out of the platoon of eight men, including Peter, who would rather rest but followed orders. He had the rest of the platoon form a perimeter in a semi-circle with the last man on each end at the edge of the rice paddy but covered inside the line of trees and underbrush. The radioman was next to him when he was ordered by the captain of India to hold fast. The colonel was having Golf pass through them and take the point, leap-frogging units toward Hai Van. Bringing fresh troops into a possible firefight gave them an advantage.

Golf passed through their perimeter and mostly didn't speak. Each man from the rear guard knew they had been in some shit, as it was called. Before Golf Company reinforced India, the firing had stopped. Now it was their turn—everybody gets their turn.

"Heard ya'll...what do we have up there?" one dark Marine asked anyone who could hear him on the perimeter.

"Don't know...ran into an ambush and they peeled back. Watch yourself."

"Yea, man." He walked on, forward; an angry gait took him and was common to each of them for having the little bastards run and hide and wait for them. He was carrying an M-60 by the handle on top of the barrel like an appendage of bondage that didn't suit him. David wondered where he was from and what he had to look forward to after his tour of duty. He thought of him as probably an inner city man from desperation who had little but the $116.00 per month he earned as a lance corporal in the *crotch,* a term used to not so endearingly refer to the Marine Corps by every man ranked less than a first sergeant. Most were proud to be associated but also saw the effects of having the last place in the pecking order for equipment and food, hot beer and mechanized transport—Marines were trained to walk more than ride. He watched as his back became smaller and disappeared into the canopy and prayed for him.

"India! Saddle up in twenty minutes!" Lieutenant Rapier ordered as the chopper could be heard coming for Billy's body and three more who were wounded.

While PFC David S. McCray was in the bush as a member of India Company, Henry Lee Jr. was in Washington, sweating during his sober moments. He was not a leader in the movement but a determined follower. His hair reached beyond his shoulders and allowed him to fit in pretty well by appearances. His work in the college of education wasn't going well for him and his draft number was close—so close that he could be called up within the year if he lost his student deferment at Georgetown. His mother sent him money regularly and his father had bought his car out of guilt perhaps, but nonetheless supplied him a used compact Renault station wagon. It was light beige with a personal touch of his own—a peace sign sticker prominently displayed on the back window. The four speed and four cylinders took him to each event and had enough room for a few friends to make the trips with him.

Henry Lee, Jr. heard about the concert at Woodstock and figured he would drive the few hours to the New York countryside that summer even without tickets. He knew there would be plenty of dope—acid and grass; and there were bound to be plenty of girls for his temporary escape from school—a tidy vacation as he considered everything he would need to move to Canada. This would put him close and he could learn more about where he could cross for the dodge.

He dated Carol Adamson beginning their freshman year and had her body using prophylactics each time they got together in the back of the Renault and even bought her a cheap engagement diamond. She was the daughter of a business owner and was studying to teach social science and art—a double major she could use in the Baltimore school system. On a weekend she went home, he asked one of her friends out and when she found out, she brought the cake she baked for his birthday with the ring stuck in the icing and raced back up the stairway crying. He felt only slightly embarrassed, standing in the lobby of the dormitory that day holding a cake and quickly left and pawned the ring. *Damn!* he thought, *I'm not getting any tonight.* He tossed his hair back, edged the sides with his fingers and rubbed it back to open his face. *There are others! There are plenty of others!* he told himself.

His sister Elizabeth remained in Atlanta and was transferring to a different college the next year—she wanted to try Berkeley—as a failing sophomore student in general studies. Her father did not make the same offer to her to help with school expenses and an automobile, but her closest friends offered a trip to Kabul, Afghanistan. There was a great deal of money to be made bringing back dope, and she was promised a wonderful time while in Kabul as well. Elizabeth was known as Beth to her friends and had also experimented with drugs and love.

Beth liked to make love to her select of either sex when she was high after swallowing cocaine through her nose or shooting heroin into her veins. Claire was unaware and thought her daughter simply had to find herself and that she would, given time. She dedicated herself to the growth of a law practice in Atlanta and came to see Helen less and less, until finally no time at all. There were suits to file and court dates to make, settlements to bank, and on the horizon, new opportunities for her business because of government regulations. There were legitimate cases and phony cases, and it didn't matter from which she received checks; there were bills to pay!

They heard the firing and explosions about five hundred meters to their front out of sight, near the place a village was marked on the map. David looked to Peter and saw his jaw clinched. Kannawaa stood for a moment and took in every sound. The lieutenant waved his arm and had the platoon double their pace toward the fighting.

"Move it! Move it! Sgt. Gunnels, take first and second squad to the right and close!" he ordered, as he tried to raise Lieutenant Cahill on the radio.

Rapier finally arrived to the scene and found Lieutenant Cahill standing in the middle of the nine straw hooches talking to himself. He noticed a lot of gear on the ground, from clips to rucksacks and weapons. This wasn't right. Something had gone terribly wrong because Marines wouldn't leave their stuff like this. He carefully walked up to Cahill and grabbed his shoulders.

"It's alright, Bruce," he said softly, determining the man had his mind by looking into his watered eyes. "We've got you covered." He sent his platoon to take the perimeter and that's when Peter found them. He was the first man from India to see the trench. "What happened here?" Lieutenant Rapier asked the officer who was repeating names of Marines.

Peter rushed back to the village and found the lieutenant. "Sir... there's six of them up there, stripped and dead." Lieutenant Rapier quickly had him stop talking by taking his hand across his lips to tell him to zip it.

"I sent them on a point patrol, Dan...George, Phillip...Shit! Rich, Louie...they're not back yet. I'm waiting for them to come back!" he sounded strange, mental, his voice like some kind of imaging from somewhere else, someone else, and he stood there with a blank, faraway stare. Dan took him by the arm and led him to a seat on the wooden floor of one of the hooches. He called for the corpsman and left Bruce, taking Peter with a strong grip on his arm, leading him toward his position on the perimeter. Once they were out of earshot he let Peter's arm loose.

"Tell me what you have, Private... The lieutenant is fucked up."

"Aye, aye, sir."

"Take me there."

He came up to the trench and saw six bodies of Marines and an NVA helmet, which surprised him. They must have closed near regular army, not Viet Cong. They had been executed after the firefight and before the Vietnamese soldiers took off. He saw there were wounds on their arms and through their hands where they had tried to fend off the final shots. Gear, boots and blouses had been stripped off each of them. NVA regulars had taken them prisoner for a few minutes, led them to the trench where they shot and executed every one.

"Take a position to our front, Private. I'm going to have these men moved!"

"Aye, aye, sir." He walked away with his head tilted slightly down, angry and thirsting for revenge.

The lieutenant had a group of men that included David come to the trench to remove the bodies. David noticed one of them was the black guy he met for one instant and didn't have time to even hear his name. He felt tears form, but had work to do out of the dirty, bloody, and wasteful scene—just to show a little respect for the fallen Marines. He knew he could have easily been one of them but for an order. They were no different, no better, no worse, than he and had been taken out of the world in a rush by Vietnamese soldiers who showed no mercy to villagers and enemies. *Alright then,* he thought as he lifted the legs of one of them while Kannawaa lifted his torso.

Chapter 22

"Tell me, John. How is Kelly really doing?"

"She's coping, Jane. That's about it." He stopped and looked at her eye to eye. Jane nodded. "She has many moments where she is bottled up somewhere and lost in deep thought. I know she misses her mother terribly and it's going to take a while."

"The poor darling."

"But you help her tremendously... thank you, Jane," he said.

"I wish I could do more."

"No, ma'am...the fact you see her is wonderful. I don't want you to ever feel you have to do anything...we're okay. I know you're very busy with your practice and all."

"I do love her, John. It's no trouble for me."

"You know, I didn't think you'd go out with me...mighty glad you did. Would you like for me to take you home now? I don't want to because you're beautiful of course, and it would be wonderful to have more time tonight," he said shyly.

"I don't have to go home. Thank you for saying such a nice thing." She laughed. "I think you're pretty too!" she said as she leaned closer toward him at the table. "It's early and all we've done is dinner." She smiled. "I can think of something else I would like."

On the way to her house he reached for her hand while driving with his other hand; he held her hand gently. He caught glimpses of her turning his eyes off the road and taking her smile and lovely vision in deeply to his heart, feeling his body stir. She had been a great friend to Darla, and he knew her as well as she knew him. The times were different then and the wall of loyalty certainly precluded such an advance; he or she never considered it. Now they were free to explore a different and closer relationship as though providence overseen by Darla was taking them to a new step for the sake of Kelly and each other. Darla would approve.

"You know I was married before I met Darla."

"No, I didn't."

"Yes. I was married before…Debra Jones…and ironically she ran off with a Jones." He laughed out of pain. "We were together for a little more than six years, but I guess she felt the basketball coach was more her type so she left with him one day."

"That's awful!"

"Well, I could have seen it coming if I had my eyes open," he said seriously. "She acted like she was trapped and didn't seem to want to do anything…no children, no work, only hanging at the house waiting for me to shower her with attention I suppose."

"I see."

"She was on painkillers and became a kind of wreck around there. You know, I would come in and be tired and all, real tired."

"She didn't help much, did she?"

"No, Jane. I just wanted you to know.…I picked bad the first time and struck gold the second. But I'm no loser—Darla came and we were good together."

"I would never think of you as a loser, John. I've seen how wonderful you are with Kelly and I saw how wonderful you were with Darla. But you didn't have to tell me anything!"

"I won't go on with you with any secrets. You'll know everything. I feel it's important. That way, you won't be disappointed or surprised some day."

She smiled at him. "I'm not at all…I think you're a great guy!" she said as she kissed him on his cheek. "I've never been married. There just wasn't time to even think about it." She smiled. "I've dated a little, but I think the way we met and knowing each other over the couple of years is the best way for me. It has meant I knew you well before anything else."

"I guess that's so." He smiled. He caught a glimpse of her profile, the long lines of a well dressed, pretty woman in the simple way, topped by blond hair cut short to her shoulders, and just right for her angular face.

She invited him in and took him by the hand to a large, plump sofa and asked him if she could bring him a drink. He watched her leave the room and couldn't help but notice her heart shape from behind. He felt the urging and held it in check; he practiced good manners. He was attracted to her in every way now and would tell her; he was an honest man.

Beth told her mother she wanted to fly to Kabul with friends. "We have a month before the next term starts, Mother, and I am going!"

"Why Afghanistan, Elizabeth? That's so far and there's nothing there. My God! What are you doing?"

"Don't be so bourgeois.... Everyone is going for spring break and Hiram and Polly have asked me and I feel I must go to learn about other cultures. You won't stop me." She paused with a sassy expression on her face. "Will you?"

"I don't suppose." She stopped and began walking out of the room exasperated as she had been many times before with her children. "I have work to do anyway and you and your brother never understood that. Someone has to pay the bills around here!"

"Go on! I don't need anything from you! I already have the ticket!"

Claire wondered how and when she lost control. It seemed like the world and every young person have gone mad. Nothing was like it was even a few years ago when she made the move to Atlanta when she was ready to start her practice. She thought it would have been a good move; there were so many more opportunities here than there was for her near Tampa, and she had fared well enough to buy a nice house with a swimming pool and give the children practically everything they wanted without help from Henry. He was moving from one woman to another all the time and did very little for the children and never saw them. She felt dizzy and couldn't focus her mind.

What had she done to deserve this? Her life was sad, so sad she felt no anger but only confusion and what must be depression, she thought. She had no control and couldn't force any of them to love her. It seemed there was nothing for her at home or anywhere. She began to tuck her emotions inside herself and avoid people and issues, resting sadly inside a locked house when she could, cuddled with ice cream and coffee and cigarettes for a smidgeon of comfort. There were moments when she didn't want children or any lover, and these moments grew to occupy more and more time when she wasn't working.

She felt more years than her age; she hadn't even broke fifty yet but felt older and more used up. She had gone to the best schools in her mind and had smart parents who were professionals and had every advantage, yet life seemed to hold out on her. She looked at a full-length mirror and studied every line and wrinkle formed out of frustration and worry. She stripped her clothes for an honest view and saw a woman who had some defects but was still attractive, smart and able. *Why isn't it working for me?* she wondered. *What in the hell can I do about it?* She stumbled into her living room and dialed Clearwater.

"Mom? This is Claire."

"Hello, dear! Glad you called! How are you?" she asked, her English accent still intact.

"I'm fine, I guess...no, not really."

"What's happened, dear?"

"I can't tell you all....You wouldn't have the time," she said mournfully. "How's Dad?"

"He's fine. He's gone to play golf with some friends. I'm worried about you, Claire. Tell me what can we do, please."

"I don't know, Mother. So much of what is happening with the kids is unreal, and I don't know what to do. They've gone wild. Henry Jr. is flunking out and doing drugs. Elizabeth is going to Afghanistan and probably doing drugs and no telling what else. Mary's in a shell and doesn't seem to care about finishing high school. I'm at my wit's end."

"I understand, dear. You worry so....I don't want you to suffer because of the children. You know everyone goes through the process of growing. I'm quite sure they'll come around."

"I don't know, Mother. They are into some things I don't understand and I'm afraid....I shouldn't bother you, but I don't know what to do!"

"I know. They say it's a more complex world we live in, but it's really all the same. I don't believe much has changed." She paused and smiled on the other end of the phone line. "You can pray and be there for them, dear. I believe it's a phase, and they'll grow up. I can come up and stay with you a while. Maybe I'll have a chance to talk to them."

"That would be nice....I miss you and Dad. But don't be surprised about what you hear and see....I can't do anything with them."

"That's alright, Claire. I'm their grandmother and nothing will put me off."

"I am looking forward to your visit, Mom. I love you."

"I love you too, Claire." It was the first time in years since they expressed that to each other in words and not written in birthday or Christmas cards. Agnes knew her daughter was experiencing the touch of the bottom and that life provides everyone with the hard surface through which they cannot pass any lower and it always rises again—as she would. She needed some encouragement and assurance that was all it was and nothing more.

Henry Jr. made his way to Woodstock and spent three days in a fog, high on beer and grass. He took a hit of acid and heard the echoes. The music was great and the crowd was greater. He felt empowered and that the movement was stronger than anything Nixon could stop. He found nirvana, home; he thought, and he never wanted to leave. These people would accept him, and he could do his thing with the women. By talking a little about the tragedy of war, he was able to have it all. It ended and he felt washed out, empty, alone.

David S. marched to Go Noi Island where a daylong battle and horrible, unimaginable confusion ensued for control of the patch. The thousands of rounds discharged from the Marines exchanged with thousands from the NVA deafened the hearing and dulled their reaction time. While making a slow advance and popping figures he could see, a hand-thrown chicom landed near him and blew him down; he felt burning in his shoulder and back. Then two or three more were thrown toward his position, followed by more explosions. The radioman was killed and a man on the other side of him was moaning in soft, low tones of distress forming the words, "God, please stop it." David quickly rose back to his knees and began firing again.

It was done and there had been an awful cost. The Marines swept through the island and checked bodies. Some were still living but had been mortally wounded. He came across an NVA soldier whose eyes were peeling backward into his skull while he was still barely breathing, gurgling. He checked his pack for food and cigarettes. He ate the rice balls he found and smoked the French cigarettes, waiting for him to die. The Americans had opened up Highway 1.

"Saddle up! Hodges...take the fourth squad and move the bodies out of the DMZ," Lieutenant Rapier called out to Corporal Hodges, a Midwesterner who wore a cowboy hat while in garrison and heard the taunts from some men who bought into the hippy culture. They were the ones who opted for more than beer too and at times would be so stoned as to be incommunicable. He paid them no mind and figured the more people who "dropped out" the more jobs and work he could enjoy.

The choppers filled the sky and swooped in to recover everyone who was killed or wounded, and the colonel ordered India and Golf Companies to march back to Phu Bai. David and Peter made their way through thicket and narrow paths with Kannawaa in front. His thick, powerful legs tore through the brush easily, it seemed, and cleared the way for an entire squad. It was good to have him on their side.

Captain Hollis arranged for a delivery of hot beer to his troops who had been on a three-week, exhausting campaign, and needed some food and rest.

"Get your gear checked before you sack out, men," he said. "Make sure your weapons are serviceable and clean."

"Aye, aye, sir."

"Lieutenant...we'll meet at 0530 in the CP," he said. "Post your watch and report."

"Aye, sir."

Galveston was far away and David remembered his dad taking them to the beach and playing with them. The sun and shore, the sound of the waves, and Dad's discipline making sure no one went too far out into the surf. He remembered the gulls and picnic basket Mom prepared with her loving hands and how she made sure each child's favorites were always included. He felt the heat on his back from those days and tasted the salt in the air. It was the first thing he wanted to do when he returned; go to Galveston to feel and watch.

Luke was made the offer to work with veterans at the University of Virginia. He wanted to return to life more than anything he could think of in the world and happily took the job. He knew the horrors they had seen and knew he could talk to them in ways they would understand. Maybe he could help even one come through and live a normal, happy life, and his efforts would be successful. *One boy who thinks he's a man could make it,* he thought. *And show them all and prove to himself that there is life—that there is more and good things; not the killing nor the grip of an absolute fear but more and better and peace...*

John and Jane along with Kelly picked him up at the V.A. hospital in Richmond where he had been transferred last year in the final phase of his recovery. He had been put through a number of procedures and had been given a number of drugs to cause his mind to control impulses and thoughts and bring him out of the semi-conscious state he found himself suddenly drawn into like a magnetic pool of mental slush without coherent thought and only a dull awareness. He endured the doctor's attempts, which were all made in good faith but made without surety and only minimal results. The priest was able to bring him around slowly, painfully and finally by talking to him about the war and what he had done as only one of the two surviving chaplains of the 29th Infantry during Operation Overlord and his landing on Omaha in the second wave. The sights, sounds and smells he could recall on command gave Luke something he needed—another human being who was there and saw as much and did as much as he and the men who were with the 101st.

"I'm so glad to see you, brother. It's been a while and we've worried about you. It's good, damn good, to see you like this again!" John said.

"I know it's been something and I'm sorry to have put everyone through this mess. I'm okay and will make it now, thanks to Father Wathem."

"Father Wathem...I remember you told me about him last month. Well, I'm happy for you."

They loaded into the 1970 Monte Carlo John bought during the fall and left the campus toward Fairfax. Kelly looked at her uncle and smiled her precious smile, showing the whitest teeth in the family—a trait she inherited from her mother.

"And it's good to meet you, Dr. Bray," Luke said and smiled humbly.

"Please, call me Jane. It's good to meet you too, Luke. I've heard so much about you and really admire you and John for what you've done." She smiled.

"Well, I haven't been as fortunate as John here." He smiled. "He has done himself proud to have you with him!"

"Thank you! But I am the one who feels lucky!" she said and clasped John's hand. "I'm glad he came along." She paused. "So what do you do now if I may ask?"

"I report to the University of Virginia next semester. There are a good many veterans returning to start a life, and it isn't easy. Especially these days with all they hear. I hope to help them."

"A counselor?"

"Yes, ma'am...of sorts. I help them with registration, G.I. benefits, housing, and whatever else they need to have a decent chance."

"That should be rewarding, Luke. That's great!"

"It's the only thing I want to do for the poor guys...so much of the country have given up on them but not me. I know what they have in their hearts, and they deserve a chance."

"That's wonderful!" she said.

"Yea, well...Hey, they come back to a bunch of crap—as if no one cares about what they did—and they don't! It's a damn thing what so many people say about them and to them." He thought for a moment. *I wished I could be as good as Father Wathem. That man is a true man of God and seemed to have exactly the right words at his full command! I miss him already.* "You know he told me he killed some Germans and that God was looking at the carnage and blessed him for it. Can you believe that? But he had such tenderness; he didn't want to kill them but had to in order to live—and he didn't want the slaughter of innocents to continue either because he didn't pull a damn trigger!" he breathed.

"I understand, Luke," John said.

"He convinced me there was a blessed connection. The way he saw it, we were there by the grace of God to end the madness and it cost us dearly too, so dearly, so many men never to see the world as we have it today," he said. Luke's breathing was becoming labored. John figured to change the subject from the sadness and doubt caused by so many they thought they were fighting for—at least their sacrifice saved them from going, but it didn't matter to the generation of pleasure. He knew many of them and of their shallowness.

"Luke…are you hungry? I know a great barbeque place off the Fredericksburg exit." He laughed. "They serve North Carolina-style pulled pork!"

India Company marched out again for another mission. This one was to the sandy bottom of the creek that ran from Quang Nam Province toward Go Noi Island. Marines had been there before and had to return because of intelligence the NVA infiltrated the area and villages in the province. For the men who went into this battle, they were each bound in destiny to *face the dragon*, a phrase widely used by troops in Viet Nam to describe an operation that would mean almost certain death.

The villagers in Viet Nam were tortured and killed in a horrific order of evil; the farmers were punished for giving aid to the Americans and South Vietnamese and burned out for giving aid to the North Vietnamese. Their sons and daughters were forced to kill Americans by the Viet Cong; refusal or failure meant members of their families were killed as examples. Their bodies were hung as a macabre display of consequence in the center of the village, often with their tongues cut out, eyes gouged and privates stuffed inside their dead mouths.

India advanced through the jungle area and reached the sandy bottom of the creek where bodies were stacked like firewood. There was gear stacked in a huge pile and weapons massed for retrieval. The crimson-colored flow of the stream brought the seeping blood flowing toward Da Nang. David saw there were NVA in one pile and Marines in another. David thought that maybe the guys were from New York, Nebraska, Florida, or Texas and gave their life to hold a line of ground of probably little or no value other than that instant in time where enemies faced each other.

"Squad leaders! Fan your men out and move north on line!" the lieutenant commanded. He led the procession of relief warriors past the creek bed, into the ravine and then up toward the jungle-covered hills. The line of Americans was moving toward the NVA to deal them a deathblow. Golf was following within ten meters and behind that company, Lima spanned the third wave. Helicopter support was standing by out of Phu Bai, fully loaded with ammunition and rockets, the rotors turning and the engines warm.

David had his M-16 at the ready and took one step at a time through the undergrowth. Since no trail could be used again safely, each man tried to find new earth to step. The danger of booby traps kept them off the familiar to be certain, but there were traps outside the trails as well and pre-sighting of mortars.

"Stay on line, men," Rapier said in a low voice. "We're close. Be ready."

David could hear his heart pounding through his chest and felt the beginnings of a kind of paralysis coursing through the veins in his arms and to his legs, but he managed to keep moving. He checked and rechecked the safety on his weapon, making sure it was off and ready to fire at the slightest sound or movement. Suddenly the tense quiet was punctuated by a long burst from a machine gun ahead and screams from some in his company.

Supersonic buzzing struck through the brush all around and over them and could be felt—like iron vomit from hell itself penetrating their space, a fraction of an inch or a split second making all the difference whether one lived or died. They had been hit and it was time to move quickly. Every man dropped to the ground and then moved forward on their knees, using their arms and weapons to gouge the earth in front of them and help pull them toward the enemy, toward sighting who was trying to kill them.

"First squad! Move to the right and frag 'em!" Rapier called out to Peter and Kannawaa, with David trailing slightly. Hoskins and Smith were with him and firing toward the origin of the sounds. The men quickly found a thicket behind which the NVA soldiers were firing and threw several grenades over the brush to silence their point. One began running back and Kannawaa stood up in an instant and cut him down with an aimed burst. He then followed the path the dead man tried. A few of the men passed out and had to be revived by the corpsman as the company moved up in line and stalled to wait for orders.

Lieutenant Rapier surveyed the thick jungle to their front as best as he could see and had the men move slowly forward until he could find the main body of NVA. Finally he needed more and sent a patrol out to report what was ahead of them.

"McCray! Harris! Brooks! Take the point and recon fifty meters!" he said and quickly added. "Watch your ass!"

"Aye, sir!" David said and picked up his gear and moved toward the unknown with Peter and Ronny on his back. It was his turn to face the dragon and either live or die. *Lord, please be with me. Please help me through this,* he prayed silently over and over.

Matthew and Marlene welcomed Luke to a warm, simple and relaxed homecoming. They had prepared Joan's home to welcome the brother with a pool party. Candles were lit and banners hung, gentle folk music played in the background and guests were treated to food and drink in his honor. Luke smiled. "I'm sorry I couldn't have come earlier," he said. "This is very nice of you all."

"We love you, Luke," Marlene said. "And we're happy to have you home!"

"Yes, please make yourself comfortable and have anything you want!" Joan spoke up. "I'm going to change into my suit. John has one for you, too, Luke, if you want it. The water will feel mighty good after such a hot trip!"

"When do you make the move to Charlottesville, Luke?" John asked him. "We will help you, you know. Just tell us when." He smiled.

"Thanks. I'll be headed that way Saturday, week...want to get settled and all."

"Well, I know it's a beautiful area. I'm sure you'll find it very nice," Joan said. "We are looking forward to seeing the place. I've heard so many great things about Charlottesville. I believe it will suit you!" She smiled and gracefully handed Luke a glassful of ice and tea. "I'm going to slip into the pool, dears," she said to the brothers, turning, her heart shape prominently outlined but modestly concealed by the bottoms of a yellow two-piece swimsuit.

"You done good!"

"Yes, I have." John looked down and smiled a gentle smile. "You will too, Luke. How can they resist you?"

"We'll see. I don't know anyone, John, and it seems no one wants to know me."

"Don't worry. A good one will come along... just be patient."

"Well, congratulations, brother! She's fine, mighty fine."

"Yes, she is. I'm a lucky man." He paused. "We're both lucky."

"I know. Hell, we might not have ever made it out of Iwo except by luck."

"And God's grace."

"Yea...I know."

The evening turned to nightfall and the group had a meal John prepared on the gas grill, a new gadget for him. They ate and then embraced each other goodbye in the soft, warm breeze of summer and comforting shade of black. Here was peace of mind and happiness of heart for Luke. He had returned and would never go back to the place his mind took him for a while—away from all that was good and safe and clean in the world for those who made the slightest effort to recognize and stay the course.

Beth stepped off the plane in Kabul and left the airport in a rented van with several friends from Atlanta. Christy Burroughs led them. She was an older student they came to know in school from Cleveland and had made the trip before. "Now, be cool!" she said. "We can get all we can carry before we leave, but there's a lot to do while we're here! It's going to be so hot!" she said, excitement clearly in her voice. "Jan, you can drive us… just watch out for Christ's sake!" She laughed. "I'll tell you where to go."

"Where are we staying?" Beth asked.

"Don't worry about it. It's already taken care of."

"That's good! Now pass the joint!" Jerry Vaca, the only male with them said. "It's party time!" He laughed, shaking his head, slinging his hair and pulling the long brown strands back like a woman might who had locks which ran the length to her breasts.

Elizabeth kept her eye on the sights outside the white van; Jan steered out of the airport and toward the countryside. It was a place as she had seen only in the abstract somewhere, perhaps in the *National Geographic* magazine or some such; a place trying to swim away from primeval custom with two societies both which profited from the sale of the poppy. She noticed the veils and the miniskirts on the same streets. There was little color and few lights, not what she expected if she had thought about it before making the trip. It was a strange land with strange people, and she began to feel unnerved.

"Did you see them?" she asked the crowd above the hum of the engine. "They were wearing long robes and veils…what kind of place is this?"

"They're Muslims. Traditional, I'd say," Jerry said. "Do you like their outfits?" He laughed.

"It kind of freaks me out, Jerry," she said. "Where are we going?"

"Don't worry any, Beth." He laughed and took a long suck on the cigar-shaped joint, holding his breath with the smoke buried deep inside his lungs.

"I asked you where we're going!" she repeated, glancing out the window and seeing a much more barren landscape all around and ahead.

"Azzar's ranch. He likes Americans!" He laughed. "He likes our dollars a lot more!" He tossed his hair back again. "He's a chieftain...of a tribe. They have those here." He suddenly sang out, "All the chiefs and more good dope than you can count!" He laughed and drew more of the sweet-smelling smoke into his mouth, squeaking his voice. "You'll have a good time there. Plenty of dope and a twenty-four-hour party!"

Beth suddenly felt Christy's hand on her thigh and turned to see her staring into her eyes. "Sounds like fun, doesn't it Beth?" she asked softly wearing a subtle smile intended only for a special friend.

"Give me a hit of that, will you Jerry?" she smiled and asked. "It's been a long trip."

"It'll be worth it! Boy, are we ever gonna score!" Jerry said and laughed. "And I mean big time!"

"Cool! Now how long before we get there?"

"Another few miles. He's on the plain just over the mountains," Jerry said, his speech sounding slightly slurred. "Pass the joint back!"

Another hour and Jan turned into a winding, compacted dirt and rock roadway that traveled like a snake moving. The sharp curves and dust kicking back from where they came made seeing ahead farther than a car length impossible. They passed a couple of bearded men in long robes carrying large bundles on their backs, walking along the road with a labored gait, using long sticks or poles to aid. Jan stopped the van when she noticed a poppy field as far as she could see, purple and yellow heads covering the land like grass does in the States. At a distance they noticed more of them stooped and working the harvest reminiscent of a painting Elizabeth saw once when she wasn't paying much attention in art class.

The dwelling was a complex of five buildings, each of them one level and stone-dust colored with wide openings into darkness. She pulled the vehicle close to others parked in front of the largest structure and stopped as several men in long robes approached them. They were Azzar's men, each armed with an assault rifle, easy to come by in the border towns with Pakistan. The chieftain, the warlord, the boss, supported a small army of fighters and protectors to make certain the enterprise was safe from raiding—a hostile takeover, Afghan style. They noticed a herd of goats grazing nearby, lazily moving about a little and not deterred by their arrival. Vaca said he would do the talking. "Azzar is expecting us!" he called out to them in English. He heard the men mumble between themselves in fast tongues Arabic and then motion for them to get out of the vehicle. As they did that, Azzar appeared in the doorway and walked toward them, smiling widely, showing his stained teeth through his dark and hairy face. As they approached, they could hear the unmistakable music of Hendrix playing inside the house.

"Well, I feel better now!" Jan said. "Sounds like home!" She smiled.

Christy clasped Beth's hand and walked with her as Azzar led them inside. The interior was a collage of movie billboard posters, modern art pieces and statutes of nude female forms, some modern and nearly indistinguishable as human and others realistic poses standing, leaning, sitting, and lying as ladies in plaster at leisure, undressed and exposed for only one purpose. Azzar also used oversized, gaudy, painted but empty vases, hanging beads, bamboo and oriental rugs layered on top of one another and several wall paintings of couples engaged in the sutra to inspire the particular fantasies of men living in a desert wilderness. His place was his island of decadence bought with the proceeds of America's decadence. Azzar invited his guests to sit; his eyes and dirty smile lingered on Jan and she knew making him happy fell first to her on this trip. Last time she was third or fourth—she wasn't sure.

"Take this…enjoy!" Azzar passed the pipe to Jerry after taking a long pull from the length of narrow hose attached to the base of a large, round, smoky, full, painted glass vat. Before eating, the Americans and Azzar completed a first round of close encounters and engaged in every form of sexual expression in the same garish room. It was part custom of recognizing trust in friendly commerce of goods forbidden in the United States and part courtesy on behalf of strange visitors to this man's house and was no major quandary of conscience for them to quickly free deepest inner desires to action, unburdened by convention or what their parents taught them about right and wrong.

The small group of Marines sent on patrol made their way two hundred meters to the front of India Company in thick jungle cover, walking through where there was no trail. Peter Harris had the point, with Ronny Brooks and David McCray following closely. He led them down a ravine and stopped behind the large leaves just short of the bank of a fast running stream, filled with rock and dead wood. He whispered to David they would be exposed if they crossed here and couldn't see if any NVA were waiting in ambush or not.

"I swear, I can smell them, David!" Peter said under his breath.

"Maybe we can cross up stream…I will radio the coordinates to Lieutenant Rapier if we move off the reading."

"I don't know. I just simply don't know." He shook his head in confusion and indecision, his soft English appearance changed to something red and dirty, tough looking like a farmer from Alabama.

"We have to recon...the company is coming up I figure not more than ten minutes from us," David whispered. "Let's scope it here. I'll move up a couple of first downs worth. Maybe you can move down some and see if they're around," David said to Brooks who nodded in agreement, his steel pot covered with camouflage cloth and a few twigs and leaves moving up and down gently, protecting the head from bumps and flying rock and dirt but little else when the lead and steel starts flying. Brooks had a peace symbol inked on one side in black and the Twenty-Third Psalm written in small letters on the other. The Psalm was a favorite of a number of Marines with some variation in the words including a profane description of the owner in the last part of it—*I will fear no evil because I'm the baddest son of a bitch in the valley.*

"Okay, David," Peter said as he moved through the brush to get a better view of everything on the other side of the stream. He looked for any movement, even the movement of a man breathing behind cover—any change of bush or leaves or sound that would give the enemy away. At least they would know and could try to bring in artillery fire or aircraft loaded with napalm to clear their path—at least it would kill some and run others back, he thought. He stared out to his front until he did see them.

As David was surveying the opposite bank, and behind from his position, he heard the unmistakable sound of troops moving toward them. The muted sounds of limbs and leaves scraping the sides of men's uniforms and the barely discernible sounds of footsteps on the soft jungle floor were those made by the enemy moving quickly toward India. He returned to Peter and told him they were coming. "Where's Ronny?" he asked quietly.

"He's to my left a bit."

"I'll get him while you fall back and radio what we have. We need to get the hell out of here."

"Very well, David. I'll be ten meters back."

"Gotcha."

Brooks felt his hand on his shoulder and the two met Peter and quickly made their way to Lieutenant Rapier who was leading the company toward the stream. He knew a village laid on the other side about two clicks farther west and that it was probably being used by the NVA and Viet Cong. Every time one was cleared and checked, it seemed to be revisited by the enemy after the Marines left a shaken populace. The lieutenant called in air strikes on their word and had the company hold their positions a click away from the stream until they arrived.

"Watch!" Rapier ordered. "Take turns grabbing some chow and stay alert in your fighting positions," he said, having the company form a semi-circle on line, curved away on both ends. He centered himself on the bulge closest and sat down next to Kannawaa on one side and Sgt. Baggett on the other.

The jets suddenly screamed overhead and as fast as a spoonful of peaches falling into David's mouth, laid in napalm and bombs, the sounds clearly heard by every man in India.

"Mount up!" Rapier called out to his sergeants. Golf is on our right flank and we're going over there!" He passed what he heard on the PRC-26 radio to his men. The jungle fire could be seen for miles and black smoke rose quickly in a spreading "V" shape into the sky overhead, boiling layer upon layer as the napalm stuck to everything and everyone close. "Damn! That's good!" He smiled. "Move out on line, India!" his voice emanated from deep in his diaphragm as he stood up and commanded.

David threw the small can of peaches to his side and checked his M-16, pushing the seating apparatus for the rounds of his spring-feeding magazine several times. Kannawaa picked up his M-60 machine gun and walked beside him, the lieutenant and Gunnels as they made their way toward the stream.

The company arrived at the bank virtually in step and stopped on hand signals from the platoon sergeants. As far as every man could see, there was fire and smoke, but now they heard the screams. David had been right. There was a battalion of NVA that had come to stop them and had been nearly completely destroyed. The Marines took the other side and put in a hot base of crossfire to their front, intersecting in a fireball only fifty feet ahead. "Let's go!" Rapier ordered, "It's a good hunt!"

As they moved through the jungle and stepped around residual pockets of fire from the deadly spew, they came across the bodies of fifty-plus NVA, their uniforms burnt off and their skin peeling deep and away from bone red, black and bloody. The rear guard had escaped and set up an ambush for the Marines instead of leaving the area. As Rapier led his men farther and deeper, he gave his life for his country and so did fourteen other Marines. David fired until he was out of ammunition and then threw his few grenades. He attached a bayonet to the end of his M-16 to fight and met the dragon eyeball-to-eyeball and would kill as many as he could before being killed. He waited. It seemed like hours.

The Marines had advanced and held when suddenly there must have been a fast retreat by the enemy. As suddenly as they had been hit, there was a quiet except for human voices in agony; there was no more firing or explosions from mines and grenades to take young Americans. David gathered himself when he got the word, shook his head to try to clear his mind and took a long, deep breath. He rubbed his eyes then had to rub them some more because of the filth he put in them.

"Peter?" he called out. "Peter?" he called out louder.

Kannawaa found him stumbling and weak calling for Peter and held him fast, removing his weapon. "Peter is gone, David," he said. "We took it bad today."

David cried, as did several others for the Marines lost and their own ordeal, confused about why it happened this way and what it meant for them to have survived one more day while others didn't. And it hit them at once.

For the balance of his tour, David had little to say to anyone. He lived one day at a time and made his thirteen months. He quietly left Viet Nam and then quietly left the Marine Corps and returned to Houston a different man than he was before. He felt much older. He saw them here and there—the people of his age who held him in contempt and thought he surely killed babies and did horrible things in an unjust war. He heard all the accusations somewhere and knew these people without speaking to them. Sarah prepared a large dinner for the family and invited his brother and sisters to welcome him home. There were a few people, perhaps the only ones, he thought, who thought of him as a good guy for what he did. His father embraced him and wrapped him in his very strong 101st Airborne arms.

Chapter 23

"I want to get the stuff and go home!" Elizabeth said to Jerry Vaca, a hairy reflection of a few rock and roll artists he enjoyed fancying as peers. "I've had enough and Christy is tired, too," she explained with her foamy mouth. Her eyes were circled by a natural black shade from the affects drugs had on her blood, and her arms were trembling in weakness.

"Oh, baby! Can't we talk about that later?" he asked as he held onto Jan who leaned into him, stoned, and wearing nothing on top. "I promise!"

"Shit! Jerry!"

"Just give us a few minutes, okay?" he asked. "And close the curtain on your way out, please," he said as he caught Jan and kept her from falling.

"Okay. But let's get it settled today, Jerry. We're hungry for some decent food and more than this f'ing place!" She took Christy by the hand and went to Azzar for one last favor.

Azzar was a Muslim most of the time and contributed heavily to the mosque but his proclivities and taste for American women were so strong that, in his words, he succumbed; it was their evil ways and intentions that drove him to sin against Allah.

In Atlanta Agnes and Claire reunited and were working on their mother-daughter relationship. Since Henry took over her life for so many years, he convinced her that the McCrays would never be the family he wanted. To him there were too many imperfections in the bloodline and would, it seemed, never be social enough with the rich and powerful because of their dogged grounding in faith and other such superstitious notions. He explained to her that was bad for business. Claire listened to him because the marriage was at stake, she thought, and even if she didn't fully buy his story, she had to show support for the Lee partnership.

"Claire…it is so nice to see you again. May we meet more often?"

"I would like that, Mom." She looked downward. "I've been so wrong about so much!"

"Dear…don't worry like that. Everything will be all right. I believe that." She smiled at her daughter. "You were always right in your father's eyes!"

"I can't believe I've been such a fool!" She began crying. "Henry Jr. isn't doing anything but living off me and what little he can get from his father. Elizabeth…well, Elizabeth has gone wild and I'm afraid for her." She wiped her eyes.

"I would like to see Henry and Elizabeth," she said. "And sweet, gentle Mary… what is she doing?"

"She's the one, Mom." The thought brought a smile back. "Mary is winning a scholarship to Emory and she'll stay here at home!" She took a long breath. "But I'm afraid you might not see the other two. They're off on their own and hardly come here any more. I'll hear from them when they need money."

"I see. Have you thought not to give any to them?"

"I'm afraid to do that, Mom. They may be hungry or need to get home. I keep hoping that's what they'll do with it—and I believe in my heart they will one day."

"Do what you feel is right, Claire. Have they ever called and told you they are hungry?"

"No, Mom."

"Have they ever called and asked for fare to return home?"

"No, ma'am."

"Well, then…all I can do is recommend a course because I love you and I love them. It's hard to be firm, but I suggest you tell them today there will be no more unless they are home and follow your rules."

"I'm not sure I can. That sounds so hard." Her eyes became wet.

"Did I ever tell you the story of your family when they came to America?"

"Dad tried to share a little, but I was so young and so easily distracted."

"Like Elizabeth?"

"I guess so." She smiled.

"Of course these days are so different. Her being distracted now carries far more consequences than when you were young, but it's still the same, isn't it?"

"I don't know if they'll listen."

"Well, dearest…tell them of the McCrays and their fight to make good in this country." She looked away and her voice changed to something stronger and fiercely determined. "Tell them about Lucious and Katy farming in Alabama and how their sons fought for their land, about your own grandfather and how he endured Matthew's mother being murdered and still did his family proud, and tell them about the McCray men who fought and died in every war for their freedom they enjoy today, and it wasn't just a handy phrase for them. They must see. One day they will."

"I don't think they'll care one little bit about all of that, Mom."

"They will in time."

"Can I get you some coffee?" Claire asked her.

"And tell them no more and when you do, you mean it! They will hear it in your voice." She looked back toward her daughter. "And stick to your guns, Claire. No amount of begging, no sad story...nothing will cause you to return where you are now with this."

Claire felt power come suddenly, unblocked, and not rationalized away, not slow. She knew she had the strength and would do what was right. She smiled, her lips curved on end, her eyes more focused than she remembered they had ever been. She was a McCray and it was time.

Dave and Joan Creeless made love in the sands near their place because they enjoyed the constant sea breeze and clear stars balanced with moonlight, providing a perfect, subtle illumination to match the beautiful sight of each other's skin with their touch. As the couple neared their fifties, they were still very much in love with each other and had the desire and passion of their younger years. They each had their own shortcomings, but allowed each other to be the person each was with all of them. The club was doing well enough since tourist season was year-round on the islands, and they still served reasonably priced beer and food to the well-prepared visitors alongside Naval personnel—something they both knew was important for them to do. Dave had decided before the business he would never be in something the enlisted man couldn't afford. Too many of his friends were buried in the place and he often kidded that if he ever, they would kick his ass when they saw him in the next life.

Dave still enjoyed living parents, and he and Joan made the trip to the mainland several times each year. She still remembered the awkwardness of staying with them the first month, and how the good people in the house made her feel as one of them before the many months she was there ended. There had been no pretense, no pressure, and no questions. They acted in faith and were right again. Jules and Ruth were retired and living in the same home in San Diego and still walked the beach and dreamed.

Ruth thought of what went with the years. It seemed they suddenly passed and here she was, still the same woman who moved from Marshall County to

California with her lover, one of the Creeless boys. She walked slower now and took more time to do everything it seemed. Time passed too fast for the good things. She looked at Jules and could still see the man she married so many years ago and loved him as much. She remembered the cruises to Hawaii, a protectorate at the time, somewhat primitive compared to her home city and a beautiful secret found. She thought of Tommy every day and cried when she thought of his death so young, innocent and hopeful and smiled when she thought of his childhood.

Daniel and Katherine moved to Galveston where he enjoyed fishing and hanging around the docks swapping stories and jokes with other men who enjoyed the same schedule of sunshine. She waited for him every night and as had been their custom, they embraced every evening. She knew it was a habit that kept them close and was God sent, as they must have been for each other. He still thought of Paul and the horrible loss and change in his life because of those damn German bullets. It was such a thing that could not be described. He thought of his quiet father, Samuel McCray, a name to be proud of for all time and of his father, Jebediah. He hoped to meet him again someday and have a nice visit though the appointed place was in a realm no living man has seen.

"Thank you, Katherine," he said gently.

"For what, Daniel?" She smiled.

"You know you still have the prettiest smile!"

"Oh, go on!" She laughed. He reached for her and took her in his arms. Their lips met and tongues danced, telling each other of affection and goodness, sweet tastes of passion, giving, helping, and loving. She sighed still and he moaned still when they were together.

"Come to the marina with me, dear."

"You all don't want a woman around there."

"I do. I do very much, dear. Every minute that I have belongs to you as much as me." He smiled and kissed her again. She packed a basket of sandwiches and drinks for them to take to the docks.

John Riker took Jane and his ten-year-old daughter Kelly to the mountains in North Carolina that winter. He intended to ask her to marry him during the weekend and planned to surprise her with a ring over dinner Saturday evening. Luke brought Gail Pennington, a widow he met at the V.A. who worked in administration. She had processed his paper and during the interview, liked his smile, and taking her daughter's advice for the first time in matters of the heart, asked him to call her. Matthew and Marlene Riker also met them in Boone to share the large rented chalet perched on the side of a steep slope that came complete with a broad view of the white-covered mountains.

"Can you start the fire, Matthew? You're the engineer!" John laughed. "I'll help Luke unpack." He heard him park in the drive that circled in front of the upper third of the chalet. The doorway led to the second floor, passing a loft and two bedrooms upstairs. Downstairs the large living room included a hearth and for view, an entire wall framed in glass. There were two more bedrooms and a kitchen off sides of the comfortable den.

It was the first time the sons had been together since the funeral in Atlanta. Helen had lost her third and consoled herself through her sons and knowing hers had been a good life after James, whom she barely remembered anymore, and the move to Washington. She smiled for Horace, knowing he was free from pain and at peace in God's arms. He was a man who always did and said the right thing—a rare man it seems, not selfish or self-centered to any degree, who shared her bed and made beautiful love. His love for her sons made a difference too that was natural for him but still she appreciated.

As they were together to cook and talk, there was never a mention of war.

"Isn't she wonderful?" John asked the crowd in her presence as Jane brought a tray of drinks for everyone. She blushed and murmured he was embarrassing her with such talk. He watched her heart shape leave the room as she returned the tray to the kitchen and stayed to help Marlene and Gail finish the chicken and potato salad. He could hardly wait for the evening to progress when they would have some private space and time.

"You're a lucky guy!" Matthew said. "And so am I!" he laughed. "I have some news for everyone but have to wait until Marlene is out here."

"I'm lucky too," Luke spoke up. "How do you like Gail?"

"She's a great looking woman, Luke. Yes, sir! I'd say you've done well and it's about time!" John said and laughed. "Geeze! I thought you were destined to be a confirmed bachelor!"

"My bachelor days are over. I'm going to ask her!"

"When you're ready, tell us and you'll get the time!" John said.

"This is turning out to be some kind of weekend, isn't it?" Luke said. "Here they come."

"Hello, ladies! Is everything ready?" Matthew asked. "Marlene and I have some news!"

"Knock off the suspense, little brother…what is it for you two?"

"We're expecting!" Matthew said as Jane embraced Marlene. Standing nearby Luke's shoulder, Gail smiled also and went to her.

"Congratulations!" John said. "I'm very happy for you. It's a good life!" He smiled and turned toward Kelly. Luke smiled as he watched Gail and thought how wonderful it would be.

Luke was doing the job at the University and most of the time he saw the difference in the eyes of the veterans who came to him. They were slightly older than most students and some did well while others failed. The innocence of youth had been spent in Southeast Asia and even though most spent a short time there they were scarred and reentry to society, finding normalcy, and picking up where they left off before the service was proving to be more than they thought it would be while daydreaming behind a sandbag wall.

Luke had trouble with most of them; it seemed they were different, yet in ways the same, and whether they made it was their own mind and heart. He tried to counsel and encourage but with some he was trying to encourage the inconsolable—their minds near wasted, burnt, bitter and left in Viet Nam with the consciousness of politicians who failed them.

They weren't allowed to win it. He watched some stray into drugs as a temporary escape or phony cure sold them by the peddlers. That wouldn't work and he cried silently for them. But there were a few who made it. Maybe they put thoughts of things past behind them, which he knew now, that was what one must do to return. Others made it out of sheer determination that those who dodged and complained loudly and hated them were not going to be more successful. It was a form of hatred turned toward in the spirit of winning one. Gail helped him see himself and enjoy good things. While in the mountains with her, it was easy for him to laugh and feel the surges of happiness he remembered as a boy in Washington.

Father McCray was an elder now and still in Houma working as the parish priest. He slowed little and knew his days were coming close to the end. It was the wine and food, and more the wonderful people who talked to him and asked him to tell of truths. He loved his home and invited the lost in, the hungry to eat, and the lonely to find comfort. He felt it and knew. He would see the Lord soon and would have to thank Him in person for everything He gave such a lowly and imperfect man in this life. He thought he may say hello to the Frenchman he pulled into the trench to prolong his horror perhaps—maybe he had life later. He never knew what happened to him, but it was so long ago, he was certain he would be there. Maybe he could ask his name.

Maybe he would learn he had children who went on to do well for their world, in the world. He smiled at the thought. Maybe he had many tales of his experiences after the war and every one of them would be important touches of other people. He sat on the porch and watched the gentle, warm breeze move the moss as a woman's hair beautifully moves when she walks. These people had been his life and the parish his mistress whom he loved with everything. He thought of his father and mother and would see them too. He would tell them he loved them and loved the wonderful life they gave—that although it could be said it was of little consequence. He knew the Lord looked on the imperfect, the ones whose voices are not so pleasant when they sing, the defective, the honest sinners, the ones not thought of as much in this world; these are His people whom he looks more kindly on and mercifully propels to the highest place when it is done.

Within the month Isaac was taken without protest or worry while sitting on the porch; a fixed smile on his earthly face. Matthew and Helen came to Houma once more to see him and pray. Peter and Maria's children had done their parents proud.

At the same time, David S. was offered a job on an offshore oilrig, and took it rather than going to school. Sister Katy was dating and about to be engaged to Bob Short who had been in the Navy and was a graduating senior at the University of Texas. His brother James followed him into the Marine Corps and had just completed basic training and was off to his M.O.S. training in air control, a good job, David thought—his brother would be working in an office rather than mud. The youngest sister, Jesse, was working a couple of years in Houston before college. His parents held several barbeques each year for all of them to attend and be together as they were before. David and Sarah McCray were also invited to Marshall County for a probate reading. The farm was vacant now, and the family had to decide what to do with the property.

The house had become empty and began to show the wear of the years, its layers of paint peeling away revealing bare wood and the porch Daniel and Irene enjoyed sitting on began to fall back to earth. The fields were grown in browns and greens, haphazardly now and surging as a low jungle of confusion and neglect. Farm implements were nearly covered by grasses and weeds and stuck to the ground where they rested for years. Vandals and thieves, modern versions of bushwhackers, came from other parts on a prowl had taken a toll as well, stripping as much as could be salvaged from inside the dwelling when no one could stop them. David's younger brother Thomas had stayed as long as he could until the sudden and massive stroke finally caused his retreat. There was no McCray left to live in it as generations had before the children moved on to their own lives.

It was more than a passing thought for him. To return to the place and live there, throwing his lot into the home place, and working it as his family had worked it for a hundred and thirty years. He knew there must be something drawing him back he couldn't explain, some deeper meaning that was forcing him to confront his life. The job with Texaco was a good job but not what he would do if he had a choice—the routine, the boredom, the surface and base nature of it provided a good living, but that was all. Should he give up all he earned for something he could not be certain and knew would not be as financially rewarding, or should he sell the farm? Somehow selling the place didn't suit him; he couldn't do it and feel he had done the right thing. Sarah didn't care as long as she was with him.

President Nixon pulled all of the troops out of Viet Nam and the country fell to the communists. Bob and Katy married and moved to New Orleans where he had taken an offer of employment to begin an internship in hospital administration. David S. stayed on the rig in shifts of seven days at a time and spent a lot of time in the bars when he was on shore. His efficiency apartment was all he needed and was sparsely furnished—the most prominent fixture was a Marine Corps flag he was proud of despite the contempt from so many of his generation.

He usually brought any willing woman he could find to the place for a night or two. He liked Black Sabbath, Lynard Skynard and Zeppelin and would play them loud, losing himself for a while in the strong rhythms; he liked George Jones and Merle too and would play these artists softer when he was in one of his moods. Faster cars, mini-skirts, nude dancers, women's liberation, animal rights, a determined drug culture, *Sonny and Cher*, *Laugh-in*, the pill and anything goes as long as it was harmless to others took hold across many parts of America. Freedom had been protected and people used it to suit them, which suited David fine.

Chapter 24

"Take this job and shove it! I ain't working here no more." They were words to a song David S. heard on his way back to the rig that Sunday. He asked himself what he was doing with his life more than once and wondered what else he could do to find peace. It seemed it didn't matter much. Having killed others worked him miserably even though he heard it said he had to kill to defend himself. Watching other Marines being killed was worse. Neither time nor words could put away what he'd done or veil what he'd seen; it was hard to live with the inglorious truth of Viet Nam, especially now that it was so worthless.

David McCray watched his oldest son from a distance and worried he would stay in the downward slide. It was for his sake, for some connection and happiness missing from the boy he diapered and held and taught through those early years. He owed David S. for the portion of happiness he freely gave then that made him whole. And what could he do now? he thought. Were it simple, he would have already done the right thing, but it is never easy, never a task one could simply grab and finish.

Sarah stayed in vigil, almost a silent one for her oldest, without so many words, David knew her heart was breaking slowly, and each year was worse. She watched David S. live in a vein of self-destruction and felt unable to stop it. She did not know what to do. This generation was new—and different than anything she could have conjured in the past when she remembered their life. She found some solace in David's arms though an ever deeper void of black confusion kept her from fully feeling the goodness between her and her husband. There had to be answers, something, she thought, and somewhere, that would reveal him to his true heart and cause him to live without the anger and start caring. She could love her son though until God answered.

"Hi! Excuse me, but I saw you sitting here and wanted to see if you would talk to me," David S. said to the woman sitting at the last table in the back of the Injured Pelican, a club near the wharf, which catered to longshoremen and oilrig workers. It was opened in a location that was the first bar one would see as they came ashore. The windows were filled with neon and beer posters centered in an iron and brick, sloppily, quickly laid mortar encasing vertical bars in used stone. She was drinking one beer after another, perhaps to feel happier than life was for her, and she managed a distant smile. Her eyes looked past him and then she pulled her lips back saying with no words that she was tired of the routine. "May I sit with you a while and buy you a beer?" he asked.

"If you'd like…but I'm about finished here," she said against the brash, pounding sounds of Hank Williams Jr. in over volume for the club's speakers. He saw she was a bleached blond, straight and statuesque in posture, wearing a short black skirt, a tightly fitting red top and red high heels. Her face was obviously quickly prepared as if she rushed and splashed makeup and lipstick she didn't worry would stay. He could see pain in her face that came from somewhere—probably because of someone—and thought for a moment he should leave her.

"You seem sad tonight," he ventured. "Was it something I said?"

"I'm fine," she said unconvincingly as she looked away from him. "Look, I'm sure you're here for one thing and I'm not really in the mood for it."

"I understand and I suppose you're right." There were a few long moments where nothing was said between them. "Why don't we just talk?"

"I suppose that would be all right. But like I've said, I'm about ready to leave. Is that okay?" She half-smiled toward the sandy haired son.

"So…do you work close by?"

"Yes. You?"

"Off shore," he said too quickly, he thought. He fumbled with his hands, nervous about the rejection. "I haven't seen you here before and I drop in every couple of weeks."

"Well, I don't come often. Usually I have a beer or two at home, but I ran out yesterday."

"I'm David McCray, and it's a pleasure to meet you."

"Hello, David. I'm Julie." She smiled more fully, hopeful against the odds, wishful it were true someone would simply talk to her. There was something in his eyes, a look, which made her think it was possible.

"Would you like to share your story with me? Who are you?" he heard himself say out of reflex, guided by no thought he was conscious of, but the words came. "Geeze! It's hard to hear, isn't it?"

"Yea. But that song is almost over." She smiled and waited. "Do you really want to know or are you just talking?"

"I want to know. Since we're just going to be friends, I'll settle for some good conversation." He smiled and lit up a cigarette.

"May I have one of yours? I've been meaning to try that brand but you know, I'm hooked on these. They're getting harder to find." She pointed to a pack of Territons. "I believe they're going to stop making them."

"Sure. Well, are you going to tell me a little about yourself?"

"There's not too much to tell. I'm not looking for anyone really, though when I may have thought about it—don't know why. I've been cheated on and lied to and I'm sick and tired of it." She looked down. "I'm divorced and doing fine by myself...have a dog, a cat and no kids. You?"

"No dog, no cat and no ex-wife." He smiled. "But I do like beer and music, and that's about all."

"It seems we have something in common!" She laughed slightly. "What else, David McCray?"

"You remembered my name! I'm impressed!" He laughed then turned serious. "I don't lie." He looked down and then raised and caught her eyes.

"Somehow I believe you."

"I don't. When I saw you, I figured on trying the same thing I've always done and maybe get lucky...you know. But it's okay."

She thought he was attractive enough, cute, and so far, able to talk to her as a human being not just a flirt. She saw him differently and felt safe with him.

"So tell me where you work."

"I'm a teacher at Brighton Street Elementary. Can you believe that?"

"Well...I'm impressed. Didn't expect to meet a teacher here—especially an elementary teacher." He smiled.

"I know. But I needed a beer. The children do not need to know everything about me."

"No, of course not. Do you like it?"

"I love it! It's the one thing in my life I haven't lost or been screwed with—although some parents are unbelievable!" She laughed in such a way to tell him there were some uncaring parents whose lifestyles were lower than base. "I sometimes wonder why they had children to begin with. Some are so sorry!" She paused. "Let's talk abut something else; I don't like thinking about them. Tell me about you, David McCray. Who are you?"

"Just a working man. Nothing special."

"I'll bet you're more special than you give yourself credit for."

"No, ma'am. I'm not." He smiled. "I'm pretty much what you see."

"No agenda?"

"No agenda." He looked into her eyes. "Sometimes I think I should have one, but it's not me. Your eyes are beautiful."

"You're not bad yourself," she said. "You're a quiet guy, aren't you?"

"Yea. I try though. I'm just not one full of B.S. I guess. I hope not."

"It's about time for me, David. I wouldn't mind you calling me sometime. Would you like my number?"

"Yes, ma'am, I would like that and I will call."

"Okay then. I'm free most nights and weekends and will talk to you."

He watched her leave the place and noticed her every subtle feminine curve, the way the skirt held her hips, her arched back and free hair. There was an air of class about her he was unaccustomed to meeting in a place like this. She was not the kind of woman he usually met and did seem of another element, an outsider in his world and one who made him curious. She certainly hadn't been shopping like he may have been as a sidelight.

David clutched her number and made sure it was securely in his pocket. He touched the fabric and felt the folds of paper several times before he left the bar himself. The eighties had come, he was past thirty and tired of the routine, working the rig and drinking when he was off and that was all.

His sister and Bob made their way through Bourbon Street, saw some tantalizing flesh and heard some persuasive blues before stopping into the restaurant to eat. The sights and history had been interesting and stimulating of this part of their hometown. The rain started and there were tropical storm warnings paid little heed by the revelers, as the party was early. They were to meet David S. at Coleman's that evening and he was late. Katy worried about her brother and until she saw him the unsettling caused pain in her hair. His work and lifestyle put him at risk in her mind, and anything could happen to him any time.

Elizabeth was working as a traveling registered nurse—on contract and free to fly to any city where her services were required on assignment, lasting from a month to several months. She remained single over the past ten years and managed to get her education after a brief period of incarceration owing to a failed smuggle from Afghanistan. Customs had stopped her group and arrested them shortly after landing at the Los Angeles LAX airport. It was enough to shake her as her time inside a federal penitentiary was spent in fear and dread, often not knowing what would happen to her while she slept. The hatred and violence that permeated the place and put her on notice was seated because of elements she was born with and her perceived standing outside prison walls. Resentment took its worse form inside those walls and she learned whom she was and what she wasn't. Claire told her to come home after the time was used to pay her debt and she did; she followed Claire's house rules.

Henry Jr. passed his ninth anniversary working as a machine operator for a manufacturing firm in Memphis. He couldn't finish school as the contents of his mind failed him; he could handle the routine for his living and found the work enough. It had been twelve years since he left Woodstock, his last great party, and he watched the movement die as quickly as it started. He asked one woman to marry him six years ago, but she returned the hundred-dollar ring after he screamed in rage one night and struck her face with an open hand. His selfish instincts were still intact.

David S. walked into Coleman's holding Julie's hand. They became a couple quickly when he listened to her and she learned he was genuine.

"My! It's been a while, David!" his sister said as she embraced him and he kissed her cheek. "Bob said to give you a while because you're always late." She laughed.

"I'm glad to see ya'll!" He smiled. "This is Julie and she will marry me!"

"You're not desperate are you, Julie?" Katy asked and laughed.

"Oh, no...he makes me happy! And I want to make him happy."

"So, David...are you still on the rig?"

"No, Bob. They brought me into the office to do the hiring. It's tough to find good help these days and they figured I could."

"Congratulations!" Katy smiled. "So when is the date?"

"We are going to keep it simple and get married in her hometown. It's not far from here," David said.

"Well...I hope we're invited!" Katy said.

"Of course you are...do you know Houma?"

"Yes, I heard of it...the town is Cajun over there and in the swamps. Ought to be real nice for you two. I'm very glad to meet you, Julie!" Bob said.

"Her family is really nice and have accepted me pretty well." He looked at Julie.

"Yes...they think he's a good one!" Julie said. "And I won't tell them different!" She laughed.

"Let me buy a round for the happy couple! What will you have?"

"Thank you, Bob. I'll have a Coors and Julie drinks wine."

"A light Chablis for me, please," Julie said.

"So, can you make it the weekend of the thirtieth?" she asked Katy and Bob. "We'd love to have you there."

"Yes, ma'am…no problem with that. I'm looking forward to it. I've never been there, and it'll be interesting. I like the music." Bob laughed.

"Do come. We'll make you feel welcome!" Julie said. "His parents are driving from Houston. Jesse's coming as my maid of honor and James will be in on leave so I'll meet his family and we'll all be together. He's the only one I haven't met yet."

"Cool!" Katy chimed as she turned up the oversized wine glass of vodka, lime, and lemon.

"The Broussards would be proud!" Julie laughed.

"Well, David…you didn't tell us she was so beautiful!" Bob said and laughed. "I'm proud of you!"

David felt like a whole man since he met Julie. She had left a marriage taking little with her except the world's scourge of sourness penetrating a sweet, innocent naivety she brought from Houma where her mother and father raised her to assume the good in people. She walked in on her husband the night she was scheduled for a full shift in the emergency room and was released early. She found him with Kelly, the wife of a couple befriended early in their move to a new apartment complex. She sensed the hole in his character before that night but didn't think about it and dismissed it in hopeful love—but there was something not in him out of the grasp of explanation until she saw him with her. David had no hole; he was, as he seemed to be. He loved her, and she knew it was good with him.

Luke and Gail Riker retired to a campground on the Florida panhandle where they chose to live in a large camper-trailer and enjoyed the mild weather and their neighbors who moved down mostly for the same reasons. There were community cookouts and parties, costume balls, fishing and swimming; he smiled every time he laid eyes on her. His brother John and Darla remained in Fairfax where they were helping Kelly finish her degree in history. She accepted the marriage proposal from Joseph Saxon, a senior in the business college she met while volunteering with disabled youths, a program sponsored by her church. He was a tall, dark, curly haired Italian attending the University of Virginia on a partial scholarship owing to his father having served in the Army and being wounded in Korea.

Mary Lee remained in Atlanta and married a young version of her father. The marriage was rocky from the start as he always had something to do that didn't involve her, and she became a lonely woman wondering if this was all there was. Her mother, Claire, and her grandmother, Agnes, buried Matthew within the past year—although the person they lost had no longer been the energetic reporter who retired from the *Times*. After he passed eighty years old, he slipped into Alzheimers and the family lost him over time—perhaps a gentler way though the sadness was prolonged. At least they could see him and care for him his last years.

James McCray was a father of four by the dawn of the eighties. He was paying for private school for all of them. Jesse worked and shared an apartment with a French immigrant, Lacey Pétain. They both worked social services in Houston County. David and Sarah moved to Galveston and set up a bait shop where they lived in quarters overlooking the Gulf on top of their part-time business. The large sky and great body of ocean provided a panorama of color for Sarah to paint in acrylics on canvas, a hobby she began after the children left home.

The day of the wedding was a hot and dry one that caused each of them to sweat sticky to their clothes. His father stood as the best man in the outside courtyard fashioned by the Broussards and Hebérts; he sipped the wine served and embraced his son and daughter-in-law. James attended wearing his dress blues, the number of chevrons figuring prominently as he was a master sergeant stationed at Cherry Point, North Carolina. Jesse stood next to Julie in a long blue satin gown; throughout the day she noticed she seemed a young Cajun's main interest. She smiled at him while placing small portions of food on a plate. He was a burly hunter and trapper who came to every parish function. She felt compelled to ask him.

"Hello—Jesse, sister of the groom here. What's your name?" she said and smiled slightly, showing her very white, perfectly aligned teeth surrounded by soft red lips. Her eyes were open and pretty blue; her hair strawberry blond and wavy past her shoulders.

"I'm Jack. Jack Mouton. Please to meet you!" He shook her hand by gently clasping it with his thumb and two fingers. His beard was long and wooly around the edges, an odd look for the large man dressed in an ill-fitting suit. The necktie didn't fit him well either and seemed to uncomfortably choke him. She liked his style—much different from the men in the city who tried. So many seemed overly sensitive and too gracious to be masculine, but Jack was not one of those.

"I'm so glad you came to their wedding, Jack."

"I would not miss such a thing," he said in a Cajun accent. "I've known the Broussards all my life...and, Julie! Aye! Julie is a sweet woman who went away to the big Houston! We surely miss her here 'bouts." He smiled, revealing imperfect teeth, jagged and stained. Two older men were tuning up their fiddles and a grandson was chiming an accordion to begin the celebration.

She wouldn't have thought him to be her type, but she was unsure what her type would look like. She felt it inside her and, as unlikely as it would have seemed to her had she been told before, he did cause a stir inside her heart somewhere, and it was a feeling she hadn't known. *Jack Mouton,* she thought as she studied him, *Jack, manly Jack...has a nice ring to it.*

"I'm glad to meet you, Jack! Care for some of these?" She steered the serving platter of shrimp Creole toward him.

"Thank you, ma'am. Oui! It be that I do, Miss Jesse." He took one after another and was able to peel with one hand and eat several very quickly. She began laughing as she tried to copy his technique and dropped several. "No, no!" he said and laughed. "You mustn't use too many fingers! Do like this, Missy."

"I'm afraid I'm having too much trouble, Jack."

"You are fine, Miss Jesse." He took her hand and kissed it. "Are you here long?"

"I have two days on the room in Metairie."

"I have a cousin who stays there. I be from Bayou Carie, close by." He laughed. "Swamps all 'round the road." He looked into her eyes and found her engaging him. "Would you like to dance with me?"

"I would, but I fear I don't know how. What is that?" she asked as couples began.

"That be nothing more than a two step. Come with Jack, darling, and I show you." He took her hand and led her into the dirt and pebble stone patch carved out alongside two weathered, gray-boarded frame houses and a hastily built plank stage that barely rose off the ground. She began laughing and didn't stop.

"I've never had such a time, Jack!" She moved with him, their arms crossed and both hands clasped.

"I say to you, you're a pretty woman, Miss Jesse! Thank you for favoring me."

"Oh, Jack..." She laughed. "You favor me!"

"Oh, but Miss Julie, it is me, Jack, the lucky one!" He smiled. "I take you on to Big Easy one day and we sing and laugh!" he said, his deep Cajun accent in form.

"I may go, Jack! You better not say unless you mean it!" She smiled, unsure of what it was or why she felt safe with him but happy with this large, grounded stranger so far.

"I see you two are having some fun!" Julie smiled, having been making her rounds to all the guests. "She is David's sister, Jack Mouton. Her parents and brothers are watching you!" She laughed. "I'm so glad to see you! Ya'll have a good time!"

"Thank you, Miss Julie," he said, a harmless bear of a man who usually feigned dancing preferring short visits and a quick return to the bayou. He decided today to dance with one of the pretty ones and put aside his shyness toward social settings.

"You have a nice smile, Jesse. May I call you after today?"

"I would like that, Jack! I want to see New Orleans with you sometime, like you said. What about that?" She tugged on his arm slightly, feeling a strength and warmth that caused her to want feel more of it.

David and Julie were now Mr. and Mrs. McCray of Galveston and would return to the bay to take up a life similar to his father's and mother's, her father's and mother's, and the many Broussards and McCrays.

"I hear you are related to Isaac McCray, our dearly beloved priest who passed away a little while ago." old man Jimmy Boudreaux asked David S. without even a hint of a smile.

"Yes, sir. He was a distant cousin from up in Boston. We knew little of them."

"He was a good man, by the by. You are from good stock. Take care of your wife now, young McCray, and she'll take care of you…that's what it is for our folk."

"Yes, sir…I surely will."

"He is missed here. He was our priest and never will there be another like him," he said, his accent so thick, David could barely understand his words. "He was in the Great War you know and saw our boys off in the second one. Not all of them came back, but he's attending to them now for sure. That's who he was you see, and he'd never quit them." Tears formed in his eyes and he was unashamed, letting them run their course unmolested and through falling off his chin. He was one of the young soldiers who listened that day before leaving Houma for Europe. "I believe he saved me."

"I'm glad…Mr. Boudreaux, isn't it?"

"Yes, son. That's me."

"My father was also in Europe during the war."

"I know. Father McCray told us of him."

"He's a man...I only hope to be half as good."

"You got the right attitude, young McCray. You be fine for our Julie."

"Thank you, sir, and I'll try." He smiled toward the elder who began to recite. He learned more about the Creeless family in California and the Rikers who he knew little, but were also of his blood. Jimmy knew dates and places and names as though it had been a lesson from Father McCray he committed to memory almost as important as the frequent Bible studies. David S. took it in and felt his heart fill with pride. There had been people in his family who did so much. There had been success and failures in their humanness, but they survived as Americans truly pursuing their dreams and taking care of family first, defending their country and coming back to God. He was humbled and speechless by the words of the man. It was as if he adopted the McCrays as his own, taking the Scottish immigrants as his history and answers.

"You are of a strong, sweet family, David. Julie and you... are strong and sweet; stay the course. I must go." He left him, his shadow abruptly swallowed by the thickness of the bayou. The paratrooper's son never saw him again. The old Cajun knew more than he had ever even been told about his family. The impact of the stun kept him in place, standing frozen, his mind scattering in points of light flying out and around him to a peace and harmony he never knew before. He gazed toward the gray and red sky and felt those who had gone before him accepting him, approving.

"Thank you!" he called out toward the mass of wood, moss and water of the dark swamp. Sound returned he could understand; he heard the Cajun band. Feeling returned and he could react to as his father, who took his arm near his shoulder and smiled. He welcomed him back from Viet Nam and loved him without a spoken word. He approved of him. He was proud of him.

"This has been beautiful, David, son. Your mother and I must go now and leave you two be."

"Thank you, Dad." He peered downward. "Julie is wonderful and I know I'm lucky to have ya'll and her...I'm very happy you came. It's been great to see you!" He looked up and smiled. "And do have a safe trip home."

Jesse returned to Houma and worked in the clinic as a receptionist and office clerk; she married Jack that year, taking up residence on his houseboat moored off the deep channel that fed the bayou. Her gentle bear of a husband was trapping and fishing for a living and cooked a dinner every night for them. He taught her how to hunt and how to live and enjoy the bayou as a warm, embracing yet edgy home where romance was—the place the same as the people.

She felt a constant tingle of nerve endings and when she thought about it, a happy heart, unexplained totally. It had to be him and the place. She became pregnant with their first child within a month and delivered Maria while at the clinic that same year. The baby was smart; she began walking before she was one and talking before she was two. She caught her first fish before she was three. Jesse home-schooled her in addition to her attending classes at the Catholic missionary school and she finished high school before she was sixteen. The scholarship she won to attend Loyola meant she could remain close to home, her mother and father, two sisters and three brothers.

David and Julie had their twins within ten months of the wedding and lived in Galveston in a town-home near the bay. The nursery room was crowded with two bassinets and two baby beds for when they were older. The boys were named Daniel and Paul after his family. As they grew, they grew strong and athletic, playing baseball as would-be highly prized recruits for every little league coach, but David had them sewn up for his team every year.

During her years at Loyola, Maria met and made a friend, Kim Russo, an out of state resident from New Jersey who came to a college in the town her mother and father visited so often it was a second home. Lenny Russo began as a contractor refurbishing old homes and buildings in Manhattan and Long Island and slipped into real estate over the years. He owned several buildings, apartment complexes and homes now in New York and New Orleans, where he intended to develop and build a casino on the Mississippi River.

Russo began meeting with financiers whose office was in the World Trade Center; James Hildebrand had known him several years, dating to the sixties before the Center was finished when they partnered to save a rooming house close to being condemned by the city. Hildebrand was his daughter's godfather the day of her baptism and remained a close personal friend of the family. He knew Lenny to be passionately honest as they caused the house to survive so the residents had a home. Several had lived there for years and couldn't move because they couldn't afford a change and were allowed to remain there as owners of their own apartment home, now with fresh paint and new appliances, better heat and plumbing, and a working elevator.

Hildebrand didn't like casinos but he trusted and loved Lenny and was close to conceding to taking time to line up investors—but it would be a group of different people than he usually dealt with, more conservative and typically only interested in conventional developments which were more sure to generate a return. The people he had to find willing to place twenty million dollars into a floating structure were not going to be the staid group who bought failing companies and liquidated assets, built new plants for others and distribution-logistics centers to further enhance their financials. But Lenny was someone worth stepping out for, and he was convincing after all. Every legal problem had been resolved through the Louisiana legislative house and governor's office and his licensing was being processed. It would mean more employment, steady tourism and tax dollars during the off-seasons and a generous amount of campaign cash—by the bagful.

Maria and Kim studied together and talked about young men they dated. Often the coffee house was full of Loyola students and they would be found in the middle of the crowd, talking economics, history, politics and its marriage or not to religion. Both women were star students and bound for graduate school if they chose it. Beyond the classroom, they researched and studied a full range of references and texts and understood more than their classmates as to the historical structure and science of business, law and the impact of capitalism on societies, the impact of the women's movement for women, the roots of economics and markets and the methods used to build business—from planning, advertising, manufacturing, diversifying, to selling and reinvesting. They planned to write and sell a program that would allow investors an ability to analyze stocks for their potential value and upside potential along with a risk ratio. While the young women worked this heady project, they wanted to test what they learned by starting something together—something small enough to work while devoting so much time to study, but large enough to get a taste of entering the system on their own. It was a new world for Maria from her life on the bayou and an opportunity for Kim to step out from her father and show him she was getting what he tried to teach her.

They set about to produce and sell a calendar by using only what they earned themselves to invest and their persuasiveness to enlist other Loyola women to pose for the photographer. They would use bikinis, stockings, high heels and automobiles for the layouts and sell space on each page for advertising. They planned to sell the calendars to eighteen to twenty-one-year-old men by setting arrangements with bookstores and convenience shops. It figured to Kim and Maria to be fun if not very profitable.

Daniel and Paul began attending trade school in Galveston, learning the math, prints, and machining for tool-and-die work. After high school they enjoyed the challenge of making something of value out of valueless chunks of steel and other metals and thought their future lay in metalworking. David S. had taught them about weapons and guns and how to build, disassemble, repair and modify instruments of hunting or defense and how to shoot them straight and true.

David S. saw her standing at the kitchen sink, her long back to him held in curved outline of the woman he loved. Her snugly fitting, sleeveless work dress was in deep purple flared below her knees—the same knees bruised so many times playing ball with the boys when they were little, but beautiful in that. She worked every day for the family and was a loving, naturally alluring woman to him and would always be the source of his appetite for life and affection.

He walked to her and embraced her body from behind, pulled her hair out of the way and lightly kissed her neck while wrapping his arms around her waist.

"Babe...are you happy, Julie?" he whispered. "I love you."

"Yes, angel." She smiled a smile he couldn't see while holding his arms in her hands. "I love you too, David."

"You're everything to me," he said quietly, turning, guiding, gently holding her to kiss her mouth and feel her body next to his. "I'm so lucky."

Retiring to their bedroom, they consummated their love again in a rainbow of light, beautifully electric sensations and pleasure and quietly enveloping passion, taking their minds away again, and sharing their very essence with each other. It was as if the world stopped its noise and went away for the time.

The boys were on their way to Houston where their grandfather and Sarah planned to talk to them about the Alabama farm—which they decided to pay taxes and arranged for a caretaker. He discussed it with his son and said if they wanted it, they could have it. Since David S. and Julie had their own jobs and commitments—a number of disabled children who loved her—they thought to offer the boys an opportunity to move and take over the property. There was plenty of work for them on and off the farm and it made sense; the space was being wasted and left to strangers and Daniel and Paul were nearing twenty-one years old and had always been thoughtful and mature for their age.

"We love you, boys, and thought this would be something good for you—not telling you that you have to go but it's there."

"It's really great! This is so much, Grandfather!" Daniel smiled, ideas and visions of what he would do there—his own place—were filling his mind in a swirl. He looked toward Paul; his near-constant companion for twenty-one years and saw him smiling ear to ear. "Geeze!" He tripped on his feet. "The only thing…the only thing is we'd miss you all and Mom and Dad."

"Don't worry about that. You can come and we can come regularly…it's only a few hours away, Daniel."

"Yes, sir." He looked down, thoughtful.

"You boys think about it. We know you'd do a good job and whatever you decide is fine," Sarah said.

"Thank you, Grandmother."

"You're so welcome. Now I have made you some cornbread and beans with fried chicken and an apple pie. Are you hungry?" She knew she didn't have to ask. The boys were well fed and filled out as very strong and capable young men, with muscles that moved every time they even slightly moved an arm. Both were light haired and six feet tall; their necks uncomfortably stuck out of their collars like a thick trunk larger than their faces.

They had been raised to be gentle and caring individuals and during the high school years, when so much petty, silly harassment of other kids not as physically commanding or different in some way was sport for some, Daniel and Paul were there for them. The twins quickly replaced unseen or seen tears of the victims with delight over the fate of their protagonists—and they did the job every time. After their sophomore year, they never had to throw even one punch as no bully or jerk wanted to suffer the consequences.

The closing of the year of the anticipated computer shutdown came and went without incident. The year of the *Space Odyssey* began and Daniel and Paul were at home in Alabama. Daniel worked as a machinist with Pat Dooley of Etowah County and built tooling for foundries, and Paul worked as a die maker for Lockheed in Huntsville. When they were off they tended the farm and raised a few head of cattle, refinished the house and built a new two-story gray and crimson painted barn, the largest and most beautiful seen for years in the area.

Maria and Kim earned their degrees and launched the software with marketing firms using the Internet. They were selling their work but also their capability; Hildebrand offered both young women jobs with his firm in New York. Jack and Jesse held their daughter when she announced she was moving and cried together for her success and because they would miss seeing her as often, but she had to be allowed to take flight.

Russo had a town home for both of them situated in Manhattan next to each other. He owned the property and gave his daughter and her best friend a valuable gift as long as they wanted. He remembered what it was like to struggle with finances and wanted to see them prosper and live unburdened with worry for anything other than their work as they started. He was like family to Maria and loved her as much as his daughter did. Her pure honesty, down-to-earth ways and sense of humor captured his heart. He didn't care about convention or political correctness; he saw her and his daughter as vulnerable to both the wilds of business and in what could be an unsafe city in parts at the wrong time—Rudy Giuliani made a difference—but still.

Chapter 25

"Tell me, Ms. Mouton… what do you think we can do with Cumming's short fall?" Hildebrand asked her.

"I see leveraging our options in Cummings at BB&T and financing their move to Georgia—but a facility available, not new brick and mortar," she rattled off as the professional she was. Her business suit was a perfectly fitted skirt and blouse ensemble centered by a white ruffle tie. It fit her well; she was curved and pretty, her lips full and red and her hair perfectly manicured in a straight fashion with blond highlights. Her eyes were wide and blue partially concealed by large-framed eyeglasses, but matching the rest of her, a very attractive presence in the office on the ninetieth floor. "Hawkins tells me he can move the equipment within two weeks. The start-up will then take six months," she said. "It's a logistics issue and we can identify a location closer to the customer base."

"Very well. Kim is coming in from Boise tonight, and I want you two to work out the details and take this project."

"Thank you, sir!" she said. It was her first major assignment and meant a large commission and performance bonus. She planned to buy her parents a new truck first and help her brothers and sisters stay in school without as many loans. The weekend began and she would tell Kim and thought they would celebrate by going to Ruth Chris.

Who would have ever thought? she asked herself, proud and feeling the joy rising powerfully inside of her every part, transmitted by every nerve. She called and left a message of the good news on Kim's answering machine—which she wanted her partner to hear as soon as she got up Saturday morning.

It seemed perfect. They could begin outlining their project Saturday evening and get off to a fast start Monday the tenth. Then in a matter of weeks they would see a plan take shape and form—and knew it would be a great one that would work so well as to exceed expectations. Maria knew they would surely excite investors and since every trend she saw in the plastics market was moving solidly up, their risk would be handsomely rewarded.

"I got your message, Maria!" Kim said through her sleepy haze. "This is so wonderful!"

"Yes, it is! And we'll do it again—you and me, Kim, partners to the end!" She laughed, her voice growing in confidence and clarity. "I can't wait to get started. I could hardly sleep last night! I'm already working the list of calls, and one name after another kept me awake!" She laughed. "I had to get up and make notes!"

"I'm glad I got some sleep!" Kim laughed. "You would have had me working through the night! Things went okay in Boise, but I never expected to be assigned a project this soon! Damn, girl! Good job!"

"You prepared it too!" She smiled from ear to ear. "So, now! When can we meet? I have some ideas on the presentation and need yours, of course. We'll hit 'em with a two-fer, one after another. Know what I mean?"

"Absolutely! I can be showered in twenty."

"Let's meet at Starbucks then at 10:30…Okay?"

"I'm already there, girlfriend!" She laughed.

Daniel and Paul were dating women they met in and near Marshall County at different times and places. Daniel met Sherry at the Farmers' Market when she was delivering produce. A short conversation and large lemonade later they decided to see each other. Paul met Amy while attending St. James church in Gadsden, one of the few times he went so far for Mass. He heard her sing and asked about her after the service—she happened to be standing behind him when he did and she answered him herself. His embarrassment was evident as he ducked his head in shy repose. Nerves and blood caused a bright red to reveal him without a chance. "Come next week and we can talk more," she told him with a half smile the first time. "It's my birthday and we're having a lunch after Mass."

"I wouldn't want to interfere or anything," he said shyly.

"No, you won't at all. There's going to be a number of people any way and we always want to meet someone new to the church." She smiled fuller, deciding to take the conversation a little further with the good-looking stranger.

"I would like that." He smiled toward the brown complexion of her face and her arms and neck revealed enough by the narrow strapped black dress she wore, accentuating her Panamanian color as a result of a union between an Army Ranger father and his native wife. After his retirement from the service, the family moved to his original hometown of Gadsden, Alabama, where he was able to start up a security firm for local industry.

"You're welcome to come. Tell me your name though!" She laughed.

"I'm Paul McCray, Amy. And happy birthday next week!"

"Thank you...Born nine, nine of seventy-nine! That's me!" She laughed. "It's an easy one to remember!"

Her smile threw his imagination into a stir and caused him to think how wonderful it would be to kiss those beautiful lips that curved so nicely into deep dimples at the ends. "What brings you to St. James?"

"I'm new to Alabama and looking for a congregation and priest and all…"

"Where are you from, Paul McCray?"

"Galveston. It's in Texas," he said and felt like a dummy for saying. "I came over last year but have been working a lot of Sundays." His smile was engaging her, wanting to be closer, wanting her to know him as a decent guy.

"Well, you come next Sunday, and we talk more, okay?"

"Okay, Amy. Have a great day, and I'll see you then!" He left knowing he had to but not wanting to, but the woman did invite him and things may improve more than he could have imagined. He thought maybe he could have the same kind of relationship Daniel had with Sherry—although she was having fun and as much a good friend to both the brothers as a sometime lover to Daniel. She helped them on the farm doing anything—from the all night tending of the birth of their one foal to repairing fencing on the east five acres beyond the pond. She was all country and reveled in the space and work and loved Daniel.

Maria and Kim worked the project hour after hour Saturday and through Sunday morning when their eyes gave way and their brains finally ceased functioning entirely. The women had compiled a fifty-page report and several financial spreadsheets to present to prospective investors, except for exact figures on the cost of the lease in Georgia—a negotiation trip would be required to finish, and until then they decided to use conservative figures to complete the analysis. Plugging in the actual would be fast and easy now; they were two weeks ahead of schedule as usual. Hildebrand had already learned his new associates were far more productive than anyone he had ever seen.

Monday morning they reported to their office in the Trade Center early enough that the third shift security guards were still on duty. They scrambled to enter all the data in the company's computer system, ready to give

Hildebrand a great start to the week. They could hardly wait to make the calls and ask Holly to make reservations for their travel. Cummings was going to be successful and deliver the specialty plastics needed in manufacturing various high value products to every company in the Southeast before the year was over and the neophytes from Loyola would be largely responsible!

Paul went to Mass that Sunday and heard Amy sing again. As he listened to the words she used her voice to exclaim Christ's suffering in "The Old Rugged Cross", and Christ's steadfastness of saving help in "The Garden", he began crying in emotional, spiritual turmoil caused by the great mystery. Her voice filled his spirit with peace and contemplation at once and an appreciation for his blessings, all he was and all his parents and his brother, and the United States of America had given him. It all came to a powerful climax as he heard her every word of the old songs, once not heard in the Catholic Church. He knew he loved the message and the messenger. He avoided looking toward Daniel, who he had invited to attend along with Sherry.

"You have a very nice…No, ma'am." He cleared his throat. "You have a truly rich and powerful voice, Amy!" he said, thinking he hoped she didn't detect any evidence of tears he tried so hard to stop earlier. He quickly introduced Daniel and Sherry. "They're with me, of course." He managed a laugh. "This is Amy, the girl I told you about."

"Nice to meet you, Amy! You are very beautiful—what are you doing talking to Paul?" Daniel laughed as Sherry tugged his arm.

"Stop it, Daniel!" She laughed. "It's very nice to meet you, Amy. Maybe one day you can come to the farm. We can have a cookout or something." She smiled.

"That would be nice."

"Well, I understand it's your birthday! And it's O'Charley's?"

"Yes. But I'm afraid I'm going to be embarrassed there," Amy said.

"Yea. They'll sing at your table," Paul said.

"Well, I'm hungry! Let's go!" his brother piped. Sherry kissed him on the cheek. "Oh! That's nice."

"You're so sweet, Daniel, but so red." Sherry smiled. "I guess that's part of what I love about you. Forgive him, Amy." She laughed.

Sherry came dressed in a snug burgundy dress and her blond hair and fit body caused more than one head to turn in church as they took a pew close to the front with Paul. The boys also made a good impression because of their gentleness and good manners, traits taught to them by their mom and dad in Texas.

"It's a wonderful day!" Sherry exclaimed and smiled widely. "It's beautiful!"

The sun was out in full glory warming the land, the people, and their hearts. They were in the right place and felt the power of light and good spirits. It was safe and secure, wonderful and happy to be alive and praising God and bound for a good meal with good friends.

"Yes, it is, angel," Daniel said softly, holding her by her waist as the perfect escort, opening the truck door for her and holding her hand until she was seated.

"Paul! You have a wonderful family!" Amy smiled and said, "I hope to see all of you many times over! Now I must have you meet mine. My father and mother are standing over there with the priest." She nodded toward the church door.

Maria and Kim finished the day and retired to dinner at their favorite Italian place near the town homes. Hildebrand accepted their proposal with a wide grin and told them he was proud of their work and that he would be certain to recognize them at the next board meeting. He congratulated them and told them they had just made the big time—a great start well beyond their age and experience. The future appeared to be limitless.

Both of the young women brought along casual dates for the dinner and a few cocktails. Webster Groves had asked Maria several times and she put him off before she finally asked him earlier that Monday. Kim's date was her long-term boyfriend who was finishing medical school at the University of New York and was only able to see her occasionally because he was in residence and worked all hours in the emergency room at New York General. Heath saw everything there, from the frequent and sadly typical gunshot victims to lacerations, contusions, and fractures caused by a variety of accidents or provocations, and he worked every one of them as though they were his own family.

"Best of luck to you, ladies!" Heath said. "I'm happy for you and thank you for inviting me tonight. I'm lucky to have you as friends." He smiled and turned the wine goblet up.

"Yea! Way to go!" Webster said. "And I'm sure glad we could get together, Maria! It sure was a surprise." He smiled.

"I know. I'm sorry, Webster. It's just that I haven't thought about going out much on the new job and all."

"I understand. It's hard to make the adjustment, but you're on the way now!"

"Let's drink to success!" Kim spoke up and raised her glass.

"To success!" Three other voices chimed in harmony; their confidence and happiness seemed to be contagious to everyone in the dining room and the place became happier for every visitor. A few hours later their evening was ending and they would retire for a night's peaceful sleep after doing the work.

"I'll be in at eight in the morning, Maria."

"Very well. I'll be there too. We need to wrap up a few small details this group might expect. Ten will come quickly and we have to have everything ready for them."

That Tuesday morning the boys drove their regular opposite directions to work. Etowah County was south and Huntsville was north. Daniel began working a fixture Pat had contracted to design and build for an electrical cabinet factory that made power facilities, and he had to finish it today. The steel had been cut and parts accumulated during the week, and all he had left was to weld them together to make the tool that would let operators turn their parts as they welded it together making a watertight cabinet for the transformer, controls and the power supply.

Paul checked through the secure gate at Lockheed and walked to his workstation. His project was a component for a missile deployment system in development. Most of his day was spent carefully studying procedures and making quality checks every step of the way as he worked to perfect the launching and release gearbox and electrical feeds. For both it was routine and what they had to do to support their true vocation— farming Marshall County as did their forebears so faithfully work from the heart—the work that gave hope and a future to their family.

The sudden, violent, and instant shaking of the building beneath them was far worse than their worst nightmare, far different and real than their worst experience. They felt it as they heard the deafening explosion with a loud afterlife. Maria and Kim stared at each other. It was a worse fright than the most frightened they had ever survived and felt even for a second during their life and there was no stop, nearly paralyzed, unable to think, unable to move for a few minutes and what seemed too long. The smoke was pouring up the sides of the building and covered every view. It was beginning to roar through the impervious floor and walls. "My God! What happened?" someone shrieked in volume above a scream, but it wasn't a scream and seemed to be heard across the entire floor, through the doors and walls; echoes in different voices with the same question devoured the residents.

"My God, Kim!" Maria cried out and ran to her friend.

"Oh, Maria! What is happening? What is happening?"

"I don't know! I don't know! My God!" She quickly turned her head to see all around the few windows closest to them and the hallway outside their office where the smoke was constant and coming toward them in large clouds of white and gray and black. The vibrations were becoming stronger as though the building would fall on its side. They had to get out of the building and fast. Webster ran past them as Hildebrand walked to them. He shouted at several men to find the exits and get the doors open.

"Let's go!" he said. "One at a time! Don't run!" he remembered to say as he watched his employees file toward the exit one after another. He would be the last to leave after checking for everyone else, he thought.

"Back! Back!" a voice from the hallway exits shouted upward to the mass of people trying to use the stairs.

"What is it?" Maria asked, bending toward the stairs to hear something, anything.

"We can't get out! Everything's on fire down below!" someone else said.

"Try another! Let's go over there!" another voice added to the confusion.

"They already tried that and there's fire covering that one too!" Hildebrand shouted.

"See if we can call out on the lines! We've got to talk to the firemen!" a voice from the group standing in the dense fog offered.

"I got through with my cell and they're on the way! They said that we might have to stay put! Damn it! Get something to stop that smoke! Wet it! Wet it! Get it around the doors!" Hildebrand shouted to everyone as two dozen more men and women appeared in the foyer.

"They don't know yet!" a voice called out in the smoke and deafening noise. "Oh, my God! There's fire!"

"We'll be all right!" someone else said. "We just need to wait!"

"Stay away from the windows!" Kim shouted. "You pull it in on us if you break one!" She felt more heat from below, through the floor and told Hildebrand, worried it could break through somewhere at any time. She called Heath and told him something happened.

"I don't know," her voice was shaking over the receiver. "We've had an explosion and now there's fire and smoke…I don't know what it is." She began crying.

Multiple sirens could be heard on the ground outside and people began pouring out the lower floors, running, shouting, confused, dazed and covered in ash. The second tower was hit with a hellish sword; another plane loaded with fuel exploded on impact and fired up the several floors it destroyed in an instant and all those inside the sudden killing inferno. The impact of the second shook them violently again. It was clear what happened.

"That's another one!" several voices shouted at the same time. "My God! We're all going to die!" a woman's voice cried out from the same direction.

"That was a plane! A plane has hit us! My God!" a voice called out with an Indian accent.

"Those poor people!" Maria cried and called home to speak to her parents amid the dizzying heat, dust, smoke and noise of human beings trying to survive something they didn't understand and couldn't see.

At Lockheed, Foreman Locklear came to the group of men in the die shop and told them he heard a plane had hit one of the towers of the World Trade Center. Before he finished another man ran toward them. "There's been another!" he said, the worried expression on his face clearly visible.

Paul had a cousin who worked there and felt a shock of nervous fear surge through his body that shook him away from the mill he set up that morning. Each man and woman of the crew shut his machine down and raced toward the break room for the television. Paul was slower and peered at the screen from a distance at the corner of the large room.

"Son of a bitch!" one of them said quietly, contemplating the fate of so many people. Video of the huge mass of the early fire and smoke was repeated time after time while the camera fixed on both towers to stream live coverage. On the ground, emergency crews of firemen and police were shown scrambling toward the burning icons of American business and free enterprise. Interspersed in the television news was video of the second plane, striking and exploding into the belly of the second tower like a knife into something soft and the smoke pouring out of the Pentagon's side, a wounded lion destined to rise from its repose and do more soon. The section's production scheduler known as preacher said they should pray for them. Otherwise there was nothing they could do except watch the horror unfold.

"Damn!" Joey Taylor said as he ducked his head toward his lap. Men began crying while watching and listening to the coverage of an event that could only mean unnecessary suffering, death and war. "Why would anyone do this? The bastards!" Someone shushed the man. Every soul felt a smoothly overpowering, unavoidable empty.

The crowd was forming larger and hardly a word was spoken as they watched a true horror unfold in front of them all. Suddenly the cameras captured visions of someone's sons and daughters jumping from more than seventy stories high. Preacher wept with many of the men in the break room.

Maria felt a growing vibration that got louder and larger, shaking her to the floor, and then she felt the floor give way beneath her. She and everyone on the floor rode it for an instant as those who looked up saw the ceiling and beams falling toward their heads. The awful noise screaming from the building silenced human voices. She could feel herself scream but couldn't hear her own desperate call to God above.

I just had my twenty-third birthday.

I have to take my wife to Bobby's recital.

I plan to use the weekend to take my daughter to Coney Island.

I must make dinner for my family.

I was going to ask her to marry me tonight.

I wanted to go for the interview.

My son is returning to school this week and I have to help him move back to the dorm.

I never hurt anyone.

I want to see them again.

I have to pick Jason up before six.

I planned a vacation with my wife for next month; we are going to Tennessee to see the colors in the mountains.

I can't miss my boy's Bar Mitzvah this Saturday.

I was retiring next year.

I haven't seen my son walk yet; he's only one.

I have to go home now.

Why me?

Why us?

  The mood in the break room turned to anger as many seethed in hatred for those responsible for taking so many innocent lives. The count was unknown but was surely going to end the lives of thousands. There was nothing any of them could do to exact justice from the cowards who arranged for these animals to take over planes and fly them into occupied buildings. The reporter said the third plane had crashed in Pennsylvania; that it had been taken back by the passengers. A chorus of hoorays and flying fists into the air followed the announcement and one of the workers had his own announcement. "We got some of the bastards!"
  "They didn't make it, the sons of bitches! How does it feel now, asshole?" Someone else shouted toward the screen. Another shushed the voice wanting to hear more.
  David and Sarah watched the news along with millions of Americans. He had trouble breathing, drowning in his living room, and she began crying, sweat pouring out of her every pore. Both knew sudden loss of the worse kind; each soul was ripped empty that morning as a wordless spirit brought them to the empty table; one of their granddaughters had died.
  David S. was at the office and sick when the planes struck New York and Washington. He called Julie to hear her breathe and make the only connection he could. "I'll be home in a minute," he finally said, interrupting silence

through the weeping. Jack and Jesse had to leave the house and every television set with their children. Numbed by grief and the likelihood, they went into the bayou to watch until they could speak to the teenagers and each other.

Daniel heard the news too and left work to watch it on cable. He wasn't sure his cousin was inside and thought surely she got out or wasn't there and was safe in another place. He answered the phone and listened as Paul told him not to get his hopes up—that it is very likely she was inside. While he was on the line, the tower collapsed and then the second one followed. "My God! They've just fallen down, Paul!" he shouted into the receiver to his brother who took the news without a word. Russo was rushing toward the scene in New York and having little luck getting there. He ditched the car and began running and walking as fast as he could breath and move his legs. But there was nowhere to go to and find his daughter, Maria and so many of his friends. Before him were policemen and others keeping a strict but bent line of no trespassing in front of a vast scene of destruction like he had never seen or imagined. Ash and smoke choked the whole city and people ran away from hell covered in whitish-gray soot and ash, ghostly human forms of all rank, all fixed in the gaze of horror and grief.

"Oh, my God!" he said it loud time after time toward the streets as the mass of people passed him and kept coming, tears caking their faces, crimson blood caking patches on the clothes of some.

The weeks that followed were filled with response—desperate yearnings from all corners—from the smallest hamlets and crossroads to the largest cities, people were doing something. Frustrated and loving, they sent money and gave what they could—blood, coins, dollars, cards and flowers; companies raised money; and signs and flags flew and stuck on all manner of vehicles and porches, windows and yards and America was angry and had to fight. The country had been hit as horrific as Pearl Harbor and for even less a reason as there was no reason then. Young men and women were enlisting in the armed services and stepping toward the unknown because they loved. Maria and Kim had not been found. Pitiful photographs posted around the site did nothing but remind those who passed there were human beings—sons, daughters, brothers, sisters, wives, husbands, fathers and mothers—left in the ruble that was still smoking.

"I'm going in," Paul said.

"What do you mean?"

"I'm joining the Marine Corps, Daniel."

"Like Dad."

"Yea, like Dad," he said to his brother whose face mirrored his—his own reflection of a solemn warrior willing to risk his life in the hunt for justice.

"You're not going without me."

"I didn't think so," Paul said.

"Surely we'll go after them this time," Daniel said, gazing out the large bay window across the fields.

"Surely."

"I'll call Mom and Dad and tell them. They need to know." He sighed. "That's gonna be the hardest."

"Yea...I think they'll understand—it's gonna be tough though. But I don't think Sherry will. She won't want you to go, Daniel." He paused and opened the bolt on the 30-06 he was cleaning. "Are you sure?"

"I'm sure. It's not what I expected but neither was 9/11."

"Naw. No one expected that." He closed the bolt after a tedious but quick inspection. "I sure would like to have Bin Laden in these sights." He brought the rifle to his shoulder and aimed at the wall.

"Maybe you'll get your chance," Daniel smiled. "When are we going?"

"Tomorrow morning. We'll get with the recruiter and see."

The brothers brought Amy and Sherry to the farm that weekend where they put out the beer and grilled chicken for them. The disc player was softly rumbling in the background with mixed melodies sung by Clint Black, Tom Petty, the late Roy Orbison and the group Alabama—some of their favorites and liked or at least tolerated by their guests. The occasion was set up to tell the ladies of a decision that would alter their plans into some more concrete and fixed—and would involve years. Amy remarked to Sherry that the twins were acting differently—strangely—as if they were keeping something from them. Neither was as flirtatious or talkative as they usually were.

"I see it, too."

"What do you think it is?" Amy asked.

"I have no idea, but I'm sure we'll find out soon enough." She smiled.

The yellow footprints painted on the asphalt at Parris Island were in the same place their father stepped, only repainted and brighter. The regimen was the same. The feel of the air and the smell of the place was the same. The drill instructors were different men who sounded the same. The tactics they learned were the same. The general orders they stood at attention and recited were the same, and the ditties repeated to their rifle and Chesty Puller were the same. Their hearts were the same as their father and his father's were when they were young and still are now—full of love and hope for the country and the safeguarding of freedom for people they don't know. They knew their own future was tied to what they could do by standing up for the most precious gift their forebears fought for and passed to them and every American. Daniel and Paul loved enough to do what they could do. This time was theirs to massage their heart in the sweet act, the essence of removing from the earth enemies who would kill people who wanted nothing more than freedom to worship and work in peace.

They had the strength to stop the evil from taking everything away from those they terrorized and killed and it was for this purpose there were McCrays preparing again. Kabul was again being visited by Americans; this time the men and women came in far greater numbers, disciplined, bone hard, and in uniform, anxious to start their fourteen hour or longer patrols to root out those people who hated them and their families enough to randomly destroy them and try to crush their faith.

The iron poured so early in Pittsburgh had been transformed many times over and finally made into the steel barrels of death and destruction carried by men and women who left America's shores with the flag proudly passed by New York firemen and police.

PFC Daniel McCray watched the AC-130 gun ships make one pass after another and put a stream of lead and explosions into the rocky and barren crease of earth two clicks to their front. The Twenty-Sixth Marine Expeditionary Force had arrived with the prayers and hearts of America after the air assault across targets in Afghanistan and was responsible to find targets of opportunity and destroy Taliban and Al Qaeda west and north of Jalalabad. Maria and everyone with her deserved their best response. The police and firefighters who were lost that day deserved their best response. The Afghan women who were driven into a soccer coliseum to be executed by a single shot to the back of their covered heads deserved their best response.

A day didn't go by in the field when Paul and Daniel didn't remember why they were swallowing sand and eating MREs and marching on line for miles to hunt perched-mouthed men. They were hunting those who cloaked themselves in distorted religion to justify slitting throats of airline stewardesses and murdering innocent Americans in a war of their making against mankind's most powerful drive and motivation out of heart and soul to freedom of thought and worship of truths no one on earth can dictate although some try by the force of the gun, the evil of the knife, and the slavery of bodies.

It had been a good start, Daniel thought, as he heard the body count of the long shirts armed with AK47s and RPGs. A number of figures were swirling through the grapevine and only the lesser of these discouraged him, but still it had been a good hunt and the Taliban were displaced from their atrocities in a mere few days. His unit with the Twenty-Sixth Marines was relatively new to the scene and anxious to see the test and work through whatever it proved to be and live the results.

"Paul...take this." He handed his brother a package of beef and noodles with a small bottle of Louisiana hot sauce that had become a staple for them since their days in Galveston. He noticed his brother sweating around his neck, the speckled bits of sand and dirt illuminated against his wet tan.

"Thank you, Daniel. I'll swap you some chicken."

"Do you think we'll get Bin Laden?"

"I think we will...." He stopped and thought. "But he's such a coward, we should have known he'd run away and hide."

"Yea, the friggin' ass! That piece of shit sent others to do what they did while he was safely hiding behind rock. I swear it makes no sense!"

"Yea it does—but only to them....Hell, Paul, these people have been teaching hate for years and we're just now catching on to what that means. He thinks he's near God and is suppose to send others and protect his ass," he said as he opened the bolt on his M4 and checked it for a light coating of oil to make certain he'd be ready when the time came.

"I heard we'll move out tonight...I think we've got a surprise for somebody!" Daniel laughed. He checked his action and tapped the ten clips he carried to make sure each one of them was firmly seated with twenty rounds of Al Qaeda killer projectiles.

"Damn right!"

Daniel dreamed of Sherry that night while bivouacking in a shelter half tent he shared with Paul. He saw her bending over at her waist and picking up timbers they were using to build and repair the old barn. In his sleep relished the vision of the woman who seemed very much at home. His sleep sightseeing suddenly changed to his great-grandmother as she was walking to the same barn, and that's all there was to it. He wanted to get back to Sherry and tried to steer his mind toward her face and hair, the soft deep blond she kept straight, naturally full and free, wild with the wind, but comfortable on her, beautiful to him. *I should have told her I loved her,* he thought in his dream. Several hours later, he was studying her when suddenly his deep sleep ended, his body and mind awakened by the voice of the platoon sergeant telling them in a steady tone it was time.

"Aye, Sarge." He rolled over and made sure Paul was awake. "Gotta saddle up, Paul," he said knowing that instant he was determined to ask Sherry to marry him and have their children after he finished the work before him and returned to Alabama.

Paul thought of Maria. This was a chance to go after some justice and show them America had arrived—something they hadn't expected, but was on them in full measure. It was a consequence many of the enemy would not live through and others would long remember. "This will teach 'em about us, Paul! You can't rape Lady Liberty and kill her children! She'll come after your ass!" He knowingly laughed.

Americans were thinking of all of those people wretchedly and horribly lost for nothing as they watched the war unfold on their television screens and cheered loudly for all the sons of immigrants privileged now to be pulling the triggers in defense of country, freedom, peace and liberty from fear. Every generation has had to be ready to defend the land and most have sent sons and daughters to face the dragon.

Now their target is an enemy that hates freedom as much as it is loved by thoughtful and loving human beings who, by the courage of other generations and out of their own hearts, came to the shores of a new land full of promise, hope and happiness as one can will it. The toll has been high and is and will always be. The work is hard to keep it. Faith, hope, love, and courage are American families.

Continuing

Printed in the United States
33188LVS00009B/37-63